Where the Road Begins

Where the Road Begins

Tattered Glory Series
Book One

By
Nancy Dane

NDB Publishing
Russellville Arkansas

Books by Nancy Dane

Tattered Glory
Where the Road Begins
A Difference of Opinion
A Long Way to Go
An Enduring Union
A Reasonable Doubt
Sarah Campbell, Tale of a Civil War Orphan

To My Family

You are the best on earth

WORD FROM THE AUTHOR

Write what you know. That sage advice led me to use Arkansas as the background for this novel. Research, however, took me on a detour, which ended with the compilation of a documentary history of the Civil War titled *Tattered Glory* on which this book is based. I had assumed Arkansas, and especially the area in the mountains where I live, played a minor role in this conflict. Official documents and diaries proved otherwise. The military action portrayed is as accurate as years of study can make it. With these facts, the story, although fiction, shows the reality of the time and place.

Even though education has now changed the speech of hill folk, many old-timers retain a distinctive dialect. I have had the privilege of hearing the authentic—the soft, pleasing drawl that sometimes says hit instead of it, yer, yore, or yor'en as a substitute for your. The word *an* is seldom placed before a vowel, and rarely is there a waste of breath pronouncing the final g on anything. There are words and expressions well known although found in no dictionary; a squirrel *squacks*; koutou is rendered *kowtow*, meaning to cater to another's whims; foolishness is replaced by *foolishment*; *in no wise* is an expression meaning in no way. To the purist, please note for easier reading I have refrained from using some hill vernacular.

Other than known historical figures, the characters in the novel are figments of my imagination and meant to portray no one. The few exceptions are real people briefly mentioned: Colonel John Hill, who led his men at Pea Ridge; Major Hall McConnell, killed while leading a Rebel charge at the White River; James Cheeks, a mountain man hanged for refusing to give information about loyal Unionists; Joel Smith and Vince Blackard, two Johnson County men killed at the battle of Wilson's Creek; Benjamin Pelts, whose son was hanged near Little Piney Creek; Batson Cox and Thomas Fiddler, who were both killed by bushwhackers; Quinton Beasley, who piloted General McNeil through the mountains and across

Little Piney when the Yankees chased Colonel Joe Shelby across the Arkansas River.

I have many to thank for support and aid, especially Tom Wing for his endorsement and help with research. A big thank you to Kenny Preston for critique, to Shanna Kalicki for editing, to Becky and Sharon for scrutiny, and to Nancy Cook for one last perusal. Thanks to Janae Glass for the cover design and to Chris Kennedy for the fantastic cover photo. Special thanks to Dr. Fritz Ehren for his kind words and endorsement, and to Ira Taylor for his endorsement and his encouragement for many years. Most of all, thanks to my family for your love, support, and prayers. To my readers, thank you very much. I hope you enjoy this trip to Civil War

Arkansas.*Official Records Vol. 22. Part II:*

FORT SMITH, ARK., October 31, 1863

Major-General SCHOFIELD:

.... Although we did not overtake Shelby, we kept him from extended pillage, punishing him severely, and drove him across the river at a point near Clarksville. We took about 75 prisoners, killed 20 or 30 of his men, including 1 captain, and captured a number of horses.

We have to mourn the death of Lieutenant [James G.] Robertson, of the First Arkansas Cavalry, who fell, mortally wounded, on the 26th, while bravely leading a charge against the rear guard of the enemy on Little Piney Creek....

JOHN McNEIL,

Brigadier-General, Commanding.

Chapter 1

1861

The redbone pup yipped as she eyed the twisted treetop bent far over a deep, wooded hollow. The leaves of the hickory were small and glossy with spring, and yet the bushy top made ample cover for an intruder. As high as frantic feet could reach, the hound reared and scratched the scaly trunk.

The young man grinned. He hunkered to give the bobbing head and floppy ears an affectionate rub. "That old bushy-tail fooled you. She's not up there. She already jumped out."

With flared nose still pointed at the leafy hideaway, the dog bayed. The doleful rumble filled the hollow and echoed off a far rocky bluff. Once again she gave excited yips.

"Belle, sounds like your voice is changing." Elijah chuckled. "Come on." He pulled the long-eared pup from the tree. "By now that squirrel is halfway down the holler." As the dog's tongue wet his face, he drew back and wiped his chin, feeling satisfaction at the stubble scratching his palm. His beard was getting thick. Soon he would have to shave every day like Pa.

After a reluctant glance at the treetops where the squirrel had fled, Elijah turned away. He wished it were fall already. The mountain air was crisp, then, and tangy with the scent of ripe muscadines, and a body could hunt squirrels without fear of killing a sow with young ones in the nest. He glanced around. Of course spring was fine, too. Now the woods were lacy with dogwoods spreading the hills as white and pretty as Ma's Sunday tablecloth.

He squinted east where sun had just crested the ridge to poke yellow fingers of light through the trees along the high rim. Sun and shade dappled his dark hair and the shirt where youthful muscles held taut the butternut homespun. The cheery call of a wren fit his mood. His heart quickened with anticipation of a rare trip to Clarksville. He must hurry. There was work to be done before tomorrow.

The pup trotted ahead through short, dewy grass alongside the trail. Occasionally she ran back to keep pace with Elijah's loose-limbed strides. When a covey of bobwhite quail, in a feathery flash of white and brown, whirred from the trail ahead, the pup gave chase but soon lost interest as the birds flew away.

Just as the pup began to bark, the boy stopped and threw up his head. He hunkered to grasp her muzzle.

"Hush, Belle!"

He held down on the squirming hound and cocked his head to listen, but there were no more shots. Now all was quiet. Even the birds had hushed. Since this was Pa's land there was seldom anyone else on this ridge. Elijah supposed someone might be after the turkey that had gobbled down in the holler just after daylight. But more than likely it was someone just passing through who had shot a varmint, a snake, or a bobcat or some such. No one hunted squirrel or deer in April. No one risked killing game with new offspring. Besides, all the folks he knew in the mountains still had plenty of smoked meat left from the winter's butchering.

He frowned. Of course it could be Lew Willis. That no-account was apt to be anywhere. Lew was forever slipping through the woods as sly as a panther to disappear before a body hardly saw him.

"Come on, Belle," he said. "Let's go check. "Pa will want to know who's shooting this close to home."

Glad for freedom, the pup shook long ears and ran ahead. As the boy left the trail and went forward, his keen eyes probed the woods. Briars were greening, but the underbrush was sparse here and the leafy loam was deep. He could tread softly in the morning dew, wetting his tough, bare feet.

He stopped. Up ahead, through shaggy ropes of grapevine, he spied a shadowy figure. He crept forward, stooping to get a better view. After expelling a deep breath, he stood and strode into the small clearing.

"Michael, what you shooting at?"

The ragged, scrawny boy, a head shorter than Elijah, held a limp gray squirrel in one hand. The other cradled an ancient flintlock musket.

"Howdy, Elijah." Rather than meeting the friendly brown eyes, Michael looked shamefaced at the ground. "Squirrel fer breakfast," he mumbled.

So the Lanes had no meat left.... On second thought, Elijah realized Johnny Lane might not have even butchered. Johnny seemed too happy-go-lucky to worry about his family. But the lines between Michael's eyes and the pinched, down-turned mouth proved he worried a lot.

In a rush of pity, Elijah said, "Hey, you want to come to town with us tomorrow? County militia is gonna drill. There'll be lots of food and a horserace."

Michael's face fell. "I better not." He hunched thin shoulders and swallowed before adding, "Ma is gettin' worse. She coughs all the time."

Elijah quickly put in, "I spent the night at Granny's. She sent Uncle Caleb over to your place with some medicine for your ma. I bet it'll fix her right up. Granny always doctors us with her roots and berries and such, and we're never sick."

"Tell her, much obliged," mumbled Michael. He turned away. "Reckon I better get on home and fry this squirrel." His voice choked.

Elijah watched him trudge away. He hated that Michael would miss the muster. Maggie must be awful sick. Even Granny was worried.

With some of his own pleasure dimmed, he retraced his steps back to the narrow path made mostly by his own feet on the shortcut to Granny's. Here it snaked the mountainside to finally drop into a hollow. Before descending he hunkered on bare heels to gaze at the view. When Belle snuggled at his feet, he rubbed her floppy ears.

Far below, Little Piney Creek hurried a rocky bed of deep pools and sandy shallows. Swift from last night's heavy rain, its rushing tumble echoed through the hollow where a blanket of morning mists lay, too lazy to rise and greet the sun. Elijah eyed the timbered ridges. Oak, hickory, gum, ash, and pine stood proud and green against the sky. Then he looked beyond, as far as sight, where rounded mountains overlapped into blue distance. Except for the crooked trail he would travel, there was no sign of man. He figured it had looked exactly the same to the Indians who once roamed here. He loved the wildness of it all. If it were up to him, he would stay out in the woods all the time. He gave a crooked grin. He reckoned that would make him about as sorry as Lew Willis. As far as Elijah knew, Lew had never worked a day in his life.

When Belle barked, he stood. "I know, girl, it's time to go. Pa will be wonderin'...." The word died in his throat.

Lew Willis stood less than ten feet away. A nasty grin split his unshaved face, but the cold eyes were what chilled Elijah. They were tawny and glittering like a cat's. With hair as black as midnight, his long, lean face tense and watching, the yellow-brown eyes hooded and staring, Lew looked like a panther ready to pounce. Elijah felt as trapped as he had long ago, the day the hissing cat with eyes of yellow fire had him cornered in the barn.

When Belle kept barking, Lew reached a moccasin toe to nudge her. "She'll make a good coon dog one of these days," he said. Then he turned and melted into the woods.

Elijah sank back down. His heart beat faster than Belle's thumping tail under the hand he pressed on her back. He had never believed it possible for any man to get that close without him hearing. Pa often said he had ears like a wolf. But this time he had not heard a thing, not even a whisper of sound.

It had been five years since Lew had scared him this badly, since the afternoon Elijah had rounded a bend and come upon Lew washing his hands in the creek. Lew had whirled and jerked a knife—a long, wicked Arkansas toothpick—from bloodstained leggings and hefted the blade. Elijah had dropped the stringer of fish and almost wet his pants. When Lew had grinned, he figured Lew was only funning. Nonetheless, he was scared, and he knew that had given Lew mean pleasure.

The paralyzing fear had come the next day, when just a short way up the creek, Bessie Hadley was found hacked to death in her cabin. Elijah told Pa about the knife and the blood on Lew's leggings. Pa had laughed and said it was deer blood. He had seen the fresh haunch of venison that Lew brought to Maggie Lane. Pa said Lew had no reason to kill Bessie, but Dub did.

Elijah knew what folks said about Bessie. While waiting at Dub's mill to get corn ground, he had seen men wink and nudge and whisper that the boy didn't look a thing like Dub. And they had great fun guessing.

Uncle Caleb said at the trial Dub swore the blood-soaked body of his wife was on the floor when he came home from the mill for dinner. And on the way from the creek he had glimpsed a tall, skinny man slipping through the woods behind his cabin. When Elijah heard that he had broken out in a cold sweat. Lew was tall and skinny.

The jury figured there might have been such a man. The evidence, however, pointed to Dub. He was a fiery, jealous man, a wife-beater, as time and again Bessie's bruises proved. Although with his dying breath Dub still swore his innocence, even Uncle Caleb, his good friend, thought him guilty. Although Caleb and Pa were usually right about everything, Elijah was unconvinced. Just now, after staring into Lew's wicked eyes, he could imagine him capable of anything.

Elijah stood on shaky legs. With Belle scampering ahead, he descended to the bottom of the ridge to follow the trail until it crossed the creek. When he saw the cabin in the distance, he gave a relieved sigh and on much steadier legs crossed the rushing stream on polished stones that rose like wet turtlebacks above the water.

Alongside a plowed field the gray cabin shouldered a pine-covered hillside. The house had been built of logs as thick and long as Elijah's Great Grandpa Tanner's ax could find, three rooms, one large and two small and a loft over all. Elijah's pa had added a lean-to on the back for a pantry. There was a low front porch, the lone step a flat rock smoothed first by the rushing waters of Piney and then polished by the comings and goings of three generations of Grandpa's offspring. A rambling rosebush stubbornly clung to the jagged rocks of a tall chimney. Although it was too early for the sweet-smelling flowers, the promise of tight red buds hid among the thorny leaves. In summer a cinnamon vine, with tiny star-shaped blossoms, climbed the porch and twined around the rails, filling the air with spicy goodness.

Elijah saw Ma in the doorway, shading her green eyes against the bright morning. In the blue dress, with the sun glinting off her fair hair, she looked almost as slim and young as Cindy. He supposed she had heard the shot and been anxious about him. He waved. She waved back before returning inside.

Ned Loring stepped from the barn. "Howdy, son. Heard a shot a bit ago." He wiped calloused hands on an old rag. Like Elijah, Ned's hair and eyes were brown. Although he was not tall, the wide shoulders beneath the sweat-stained shirt dispelled any thought of smallness.

Elijah decided not to mention seeing Lew. Pa already thought him notional where Lew was concerned. Of course, Pa was not afraid of the devil himself.

"Yeah. It was Michael shootin' a squirrel for breakfast."

Ned's face clouded. He pushed back a shabby hat and propped a worn boot on the bottom rail of the fence. "Poor boy," he muttered. "For a youngster, he carries quite a load. Good thing he's a crack shot or they'd go hungry."

"I invited him to come along tomorrow, but he said he couldn't. Said Maggie was too sick."

"I guess your ma ought to go check on her."

Elijah knew the only one who would like that less than Ma was Maggie. He hurried to say, "Granny sent Uncle Caleb over this morning with some yarbs."

He could almost hear Ma correcting, insisting he say herbs instead of yarbs. But in spite of Ma's efforts, he figured mountain ways came as natural to him as runoff flowed to Piney.

"Granny will fix her up if anyone can." Ned glanced at the sun. "Are they coming with us?"

"Naw. That heifer ain't calved yet, and this being her first, Caleb won't leave her. I invited Granny and Viola to ride with us. But Granny said with Viola being so poorly she reckoned they'd just stay home." Elijah stopped for a slow grin. "Pa, you should have seen Viola's face. Before I had a chance to give the invite, she lit into tellin' me how terrible she felt, how she could hardly get out of bed this morning." Elijah's grin widened as he experienced again the wicked delight of seeing Viola caught in her own trap. "I just about laughed right out. You know how she loves a trip to town."

Ned chuckled. "For a sickly woman, she is right fond of a wagon seat."

With a broad grin, Elijah went on, "Granny was getting a kick out of it, too. She loves a good joke, especially on Viola." Then he sobered. "Why did Uncle Caleb marry such a sourpuss?"

Ned took his boot from the fence, stooped, and ruffled Belle's ears. "Oh, Viola's a good woman," he said slowly. "We've all got our faults. Some have sour dispositions and some have sour tempers."

When Ned pinned him with a look, Elijah looked at the ground. He knew Pa must have seen him sling the milk bucket across the barn last night and kick the cow because she had stepped her foot into the bucket and spilled the milk. No matter how hard he tried, his temper was forever getting the best of him.

Ned went on, "No doubt about it, though, a man ought to pick his wife real careful. 'Til death do us part is a long time if she's ill natured." He stood and nodded toward the empty wagon. "We need to grease the wheels and get loaded, but first go ask Ma if she wants me to take her over to check on Maggie."

Elijah nodded. He started toward the cabin, his mind once again on Michael's plight. It hurt to think the Lanes had barely enough to eat. Elijah had never known hunger. He was suddenly struck by the prosperity here. Fat cattle grazed in the pasture, chickens sang and scratched in the dirt, a large herd of spotted hogs in the edge of the woods ran free to fatten on acorns. There were wide, plowed fields ready to plant. By summer's end there would be rows of corn with firm, white ears to grind into meal or to make into grits or plump, tasty hominy with plenty left over to feed the stock. The tall corn would shade long, fat melons as pieded as rattlesnakes, their seed brought from Tennessee to the Boston Mountains years ago in Great Granny Tanner's wagon. Elijah's mouth watered just imagining the sweet, red meat.

Near the creek was a patch for sorghum cane for making molasses to sell or barter for the few things they must buy. Closer to the cabin was freshly turned black earth waiting for garden seeds: string beans and summer squash and plump red tomatoes and rows of yellow corn with ears of juicy sweetness. There would be peanuts and beans and peas for shelling and sweet potatoes with thick vines that crawled and spread and took over the ground and Irish potatoes and winter squash and huge orange pumpkins that kept well in the cellar that was dug into the hillside behind the house. Along with what the smokehouse held, there was always plenty to eat.

Compared to the Lanes they were rich. Elijah's dark brows drew together and he frowned. Funny how Johnny had trailed around after Pa ever since they were shirttail boys, but while Pa had prospered, Johnny had grown poorer. Oh, he was not as worthless as lazy Doc Lucas who wouldn't work enough to feed his hungry brood. Johnny would work hard in spurts, not steady at it like Pa, and bad luck dogged him. If his sow had pigs, more often than not, a bear ate them. His crops often died of drought or blight. Last summer his only milk cow ate larkspur, bloated, and died. It almost made Elijah feel guilty until he remembered how Pa kept his sows in a good, tight barn when they farrowed, and he kept his fields free of larkspur. Maybe Johnny's bad luck was due more to slipshod ways than to some evil curse.

The thought of a curse conjured Lew to mind. If anyone on the mountain was cursed, Elijah figured it was Lew. As he lifted his eyes to the far ridge, gooseflesh peppered his arms. He shook off a feeling of foreboding and went to find Ma.

———⌒〜⌒———

The next morning Elijah stepped outside into a pearly-pink sunrise. Damp splotches wet the dirt and crystal drops clung to shining leaves. It had rained just a spattering the night before. Wisps of fog rose from the creek to drift away on the breeze. He breathed deeply of air still fresh and soft with morning and, with exuberant anticipation, did the chores, whistling all the while. After a hurried breakfast of cornbread and milk, he coaxed Belle into the barn. When he shut the door against her howls, he frowned.

"Aw, you'll be fine," he called. "You've got feed and water, and Johnny will turn you loose this evening when he comes to milk."

Elijah hurried to the wagon where Ned and Becky already sat shoulder to shoulder on the hard board seat. Climbing into the wagon bed, he perched alongside six-year-old Deborah on a thin, ticking-covered mattress that was rolled and tied with a rope. He leaned to tug her long, golden braid.

She slapped his hand and scooted farther away. "Stop it!"

"Aw, you ain't hurt."

Without turning Becky Loring spoke, "Behave yourself, Elijah. And don't say ain't."

He grinned, wondering if Ma would ever give up correcting his grammar. He handed Deborah a fat molasses cookie from the handful he had just sneaked from a stuffed basket. While savoring the sweetness, he studied the sparkling morning. It was a grand thing to be heading to town for two days of fun and excitement and no chores! He looked at his family and felt warm pleasure. Granny said vanity was a sin. Maybe it wasn't vanity to be proud of someone else. Everyone did look extra nice today—Ma in a pretty green dress and bonnet, Pa with his dark hair wet from the recent combing and his wide shoulders stretching tight the starched brown shirt, Deborah in blue ruffled calico. Elijah wore his former best today, brown pants and a green plaid shirt. For tomorrow he had a new outfit: black trousers, white shirt, and a black string tie.

The mules had just splashed through the creek and started along the broad wagon trail when Ned whoaed them. Johnny Lane came cantering up the trail on a dappled-gray mare. He grinned ear to ear and his blue eyes sparkled.

"Howdy, all." He briefly doffed a hat off curly black hair. His handsome face sobered as he nodded to Becky. He turned quickly to Ned. "Think I'll ride along if you don't mind the company...now don't go thinking I forgot about promising to do yore milkin'. I told Michael to do hit." Johnny gave a hearty laugh. "Truth to tell, he's better at it than me, anyway."

Becky raised her brows and said, "I suppose Maggie must be much better today, or you'd never leave her."

Johnny gave her a sour look. "Michael can manage ever' bit as good as me."

Elijah frowned. It seemed wrong to leave Maggie sick abed and Michael to do all the chores, especially since Mattie and little Johnny were too young to help. Johnny was a fine-looking man, full of jokes and laughter, but he was a rascal. Elijah liked him anyway. Everyone liked him. Everyone except Ma. Under the bonnet brim, her mouth had narrowed and her full lips had turned down. Her back had gone as straight up as clock hands at noon. Ma had no use for Johnny. Johnny didn't care much for her either. She had looked forward to this trip for weeks. Elijah hoped having Johnny along would not spoil it. Although Pa was being jovial, he darted apologetic looks her way.

Johnny turned to Ned. "On the way over here, I stopped by Caleb's. Did he tell you about seeing that genius Vernon Millsap at the mill yesterday?" he asked.

Ned shook his head. Elijah perked up his ears. By any stretch of the imagination pudgy Vernon, the school bully, was not overly bright.

"Well, Caleb had took some corn to mill—when along come old man Millsap and big, fat Vernon. Right off Vernon got busy lookin' over Caleb's fine team. Then he asked the mules' names.

"'Sam and Pet,' says Caleb.

"'Which un's Pet?' says Vernon.

"'One on the right,' says Caleb.

"'Which un's Sam?' says Vernon."

Johnny's eyes began to dance. Elijah laughed along with Pa. He noticed even Ma had smiled. Having Johnny along would make the long trip lively.

Here, the narrow trail wound between massive white oaks thrusting up candle-straight from a rich loam of decayed leaves. Without bridges, the route crossed and re-crossed Little Piney, the water crystal clear, not yet warmed by spring sun. The woods were alive with creatures: deer, squirrel, fox, and rabbit. Thin and lank, they scurried in search of food, but Elijah knew it would be a while before their hungry bellies filled. Dogwood trees were blooming and bird's foot violets dotted the woods and hollows, but the nights on the mountain were still too cold to grow much forage.

They passed no dwelling until finally in the distance rose the sagging roof of the Lucas hovel, a pencil of smoke coming from the crooked chimney. From the looks of the chimney, Elijah figured Doc had put the same effort into building that he did into other work. Granny claimed there was not a lazier man in the hills. A mile further was the Matthers dwelling. Elijah thought the place just suited burly Red Matthers. It was big and rambling and untidy. The rail fences had tumbled down, allowing a fat sow and half-dozen pigs to root right in the yard. The cabin and outbuildings were in shameful disrepair.

Red stood in the barnyard beating a plowshare on an anvil. A red-hot forge glowed nearby. "Howdy," he called, and then raked the share twice into a tub of water to cool the molten iron. He dropped the share into the tub and strode over. Elijah wondered if Red got his name from the coppery hair and beard or from the constant whiskey flush on his face.

Elijah did not like the Matthers. He could not figure out why Pa and Uncle Caleb did, unless it was because they occasionally liked to pull a cork and Red Matthers made the best whiskey in the mountains, or so folks claimed.

Before shaking Ned's hand, Red wiped his own broad, hairy hand down a ragged pant leg. "Ma'am," he nodded at Becky before turning back to Ned. "Reckon yo're off to the muster."

"Ain't you coming?" asked Johnny. "Won't be much of a shindig without some of yer refreshment."

Red, scratching at the thick red beard, gave a hearty laugh. "Somehow I never got around to fixing my plow this winter. I got to get some corn in the ground or there won't be any more of that-there refreshment. Besides, Allen took some jugs on down. I figure to head down tomorrow."

"Hope you do," said Ned. "We'll be camped in the wagon yard. Look us up when you get there."

"I'll do that," said Red.

"We better get along. Eighteen mile is a far piece to make before night. And I don't want to be driving in the dark." Ned flipped the reins to urge the mules along.

"Take care," Red called. He waved before returning to the barn.

Dillon, the youngest of the Matthers clan, stepped from the barn and waved. While everyone else cheerfully returned the salute, Elijah barely put up a hand.

"That Dillon," said Becky, "is certainly a fine-looking boy."

Elijah glowered. He wished Dillon were not so good-looking...and so sweet on Cindy!

Becky went on, "I'm glad he's getting an education. He'll have a better chance than the rest of them." She lowered her voice. "I'll swan, Ned, how can Kate stand to live in such squalor?"

Ned glanced at Johnny. "It ain't our way, but they seem happy."

Elijah agreed with Ma about the disgusting way the Matthers lived, but in some ways he envied them. Red and his six sons were all as big as Goliath. Elijah felt dwarfed alongside them. The rough-and tumble brothers were as lusty and raw as the whiskey they made and drank. They won every fistfight and every horserace. They could ride anything with four feet. They could sing and dance. And they were great musicians. Granny said it was the way of the Irish. Elijah wished he had a bit more Irish in him. It still smarted to remember his failure at fiddling. Uncle Caleb had tried and tried to teach him but finally had scratched his baldhead and given up. That had been three years ago. Elijah wondered if he tried again now....

Deborah jumped up, interrupting his reverie. "Look, Pa!" she cried, "a big fat bear!" The furry brown creature lumbered across the road ahead. Crashing through the brush, it disappeared into the woods. The mules seemed oblivious, but Johnny's horse perked its ears, sidestepped, and snorted.

"That bear ain't none too big nor fat," said Ned. "His ribs was pokin' out. But he'll soon fatten up when the berries ripen."

"Hey, Ma," teased Elijah, "why don't you ever correct Pa's grammar?"

Ned chuckled and gave her a quick wink. "She gave up on me years ago. That's what a city woman like your ma gets for marrying an old country boy."

When Johnny frowned, Becky's back stiffened again.

"Think I'll ride ahead a ways," Johnny said abruptly. He did, however, return when Ned stopped at the foot of the mountains, and in a shady grove of white oaks, Becky set out the picnic.

Elijah devoured the golden-crusted fried chicken, buttermilk biscuits, and flaky dried-apple pie and washed it all down with cold water from the nearby spring. After polishing off four more cookies, he was stuffed and drowsy. Using a sack of feed corn for a pillow, he nodded off and awakened only when the mules' hooves pounded the long covered bridge spanning Spadra Creek at the east edge of Clarksville.

Elijah sat up and his eyes grew big. There were five new buildings around the courthouse square. Two were made of red brick, and except for the high peaked roof of the courthouse cupola, they were as tall as the two-story courthouse. Main Street was still a short, dusty road; although to the west there were skeletons of new construction. The street was choked with wagons, buggies, carts, and horses. Elijah had never seen so many people.

"Whew wee!" exclaimed Johnny. "Never seen such a crowd for a mustering."

Ned pulled up to let a buggy turn onto the crowded road. "Must be secesh fever," he noted.

Becky turned worried eyes toward him. "Ned, you don't really think we'll secede?"

His eyes swept the crowd and he chewed his lip a second before answering. "Folks seem right stirred up," he admitted. "Last time I was in town, Phillip said he feared it was heading that way."

Uncle Phillip would know, reflected Elijah. Being owner and editor of *The Star*, Clarksville's only newspaper, he kept abreast of all the news around the state and even the nation. Elijah hoped they got to see Uncle Phillip and Cousin Nelda this trip. But he could leave happy without setting eyes on stuffy Aunt Louise. She had never forgiven Pa for marrying her sister. Elijah knew she was not fond of him, either.

"You want to stop by Louise's?" asked Ned.

Becky dropped her head and stared at the work-reddened hands clasped in her lap. She shook her head.

"Then we'll head on to the wagon yard," he said, "and get set up before it gets too dark."

He guided the team through the throng and turned the corner at a red brick building that was across the street and catty-cornered from the courthouse. Behind the building was a large lot filled with parked wagons. Small campfires already dotted the twilight. Ned soon found a likely spot under a spreading oak and not too close to the other camps. Elijah jumped down stiffly; glad to be out of the jolting wagon.

When Johnny tied his horse and walked off, Becky put her hands on her hips. "As usual he ate our food. But instead of helping set up camp, Johnny's off looking for a jug and a card game."

Ned looked after him. "Oh, he never meant any harm. I don't reckon it occurred to him to lend a hand."

Becky snorted and began unloading pots and pans.

Lately Elijah had begun noticing such things like how Pa was not flighty and selfish like Johnny. Unlike Johnny with Maggie, Pa was considerate of Ma, like now as he staked down a small tent for her. While most of the women here would sleep on a hard wagon bed or a quilt on the ground, Ma and Deborah would sleep in comfort on the straw-filled tick. Elijah intended someday to be thoughtful like that for Cindy.

When the milling crowd finally quieted, he was too restless to sleep. He lay in the wagon and stared at a sky bright with stars. But his thoughts conflicted with the serene night. War talk had filled the evening. Everyone was in a dither. Although Elijah felt no particular loyalty to any government, all this talk of secession made no sense. Back in February, when Pa had braved the icy weather for a trip to town to vote against the secession candidate, most people in the state had agreed. The anti-secession candidates won by more than eight thousand votes. But if this night's talk was any indication, things were changing. Hardly a soul had spoken out for Union. Feelings were running high against it.

Elijah had only a hazy understanding of state's rights. And slavery was no concern to him. There were few slaves in the mountains. The few he knew appeared content. It seemed impossible that they might rise up against white folks as some were saying.

Pa had been unusually quiet during all the chatter. Ma had cast worried looks at him all evening as if reading his mind she disliked what it said.

The night was filled with the chirping of crickets and the stamp of livestock stirring at their pickets and Ned's deep breathing beside him. A raucous laugh echoed through the darkness. "Probably some drunk winning at cards," thought Elijah as he sighed and turned on his side, hunting a more comfortable position. He wished tomorrow would hurry. It would be a grand day. Eventually, he slept.

Chapter 2

Ned guided the mules across Horsehead Creek and topped a rise where James Wilson's broad, grassy field spread out below. Elijah stared pop-eyed. Like a busy anthill, the field worked with booted farmers in crude homespun and women in poke bonnets and calico who mingled with silk draped ladies and frock-coated gentlemen in tall black hats. Before the mules stopped, Elijah looked about for Cindy. She had said her folks might come. Instead he espied a slender, one-armed figure in the distance. He jumped down and weaved through the crowd.

"Hey, Uncle Phillip," he called.

Phillip turned. A smile lit his scholarly face and deep-set eyes. He was a well-groomed man with short hair and neatly trimmed beard of silver-white.

"My word, Elijah, you've grown a foot since last summer!"

Elijah shook Phillip's left hand. The right sleeve of Phillip's crisp white shirt was empty and his frockcoat sleeve neatly penned up at the shoulder. The arm had been lost years before in the Mexican War, but Phillip was so capable, Elijah rarely noticed the handicap.

Where are your folks?"

"Over there." Elijah nodded toward the road. "Uncle Phillip, I've never seen so many folks. Pa says there must be a thousand."

"At least." Phillip's troubled eyes swept the crowd. "An amazing crowd for our little town."

Nelda joined them. "Elijah Loring! Don't you look handsome!" With a sunny smile, she looked him up and down. "I've never seen you so dressed up."

He straightened the string tie and looked sheepish. "Aw, Ma said I had to slick up." Then he quickly added, "You look nice, too."

It was not necessarily a lie. Tall, thin, and all angles, Nelda was neat but as usual void of frills. Although her hair was pulled back in the customary knot, she was the only woman present with neither hat nor bonnet. Elijah thought Nelda was almost pretty just because she was so nice. She was as different from Aunt Louise as a pea from a pumpkin. With apprehension, he quickly looked around. "Is your ma here today?"

"No. She has one of those awful headaches."

"That's too bad," he mumbled, feeling like a hypocrite.

A portly, well-dressed man climbed onto a stump and called for quiet.

"Hall McConnell," whispered Nelda. "Important family. His Pa was the first doctor in town."

"Ladies and Gentlemen!" Hall's voice boomed and the crowd hushed. "The brass band has marched out from town. They're just over the hill. Let's give them a grand welcome!"

Rows of infantry began forming quickly. With muskets and rifles on shoulders, men fell into line. Elijah thought they looked grand. The distance reverberated with the cadence of drums. His heart took up the rousing beat. First into sight came a flag popping in the warm morning breeze. Over the horizon it drew ever closer until blue bars and white stars were clearly visible on a field of blood red.

When Nelda gasped, Elijah turned. Her face had gone white. With hand to throat, she stared at the huge banner held aloft by a racing horseman. Men began cheering and waving hats high in the air. Nelda and Phillip exchanged dismayed looks.

Pa had said Uncle Phillip and Nelda were strong against secession, so Elijah supposed that was why the flag upset them. Nelda was as big on politics as Uncle Phillip. She even wrote articles for the paper, and according to Pa, they were very insightful. Elijah never read them. He did not relish politics. Adventure stories were more to his liking.

The band marched into sight, kettledrums pounding, cheeks puffy and lips glued to all manner of horns. It was Elijah's first glimpse of a brass band. It was a sight to behold! Whistles and cheers muted the music. He could barely hear the rollicking tune. As the horseman galloped the flag through the open columns, the infantry presented arms. Elijah thrilled at the splendid sight. Caught up in the excitement, his heart beat high. Out of respect for Nelda and Phillip, he refrained from joining in when someone ordered three cheers for Jeff Davis and the Confederate States. He noticed Allen Matthers standing close by, looking oddly solemn. Most folks here were alive with fervor such as Elijah had never experienced. It was a heady thing.

When the drill concluded, men marched in rank behind the flag to stand in front of a platform. Before Phillip joined the dignitaries seated there, he reached over to squeeze Nelda's hand. She gave him a shaky smile, and then began to hurriedly scribble notes.

The crowd slowly quieted. The representative to the state legislature called the meeting to order and then introduced Johnson County's delegates to the recent state convention. As Mr. Batson and Mr. Floyd droned on, Elijah grew bored and began looking around. He noticed Allen once again. Of course Allen was a head taller than everyone and his chestnut hair was bright in the sun. Arms crossed over a broad chest, he seemed mesmerized by the speeches. That was surprising. Elijah had figured Allen had only four interests: drinking, gambling, fiddling, and women.

Dillon was not in sight, but in a crowd of this size he might be anywhere. Although Elijah stood tiptoed, he still did not see Cindy's golden-brown head anywhere. A buzz of excitement drew his attention back to the platform. A resolution had carried to reconvene the state convention. Elijah noticed tension around Uncle Phillip's mouth.

The speeches finally ended. As the group dispersed, a short, burly man with forearms like a blacksmith handed Elijah a pamphlet. It was a speech he had studied at school, George Washington's farewell address warning against "*causes which may disturb our union.*" Elijah folded it and put it into his pocket. Apparently Uncle Phillip and Nelda were not the only ones upset by secession. More often than not, however, the intended recipient either refused the leaflet or threw it down. When that happened, the fellow picked it up, dusted it off, and offered it to someone else.

Elijah overheard Ned talking with John Hill. The sheriff's dark eyes were full of fire as he tugged at a long mustache. "I say hit 'em hard, Ned. One quick action and they'll know we mean business. Then they'll tuck tail and leave us alone. If we don't stop them first, they'll come marching right down Main Street and shoot us on the courthouse square!"

Elijah walked on, looking for Cindy. Finally giving up, he pulled a grass stem to chew and then leaned with his back to an oak. With knee bent, he propped the bottom of a boot on the trunk and watched the crowd. When Nelda joined him, he took the stem from his mouth and used it to gesture to the knot of men who had suddenly congregated around Phillip.

"They're buzzing like riled bees," he said. "And it appears your pa is the one getting stung."

Nelda frowned. When she went to stand near the edge of the group, Elijah joined her.

"I've been as strong for the Union as the next man," declared a man with heavy jowls.

Elijah had seen him before in Uncle Phillip's office paying for advertising in the paper. He was Robert Morrison, who owned the mercantile and the livery. Now he held up a newspaper and thumped the front page.

"You're a good editor, Phil, but you've got your head in the clouds if you think this can be settled without a fight. I agree with Danley here in the *Gazette*. It'll take an act of God to hold the Union together now. He says we're setting ducks between the Mississippi and the Indian Territory. We have to take action to defend ourselves."

A man with a strong drawl put in, "He's right." His broad-brimmed, white planter's hat nodded vigorously. "We ought to go ahead and secede. There's no other reasonable course."

When a murmur of agreement arose, Phillip looked at the speaker, barely masking his thin-lipped impatience. "Now hold on, John," he said. "That kind of talk will start us down a road we don't want to travel. Even Danley is still against secession. He urged us to be calm and act like wise and patriotic men." Phillip paused. "It's not too late to save the Union. In February we voted down the secession candidates almost two to one."

A slit-eyed man with a thin face stood near the back. He began to elbow his way forward. "Phillip Horton, you know very well the North changed things when they elected a no-account Black Republican!"

Phillip raised his hand for quiet. "Gill, none of us are thrilled because Lincoln won"—his eyes swept the group—"but let's not act like spoiled children who grab our marbles and run because the game doesn't suit. The last editorial in the Fayetteville *Arkansan* urged giving him a chance. If he fails we can always impeach him..." He was interrupted by a disgruntled mutter.

Gill spoke again, louder than the rest. "Hell, Phillip! Give *him* a chance? I'd sooner give a fox a chance at my chicken coop. Why, he'll ruin us!" There was assent and he went on, "We got to have darkies or the South is ruined."

"Lincoln's blather has them stirred up. There's going to be trouble. What if they turn on us?" asked the man in the white hat. "Last census there was almost a thousand in this county alone."

"No matter what, we need to stick with the rest of the South," said Robert Morrison. "Mark my words; there'll soon be Federal troops down here."

Phillip's voice was lost in the swell of accord. Nelda caught her lip in her teeth. Elijah spit out the grass stem.

"Don't worry about your pa. No one is going to best Uncle Phillip. He's smarter than that whole passel put together."

She shook her head in despair. "Oh, Elijah, what are they thinking! The Union is...."

Someone suddenly shouted, "Horserace!"

Political argument quickly died as every man turned to stare. At the far edge of the field, near the end of the long lane forking off the main road, were at least twenty riders, their mounts prancing in the noon sun.

Elijah pointed. "Hey! That's Johnny Lane on the dappled gray. And there's Allen Matthers on his big sorrel."

A pistol fired and the crowd yelled. Dust from the pounding hooves fogged the air. For several rods the horses were bunched. Johnny's gray was a nose ahead. Then a tall paint took the lead. As the horses circled the far side of the field, coming out of the turn, the barrel-chested sorrel pulled ahead.

Elijah whistled. "Look at Allen's sorrel stretch out." He loved good horseflesh, and he eyed the splendid horse with appreciation. Although a bulk of a man sat the sorrel's back, he ran with ease, powerful muscles rippling as he flashed through sunlight and shade, mane and tail flying. Like flames chased by the wind, his hooves ate up the road, leaving the others far behind. At the finish line, the big man reined him in, sending dirt and gravel flying.

The losers soon sawed to a stop. They endured jibes from the crowd with good-natured laughter as they threw greenbacks into Allen's proffered hat, all but a fair-haired, thin young man who glared when he tossed in his money. He threw the paint's reins to a Negro boy who quickly led the animal away. Still holding the quirt, which although used liberally, had failed to bring him victory, he swatted at his high-booted leg, and with long strides, started through the crowd.

Elijah was glad he had been beaten, even if it was by a Matthers. "That feller sure is a sore loser," he noted.

"Bo is a mess," Nelda agreed in an undertone. "Comes from being rich. His pa is Robert Morrison, and he owns half the businesses in town."

"Loosen-up, Bo,' called Allen, leaning indolently on the saddle horn. "I don't get riled when you out-shoot me."

As Bo stormed away, a beautiful girl reached out and caught his arm. When he shook off the hand and pushed on, she glared and turned to watch him disappear into the crowd. Her green eyes grew hot and her face flushed. Then as swiftly as a chameleon, she masked the anger and glanced about.

"Nelda!" she called. With skirts held above dainty slippered feet, she laced her way through the crowd. Her eyes strayed to Allen. Still sitting on the lathered sorrel, he returned the stare, plainly enjoying the perfect figure and the curly auburn hair hanging to her waist.

"Hello, Mary Beth," greeted Nelda. "Have you met my cousin, Elijah Loring?"

"Why, no." She held out a hand. "I'm sure I haven't. I'd certainly remember such a handsome man." As Elijah reddened and gave the soft hand a quick shake, she turned to Nelda. "That brother of mine! The way he takes on! He's such a sore loser...why, it plumb shames me. He'll sulk for a week over Allen beating him. I hope he doesn't get drunk and do something outlandish to spoil the party tonight."

"Oh, your pa can handle Bo."

"Pa!" Her eyes rolled and then narrowed with contempt. "He's never handled Bo. No one has." She lowered her voice. "He's always gotten anything he wanted. That's why he's so rotten." She sighed in exasperation, but in a heartbeat she was animated again. "Nelda, come early tonight and help me pick out my dress. I can't decide between a new green silk and a blue...."

Nelda hooted. "Mary Beth, you know very well I can't tell a fashionable silk purse from a sow's ear. Besides, I'll be working at the paper."

"But you are coming?" she cried.

"No, I don't think..."

Mary Beth rapped her arm. "Oh, Nelda! Do come. And bring your handsome cousin along." She fluttered away, calling back over her shoulder, "I'll see you both tonight."

Elijah wished he could go to the party, but Pa planned to drive a good ways before dark and camp along the trail somewhere. Pa would soon be expecting him back at camp to help load up, so he told Nelda goodbye. Although she quit chewing a pencil long enough to hug him, her mind was far away, probably on secession.

All too soon the wonderful trip was over, but Elijah knew he would always remember it. He wondered why Pa and Ma were so quiet on the way home. Why, they acted as if they'd just come from a funeral! Johnny's funning was the only bright part of the trip home, and finally even he gave up and grew silent.

It was four days before word finally reached the mountains. Another event had coincided with the muster. Allen brought the news from town. Far away in South Carolina, Confederate troops had fired on Fort Sumter. War had begun.

———————

As morning mists rose from the creek, Elijah looked north. He wondered if Lincoln really would send troops to Arkansas. On such a peaceful morning war seemed impossible, but more than likely right this minute folks were killing each other. He shook his head and then gave his face and hands a hurried wash in the creek and a swift pat to his wet hair. He grabbed up a dinner pail and book and quickly crossed the stream on the stones spanning the lazy water.

He was late again. Deborah had been gone for half an hour. He could not figure why Pa would not wait until next week when school let out to begin spring planting. Ma had warned that whippoorwills had not yet called and that meant more frost. For some reason, Pa was in a dither to get the corn into the ground. They had been in the field since sunrise dropping the golden seeds into the long, freshly plowed furrows.

Pa's mood was strange lately. He was fretting on something. And Ma knew it, too. She kept watching him with little worry lines between her eyes.

Elijah was deep in thought as he rounded a curve in the trail. He slowed from a trot to a walk, and then he stopped to let a wagon come abreast on the narrow trail.

"Howdy, Granny. Howdy, Uncle Caleb."

"Howdy yerself. Where you off to in sech a all-fired hurry?" asked short, wiry Caleb with a grin. He removed a sweat-stained hat and wiped his forehead. A full, grizzled beard flowed from his chin. With the exception of a fringe around the sides of his head, he was shiny bald.

"O'course, he's off to school. Got his dinner pail and book," declared the tiny woman seated alongside him, before she leaned to spit a brown stream of snuff. She wiped her mouth with the back of a bony, blue-veined hand and then rested it on a cane. Granny was small but so full of vinegar that she had always seemed sizeable to Elijah.

"Now that yo're full-growed, hit seems to me you ought to he'p yore pa with the plantin', instead of traipsing off to school," she said.

Elijah silently agreed. He should be doing a man's work. With the exception of Dillon, he was the oldest boy in school. But Ma insisted that he and Deborah get all the education possible, which had been little enough except her own efforts and an occasional traveling teacher. Mr. Saddler had been there only since last fall.

With down-turned lips, Granny added, "Don't know why Ned kowtows to that woman's fool notions." It grieved Elijah that Granny was so dead-set against Ma. Except for his immediate family, he loved Granny better than anyone, and it was no secret that he was her pet. She favored him over Uncle Caleb's Billy or any of the great-grandchildren. He figured it was only natural since Pa was her favorite. And more than likely that was because Pa was a baby when his ma had died. Granny still cried sometimes when she talked about losing her only daughter.

Even though Elijah had never known his grandparents, it made him sad to think of them dying. He never saw Piney Creek in flood without thinking how the flash flood had washed their wagon away. It gave him the shivers to think if Pa and Uncle Jim had not been spending the night with Granny, they would have drowned, too. Granny said the Lord was punishing John Loring for his hard ways, and in the same breath, she claimed Reeda May had been spared from the wrath to come, gone on to her reward early for being such a good woman. Like Ma often said, Granny could be mighty prejudiced in her thinking.

"Reckon you'll get educated enough to take off and go fishing with me one of these days?" asked Caleb.

"You bet." Elijah grinned, looking up at his laughing-eyed great uncle. "Where ya'll been?" he asked.

"I took Ma over to check on Maggie Lane. She's still poorly."

"Michael told me." Elijah faced Granny. "Is she gonna be all right?"

Granny and Caleb exchanged quick looks before she answered. "Life and death is in the hands of the Lord."

Elijah's heart sank at the evasive answer. It meant Maggie was bad off. He looked at the sun. "I better get along. I'm awful late."

"Come when you kin," called Granny. "Hit's time fer a dose of sulphur and molasses to keep the ticks and chiggers off." As Caleb drove off, she was still calling, "And ya need to be drinkin' plenty of sassafras. Hit thins the blood fer hot weather."

Elijah grinned and waved before beginning to run. Without slowing he passed the rambling, run-down Matthers home. Breakfast smoke curled from the chimney. Pigs and chickens roamed the yard, and a big, dingy washing hung on the rail fence. Half dozen bony hounds gave desultory barks. Belle trotted over to pay her respects. They ignored her and stayed in the shade of the sagging porch. The dogs were well acquainted with the pup because she was one of Old Scrapper's pups. When Ned's hound, Lightning, had been killed by a bear, Red had given Belle to Ned, but she had clearly chosen Elijah as her master. Now she hurried back to trot at his heels.

Red looked up from plowing to wave. Elijah threw up a hand. He wished the traveling teacher had found some place other than the old empty cabin on the Matthers' property to hold school. If he had, Dillon would not be in school. It was a cinch, Red Matthers would not pay tuition. He never had before. But the teacher had traded tuition for rent, so sixteen-year-old Dillon, the youngest, had become the first and only Matthers to attend school, and to Elijah a constant source of misery. Except for Dillon's presence, Elijah enjoyed school. He would miss going when the term ended.

In spite of running the last quarter mile, he was late. He slowed at the edge of the hard-packed clearing and walked toward the small log building with holes for windows and a crooked rock chimney leaning in one wall. Belle dropped down to wait in the shade. She would give up after a while and go home.

Elijah hated being late. It was the third time this week, and old man Saddler loathed tardiness. As Elijah came through the door, the teacher was already reading the scripture.

"*And the LORD said unto me, 'Say unto them, Go not up, neither fight; for I am not among you; lest ye be smitten before your enemies. So I spake unto you; and ye would not hear, but rebelled...'*" The droop-shouldered, scrawny man looked up over the top of his spectacles. "Elijah, late again?"

Dillon folded arms across his thick chest and leaned back in the seat. "Maybe Lige's ma is teaching him the minuet." He smirked at the laughter.

Deborah whirled in her seat. "Shut your big mouth, Dillon Matthers!"

Elijah's ears went hot. Pa had warned him not to let his fiery temper get him into trouble but he longed to smash Dillon's nose. Of course Dillon would probably thrash him. Like all the Matthers, Dillon had a barrel chest, a bull neck, and arms like bridge timbers. Barring a miracle, Elijah figured he had less chance than David against Goliath.

Elijah's scowl included his seatmate. Vernon haw-hawed louder than anyone. Elijah glanced at Cindy. She was looking down at a book. If he did not have a go at Dillon soon, she would think him a coward.

Mr. Saddler closed the Bible and shoved the spectacles further up his long, thin nose. "First grade, get your slates, rise, and come forward."

First grade consisted of Deborah and towheaded Pete Mason, who both got slates and rose. Deborah kept shoulders stiff and blazing eyes straight ahead, but as Pete stood, he gave Elijah a big, gap-toothed grin.

Elijah let out a deep breath and headed for the back row. He stopped short. Dillon's big feet were propped on the flat sawed log that was Elijah's seat. The boots had shed dried mud all over it. With a frown Elijah threw his book onto the log desktop and unconsciously clenched and unclenched his fists. "Move your muddy boots." He waited, his brown eyes ice.

Dillon hummed under his breath and kept drawing on a slate. Elijah braced himself. More than likely Dillon would come up swinging. He raised his voice. "I said to move your muddy boots off my seat."

The humming stopped.

"Right now! Move your big, ugly feet off my seat!"

Dillon looked up. With a lazy grin, he shrugged and pulled the boots back. They hit the floor with a thud, sending up puffs of dust. Elijah was stunned.

Dillon leaned forward and tossed his slate across the aisle. It landed on Cindy's desktop, a long split log held high by forked posts. On the slate was a big heart with Cindy's name in the middle. Elijah saw the blush before she lowered her head. She erased the heart, but when she handed the slate back, she raised her eyes and gave Dillon a shy smile. Elijah's gut twisted.

Cindy was his girl! Well, not that there had ever been a spoken promise between them, but they sat together every day at dinner. He always walked part way home with her. She must know he was going to marry her.

Dillon taunted him with a knowing grin. A slow burn crept up Elijah's neck. Tight-jawed, he sat down, took up a dog-eared book, and stared at the pages. It stung worse than salt in a cut to have Dillon taunt him about Cindy. She had smiled at Dillon! Elijah fumed, and yet he could not keep his eyes off her. Sunlight came through unchinked cracks and lay in golden bars across her sun-browned face and thick brown hair. Her eyes were brown with a shimmer that reminded Elijah of a sun-flecked pool in Piney. Cindy was beautiful and smart too. She made the best grades in school, even better than his, unless he really put his mind to it. He squared his shoulders. She was worth fighting for.

As morning dragged on he fidgeted to be out of the stuffy room. His eyes strayed out the window holes toward the shady creek and the towering bluff beyond. It would be a good day for fishing. He tried pulling his mind back to study. Doggone it! He didn't know what was wrong with him. He would make up his mind to concentrate on lessons. The next thing he knew, Cindy's big brown eyes were staring up at him from his slate, or he was watching the sunlight dance on her hair pulled back into a thick, pretty braid. It would take less keen eyes than his not to see that Cindy, at fifteen, had turned into a woman. That was considered marriageable age in the mountains, but Elijah had been warned not even to think about such things. Ma and Pa had made it plain that he could not marry before he was able to stand on his own two feet. Besides, Brother Simon held that child brides were an evil curse that needed stamping out in the mountains. Elijah knew the preacher would likely tar and feather anyone that came buzzing around after his daughter. Elijah had confined his courting to school.

"Mr. Loring, perhaps you'll tell the class why you sit daydreaming rather than doing your lessons."

Rather than resenting the reprimand, Elijah had to admit his mind had not been on his studies lately. His grades were reflecting it too. He would have to snap out of it. It wasn't fair to Ma for him to dawdle this way. She was paying to keep him in school. School might be over for good soon enough. There was a rumor that Mr. Saddler was heading north as soon as he drew his tuition fees. Elijah was not sorry to see him go; however, he would miss school and not seeing Cindy every day.

Without realizing it, he sighed aloud. When half the class turned to stare, he hid his face behind the history book and tried to act interested in the boring dates and far off places. In reality, his mind flew right back to his dilemma. He raised his eyes again to Cindy. His stomach knotted when she glanced around at Dillon. Then Elijah daydreamed of pounding Dillon to a pulp. His anger smoldered like coals easily fanned into a blaze.

When Mr. Saddler dismissed for dinner, Elijah went to a shady spot and sat on the ground. He leaned back against a tall elm. It was not the spot that he and Cindy always shared.

Deborah, carrying the dinner pail, raised her eyebrows and then came to join him. "Dillon's just an old loud mouth." She pulled out biscuits stuffed with pieces of fried ham. "And he doesn't make near as good grades as you."

Elijah pretended not to notice as Cindy walked past, but all the while he stared at her through downcast lashes. She was long-legged, tall, and pleasingly curved. Even though her feet were as bare as the hard-packed schoolyard, she walked with an easy grace. Head held high, she went to the shade of a nearby leafy oak and sat down on a stump. The dinner pail in her lap remained unopened while she waited for Pete.

Pete arrived out of breath from a hurried trip to the woods. His tawny hair gleamed in the sun, and a smattering of freckles dotted the fair skin of his sunburned nose. Vernon stuck out a foot to trip him. Without even slowing, Pete hopped over. "Keep your clod-hoppers out of the way!" He glared at Vernon. Then he reached eagerly for the lunch pail. "Sure is great to be preacher's kids. Bet no one else has fried chicken."

"I'd just as leave they paid Pa cash. Maybe then we could buy one or two of the million things we need." Although Cindy spoke low, her voice carried to Elijah.

"Aw, Cindy, you're just a old sourpuss. What's wrong with you? Ya ought to be happy for a special dinner." He glanced over at Elijah. "Oh, you and Lige must be fightin'."

"Don't talk with your mouth full," she snapped.

Elijah was glad Cindy was unhappy about their tiff. His satisfaction quickly faded when Dillon sauntered past and looked from him to Cindy and grinned. Dillon walked on and sat down on the ground near Cindy.

"That fried chicken looks good."

When she offered a drumstick, Dillon took it from her long fingers. "Much obliged, Cindy. That's mighty sweet of you." He gave Elijah a spiteful grin.

Heat suffused Elijah's face. He threw down the biscuit, sprang up, and charged.

Dillon jumped up. He shoved Elijah backwards. Red hair flaming in the sun, he was leeringly confident as he put up his fists.

Elijah was thankful the roundhouse that followed missed by a hairsbreadth. It would have knocked him cold. He stepped in quickly to land a blow on Dillon's nose. Before he could retreat, Dillon returned the punch, glancing it off Elijah's cheek. It stung, but in the heat of battle he barely noticed. He had put up with Dillon's needling for a long time. It felt good to finally be doing something about it. When Elijah lunged, Dillon's fists caught his shoulder, spinning him back.

Deborah screamed, "Teacher! Teacher!"

Elijah knew there was no worry on that account. He was sure Mr. Saddler had headed for the woods the minute trouble started. He was also sure the teacher's absence would last just as long as the fight.

Dillon hit Elijah's chin, and he saw stars. As they traded punches, every one that connected jarred Elijah's teeth. He knew he would never last trading lick for lick. Dillon was too big. He would have to change his strategy. Ducking under the next blow, he caught Dillon off guard and butted him hard in the chest with his head. As Dillon fought for breath, Elijah backed off and butted again, knocking him to the ground. He leaped onto Dillon's chest only to have Dillon land a hard lick on his nose.

Elijah strained to keep his perch, but Dillon struggled up and threw him off. He hit the dirt hard and rolled. Dillon shook his big head and pushed the sweaty red hair from his eyes.

For a minute Elijah thought he had Dillon winded, but his heart sank when, hardly panting, Dillon doubled ham-like fists again and circled, grinning at him like a fellow enjoying a Sunday picnic.

Elijah moved in swinging hard, but his blows had little effect. Almost spent, he was forced to stop swinging to protect his teeth, two of which felt jarred loose. From the taste of his own blood and the dizzy ringing in his ears, Elijah knew he was whipped. Weaving,

he barely stayed on his feet. It was especially humiliating with
Cindy looking on. He was amazed when Dillon dropped his fists
and laughed.

"You fight pretty good, Lige." Dillon sauntered away.

Elijah shook his swimming head and felt his swollen jaw.
Dillon had him whipped. Why had he quit?

A few faint freckles stood out on Deborah's anxious face as her
large brown eyes swept him. "Are you bad hurt?"

He dusted himself off. "Naw."

Cindy stepped up. "Are you sure? Your nose is bleeding."

He swiped a sleeve across his face and winced. The sleeve
came away with a bloody smear. And it was torn. Ma wouldn't be
pleased. He only had one good school shirt, and Ma didn't hold with
wearing patches to school. He wiped his nose and cringed.

"Here." Cindy handed him a handkerchief. "Elijah, you better
watch that temper before it gets you killed. Dillon could have hurt
you bad."

Her words stung worse than his cuts and bruises. His jaw
jutted. "He was egging it on." He licked his busted lips. "What did
you expect me to do?"

"Turn the other cheek."

Elijah snorted. "If you take up preaching, don't expect me to
pay for your sermons with chickens so you can share 'em with
Dillon."

Her eyes flashed. She whirled and stormed away.

At the moment Elijah was too mad to care.

———————

"Elijah," Mr. Saddler stopped him at the door. "Don't stoop to
coarse ways. You're different from these ruffians. Your mother is a
lady. She expects great things of you."

Although Mr. Saddler spoke low, Elijah squirmed. He was not
different! When Ma spoke of him going away to school someday to
make something of himself, he kept quiet, but he shunned the
thought of ever leaving. This was his home and he liked it fine. He
was saved a reply when Caleb rode a mule hard into the
schoolyard.

Without dismounting, Caleb shouted, "We seceded. Weren't but one feller voted nay." Then he kicked the mule's flanks and sped off like Paul Revere to spread the word.

Mr. Saddler was preoccupied all afternoon. And all afternoon Elijah ignored Cindy. He kept his eyes on the books. When Mr. Saddler dismissed the class, she hurried from the room, and Elijah walked home alone. His anger had cooled and he wished Cindy were beside him. He was in no hurry to face Ma and Pa with a swollen face and torn clothes. He suddenly wondered what Pa thought about Caleb's news. Elijah doubted secession would affect them, living way back in the woods here on Little Piney.

When Elijah set his dinner pail on the long pine table, Becky's tear-filled voice came through the closed bedroom door.

"*You can't leave me here alone!*"

Ned cajoled, "You won't be alone. Elijah will be here. Cousin Jenny is just over the way. And Caleb and Granny are close by if you need them."

"That old woman hates me!"

"Now, Becky, that ain't so. She'll help you any way she can. Besides, I won't be gone long. I figure, at most, a couple of months, and Elijah can manage fine with a little help from Caleb."

Her voice rose. "How can you even consider this! This war doesn't concern us!"

"Oh, yes, it does. Lincoln is sending troops down here. And I don't aim to sit here twiddlin' my thumbs until they march into the front yard."

"Then let the single men fight," she pleaded.

"John Hill is right. The more that goes now, the quicker this thing will be over with. If we hit 'em hard, they'll tuck tail and run." He was resolute. "You may as well get used to the idea, Becky. I am going."

Pa was leaving! Pa was going to war! Elijah grabbed the milk bucket and fled to the barn. Ma would not talk him out of it. Pa was as headstrong as a mule. But this time Ma was right. How could they manage without Pa?

Elijah put the cow into the stanchion. The milk hit the empty bucket with a tinny ring, and then as the Guernsey easily let down her milk, it became a soothing, soft, creamy swish. But Elijah's mind reeled and sweat trickled down his sides as if he were splitting wood or plowing.

It was the next day before he was alone with Ned. He had just forked a pile of hay to the mules when Ned strode into the barn and took down a harness from a hook on the wall. Ned sat down on the lid of the salt barrel.

"This harness is gettin' old and wore," said Ned as he picked up a leather punch, "but I reckon it will stand a bit more patching before it gives out."

Elijah did not answer. Pa would hear the tears in his voice.

Ned gouged at the leather. "While I'm gone, you'll have a man's load. I don't intend to be away long. But the fact of the matter is, with soldiering, a man can never tell." He looked up from the harness to meet Elijah's eyes. "A man can't afford temper fits, Elijah. They start a feller down the wrong road. Like the Good Book says—little foxes spoil the grapes. It's a foolish man won't rein hisself in when he gets mad."

Elijah had stopped forking hay. Now he looked at the ground. The words were almost a whisper. "I'll try, Pa."

Ned nodded and looked back at his work. "Be thoughtful of your mama and spare her all the work you can."

He knew what Pa meant. Pa never asked Ma to clean fish or game, and on butchering day she stayed inside until the skinning and gutting were done. Elijah must spare her that now.

"I'd not go if I didn't know you can handle it." Ned stopped to swallow. "No man could ask for a better son."

———— ∽ ————

The east sky had just pinked when Ned picked up the pack and slung it onto his back. Becky was a statue. A rooster's crow split the stony silence that had fallen between them.

"I'll be back 'fore you know it."

"I'll know it," she said. Her words were dead and cold.

Elijah had already hugged Pa goodbye. But now he wanted to throw his arms around Pa's neck, to hold him tight and beg him not to go. Instead, with a hand on Deborah's shoulder, he stood resolute while Pa told him again to take good care of Ma and Deborah.

Just then Johnny Lane rode across the creek. His face shiny with excitement, he stopped at the edge of the yard. "You about ready, Ned?"

Becky did not look at him, but her nose flared and her lips narrowed.

"Be right there."

Ned took her in his arms. For a minute she held back. Then she sobbed and melted against him. Only once before had Elijah seen Ma cry like that, the day they had buried his twin brothers on the hill behind the cabin. She had wrapped the tiny, lifeless bodies that had not lived long enough to see a sunrise in her best quilt and wept great racking sobs as she was doing now. Pa had stroked her hair the same way then.

Finally Ned stepped back and hurried from the yard. As Johnny's mare fell in alongside, he asked, "You ain't riding?"

"I figure to get a mount in town. The boy and Becky will have need of the mules."

Becky went inside and shut the door. Elijah watched until Ned was out of sight.

Chapter 3

"Feels like a funeral," fumed Elijah. For days Ma had mostly stayed in the bedroom as silent as a corpse, and Deborah had crept around, big-eyed and frightened. At school things were no better. Cindy ignored him. He kept his distance, but in spite of wounded vanity, he wanted to patch things up. School would be out soon. There would be little opportunity to see her all summer.

She rebuffed his advances. On the last day when he tried walking home alongside her, she quickened her steps. He kicked at a rock and let her go. After a week had passed, he wondered if she regretted their quarrel as much as he did. Finally on Sunday he rode over to see her. Brother Simon invited him to step down and come in, but the preacher did not looked pleased when Elijah asked to speak to Cindy.

Polly looked up from the quilt frame. "Cindy and Pete are over visiting at my cousin Myrtle's."

"Elijah, let's go sit outside where hit's cooler," invited Simon. He sat down on the porch in a rocking chair, picked up a piece of wood, and began to whittle. "Have a seat."

Elijah sat down.

Simon shaved off a long curl and then felt the wood with his finger. "I'm makin' Polly a fancy shelf for her doodads." He put the knife to the wood again. "Elijah, yo're a fine young man. A couple a' years from now, I'll be glad to see you come courting. But not yet."

Elijah nodded. It was just what he had feared. Simon had shut the door on any courting. And so far as Elijah knew, so had Cindy! He was miserable. He rode home feeling doomed.

His thoughts stayed full of Cindy, but as May gave way to June, the demands of work kept him busy. Crops needed hoeing, animals needed tending, and Ma often needed help. She was overwhelmed with chores. Butter needed churning, clothes needed washing, and food needed cooking. The house needed cleaning. She made jelly from wild plums and from juicy, ripe blackberries that grew in thickets at the edge of the fields. And she dried fruit spread out on a sheet in the sun. She chopped cabbage and salted it down in crocks for kraut, and when the green beans produced, she threaded them onto long strings to dry into—as Granny called the tough dried beans—leather britches.

Ma had actually been cheerful since the day before when Caleb brought a newsy letter from Ned. Elijah hoped it lasted. Just now, she laughed when Belle got tangled in his feet causing him to fall and spill the bucket of water.

"Get!" In pretended anger, he kicked at the pup. He hid a grin, overjoyed to hear Ma laugh in her old cheery way. She looked pretty today even though the old work dress was faded and growing threadbare. Sunlight dappled through the elm leaves onto her fair hair where she stood, sleeves turned up, her arms elbow deep in the washtub.

"Oh, no," she said. "A button is missing from Deborah's best dress." Her hands searched the bottom of the tub. "Thank goodness, here it is." She lifted a shining gold button and laid it aside on a stump. "I'm glad I found it. I'd never be able to match it." She plunged the dress back into the water and scrubbed and lifted. "I don't care what your granny says, this store cloth is as durable as can be."

Elijah knew Granny could not get over the fact that Ma did not weave or spin, and although Ma sewed, she bought the yard goods in town. Granny prided herself on fine weaving, raising her own sheep for Uncle Caleb to shear. She had a small field of cotton and another of flax for spinning. Her dyes were the envy of all the womenfolk. Granny, because of a special knowledge of herbs, roots, and berries, made the prettiest and fastest dyes in the country. But Elijah liked the store cloth just fine.

As he returned to the creek for more water, he digested Pa's news. It was a relief to know Pa was fine and still in camp in northwest Arkansas. He had not fought any battles yet. Elijah missed him and he missed things not being like they used to be. He hoped this silly war would be over soon. It still made no sense to him. Pa's explanation for joining up made no sense either. Why didn't he just wait to see if the Yankees came? Better yet, why didn't everyone just let other folks be? Elijah didn't care what folks in Maryland did, and he didn't see why they should care about Arkansas either. He felt no loyalty to any government. He had rarely been off the mountain except for a yearly trip to Clarksville, and sometimes not even that. But he did feel loyalty to Pa, so he hoped they whipped the pants off the Yankees so Pa could come home.

Caleb's news was a poser. Why would Uncle Jim's boy, James, join the Union Army? At least that was his intention when he left last week for Kansas. Caleb figured it was because Uncle Jim had talked him into it. Grandpa Loring had been from Indiana and Uncle Jim idolized his dead Pa.

Although Granny had raised both Pa and Uncle Jim, she had never cottoned to Jim as she had to Pa. She said Jim had a mean streak like his pa. Although Uncle Jim rarely laughed and joked like Pa, Elijah did not recall seeing any meanness in him...but even Pa had said his brother could be a hard man.

Elijah stopped in his track. If Pa had remembered Grandpa Loring and his stories of Indiana, would he have fought for the Union? All Pa had ever known was Granny and Uncle Caleb. With Granny feeling like she did about John Loring, she had never encouraged any goodwill for his memory.

Uncle Caleb said Granny would be hopping mad at James. Elijah figured he was right. Not that Granny was a patriotic Confederate, but now that Pa and Uncle Caleb's Billy had both gone off to fight for the South, she would be right put out at James for fighting against them. Elijah shook his head and went on toward the creek. Every time he tried to sort things out, he got about as far as Belle did chasing her tail.

Heat waves danced in the yard, but it was cool in the shade. The water was crystal clear today and not too cold. Down the creek a bullfrog croaked. Elijah decided to go for a swim when the chores were done. He dipped the pail full and made it halfway back to the washpot boiling near the cabin when Belle barked, her nose pointed toward the creek. He glanced back and instantly stilled.

Lew Willis! He sat on a chestnut-brown horse in the shadows. Elijah, his neck hairs rising, again envisioned a cat eyeing prey. Lew stared. Then, kneeing the horse, he crossed the creek. He dismounted near Becky and hunkered on the ground. Elijah stepped near the shotgun leaned against the porch. He would not lift it and insult Lew, but he intended having it close at hand.

Lew wore a frayed homespun shirt and trousers, but the leggings and moccasins were fancy, fringed and beaded like the handiwork of an Indian. Elijah wondered if he might be Indian. His dark face was narrow with high cheekbones. His skin was leathery and roughened by a short, scraggly beard that never grew longer. Elijah doubted he ever shaved. If he were part Indian, perhaps the beard would not grow. Pa said Indians had no face hair.

When Lew lifted the dilapidated hat from long, greasy hair, his eyes slid everywhere. They flickered when he saw the shotgun.

Becky gave a nervous smile. "How are you, Lew?"

His eyes slid over her. "I heard Ned was gone. Thought you might need a hand with something."

"No," said Elijah. "We don't need a thing. Besides, I thought your back was so bad you couldn't go to the army."

Resentment washed Lew's face and his eyes tapered into glittering slits. He turned to Elijah. "That's a fact. But some things I kin still do real good." Briefly a dark hand rested on the knife butt protruding from his leggings. Without another word, he stood, mounted, and rode away.

Elijah stared until he was out of sight. Would he ever get over being jittery when Lew was around?

"Your pa thinks Lew is harmless"—Becky bit her lip—"but I don't know. He gives me a strange feeling."

"Don't trust him, Ma, not as far as you can throw him. Pa is so quick to see the good in everyone; sometimes I think he turns a blind eye to their bad."

"Perhaps. But that's one of the things I love about your pa." She gave a faint smile and turned back to the rub-board. Her eyes fell on the stump. She leaned over and looked all around. "Elijah, do you see Deborah's button?"

Only half listening, he shook his head. He did not like Lew coming here, not one bit.

"Oh, I forgot to put the beans to soak for supper," said Becky. "Hang up these last things for me, please."

"Sure, Ma."

The laundry was almost all spread on the fence when Belle began to bark again. Elijah tensed. But it was only Cousin Jenny crossing the stream, surefooted but careful of the white topped water rushing past the stepping-stones. Rain from the night before had swollen Little Piney to twice its normal size.

"Howdy, Jenny," he greeted.

"Howdy, yerself," she answered.

She wore no bonnet and her dark hair glistened in the sun. Elijah found it odd there was a kinship between his ma and this big-boned, dark, silent woman. Some folks held Jenny at arm's length, the ones who disliked Injun blood even if it was mixed with white.

Her broad, tanned face crinkled with a smile. "Hit's a purty day, ain't it?"

"Yep, too pretty to be doing chores. I'd rather be fishin'."

"I just passed Lew Willis a ways back on the trail," she said.

"Yeah," said Elijah. "I'd sooner meet a razorback hog in the woods than him."

Jenny raised one eyebrow and nodded. "He does sort of make a body's flesh crawl...but I never heared of him doing no harm."

Elijah was tempted to voice his suspicions. But he had promised Pa, so he kept silent. Instead he said, "Come on to the house. Ma's inside."

He followed Jenny inside. "Hey, Ma," he yelled, "Jenny's here."

"Hello, Jenny," Becky called from the loft, pleasure coloring her tone. "I'm just getting some dried beans. I'll be right down."

While Jenny took a seat at the table, Elijah sat down on the opposite bench. She glanced around the neat room.

"I keep my place scrubbed clean," she said, "but I declare, I ain't got yer Ma's knack. She kin turn a cabin into a palace. Some might think them quilts hanging on the wall and them pretty pillows in the rocker foolishness, but I think they're awful purty." Then she bit her lip, realizing she had let slip the criticism of neighbors.

Elijah pretended not to notice. "How's Pappy?" he asked.

"Not so good...."

"Jenny!" Becky came swiftly down the loft ladder and rushed to give the tall woman a hug. "It's so good to see you! I've been starving for company."

"It's been a while since we visited," Jenny acknowledged. "I been wonderin' about you. But mostly I came today because Pappy wanted me to warn you about the bushwhacking going on up in Newton County. A feller Pa knows rode through yesterdee and told us. Hit's bad up there. Bound to start here, too, with so many of the men gone. He said for you and Lige to be careful and keep a gun handy."

In spite of the bad tidings, Elijah was glad Jenny had come. Her visits always cheered Ma. Becky declared it a holiday so they could have a nice, long visit.

That afternoon Elijah went fishing and Deborah swam and played in the creek.

———⌒———

Time for playing and fishing grew less as the summer wore on. The crops were good. They worked from morning till night gathering and preserving food. The attic and cellar were soon bulging. In early July the bean vines hung heavy, waxy, and full with shell beans swelling the pods. Elijah wiped sweat from his forehead and reached to strip off another pod clinging to the vine. Cawing crows set up an alarm and then lifted in a wave at the far end of the cornfield. Eyes shaded, Elijah tensed.

"Riders coming fast, Ma," he called. "Get to the house." Heart pounding, a shivery chill swept him. "Hurry, Ma!"

Becky left the half-filled basket and motioned to Deborah who worked farther down the row. "Run, honey." They ran from the garden, managing to arrive on the porch just before the riders.

"Get inside," Becky ordered Deborah, "and stay there." Deborah's eyes grew large but she stayed rooted. Becky shoved her. "Hurry! Get out of sight!"

"You come inside too, Ma." Elijah stood in the shadows of the doorway. He gripped the shotgun in sweaty hands.

"No," said Becky. I'll tend to this."

The riders slowed. Of the five rough-garbed men, three held the reins of pack mules while the two in front advanced, hard-faced and eyes searching, right hands empty and handy to pistol butts poking from worn leather holsters. The nearest man was big-bellied and fat, the second dark-haired, lean, and handsome. Seeing Elijah in the doorway, the fat one pulled rein and spoke low, but the coarse mutter carried to Elijah.

"Rooster's young, Jess, but he's got spurs."

Jess peered where his partner nodded. Elijah cocked the shotgun. The click echoed in the stillness.

"Just passing through, ma'am." Speaking loudly, the man called Jess touched a finger to his hat. But Elijah's ears went hot seeing the man's bold gaze insultingly rove up and down her body.

Softly, Jess added, "Ma'am, I'll come back when the bantam's not around." At her angry flush, he chuckled. Turning his mount, he cantered down the trail with his gang in tow.

With a scowl Elijah stepped from the house and watched them disappear. "Next time, Ma, you get in the house. I'll tend to them. And if they come when I'm not here, don't you go outside. And no matter where you're working, always keep a gun handy."

Becky nodded, and although the day was warm, she shivered and rubbed her arms. "I'm glad you were here, son."

Elijah hated to think what might have happened otherwise. That night his sleep was fitful, filled with nightmares of fiery-eyed bushwhackers on charging horses. The next day he jerked at every noise. As his eyes constantly swept the horizon, he kept the gun in easy reach. Late that afternoon Becky asked him to take a basket of garden truck to Maggie. He hated leaving her and Deborah alone, but it would be a good chance to ask if the bushwhackers had struck elsewhere. They had come and gone the wrong direction to strike at Michael's or Granny's or Simon's, but a body could never tell about bushwhackers. On the way to the Lane cabin, Elijah ran more than he walked.

He was relieved. Michael had seen no strangers. Simon had been by earlier to check on Maggie, and things were fine at his place and at Caleb's too. Elijah tried to quickly take his leave. It was not a pleasant visit. Something was sapping the life from Maggie. She was growing weaker by the day. Michael was scared and he had every right to be.

Michael followed him outside. "Ma looks bad, don't she?"

Elijah swallowed. "I don't reckon Granny's yarbs are helping."

Michael shook his head. "I can't see as they are."

Elijah scuffed his foot through the dirt. He could think of no words of comfort. Besides it was useless to lie.

"I gotta go. That cow will be at the barn needing milking."

Michael expelled a deep breath. "Well, tell yer ma thanks for the stuff."

"I will. Come when you can," he called back over his shoulder. He looked back to wave. Looking desolate, Michael still stood in the yard.

Twilight purpled. Elijah hurried along the trail not even taking time to peer about for Lew. In the evening shadows tree frogs sang for rain.

"Elijah! Wait up!"

He froze in his tracks.

"Oh, Elijah!" Breathless, Cindy arrived, smiling. "You almost got away before I caught you. My, you walk fast!"

Elijah's heart soared. She acted as though they had never quarreled!

"Good to see you." If he dared he would take her hand.

Her eyes were soft. "I've missed you."

"I came over once but...."

"Pa told me. I tried talking to him, and so did Ma, but Pa is awful stubborn"—she quirked an eyebrow—"especially when it's about me." She sighed. "I reckon I should be glad. Ma says I'm the apple of his eye. But sometimes, I wish..." Abruptly she brightened. "But he said you can come Saturday. Ma said we young folks could have a taffy pull while Ma has that quilting for Laveney Sorrels. She's marrying Tod Dougan before he goes off to the army." She lifted her eyes for his reaction.

Elijah nodded. His heart beat fast. He wished it were Saturday already!

"What time?"

"Oh, just as soon as the morning chores are done. Some will likely get there earlier than others. Ma said to invite your ma."

"I will. Tell her thank you kindly. We'll be there."

Cindy waved before disappearing from sight. He walked on, smiling. It was a beginning. Simon had said he could come. And it was nice of Polly to invite Ma. He hurried home to tell her.

"A taffy pull...in this heat?" Becky's brows rose. "What is Polly thinking? Her cabin will be an inferno."

"Aw it won't be too bad with the doors and windows open."

"No, Elijah." She shook her head. "We shouldn't leave the place. Just think of those men who rode through yesterday. It's just not safe for all of us to be gone from home."

His face grew long. It was an excuse. Mountain gatherings made her uncomfortable. He wondered if perhaps Deborah had tattled and Ma disapproved of him liking Cindy. She soon put his mind at rest.

"You can go. If you leave us the shotgun, Deborah and I will be fine alone."

Disgust filled his voice. "Aw, Ma! Wouldn't that look just grand! Elijah Loring attends quilting while mother and sister stay home."

"But, if there's to be a taffy pull...."

He was not about to go off and leave Ma and Deborah at home. What if something did happen? "Forget it, Ma. I'll stay home and let you and Deborah go. She would enjoy it." He added, "A little fun wouldn't hurt you, either."

She shrugged. "No, I suppose it wouldn't. But I think we'll just all stay home together."

The next morning, he sulked. But it did no good. Ma had made up her mind. He was still fuming when he went inside for dinner.

Deborah called from the yard, "Granny's coming."

As Becky hurried to her room, Elijah stepped outside. Viola drove the mules and wagon into the yard, scattering scratching chickens and sending Belle nipping at the wheels. Granny was perched alongside Viola on the high seat.

"Howdy, howdy," Even before the wagon stopped, Granny was talking.

Deborah ran and climbed up on the side of the wagon. She stared in fascination at the mole on Granny's sagging double chin. The long white hair growing from it seemed to intrigue her.

"We just found out bushwhackers hit Red's place day before yesterdee."

Elijah grew grim. "They came through here. Five rough-looking men and a bunch of pack mules. They rode up real fast. But Pa left his old shotgun, and when they saw it cocked and ready, they rode on."

"Thank the Lord!" breathed out Granny.

"Anybody get hurt at Red's?" he asked.

"Naw. Kate was home alone when they hit. Later on, Allen jumped the scoundrels and got their stuff back. He took their guns and horses and sent them skeedaddlin'. But we're gonna have to be all-fired kerful to keep our guns handy. With our men gone, that kind of scum thinks they kin just take over!"

Viola spoke up. "Ma, it's past noon. We best get along. Caleb will be wanting his dinner."

Granny's fiery eyes cooled. "Yep, we best get on." She leaned to spit. The amber stream hit a rooster in the back of the head. She cackled when he fled with wings flapping. "Bull's eye," she said, wiping her mouth. "My aim with a musket is jest as true. Them thieving rascals come around my place, I'll show 'em." The old woman winked at Elijah over the top of Deborah's head. In a conspiratorial, hoarse whisper, she teased, "They'll not find my buried gold."

With disgust, Viola said, "The only gold we ever had was still in Pappy Tanner's teeth when we buried him."

"Like I said, no one's ever gonna find my buried gold." Elijah joined in as Granny's laugh cackled out.

"Ma!" Viola was scandalized.

Granny rapped the cane in her withered hands. "Oh, Viola, you was weaned on pickle juice. Pappy liked a good joke better'n anyone. He'd be laughin' too."

Elijah thought Viola did look puckered with her gray hair drawn on top of her head into such a tight knot. Once again he felt sorry for Uncle Caleb.

The old woman smiled fondly. "Laughing is the only way me and Pappy made it, scratching a livin' out of these old mountains."

"Granny," Elijah put in, "Lew Willis has been nosing around. Do you think he might be up to something?"

"Lew? Why, that poor tetched feller rambles everywhere," began Granny.

"Now, Ma." Viola tried to shush her. "He might be hiding in the woods right now, hearin' every word." She lowered her voice. "He wouldn't like to be called tetched."

"Piffle! I ain't scart a' Lew Willis." Granny's black eyes snapped. "Viola Tanner, I've always spoke my mind, and I ain't likely to stop now! If Lew ain't careful, I'll spit in his eye!" She emphasized the statement by letting fly a stream of snuff, splattering a hen, and then she waved her hand in scornful dismissal of Lew.

Her eyes twinkled at Elijah. "I kin hit where I spit. I'm a'tryin' to teach Viola, but she's not catchin' on so fast." The gaunt woman beside her rolled her eyes as the old woman chuckled. Then Granny added, "Oh, poor Lew ain't got enough sense to be up to nothing. I feel sorry fer the poor creature. He ain't never had a chance. Never even knowed who his pa was. Could a' been one of a dozen."

Viola muttered, "If you ask me, he's the get of the devil."

Granny ignored the remark. "And his ma! Why, Leona never had sense enough to keep herself out of the fire. She never cared a hoot fer him. I misdoubt he had enough to eat most of the time." She shook her head sadly. "Even before Leona died, he mostly stayed out in the woods like a little wild critter."

Elijah raised a brow. Lew was wild all right. But not in the way Granny thought.

She went on, "I recollect he loved bright, shining things...seemed fascinated by 'em like a coon is. Once I give him a sparkly broach pin. Hit was old and had a broke clasp. But the ways his eyes lit up, you'd have thought I give him the moon."

"Well, I don't trust him no more than I would a coon in my henhouse," said Viola. "Like the Good Book says, as the twig is bent, so grows the tree."

Granny snorted. "Bible don't say no such thing. But I reckon it is true. Lew is twisted. But I still say, hit's because he never knowed love."

"Caleb heard tell he had him a squaw over in the territory once," protested Viola.

"I'll swan, Viola!" Granny snorted. "Yore head's empty as last year's bird's nest. That ain't love!"

Becky arrived in time to hear the last remarks. When she winced and cut her eyes at Elijah, he realized with an inward smile that Ma thought him too green to hear such talk. But a body learned things early on a farm. What animal breeding left out, bawdy mountain talk filled in.

Becky's hair was neatly arranged. She wore a fresh purple-striped dress and no apron. Elijah was disappointed that she also wore her stiff company face.

She nodded at the women and then asked, "Won't you ladies have a cup of tea?"

"No, thank ye." Granny looked down and smoothed her starched apron. "We best be gettin' home."

"Caleb is expecting us. Hit's way past his dinner time." Viola gathered up the reins and guided the team from the yard.

With hot eyes Becky watched them leave.

"Ma, why do you do that?"

"Do what?"

"Get all dressed up every time they come. If you'd just wear your work dress and act friendly, they'd like you better."

Her face reddened. "Like me! I've tried for seventeen years!" She exhaled sharply. "But that cranky old woman won't try! She's never once stayed for tea."

"Ma," he groped for words, "they aren't tea drinking folks. More than likely, they're worried about using bad manners or breaking your fancy china cups. Maybe, if you didn't put on airs...."

"Put on airs!" Her eyes blazed. She turned her back and rubbed her arms. "I'll never understand them, no love of beauty or culture—content to just live and die in the same old rut. Louise swore I'd get slovenly and coarse if I married your pa. Well, I won't!"

He was quiet for a moment. "I know you don't mean to, Ma." He hesitated. "But you treat them just like Aunt Louise treats me and Pa."

She stiffened. He shook his head and turned away. It was no use. Pa had tried and tried to tell her. There was just no changing Ma.

"Oh, Elijah, I have tried!" Tears choked her voice.

He stopped.

"Your pa is kind and good and noble. But I don't understand his kin." She paused. "Oh, they aren't all hateful. No. They treat me with respect. The men tip their hats; the woman call me ma'am. But they're cold. Cold and distant. I see their suspicious eyes, always letting me know I'm not one of them." She bit a trembling lip. "Now that your pa is gone, if it weren't for Jenny, I think I'd go mad."

He went back and put an awkward arm around her. Her green eyes were wet.

"If you'd just be yourself...let folks see how you really are. Act like you do with Jenny."

"But Jenny is not like them," she said. "She was always kind. From the very first day I came here as a bride, she befriended me. Oh! But not your granny! She resented me before I had opened my mouth to say hello. She's a mean, hateful woman!"

"Oh, Ma." He sighed. "You don't know her any better than she knows you."

Chapter 4

The Mason's front yard was crowded with wagons, saddle horses, and children. The July air was hot and dry. Dust devils swirled in the bare yard where the children played. As Elijah helped Becky from the wagon, he was still stunned that they had come, and even more so, that she wore a freshly pressed calico no finer than Granny's or Viola's.

Granny waved. On the cane she hobbled toward the cabin. "Howdy, Lige, Deborah." She nodded stiffly as she passed Becky. "Mornin'."

"Good morning, Granny." Becky's smile was tight. Long after Granny had gone inside, she hung back.

"Ma, they'll be wondering why you don't go in."

She nodded but looked at the sun-baked cabin as if a hangman's noose waited. Then she squared her shoulders and went inside.

Elijah lifted a chair from the wagon and carried it into the cabin, blinking as his eyes adjusted to the dimness. The quilt frame with women seated around cramped the small room. The quilt top, stretched tightly on the frame, had cotton-batting peeping from the ends. The hodgepodge of colorful blocks with embroidered names was set together with long strips of indigo blue and alternating ones of scarlet. He recalled seeing Granny and Viola stitching their names a few days ago. He wondered if Ma would feel slighted that she had not been asked to make a block.

The dozen chairs, all straight-backed but of different designs, had been brought from each lady's home. Vera Sorrels, with her sagging triple chins, took up two places. Beside her sat her scrawny sister-in-law, May Sorrels, with her pinched, upturned nose that forever looked to be sniffing a skunk. Elijah never saw skinny May and fat Tom Sorrels together without thinking that, just like old Jack Sprat and his wife, Tom and May must eat at different troughs. When she looked up, Elijah nodded. Then he nodded to Alice Dougan and Zora Pelts.

Everyone else looked up when Granny suddenly spoke. "Well, that handsome grandson of mine has finally come inside."

As the women laughed, Elijah's ears turned red. He ducked into a corner and waited until their attention turned to plump, golden-haired Laveney Sorrels. She sat between Polly and Viola, beaming and shyly ducking her head, plainly enjoying this moment of prominence as the women's prattle alternated between teasing and sage advice.

Elijah thought quilting just suited Polly Mason. She was a birdlike little woman, always fluttering, hands and mouth never still, her needle darting faster than a robin's beak after worms. And her tongue kept pace. But he figured when Granny got warmed up, Granny could outtalk her.

When he dared, Elijah let his eyes stray to Cindy. She hovered over a large black kettle on a shiny, new stove that looked just like Ma's! His eyes widened. Last year at Pa's barn raising, Polly had eyed Ma's stove and declared fireplace cooking was good enough for anybody. And she had said, with a disdainful tilt to her head, that an open fire made food taste better. Now with a grin, he wondered if Polly had a new privy behind the cabin or if Ma still had the only one. Everywhere else hereabouts fellows went left in the woods and gals went right, a custom accepted by all and considered as natural as the urge itself.

Cindy's eyes flickered his way. She was spooning a dab of boiling candy into a cup. Ma tested candy the same way. Taffy was done when the drop made a soft ball in the water.

The women's chatter drifted to him. War talk was conspicuously absent. Some here had husbands with strong Union sentiment before secession. Now no one was sure. All talk was of the upcoming wedding and the recent bushwhacking raid on the Matthers place. Or it was, until Granny incurred a disapproving look from Viola when she bluntly stated her dislike for the schoolmaster.

"Man was a milksop! Good thing he went north. Hope he don't never come back. I got no use fer him! He let bullyboys run over the little ones without liftin' a finger." Granny shook a crooked finger. "Now, Polly, they's no need fer you to be a good Christian and defend him. I already heared what happened at school last term. Vernon Millsap run roughshod over the little ones. Boy that size ought to be off helpin' win the war."

In a vain attempt to turn her from this course, Viola declared, "I don't like the looks of this row of stitchin'. My stitches ain't short enough to suit me."

Granny bent near to inspect the short, perfect stitches. "Oh piffle! That won't never be noticed on a galloping horse. Hit looks fine to me." She cut black eyes at Viola. "Like I was a sayin', the only reason Vernon's went to school was to make trouble. He's too dumb to learn."

"Ma!"

"Hit's true, Viola, and well you know it." She paused to spit.

"Oh, I do wish we had a decent schoolhouse and a church," said Becky, and then shrank inside herself as every eye turned.

Elijah cringed. *Poor Ma*, he thought, *she's done it again*. He knew these people. They did not resent Granny's out-and-out condemnation of one of their own, but when Ma criticized they resented it. And Ma could feel it. She ducked her head and pushed her thimble to bury the needle deep into the fabric.

Granny pursed her mouth and returned to the subject. "Come to think on hit, army's better off without Vernon Millsap." She snorted. "That boy's too dumb to pick cotton."

Everyone chuckled. Elijah noticed even Viola didn't argue with Granny's opinion of Vernon. He was thankful Vernon was no longer his seatmate.

"Cindy, hurry up and get that fire out quick as you kin," called Polly. "We're meltin' over here." She glanced around the circle and said with a simper, "But still and all, hit ain't near as hot as having a cook fire in the fireplace."

Granny snorted. "Ain't a soul here could help but notice yore new stove, Polly. Weren't no need to roast us all like chickens."

Polly's narrow face flushed and there was a brittle edge to her words. "Put the fire out, Cindy." She plied the needle with a vengeance.

Cindy shot Granny a vexed look. "I'm trying, Ma. It's almost done."

Elijah squirmed. He wished Granny's tongue weren't quite so barbed.

Soon Cindy lifted the kettle and poured the hot candy onto a large buttered platter.

"Time to pull!" she called.

Elijah took his foot from the log where it was propped behind him and ambled toward the young folks flocking around the butter dish to slather their hands. Cindy looked up and smiled as he drew near.

"Lige, would you scatter the sticks and close the damper?"

He hurried to do her bidding. The fire would smolder a bit, but with the few sticks scattered, it would soon go out.

"Thank you," she said.

When her brown eyes smiled, his stomach flopped. He would do just about anything on earth for her if she smiled at him like that.

"Put plenty of butter on your hands or this candy will stick and burn ya," she cautioned, handing him a small chunk of yellow butter. His heart pounded as he took the butter. She stood only inches away. Her hair smelled like fresh soap and flowers. As he took the scoop of candy she placed in his calloused palm, he touched her hand.

"Here, let me help," she said.

She reached for one end of the rope of candy. He tingled from her nearness. A taffy pull sure was fun!

The girls made a big fuss each time the hot mixture burned their buttered hands. They stretched it back and forth and back and forth, turning it into long ropes of candy. Elijah noticed Cindy did not squeal like the other girls. She could laugh and have fun, but she never acted silly. He liked that about her. As the taffy grew stiffer, the color lightened until soon it was as shining as Cindy's hair.

Lift and pull, lift and pull. Each time the rope of taffy looped back onto itself, her hand brushed his. He felt odd stirrings in his body.

Dillon Matthers strode through the door. "Howdy, all!"

Elijah's pleasure was dashed.

"Dillon, I'm glad you came." Cindy beamed.

Dillon's wide shoulders seemed to fill the room. All the girls suddenly grew silly. Sally Terry, June Warren, and Lucy Tate squealed and pranced as they gathered portions of hot candy and quickly shifted it from hand to hand, blowing to cool it.

Dillon joshed and talked and made everyone smile. Everyone but Elijah. He longed to be alone with Cindy. He had dreamed of it ever since she had asked him to come.

It was not to be. Becky wanted to leave just as soon as good manners allowed. Elijah chaffed at going while Dillon was still there. Cindy followed him into the yard. He wished Ma were not waiting in the wagon.

"Elijah, we were having such a good time until you sulled up like an old possum. No one said a cross word, so what in tarnation are you so mad about?"

"You were laughing so much at Dillon, I didn't figure you even noticed."

"So you're acting like a big baby because of Dillon? Elijah Loring!" Her eyes snapped. "I've always liked you heaps more than him, but the way you've been acting lately makes me wonder why!"

"Elijah," Becky called. "Deborah and I need to get out of the sun." She wiped her face with the apron. "Cindy, thank you for inviting us."

"You're welcome, ma'am." Cindy turned away.

Elijah caught her arm. "I don't want to quarrel, Cindy. There's no telling when I'll see you again."

"Well, I didn't start this. It was your nasty temper."

She was right. He wanted to apologize. But his stubborn pride would not let the words get past his throat. When he turned away, she huffed an aggravated breath and returned to the cabin.

There was no more socializing. July remained a scorching, parched month. When the garden began to wilt, Elijah carried water from the creek each evening after the sun was low. Although the plants drooped, they kept bearing enough to keep him busy. He was not sorry to see the last of July. In a few weeks fall would bring rain and cooler weather.

Because of the drought, and because Ned had planted early, the tall, red-crested sorghum cane ripened early. By the first week in August it was ready to harvest and turn into molasses. Elijah was glad that Michael had come to help. Ever since the quilting, he had felt restless and out of sorts. Even though cutting cane was hard work, it was good to have company.

It was early morning and yet his shirt stuck to his back, glued by sweat. His wrists and back already ached from stripping the long, tapering leaves from the towering cane with a long oak paddle. It was good to rest for a minute. He wiped his brow.

While Becky removed her sunbonnet and fanned her face, one arm hung limp at her side, a heavy paddle dangling. "I'm worn out! Your pa with his big arms made this look like child's play."

Elijah frowned. Although Granny and even puny Aunt Viola often helped in the harvest, Pa had never allowed Ma to do hard field work. "Ma, maybe you shouldn't...."

She stopped him. "If your pa stays gone, I'll have to do lots of things I've never done before. Now is just as good a time as any."

"At least take a rest," Elijah ventured. "Let me and Michael finish this."

Without argument she agreed and traded the paddle for a sharp knife and began cutting red seedpods from the tops of stalks which were piled nearby. Then she put the pods into a bucket to save for feed. Elijah began cutting more stalks and piling them onto the sled behind Jinks. The white mule twitched his tail at a fly and stomped a hoof, but he remained standing placidly until Elijah chirruped him down the row to stop again.

"I sure miss Pa today. He loved making sorghum," he told Michael. "Hope this war gets over with quick."

Michael's face hardened. "My pa was never home anyway."

Elijah knew it was true. Johnny had a powerful hankering for a good time. He was forever going to town and staying gone for days at a time. He looked up. "Here comes Granny and Caleb. We best get to cutting. We don't have near all of this cane gathered."

Caleb took one hand from the reins long enough to lift his slouch hat. Elijah grinned at how his hair stuck out, flying in the breeze. Caleb always joshed that it was a haircut with a moon on top. He was only fifty-four but Elijah thought he looked seventy. Elijah figured living with Viola had aged him.

Elijah looked around. "Where you going, Ma?"

"I'll be back."

Granny waved and called, "Mornin', everyone. Purty day fer makin' molasses, ain't it? Looks like you got a good crop. Appears exactly ready, too. Them heads is just the right color a' red."

"Pa planted it awful early," said Elijah. "I hope it's not bitter because the crop's early. Do you think it'll make a difference?"

"Don't think so," Granny assured. "The real trick is gettin' it ripe. Don't reckon hit much matters when that is."

Elijah was relieved. Nothing was more inedible than bad sorghum. He rushed forward to help Granny climb down. She was already on the ground by the time he got to her. "Looks like somebody got up early," she observed.

"We sure did," said Elijah. "I didn't want you to have this field already gathered before I got up."

She laughed and straightened a long skirt. "Viola would a' come but she woke up feelin' poorly today." Granny cut twinkling eyes at Elijah and they both grinned, but out of deference to Caleb neither said what they were thinking. Viola had woken up feeling poorly for the last thirty years, but she managed to feel fine whenever there was a trip to town.

When Caleb climbed stiffly to the ground, Becky arrived to offer steaming cups of coffee.

"Thank ya, ma'am."

"Thank you both for coming," she said.

Elijah smiled. The cups were Pa's heavy mugs.

Granny eyed Becky's sweaty dress and damp hair. Although she took the coffee, she set it down without taking a sip and then went to the back of the wagon to get her cane knife.

"I allowed to set the mill up right here," said Caleb. "Hit'll be handy to this-here pile."

"That's fine," agreed Elijah.

"Have you been to town lately?" asked Becky.

Caleb nodded. "Just last week...but there weren't no letter from Ned this time." He lifted a shovel from the wagon bed. "Ner your pa either," he told Michael.

Since Johnny Lane could neither read nor write, Elijah doubted there would be any letters coming. Even if Johnny could write, he might not go to the trouble.

"Has there been any fighting yet?" Elijah held his breath. In addition to being the best molasses maker in the country, Uncle Caleb always knew the latest news. It was amazing how nothing went on in the mountains or the town without him knowing.

"Not around here. But there was a terrible battle in Virginny, place called Manassas. Lincoln's whole army took a sound licking and skedaddled back to Washington City." Caleb was sober. "Folks is looking for a big push around here soon, most likely from Missouri. I reckon Billy and your pa better keep their powder dry." He stopped to spit tobacco juice and wiped his mouth with the back of his hand.

Elijah looked north toward Missouri. "I hope this war gets over with and Pa can come home before winter."

"Hit would be nice," agreed Caleb. "These old eyes would like to see young Billy comin' through the door."

Although Billy was almost thirty, Elijah realized to Caleb he was still a boy. Both Caleb and Viola idolized their only son.

"Guess we'd best get to work," declared Caleb.

"What should I do?" asked Becky.

Caleb, suddenly uncomfortable, looked at the ground and thought for a second. He cleared his throat. "Just foller Granny's lead, I reckon."

Becky looked at the old woman bending over the pile of cane. She wiped her hands on her apron, took a deep breath, and nodded.

Caleb put a foot on the shovel and began digging. The holes were shallow, just deep enough to hold the wagon wheels and stabilize the mill mounted on the wagon frame. When the holes were done, he unhitched the team from the wagon and re-hitched Sam to turn the mill. Elijah tied Pet in the shade and patted the mule's rounded belly. "Enjoy yourself. Your turn's coming."

As Caleb built a pine knot fire under the long copper pan where the molasses would boil, his rich baritone rang out. "Get along home, Cindy, Cindy, get along home."

Elijah's head jerked around. Caleb winked and Michael laughed.

Elijah grinned and finished the verse himself, "Get along home Cindy, Cindy, I'll marry you someday."

The mule ignored the singing as it walked round and round in an endless circle, turning the mill while Caleb fed stalks of cane between the rollers. Juice pressed out, sweet and clear, and ran steadily into a stave barrel with a spigot at the bottom. Before Caleb opened the barrel spigot, he closed baffles in the pan to prevent the liquid from running the entire twelve-foot length of the copper pan.

"Good sorghum has to cook slow," he remarked, while managing the baffles in the long, narrow pan. "By the time hit reaches the far end, hit ought to be done." The steaming liquid bubbled and popped, and Caleb used a flat ladle to skim off green scum that formed on top as it boiled. He leaned over the pan. A sudden breeze blew the fringe of hair edging his bald head.

Deborah came running. She gave Granny a big hug and then flew to give Caleb one as well.

"Ma, the beds are made. I dried the dishes and put them all away, just like you said. The beans are soaking and the...." She eyed the ladle and licked her lips. "Can I have a taste, Uncle Caleb?"

"Course ya can, darlin'—but ya might not like it."

"Oh, I love molasses better than cake," she said.

With a wicked grin, he stuck out the ladle. "Careful there. Blow. Hit's hot."

Elijah and Michael both stopped to see the fun as Deborah blew and then darted her tongue into the ladle. They hooted at the screwed up look on her face. She stuck out her tongue and scowled at them.

"Don't pay them no mind, darling. You can bet them two has et bitter skimmings or they'd not laugh so hard." said Caleb, his mustache twitching as he tried not to laugh. "Jest a minute." He drew out a pocketknife and cut off a short piece of cane. Feathering the end, he dipped it into the good syrup and gave it to the child to chew.

"This is probably more to yer likin', little lady."

Hesitantly, she nibbled at the cane. With the first sweet taste, a big grin replaced the pucker on her lips.

"Will you forgive old Caleb fer his dirty trick?"

Deborah's bright eyes sparkled with fun. Now that the bitter taste was gone from her mouth, she seemed to enjoy the joke.

"Now you stay back, hun, so's you won't get burnt. This here stuff's so hot if you was to fall in"—he turned for a wink at Becky—"hit'd scald all the hair off the top of yer head like it done to old Caleb. Then you'd look like me." At her horrified expression, he laughed aloud.

"Caleb, quit tormentin' that child," scolded Granny.

Becky mopped her face with her apron. "Deborah, now mind what your uncle says and stay out of the way."

"I think this batch is about ready," called Caleb. "Ma, come take a look."

She hobbled over and watched with a critical eye as he lifted a spoonful of the amber-color liquid into the air. "Spins a thread," she said, "jest right."

Caleb quickly opened the spigot at the far end of the pan and drained the thick syrup into containers. Then he closed the spigot and opened baffles to keep the constant flow of fresh juice moving and cooking. Again and again the process continued.

The sky was clear and blue. A stiff breeze eased the baking heat of a usual August day. Elijah shaded his eyes to see the sun directly overhead. His stomach rumbled. He could almost taste the fried sidemeat, cornbread, and crowder peas Ma had cooked before daylight.

"Won't you all come inside," invited Becky. I have dinner warming on the stove."

Elijah tensed.

Granny rose from stooping over the cane pile. "No, thank ye, I brung ours."

Caleb shot Granny a hard look. "That's right nice of you, Miz Becky. I'd be obliged. I could eat a horse."

"I'll tend to the pan while you eat," offered Elijah.

When Caleb and Michael followed Becky's straight back into the house, Granny got a dinner pail from the wagon and sat in the shade. Elijah bit his jaw and shook his head. He loved Granny but sometimes she could be ornery. He had no idea why she was so disapproving of Ma. Of course Granny was mighty covetous of Pa....

Michael, after filling a plate, came outside and hunkered in the shade. Elijah knew from the way he wolfed the food that he was famished. It was probably the best meal he had eaten in ages. Michael took another bite of meat and swallowed. Then he looked at it longingly before slipping it into his pocket. Elijah knew it would go to Mattie and little Johnny. He could only imagine how awful it would be to know your family was suffering. He had never been hungry. Oh, he had come in from the fields after a hard day's work, his belly as hollow as a dry well, but never had he gone to bed without eating all he could hold. So far as he knew, neither had anyone in his family. He hoped Ma could figure a way to send along the leftovers without wounding Michael's pride.

In the rising steam, Elijah was thankful for the wind fanning his face. The dark, rich smell of the syrup made his mouth water, but the steam was hot.

All through the long afternoon, Becky, her face a tight mask, worked alongside Granny. Not a word fell between them. Elijah felt as if a storm cloud had gathered, waiting to burst. In mid-afternoon he and Michael brought in the last load of cane.

"I'd like to stay, Lige," said Michael, "but I need to go check on Ma."

Becky hurried over. "Certainly, you should go. Here," she handed him a jug of molasses. "You've earned more, but we'll bring the rest over tomorrow. I've been intending to visit your ma anyway."

Michael's face clouded. Elijah figured Michael was ashamed for Ma to visit. Ma had things fixed so nice in their cabin. Maggie did not.

"I know your ma is not up to cooking lately, so I fixed a little picnic lunch so you won't have to cook when you get home. Would you mind taking it along, or would it be too much to carry?"

"No, ma'am. I can tote it." After taking the jug, Michael reached for the lunch and then hurried down the trail and across the creek.

Granny rose from stooping over the cane pile, and with a hand to her back, she arched like a stretching cat. "Liniment tonight," she groaned.

Elijah's brow knit. "Granny, why don't you take a rest? After I turn Jinks loose, I'll head what cane is left."

"I'll work till hit's done," she said. "Hit's the least I can do for poor Ned."

Becky's mouth went tight. Elijah gave an inward groan. He would be glad to see the job done. Having Ma and Granny together made him feel almost as tense as seeing Lew Willis!

When night fell, the job was finally done. Jugs of rich, delicious molasses were safely stored in the root cellar. It was a good crop. Elijah was glad. Along with table use there would be plenty left to barter. And he was glad the Lanes would eat well tonight. Ma had sent plenty for all.

Then he frowned. Always before, molasses making had been like a party, with everyone laughing and joking. But today was blighted. Without Pa around, Granny had not even pretended to act civil to Ma.

Chapter 5

Elijah emptied a basket of dusty sweet potatoes onto the sled behind Jenks. The heaping mound of orange almost overflowed the sled. "Hey you! Belle!" he yelled at the feisty red dog darting between his feet. She was getting big, turning into a hound. He gave her a shove with his foot. "Get out of the way or I'll fall on my rump." But when she sat back on her haunches and cocked her head, looking mournful out of liquid brown eyes, he laughed and squatted to give her floppy ears a pull and to rub her head. "Why don't you do something useful, like chase those crows away?" He pointed to the flock flapping and landing at the far edges of the cornfield. "They're so bold; they ain't even scared of me. Sick'em Belle. Go get 'em girl."

Although she stood and wagged her tail, she stayed put. Finally Elijah gave up with a laugh. "You'd be ready to go quick enough if I fetched the shotgun," he said. "There isn't going to be any traipsing in the woods until the sweet potatoes are dug and the corn gathered and the wood cut. Besides it's too hot for hunting. Green flies would blow the meat before we got home."

He returned to the brown, withered vines and spaded another hill to turn the cool earth, vines, roots and all up to the sun, uncovering a cluster of perfect potatoes. The spade had severed one, cutting the firm orange flesh in two. He imagined how delicious the potatoes would taste on a cold winter day dragged from hot ashes, the steaming flesh split open and laced with melting butter. His mouth watered thinking of it. He had squatted to finish groveling out the hill when Belle began to bark. She lunged forward and then jumped back. He threw a potato into the basket, stood and wiped his hands on his jeans, grabbed the spade, and hurried to her.

"You find a snake, girl?" he asked, looking carefully. The copperhead lay coiled alongside a dead potato vine, the brown mottled skin blending with the vine and the dirt. When Belle jumped forward, the snake's forked tongue flickered. Elijah brought the shovel down hard and sliced through the head. "Glad it didn't bite me," he said, giving Belle a good pat.

He looked up. It was Caleb riding Pet. The mule crossed the creek at a trot, splashing water high and wide. Elijah's heart began to pound. Caleb would not ride like that unless there was trouble. "What's wrong?" he called. When Caleb did not answer, Elijah's heart plunged to his feet. Caleb's face was a dread. Pa! Something had happened to Pa!

"Is Simon here?" called Caleb.

"No, he rode through about an hour ago."

Becky stepped through the door. She sucked in a breath and dropped into the rocking chair on the porch. As her lips began to move, Elijah knew she was praying.

"Hit ain't Ned," Caleb called. He pulled to a stop, climbed down, and hitched the mule fast to a post. "I just come from town." His words came fast and he panted. "They was a big battle up in Missouri, a place called Wilson's Creek. Ned's not on neither list —killed er wounded," he hurried on. Becky and Elijah went limp with relief.

"My Billy neither." Caleb paused and his faded eyes filled. "But Johnny Lane was." He looked first at Elijah and then Becky. "Killed," he said.

"Poor Maggie," she whispered.

Dropping his head, Caleb went sadly on, "Many a Johnson County man won't be comin' back from this one—Joel Smith and Vince Blackard—two I knowed personal."

He went on, "Sterling Price and a feller from Texas, a general named McCulloch whupped a Yankee general named Lyons. Kilt him and run his army clean back to Springfield."

"My brother Tap, Tap Brooks, was he on the lists?" Becky quickly asked. "He served with McCulloch in the Rangers. In his last letter Ned said troops had arrived from Texas."

Elijah had almost forgotten that Ma had a brother. He had never seen his uncle. When Ma, Aunt Louise, and Uncle Phillip had moved here, Tap had stayed behind in Texas. Ma had lived in Arkansas for years when she and Pa were married.

Caleb screwed up his face. "Hit's a strange name, Tap. I think I'd recollect hit... Naw, I don't think I heared it when Emmitt read the names off."

Caleb raised his eyes to the trail tracing the mountainside. "I'd rather take a beatin' than tell Maggie. Hit'll jest about finish her. Polly said Simon was headed fer Jasper. I was in hopes he had stopped by here and I might catch him so's he could tell Maggie. I thought hit might go easier with him being her brother and all. But Polly says he'll be gone until tomorrow, so I reckon I'd better tell her."

Elijah felt gut-wrenching pity for Maggie and Michael. Oh! How glad he was it wasn't Pa! It might be wicked to feel so joyful, but he could not help it and he knew from the relief on Ma's face that she felt the same.

Becky stood. "I'll come too. You go ahead and I'll have Elijah bring me in the wagon. I want to get a bit of food together." She chewed her lip. "Caleb, I know for a fact that Maggie is almost threadbare. Do you think she'd be offended if I loaned a dress? I know there'll be lots of folks stopping by...."

Caleb shook his head. "I'd not do hit, Becky. I know yo're right about her needin' it, but she's proud—poor proud—and this ain't the time to step on her toes. Food is fine. Folks always bring that and hit don't shame a body."

"Yes, of course," agreed Becky. "I'll get it together quickly."

"I'll water the mule and wait at the creek," said Caleb. "I ain't no wise in a hurry to get there." He mounted, disturbing a horsefly on the mule's neck. It flew into Elijah's face and he fanned it away. As Caleb rode off, dust puffed from the mule's hooves and the horsefly buzzed after them. Although he was in no rush to go either, Elijah hurried away to hitch the wagon.

The trail edged the side of the hill and climbed from the hollow. Elijah looked through the pines and saw dinner smoke coming from the Lane's chimney. The cabin sat on a flat piece of land a few yards from the lip of a ridge. Steep, timbered hollows fell away to both north and south. Behind the cabin the land widened into fields with dark, thick woods just beyond. He noticed the corn patch was much smaller and the crop sparser than his own.

He was surprised to see Cindy on the front porch. She was brushing five-year-old Mattie's hair. Four-year-old Johnny played nearby in the dirt. Cindy was Michael's cousin. Since she was kin, Elijah figured she had come to help in Maggie's sickness. She held the brush still in midair as they rode up.

When Caleb climbed down, Michael came running from the field. Out of breath, he rounded the cabin and then slowed to a walk. Suspicion overspread his face.

"Howdy," he said and looked from face to face. "Reckon it's bad news," he said. "Pa?" At Caleb's nod, he paled. He turned away and looked out across the stubbly field. In a minute he swiped a sleeve across his eyes. Then he glanced at the cabin and his shoulders slumped. "Let me get Ma into a chair before you go inside. She'd not want to be caught a' bed."

Caleb nodded and wiped his own eyes. "We'll not come in till you say so."

Still holding the reins, Elijah leaned forward on the wagon seat, and resting elbows on knees, looked down at his dusty boots. He grieved for his friend. Michael had never known anything but hard times. Now his pa was dead. It didn't seem fair. He glanced toward the porch. Cindy was woodenly brushing Mattie's hair, but tears streamed down her face. She was beautiful even when she cried.

It was a while before Michael came to the door. "Ma says to come in now." He lowered his voice as Caleb approached the porch. "I ain't told her yet...I jest said hit was bad news."

Caleb nodded and then braced himself before going inside. Becky followed. Elijah nodded to Cindy and then stepped inside. He wanted to reach out to Michael. But Michael's jaw was squared and he refused to meet their sympathetic eyes. Elijah was sure Michael wished Ma had not come. Even though Pa and Johnny had been friends for years, Ma had always made Michael and his ma uncomfortable.

The cabin was dreary and dark. Smoke had darkened the walls and rafters until they were almost black. Elijah's eyes traced the stark room: two small windows, bare holes just now although in winter they were covered with oilcloth; a wooden bed frame lashed with ropes and topped with a corn-shuck mattress and a faded quilt; a rough plank table and two benches; a washstand made of a wooden box turned on end; a ladder leading to the loft where Michael and little Johnny slept; two board shelves along one wall; and some pegs to hang their few belongings.

Elijah could not help comparing his own neat home, colorful and homey with curtains at the windows, wild flowers in vases, braided rugs scattered on the floor, and pretty quilts on the beds. His eyes strayed to Becky, who had knelt in front of Maggie.

Ma doesn't belong is this cabin, he thought. Of course it didn't seem as if Ma hardly fit mountain life at all. Everyone wondered how she and Pa came to marry.

Kneeling there she looked like a pretty china doll, her yellow hair gathered into a curling knot on the back of her head, a few curls straying on her neck, and her neat yellow dress setting off the tiny, golden flecks in her green eyes.

Poor Maggie looked like a worn out rag doll, limp and woebegone, her stringy hair hanging like gnarled yarn that needed untangling. Her eyes set deep in their sockets, and the skin on her narrow face looked dry and shriveled. Elijah could remember when she had not looked like that. She had never been as pretty as Ma, but she had looked nice before she got sick.

As her faded eyes darted from face to face, Elijah saw truth dawn. "Well, Caleb Tanner, spit hit out."

Caleb looked helplessly at Becky and then spoke, almost choking over the knot in his throat. "Johnny got kilt at a battle in Missouri."

Maggie swallowed. Without a word, she stared straight ahead. Elijah had expected anything but this. He thought there would be wailing, tears, anything but this stone-cold silence.

Suddenly she began to cough. It tore from her, deep, hard, and rasping. She bent, shaking and wheezing.

Elijah was thankful to see Granny coming through the door. Although his heart warmed at the sight of her, he groaned inwardly when he saw her mourning dress. He hated the heavy black dress, shiny with age. It made her look like a shriveled old crow with too many feathers, but she always wore it when someone died. Viola trailed a few steps behind.

As Granny passed, she gave his hand a squeeze. When she laid eyes on Maggie, her sad, wrinkled face quickly grew worried. "Maggie, you ought to be in the bed." She looked around and ordered, "Here you, Lige, Caleb, hep Maggie to her bed."

They hurried over, and each took an arm to lift her but she pulled away. "No!" she said, "And I'll ask you all to leave," she glared at Becky. "Hit's Ned's fault Johnny is dead. He'd not have gone if Ned hadn't egged him on."

Becky jerked back and tears filled her eyes. The tears cut Elijah to the heart.

Granny's voice was sharp. "Hesh that up, Maggie! Ain't no one's fault that yer man went off and got hisself kilt. That's what happens in a war and Johnny knowed it when he went. Now you git in the bed a'fore you fall over." Granny pointed at Elijah and Caleb and they did as ordered and helped Maggie to the bed. Then Elijah followed Becky outside. Cindy and the children had disappeared.

Becky stood on the end of the porch, her back to the door and her arms crossed tight across her chest. He laid a hand on her back. "Ma, she didn't mean it. It's the grief talkin'."

Her tear-stained face turned. "The awful thing is it's true. Johnny would never have gone alone. He's followed Ned around like a shadow all his life."

"It's not Pa's fault Johnny never had the gumption to make up his own mind about anything. Pa never asked him to go."

She sniffed and bent to wipe her eyes on the tail of her dress. "Oh, I know that. I suppose I feel guilty because Ned's alive and Johnny isn't." She looked over her shoulder at the door. "Poor Maggie. I don't blame her for hating me. I've always had so much and she's had so little."

By the next day word of Johnny Lane's death had spread through the hills. Elijah noticed that many folks who stood strongly Union were absent. Nonetheless, there was a crowd gathered at the Lane cabin. Horses were tied at every tree and bush and people filled the yard. By ten o'clock, without a bit of breeze to ease the heat, the midday sun had already turned the cabin into an oven. Even Maggie stayed outside, although Elijah knew she should be in bed. Michael took her a dipper of water when she began to cough.

Simon Mason squatted on haunches alongside her chair under the shade of a catalpa tree. Parts of the conversation drifted to Elijah. "Hit's hard, Maggie. I ain't claiming otherwise. But the Lord will see you through. He don't put more on us than we kin bear."

Elijah determined to stay close to Becky. It had been a hard decision for her to come today. When they arrived, he was relieved that Maggie had spoken to her. Although she did not say much, at least she had thanked Ma for the food.

Folks were saying Maggie would be dead before spring. "Consumption," he had heard Granny whisper. Poor Michael! He would have Mattie and little Johnny to care for. If Pa got killed it would be terrible, but Elijah knew at least he'd still have Ma to depend on.

"Well, no one came empty-handed," said Becky, eyeing the mountains of food.

Elijah looked at the table placed under the trees. Platters were heaped with golden-crusted fried chicken and thick slabs of fried ham with the edges of fat browned, crisp, and curling. There were bowls of creamy gravy and plates loaded with tall, fluffy biscuits alongside jars of pickles and relish, and garden truck of every variety: corn, peas, beans, and hominy. He lowered his voice, "No one except Salvicy that is."

"Hush! Salvicy will hear you," whispered Becky.

Stringy-haired, lank Salvicy Lucas had set a big kettle on the table, but Elijah was close enough to see it held only a dab of field peas. Doc and Salvicy always came early, stayed late, and ate all they could, filling their bellies and the bellies of their dozen or more young'uns—Elijah had lost count—and they never brought more than a few turnip or mustard greens or some other such piddling thing. Compared to Doc, even Johnny Lane had been a diligent, hard worker.

Granny's nose flared when she turned and espied them.

"Well, Doc," she said, "I knowed you'd turn up fer the service." She paused before sharply adding, "*And the dinner.*"

Elijah hid a grin. Granny despised the Lucases. She had no use for slipshod ways. It suddenly made Elijah wonder if she had despised Johnny also. She had never named it, but he wondered....

Elijah's thoughts were interrupted as Simon Mason rose. "Maggie, I'd not like to miss 'ery opportunity to spread the Word," he said as he stood, tall and skinny, his long black preacher coat open to the heat and a big, black Bible tucked under his arm, "so with yer permission, I'd like to say a few words o' comfort and warn folks that death will sooner er later wrap hit's cold coils around us all."

In spite of having no body to bury, it seemed Cindy's pa intended preaching a funeral. Elijah wondered if Johnny would have approved. He once told Pa that he liked Simon fine but he didn't care one bit for his sermons. Simon had a singsong way of preaching, starting low and quiet and working his way up high and loud, sort of like a chant. Elijah wasn't sure if that was what had gotten on Johnny's nerves or if it was Simon's warning of hellfire and brimstone.

"Folks if you'll gather round, we'll have a word for the departed," Simon called out. The crowd quieted and gathered in, the men baring their heads in respect as Simon cleared his throat and began to pray and then to exhort.

Elijah did not want to listen. He did not want to think of Johnny lying dead in a grave somewhere in Missouri, nor did he want to think how Johnny's soul might right now be roasting in hell. So far as Elijah knew, Johnny had not been the kind to "call on Jesus and be saved" as Simon was just now declaring a man must do or pay eternal consequence. Elijah felt awful for Michael, who stood dry-eyed and bleak beside his ma. Worry had plowed deeper furrows around his mouth. Michael looked old today, far older than his fifteen years.

Elijah was thinking of Pa. Pa had escaped this time, but he could get killed in the next battle, or the next, or the one after that.... Elijah didn't want to cry in front of all these folks. Instead he kept his eyes open and studied the crowd.

Maggie appeared about to keel over, sitting between Granny and Caleb. He hoped Simon wouldn't take too long warning folks about death's cold coils, or they might just wrap around poor Maggie sooner than later.

Beyond Uncle Caleb, Elijah could see the side of Viola's face. She looked as if she had just eaten a sour pickle. He figured her face would crack if she smiled. He sure was glad she was Billy's ma and not his. Thank God Ma knew how to laugh and smile.

His gaze drifted to Mattie and Johnny who stood on either side of Jenny. Her strong, brown hands were placed one on each head. Her pa, Pappy Campbell, had not come today. Elijah figured his bones must be aching awful to keep him away. Pappy loved preaching and he loved folks.

Elijah's gaze drifted to the Matthers family. All eight of them, including Kate, were redheaded, from the color of Ma's copper kettle to the dark sorrel color of Old Strawberry, the mare Billy had ridden off to war. The boys were the spitting image of their pa, thick necks, broad chests, and bright blue eyes, and just like Red, they were all as stout as mules. Granny said Red and Kate were just off the boat from Ireland. Of course she was exaggerating. Elijah knew they had lived down the creek for at least twenty-eight years. Granny had helped birth all the boys. Allen was twenty-eight and born in the cabin where they still lived.

Compared to the Old Country, I reckon most folks here are newcomers, Elijah thought to himself. *Pappy Campbell's been here longer than anybody, and he's only been here forty years. Before that it was all bears and Indians.* Then his eyes narrowed. He caught Dillon staring at Cindy like she was a stick of candy. And she had stared back with a shy smile. If this weren't a funeral, he would be tempted to punch Dillon's smug nose. He figured the Matthers clan wouldn't mind. Next to a dance, they loved a fight more than anything.

Elijah suddenly raised his head higher. Beside the smokehouse stood Lew Willis—Lew with his cat eyes peering at Ma! Elijah's arms goose-fleshed. Lew left off staring at Becky and bent, picked up something, and slipped it into his pocket. Lew saw him. His mouth twisted into a grin, and then he melted into the woods, as silent as a ghost. It took Elijah a minute to get over the nervous quiver.

When dinner was finally called, he sat alone on the ground, cross-legged, balancing a heaped plate on one knee. He was near enough to keep an eye on Cindy. If Dillon came anywhere near, Elijah intended to go sit by her. He frowned. Maybe he should anyway...even if her pa objected.

Her low voice drifted to him, "Oh! Fiddlesticks! I've lost a shoe button, Ma. And it was one of those pretty ones with the little sparkly glass in the middle."

"Don't fret," comforted Polly. "Hit ain't much noticeable."

Elijah lost track of their conversation when Caleb walked over and hunkered down. After aiming a stream of tobacco juice at a rock, he wiped his mouth before he spoke. "She's a pretty gal, Lige, and seems mighty nice and sweet, but you be careful of sowin' any wild oats, boy. I sowed some once't and lived to regret hit ever day since." His eyes strayed to Viola sitting on the porch fanning herself with her apron. "Not that Billy ain't the apple of my eye," he added quickly. "I'd not take nary thing fer him."

Light dawned for Elijah and his eyes widened. Now he knew how fun-loving Uncle Caleb came to be stuck with prune-faced Viola, but it was impossible to imagine....

"Mind what I say, son."

"Yes, sir," Elijah mumbled, embarrassed. He was glad when Caleb walked away. Here it was again, the surprising awareness, the same sort of shock he had felt when that fellow Jess had stripped Ma with his eyes. Ma was not just Ma. She was a fine-looking woman, and desirable to men. Now it was a fresh jolt to realize Uncle Caleb, and yes, even Aunt Viola, were young once and hot-blooded. Elijah glanced at Cindy and his face grew hot. He was glad she was not looking. And, he was glad no one could read his thoughts.

Chapter 6

One morning in early September, Elijah watched steam rise from a bowl of grits where butter melted into a golden pool. He was barely awake enough to hear what his mother was saying.

"This afternoon I want you to go check on Jenny and Mr. Campbell. I haven't heard from them in a long while and that's not like Jenny."

It was not how he had planned on spending his Saturday but he nodded. Besides, he'd rather visit Jenny and Pappy Campbell than just about anyone. Pappy told great stories.

"Be sure and offer to help with any chores. Jenny has to do everything now that Mr. Campbell is failing."

"Can I ride Jinks?" Elijah asked. Although Pa had two fine mules, Jinks was his favorite.

"I suppose so."

"Can I go too?" begged Deborah.

"No. I need your help today, young lady. We're cleaning house."

Deborah groaned, and Elijah leaned over to pull a frazzled pigtail that had not yet been freshly braided for the day. "I'll take you over someday soon. I promise."

Although the morning had been still and hot with bright sun, now as Elijah made his way over the ridge, thunderheads hid the sun and a stiff breeze whipped leaves from the trail, sending Belle chasing after. A few drops of rain hit his back. He should have listened to Ma and brought a slicker. He had not gone far when he heard the ring of an ax up ahead.

"Hey, Jenny," he called, spying the big-boned woman a short way off the trail. Ma thought Jenny's ma had been full-blood Seminole, and from Jenny's high cheekbones and flat face, Elijah believed it. She was actually a second or third cousin. He wasn't sure which since Pappy was Granny's brother. Heck, he couldn't keep it straight. He figured, one way or another, he was kin to half the folks on the mountain.

Jenny finished a powerful swing and then propped the ax against the ground and leaned on it. "Howdy, Elijah. Where you headed?"

"Comin' to check on you and Pappy. Ma was worried since she'd not heard from you. She was afraid Pappy was poorly."

"That's mighty nice of Becky," said Jenny while she pushed back a strand of long black hair that had worked loose from the knot at the nape of her neck. "Pappy's all right, though his joints is aching. He says the weather's gonna change. From the looks of them clouds, he's right."

Elijah slid off the mule and tied him to a bush. "Here, let me spell you. Looks like you've been at this a good while. That's a big pile of wood you've got there."

She relinquished the ax and sat down on a nearby stump. "I needed some cook wood for the fireplace. Besides, a feller can't ever have too much laid by fer the winter."

"For a fact," Elijah agreed. "Pa and I snaked in a lot of trees before he left, but I intend to get in a few more," he said, "just to make sure."

Jenny nodded and gazed off into the woods in comfortable silence. That was one thing Elijah liked about Jenny. She didn't chatter all the time like most females. And although she was not very pretty—being as big as a man, and having a broad but kind face—she was a fine person, one of the nicest he knew. She was quiet around grown-ups but she warmed up to young'uns.

As the log severed, Elijah's nose wrinkled at the pungent odor. The smell of black oak wood was not to his liking, but it made a hot, long-lasting blaze. He smiled remembering how Pa had said it warmed a feller twice, once when he chopped it and once when he burned it.

He chopped until he grew wet with sweat. Jenny stood and took the ax.

"Here, I got my second wind. I'll chop awhile." She hefted the ax and let it fall to bite into a log, and in one smooth motion, jerked it free to chop again.

Jenny's brown mare stood nearby hitched to a sled. Elijah looked over when her ears perked up and she whinnied with her nose pointed down the trail. Jenny paused when a horse rounded the bend. Then her eyes narrowed.

"Hit's that daft Lew Willis," she said.

When Lew rode past without speaking, Elijah looked after him. Then he asked, "What do you reckon he totes in that buckskin bag tied around his neck?"

"Ain't no tellin'. Injuns do that. Put good-luck charms in 'em."

"Granny says the Bible is hard against magic."

Jenny raised an eyebrow. "I don't reckon Lew reads hit much." She gave a crooked grin and Elijah laughed.

Just then lightning forked the northwestern sky. He looked up from piling wood onto the sled. Thunder cracked in the distance and a sudden wind swayed the tops of nearby pines.

"Storm's comin'," said Jenny. "You best get on home. I can haul this wood myself." She winced at another clap of thunder. "On second thought, maybe you ought to come home with me. Hit's a heap closer than back to yer place."

"Ma told me to spend the night if the weather caught me." He smiled. "I was hoping it would. You make the best cornbread in the world."

Jenny chuckled. She slapped the horse's rump with the lines and yelled, "Git up." They started down the trail with Elijah astraddle the white mule bringing up the rear.

When a small, weathered cabin appeared, Elijah waved a greeting to Pappy Campbell. The old man sat on the front porch in a cane-bottomed chair, his knotty hands gripping a blanket around him against the dampness and mists that rose from the nearby creek. Pappy nodded. A gray mustache topped a smiling, toothless mouth in a friendly face as wrinkled as an unironed shirt.

"Howdy, boy. Step down and come in."

"Yes, sir, just as soon as I help Jenny unhitch," he called.

When the chore was finished, Elijah joined the old man on the porch.

"How's yer ma?" Pappy asked.

"Just fine, sir."

"Eh?"

"She's fine, sir," Elijah raised his voice. Pappy was growing deafer by the day.

"Any word from Ned?"

"Not in a while. Last we heard he was in the mountains up near the Missouri border."

Pappy grew silent. His eyes sought the hill that stood bold and black, shutting off all view from the north. "Years ago," he began, and Elijah hunkered down on the porch, ready for a good story. The old man went on, "I come here to homestead." He nodded toward the hill. "Chose this here spot 'cause such a hill will hold off the north wind." He cut faded eyes at Elijah. "Me and Jenny's ma was young then. She was a fine figure of a woman, big and strong. A good helpmeet," he said, his eyes gone far back in time. "Had nothin' but the clothes on our backs, a spavin horse, a musket, and a ax. I was strong as a ox back then. Weren't no tree too thick fer my ax, ner no job too big to tackle."

Although he was a shrunken skeleton of a man now, Elijah judged he had been a strong man once. And big.

Jenny poked her head out the cabin door and called loudly, "Pap, what you want for supper?" Not waiting for an answer, she added, "Ya know you ought not be out in this dampness. Hit makes you ache so."

He ignored the last remark. "Whatever you fix is fine with me, daughter."

"I know." She walked out and tenderly patted his bony shoulder. "Whatever I fix, you won't eat enough to keep a bird alive. I'm worried about you."

"Afore this war's over, you might be glad I ain't got much appetite. I look for food to get right scarce."

"Well, we got aplenty now, so that's no excuse. You need to eat to keep up yer strength."

"I'll try, daughter—I'll try." He reached twisted fingers to pat her hand. "Someone's comin'."

Elijah marveled at Pappy's keen eyesight. The rest of his body might be failing, but his eyesight was as sharp as a hawk's.

"Looks to be three riders. Best get the gun, gal. These days you never can tell."

Jenny reached inside the cabin and lifted down the musket from above the door.

"How do they size up to you?" Elijah questioned softly as the men rode near. He was not sure Pappy heard. At least he did not answer.

Silhouetted black against the dusky sky, three poncho-covered figures rode the trail to the creek bank and then crossed single file. Elijah tensed.

The men paused. They advanced slowly, reining in their mounts near the porch. The leader rode a tall, steel-colored appaloosa. He lifted a dove-gray hat such as cowboys wore.

"Evening," he said. His horse danced a bit, seeming more nervous than the hard-jawed man who rode him.

Pappy nodded.

"Looks to be a wet night coming on." The man spoke again.

Pappy kept quiet. The leader took the silence in stride. Like all things common to the South, hospitality was also vanishing.

"We're from down Texas way, Rangers on our way to join up with General McCulloch."

Elijah understood the caution on the stranger's face. The fellow had no idea if they were Federal or Confederate. There were plenty of Yankee sympathizers in Arkansas, especially in the hills. But the stranger relaxed when a smile lit Pappy's face.

"I've heared tell of McCulloch. Well, well, so yer from Texas."

Elijah wondered if this fellow knew Ma's brother. He was a Texas Ranger.

Pappy rose stiffly from his chair, his tall, lanky frame proof that before age had stooped him, he had been uncommonly tall. His voice had a slight quiver.

"Step down and come in. Hit's too damp to stand out here jawin'. Put yer horses in the field yonder. Daughter'll fix us a bite to eat while ya catch me up on the war news. We ain't heared nothing since we give 'em the what fer at Manassas and Wilson's Cri'ck."

All except the man tending the animals followed him inside. The old man hobbled over to a stone fireplace and used a poker to rake ashes from atop buried coals.

"We'll need a cook-fire. Besides, a bit of heat will go good this evenin'. Jenny, where's a taper? Light the lamp—hit's dark as pitch in here."

Lamplight revealed the sparse furnishings, a table and sturdy chairs, crude and homemade. Jenny, carrying a skillet, had to squeeze past the knot of men on her way to the fireplace. As she passed, Elijah saw her sneak a peek at the Ranger. He was a big man. Jenny was tall, but she would have to stand on tiptoe to look him squarely in the eye. His sandy colored hair was thin on top, and his stomach had a paunch, but the rest of him was spare of fat and muscled. He had fine, gray eyes that sort of sparkled when he smiled—like he was doing now. Pappy must have said something funny, but Elijah hadn't been listening. He had been studying the Rangers. The other fellow was blond and smooth-faced, looking barely old enough to shave. Elijah rubbed his own chin. Why, he had more of a beard than that fellow!

"Elijah," Jenny spoke low, interrupting his thoughts. "Would you fetch a bucket of water? I'd best be getting a big meal on. That tall one is a lot of man to feed."

Elijah grinned and took the bucket. Dampness on the trail felt good to his bare feet. Long grass beside the path wet his trousers and raindrops peppered his back. The earth smelled good and clean. Wind soughed in the tall pines. Ma called the sound mournful. To Elijah it was music.

He lifted a dripping pail from the stream and trudged up the red clay bank worn smooth by many trips before. The rain grew harder. He was soaked by the time he got to the cabin. As he came through the door, Elijah smelled cornbread and his mouth watered. He noticed the big man studying Jenny while she raked coals onto the lid of the iron spider. When the big fellow spoke near her elbow, she jumped.

"Ma'am, that wonderful smell sure is torture to a hungry man."

She looked up and smiled. "Won't be long now."

"What's that you're making?"

"Hit's...It's," she corrected herself quickly, and Elijah grinned, recognizing his mother's influence. She went on, "venison stew in this pot, killed greens over here, and cornbread in the spider."

"What in the world are killed greens?" He moved near to peer into the skillet that she stirred.

"You cut up fresh greens—most any kind. These is mustard. Stir them about in a skillet with some bacon drippings, and then ya add some crumbled bacon and some onions. They're real tasty. I do think mustard greens is best."

It was the longest speech Elijah had ever heard from Jenny, and her face looked flushed. He wondered if the Ranger made her nervous standing over her like that.

The cabin door opened, and a sharp gust of wet wind scattered ashes onto the hearth, sending smoke puffing from the fireplace. The third Ranger hurriedly shut the door. He shook raindrops from a broad-brimmed hat that had covered straight, black hair. He imitated the others by speaking loudly enough for Pappy to hear and introduced himself as Roger Shepherd.

"It's starting to rain hard out there. Sure appreciate you inviting us in."

The big man turned to join him, but Elijah stayed near the fire, sniffing the food like a hungry pup. He was starving. He hoped the stew Jenny was testing for salt was almost done. He could eat the whole big kettleful by himself.

"Hit's too salty," she declared with a frown. She dipped another spoonful and blew on it. "You try it, Lige...what do you think?"

He licked his lips. "It's wonderful, Jenny. I never had better."

She gave a relieved smile and then quickly grabbed a thick cotton rag and pulled the spider from the coals. When she opened the lid, the bread was thick and golden brown. Elijah almost drooled as she sliced it into wedges, split the pieces open, and added large pats of rich, yellow butter.

When all the food was ready, she reached far back on a shelf and drew forth a tablecloth. Elijah thought that odd. He had never known her to use a tablecloth on the smooth pine table.

War news was the main topic of supper conversation. Pappy Campbell leaned forward to catch every word. There had been rumors of skirmishes in Southern Missouri but no facts.

"I allow as how this war won't be over as quick as some thinks." Pappy pushed a platter close to the big man. "Hep yerself to some more cornbread."

The big fellow patted his full stomach and declined a fifth piece. "We're hoping to join Old Ben before it's all over. Joey, here, is scared to death he'll miss the whole thing!"

The youngest of the group blushed like a girl. The other Ranger laughed while Joey blushed darker.

Pappy Campbell said, "You fellers are takin' sort of a roundabout route. Most folks don't go through this a' way."

The Ranger nodded. "I wanted to locate some kin. My sister and her man live around here someplace. Do you happen to know Rebecca and Ned Loring?"

Jenny's mouth dropped open and she and Pappy stared at Elijah. Startled, he threw up his head. This man was his Uncle Tap! He opened his mouth to speak but Jenny spoke first.

"Becky and Ned—law yes!" She pointed to Elijah. This here is their boy!"

Tap gaped. Then a glad light filled his gray eyes and a big smile lit his face.

Elijah offered his hand. "Howdy. I'm Elijah, Becky's oldest."

"Well, I'll be jiggered!" Tap shook his hand and slapped him on the back so hard his teeth rattled. Then Tap slapped his own knee.

"We live less than two miles over the next ridge," said Elijah. "Ma sure is going to be surprised to see you!"

"Well, I'll be jiggered!" Tap repeated. "How is she?" Before Elijah could answer, he asked, "And your pa?"

"Ma's fine. But Pa left back in the spring. He's in the 16th Arkansas with Captain Hill. Captain Hill used to be our sheriff."

"I stopped at Louise's in town but no one was home." Tap added, "I was hoping Phillip would know McCulloch's exact whereabouts. "Since the fight at Wilson's Creek, we've not heard where they went."

"Army leaves a trail," said Pappy. "You'll find him," he assured before yawning. "Whew! Hit's past a old man's bedtime. You boys make yerselves to home. Throw yer bedrolls there on the floor." He added before rising, "Don't take off in the mornin' afore Jenny makes a bite of breakfast."

Tap looked at her. "Don't go to any trouble, ma'am. We ate enough tonight to last a spell."

Joey protested, "Speak for yourself! I intend to stuff myself again. Do you know how long it's likely to be before we get another chance at this kind of cooking!"

Jenny flushed. "I'm pleasured to cook for you. It's no trouble a'tall."

After Pappy got into the bed in the far corner and Jenny took the lamp and climbed to her loft bedroom, Elijah lay on a pallet near the Rangers, his head cradled in his arms. The hard floor was not the reason sleep was long in coming. He was thinking of Pa and Billy and James. Almost all the younger men he knew were off at war.

Tap and the Rangers did not stay long, just a couple of hours, with Tap catching up on lost years with Becky, but it was long enough for Elijah to know he liked this uncle. He regretted not having a chance to know him better.

Before Tap climbed into the saddle, he lifted Deborah and kissed her, and as he bent and kissed Becky, her green eyes filled with tears. Then he shook Elijah's hand.

"You're a fine young man, and I'll tell your pa so if I see him." He climbed into the saddle and spoke again, "Take care of your ma and little sister."

Elijah's heart warmed from the praise. "I will, sir."

Tap lifted his hat and reined the appaloosa around. He and the Rangers rode away. Elijah felt forlorn. He had no desire to go off to war like Pa, Billy, and James, but it was hard staying behind too. It gave him sort of a left-out feeling. He sighed and turned back to the house. He needed to shuck corn. Tomorrow he had to help Ma make hominy. There were always chores to do.

Early the next morning Elijah donned a warm jacket. It was the first time that fall he had worn a cap to keep his head warm. As the morning waned, he took off both. It was sunny by the corncrib where he worked alongside Becky as they shelled corn and dropped the kernels into lye water. This corn made plump, yellow hominy. It had been ages since Elijah had tasted hominy. He was looking forward to a big, buttery plateful.

After the corn had soaked in lye made from wood ashes and water, the hard outer husk split and curled back from each firm kernel. While Becky went inside to add water to a pot of beans boiling on the stove, Elijah took the corn to the creek. He used the sieve to wash and re-wash the kernels until every last trace of husk and lye was gone. The water turned his hands to ice. He blew on them and occasionally warmed them under his arms.

Pa was partial to hominy. Elijah's throat tightened at the thought. He sure missed Pa. So did Ma. She was not prone to crying, but lately the loneliness seemed to weigh extra hard on her. He had heard her crying in the night when she thought no one could hear. The thought of winter without Pa was hard to imagine. On cold winter nights Pa had always drawn near the fireplace molding bullets, patching harness, or doing some such work. The nights he told stories were Elijah's favorite. Like Pappy Campbell, Pa was a great storyteller. Elijah wondered if perhaps Ma would let him go to town to see if there was a letter from Pa. On the way he would swing by to see Aunt Opal and hopefully learn news of Cousin James too. But first there was hominy to make and the rest of the corn to gather, wood to split and peas to pick and shell, and fall cabbage to hill.... He probably could not get to town before Christmas!

Deborah sat in the doorway playing with a worn rag doll. One of the long, brown braids hanging down her back caught on a button, making her wince. She gave a yank and jerked it free. Then she called, "Ma, Jenny's coming."

"Howdy, Jenny," greeted Elijah as she crossed the creek.

"Makin' hominy, I see," she said, stopping with a smile, her hands on her big hips.

"Yeah, Ma begged me to go hunting, but I told her I'd rather make hominy." As his eyes twinkled, Jenny laughed.

"Sure you did!"

"She's in the house," he said, rising from knees to accompany her. "She'll be glad to see you."

Becky's face beamed when she saw Jenny. "Let me put the teapot on and we'll have a good, long talk. You can catch me up on the news over your way."

Elijah was surprised when Jenny's face crimsoned. Why would she blush?

Becky set two delicate china cups onto the table and a small bowl holding brown sugar and a tiny silver spoon. "I've been out of white sugar forever. I think everyone has." She turned back toward the stove, and then glanced back at Jenny.

"Son, why don't you finish rinsing the corn?" she asked. When she asked Deborah if the chip basket was filled, Elijah knew this was going to be woman's talk.

Deborah, sensing she was to be excluded, hung her head. "No, Ma. It isn't."

Even Elijah was disappointed. Company was a rare treat. He wanted to stay. He did not mean to listen, but snatches of conversation reached his ears even after he went outside.

"Unless I miss my guess, you're not here to talk about the weather."

Jenny sounded surprised. "Well, if you don't look like the cat that swallered the cream! How did ya know?"

Elijah went out of earshot after hearing Becky's trilling laugh. When he came back inside to get the forgotten sieve, neither woman seemed to notice.

Jenny was eyeing the delicate silver spoon in the sugar bowl. Reaching to finger the ornamental swirls, she frowned, slowly shaking her head.

"No use foolin' myself, Becky. I'm like that big tin ladle in the water bucket yonder, and yo're like this silver spoon. Men want pretty, little things like you. None of 'em would ever look at a big, ugly cow like me."

"That's not so, Jenny! I think you're beautiful!"

"Yer sweet to say so." Her normally square shoulders drooped dejectedly.

Elijah's ears burned. He hurried back outside. Conversations about romance made him uncomfortable.

Later, as the tall woman left, he stood and let water run from the sieve and called, "Bye, Jenny. Tell Pappy I said howdy."

She nodded absentmindedly. When Belle ran up to tug playfully on her skirt, she hardly noticed.

As Becky came to the door, Deborah looked up from putting a wood chip into the basket. "Ma, what's wrong with Jenny?" she asked. "I spoke to her twice, but she never answered. Is she sick?"

"No. She's just in a hurry to get home."

Chapter 7

With the approach of autumn, underbrush thinned in the deep hollows, making a clear view through the woods where sassafras bushes, a dozen shades of red, blended with reddened black gums, sumacs, and yellow-gold hickories. Bright red berries crowned pinkish dogwood leaves. Sugar maples lit the ridges, their orangey coral as brilliant as a torch. Even the oaks had turned more golden than brown. Elijah sniffed the air, enjoying the smell peculiar to autumn. The crisp breeze was pungent with the scent of muscadines. To Elijah, the wild grape's odor was synonymous with fall.

Walking between rows of tall dead stalks, he twisted off long ears of dried corn and threw them onto the sled behind Jinks. The mule swished his tail at a late, persistent fly, and Elijah wiped his face on his shirttail. The day was not hot, but he sweated easily even in cool weather. With sweat dripping down his face and running between his shoulder blades, it was hard to imagine snow. But he knew it would come. He was worried there was not yet enough firewood cut. If Pappy Campbell was right, it might be a bad winter. To be on the safe side, he decided to snake in more trees after the field corn was all cribbed.

He rested for a minute, leaning on the sled as the golden sun climbed higher into a clear sky. He enjoyed the scene until his eyes roved over the rows of dried corn standing tall, withered, and brown in the field. Abruptly, his spirits also wilted. Chores! He wondered if there would ever again be leisure to go hunting and fishing. At least there was the corn husking to look forward to. It was at the Mason's and he would get to see Cindy. His heart beat fast just thinking of it.

Later that evening, however, disappointment fell like a sledgehammer when Becky declared they would not go. It was so typical, he wondered why he was surprised. It seemed Ma found any excuse not to go to a mountain gathering. But this time, try as he might, he could not push aside resentment. Ma was overreacting. It had been ages since Lew's visit and nothing had happened. Since Allen had bested the bushwhackers, they weren't likely to think it was easy pickings around here. But Becky remained resolute.

After supper Elijah stood in the dark, leaning against a pine tree. He wanted to sulk. The corn husking had been a pleasure he had long looked forward to. Everyone would be there. If only Pa were home, they would be going!

In spite of agitation, he could appreciate the crisp air and the tangy smell of pine tar that oozed from the tree trunk. He pinched off a sticky piece and rolled it between his fingers. An owl hooted. Nighthawks swirled over the fields, catching late bugs still unhampered by frost. The breeze was turning chilly. He should have grabbed a jacket.

He cocked his head. That was Old Scrapper's deep bay. The Matthers' hounds had something treed in the next hollow. Belle cocked an ear and pointed her nose toward the ruckus. She threw back her head and let out a long, deep howl. Elijah had to laugh.

"Belle, that bay was worthy of Old Scrapper!"

Elijah figured if Scrapper bayed all night no one was going to her. Like everyone else, all the Matthers would be at the shindig. Right this minute Dillon had probably found the blue ribbon tied around the ear of corn and was collecting the prize of a kiss from Cindy. Elijah's scowl deepened. He threw down the piece of pine resin. There was no use giving in to Ma's pets. She could stay home, but he was going! Without giving himself time to back out, he jogged across the yard, crossed the creek, and began to run.

He had no trouble finding his way. A full moon generous with silver light made the path easy to follow. He sped through the night, hardly slowing as he climbed the ridge. At his approach, tiny creatures scurried into the underbrush and night birds winged away in the darkness. Then Belle barked. Something had stirred in the brush. Elijah stopped, every nerve taut. The stirring stopped. When Elijah started forward, it did also. Belle's bark was frantic—like when a bear came too close to the cabin. It might be a bear, or a panther! Or it might even be Lew!

Elijah began to run. He did not stop to see if anything followed. The way his heart was pounding, even if he stopped, he doubted he could hear a thing. Out of breath, he topped the last rise. With a backward glance, he took the fork in the trail that led to the Mason's cabin. Finally, it was just ahead. Elijah bent forward and, hands on knees, gulped in air.

Then he gave a low whistle. "Belle, half the county must be here!"

The pup wagged all over.

A dozen lanterns lit house and porch and crowded yard. A crackling bonfire lit the night, sending sparks high into the sky. Wagons and horses filled both barnyard and lane. In the yard, women and girls hurried back and forth putting food onto long pine tables. Children ran around the bonfire and then darted into the night and back again. Belle began running and yipping among the youngsters. Elijah frowned and grabbed her by the scruff and gave her a shake.

"Get back home!"

She trotted off a ways. He suspected she merely crawled under a wagon. If she stayed out of sight, he would let her disobey this time. He licked dry lips and went to join the men.

There was a large pile of corn already shucked and heaped onto a wagon. Only a small pile still remained in the shuck. Pappy Campbell heckled the young men. They were shucking and throwing the ears into a wagon as if speed were a matter of life and death.

"When I was young, I never had to waste time on no pile of corn to get a kiss!" goaded Pappy.

The old men chuckled. Young hands flew, the laughter and banter only urging them on. Dillon was shucking a long, dried ear, but his eyes were not on the corn. Elijah followed his gaze. Cindy had just set a platter heaped with cookies onto the table. She wore a white dress and looked like an angel.

"Elijah, get busy!" Caleb pointed to the pile. "No one's found that blue ribbon yet. If Dillon gets it, he'll likely kiss yer gal."

It was true. Elijah did not even redden when the men all laughed. He took the jibe as seriously as a battle flag. Without looking for a seat, he hunkered and grabbed an ear and gave the withered shuck a yank. Before the bare ear landed on the wagon, he grabbed another. Dillon shot him a grin and began shucking even faster.

"Simon, you never fergot to add that blue ribbon...accidental-like, to keep your pretty daughter from gettin' kissed, did ya?" Caleb grinned at the preacher.

"You forget, Brother Tanner, there are other pretty girls here."

Caleb's eyes twinkled. "Shore they are—but I reckon Cindy best pucker up if Elijah finds it."

The comment, along with the loud guffaws from the graybeards, made Elijah's neck grow warm. He snatched another ear and ripped at the yellowed shriveled husk. His eyes popped. He could hardly believe his luck. Tied around the ear was a blue ribbon!

Dillon groaned. Then he quickly said, "I'll give ya a dollar for it, Lige. That's all I got."

Elijah did not bother answering. He stood and started for the cabin. All the men, grinning and teasing, followed. A group of giggling girls stood under a lantern on the porch. When he espied Cindy in the pool of yellow light, he slowed. He wished the ground would open and swallow him. He wanted to kiss her more than anything, but not with a crowd looking on. He wanted Cindy alone under the full moon with her body pressed close and yielding and her silky head resting on his shoulder.

There was no help for it. Even now the crowd pushed him forward.

Caleb's eyes danced. "Who'll it be, Elijah?" He gave Caleb a frown for adding, "Now, Lige, you can't kiss 'em all. You got to pick one. And don't Miss Cindy look purtty this evening!" Everyone laughed.

When Elijah's eyes met Cindy's, her face flamed. For a split second, her eyes darted toward Dillon where he stood by the wagon. Elijah swallowed a taste more bitter than Granny's quinine. He stepped forward and then surprised even himself when he gave Sally Terry a quick peck on the cheek. He felt gratified when Cindy's mouth dropped open. Her face blazed and she turned on her heel and fled into the cabin. He wanted to run home. He wished he had never come. But he could not leave now. He would have to stay, at least a little while.

Music drifted from the open door. "Sounds like Allen's got his fiddle tuned," said Caleb.

"Caleb, ain't you aiming to play too?" asked Simon.

"Oh, I might spell Allen when he gets tired."

The animated crowd drifted inside, ready to dance. Elijah swallowed. He stepped through the front door and nodded to Granny. She was seated alongside Pappy Campbell; it was obvious that she was his sister. They had the same snapping black eyes and prominent noses. It was clear they also shared the same biting sense of humor. Pappy grinned ear to ear as Granny leaned forward and spoke to Jenny where she sat, stone-faced and solemn, on the far side of Pappy.

"Jenny, I heared tell they was some Texas Rangers at yer place the other day. Heared they stayed the night."

Pa was right, thought Elijah, *You can't fart in your own cabin in the morning without the whole mountain knowing it by nightfall!*

Jenny simply nodded.

"Caleb run into them on the trail. He said one was a giant of a man." Granny paused and spit into the fireplace. Polly had said she would be more comfortable seated near the cozy fire, but in reality, she wanted to make sure that Granny's habit did not end up on her clean floor.

Granny winked at the women seated nearby who looked up expectantly. "Big man like that would be powerful good husband material."

"Didn't know you was lookin', Granny. If he ever comes back, I'll send him right on over."

Granny laughed harder than anyone as Jenny turned the tables. When the laughter died down, Granny provided information that was news to most of the gathering.

"The big man is Becky's kin. He's gone to join up with...to join the army," she finished lamely as Viola sent her a sharp look. Not everyone at the gathering shared Southern leanings. Then she turned to Jenny and laughed. "I was jist having a bit of fun, Jenny."

Jenny stared straight ahead. "Teasing don't bother me none," she said.

Elijah noticed her dark cheeks had reddened. He figured Granny's sharp eyes had noticed it, too.

The room was ablaze with lanterns hanging from rafters. All the crude furniture had been pushed back against the wall or carried outside. The bare pine floor, scrubbed to a shine, was soon covered with shuffling feet keeping time to the fast Irish reel sawed out on Allen's fiddle. Elijah looked on. He knew the steps. He danced at home with Ma and Deborah. But he felt awkward dancing in front of folks. Obviously Dillon did not. He was dancing with Cindy. He swung her around, picking her halfway off the floor. She was smiling and her brown eyes glowed as brightly as the lantern hanging from the rafter above her head. Elijah gritted his teeth.

He was glad for the diversion when his Aunt Opal and Uncle Jim arrived with their dark-haired children, stair steps from seven to sixteen, mostly girls and all pretty. Aunt Opal might have been pretty once, thought Elijah, but no longer. She had rounded shoulders and a paunchy stomach. With gray-streaked hair parted in the middle and severely pulled back into a tight knot, she looked like an old woman, although she was not much older than Ma.

Ruby smiled at him. Elijah actually smiled for the first time that evening. Although all of Jim's girls were pretty, Ruby, with long dark hair and sparkling eyes, was the real beauty. She was her pa's favorite, and Elijah's too.

There was Pearl and Emmy—short for Emerald—and then Garnet. Elijah was glad the boys had escaped Aunt Opal's infatuation with gemstones. Joe and Sam were the youngest and looked just like their oldest brother, brown-eyed lanky James. Elijah felt badly about James being in the Union Army. He hoped James and Pa did not end up shooting at each other.

Elijah spoke to Opal in an undertone, "Here come Doc and Salvicy." He screwed up his face. "I'll swear they'd drive all day and night for a free feed. Of course they waited until all the corn was shucked."

Opal laughed, covering her mouth to hide missing and broken teeth. Ruby stormed away.

"What's wrong with her?" asked Elijah.

"Aw, she's getting sweet on that one over there," volunteered young Joe. He pointed at a tall, handsome, wide-shouldered boy with coal-black hair.

"Harley!" Elijah groaned. "Aw! Doesn't she know the Lucases are about the sorriest folks around? They live like hogs." He had never been inside the Lucas cabin, but Granny said it was worse than a pigsty.

"Better not tell her that," said Joe. "She'll box yer ears."

When Ruby made her way to Harley's side and gave him a dazzling smile, Elijah shook his head. It seemed all girls preferred fellows who were as big as mules! Disgusted, he went outside to join the men congregated on the porch. When they moved into the yard and stopped in the moonlight near the wagons, he followed. Music drifted on the night breeze, and far off an owl hooted.

Red Matthers came from his wagon toting two jugs. Although Simon did not serve liquor, Elijah knew he was not opposed to a man wetting his whistle out in the yard. Red handed Jim a jug and he reached Caleb the other. Caleb pulled the cork and tipped the jug. Jim also pulled a cork, and bracing the jug on his arm, took a long draw. Elijah's eyes widened when Jim passed the jug to him. He hesitated just a second and then tipped it up. As the liquid fire ran down his throat, he sputtered and coughed and passed the jug to the next man. He sucked in a burning breath. How could anyone think that stuff was fit to drink? It tasted worse than Granny's sulfur and molasses, worse even than the coal oil he had once accidentally gotten on his tongue.

Caleb licked his lips. "Dang, if that ain't yore best batch yet, Red—e're bit as good as Tennessee sippin' whiskey."

The next time the jug made the rounds, Elijah passed it on. He was astonished at how much Doc Lucas could gulp. Doc's Adams apple bobbed as, again and again, he swallowed.

Red scowled. "Hell, Doc. Leave some fer the rest of us."

Doc wiped his mouth and grinned. Elijah realized with a shock, if Doc weren't so fat, he might be handsome. Doc's hair was as black as midnight and he had vivid blue eyes like Harley. But he was—as Granny said—too sorry to waste a bullet on.

"Don't often get a chance at such good liquor," avowed Doc. Then he eyed Caleb pulling a twist of tobacco from his pocket. He licked his lips as Caleb bit off a chew.

"I forgot my chaw," he said.

Caleb's mouth drew down, but he handed Doc the tobacco. His frown deepened when Doc crammed half the twist into his mouth and tore it off with big brown teeth.

"Much obliged." Doc wallowed the piece around, barely able to speak. "My tobaccee gets dry as powder. How do ya keep yers so soft?"

"Piss on it."

Doc stopped chewing. He cut his eye all around as several heads nodded. There was not a grin in the crowd, just silent, solemn agreement.

Finally Red spoke up, "Yep, works better than anything I ever tried."

"Fer a fact," agreed Jim. "Doc, old as you are, I can't believe you never knowed that."

Doc looked green. When he left abruptly, a soft chuckle broke out.

"Biggest dang bum in the country!" Caleb shook his head in disgust. "Wish that bunch would move back to Georgie." He looked toward the corn. "Still a pile of corn over there. I reckon we ought to finish shuckin' it fer Simon."

Elijah started forward, but Caleb shooed him away. "Naw, us old geezers will finish this. Go have a good time."

Although that was not going to happen, Elijah drifted back into the cabin. Dillon now sat alongside Allen keeping up the lively tune on his guitar. Just then Allen lowered the fiddle from his chin. "Salvicy," Allen called, looking around the room. "Salvicy Lucas, where are you? Come on out here and show 'em how to dance!"

Tall, skinny, black-haired Salvicy hung back. As the women pushed her forward, she shook her head, grinning at the insistent urging. "Naw. I ain't a-wanting to show off," she declined. But when Allen sawed out a fast reel, her head began to bob. In a second, with eyes shining, she went dishrag limp, letting her arms hang down loose at her sides. As she began to jig, her feet flew like lightning. Although her bones seemed disjointed, they jerked in perfect time.

Everyone began to clap the beat. When Allen's fiddle sped up, so did Salvicy.

"She can jig," Elijah silently admitted. "And look at her eyes shine. She loves it."

When the jig ended, the rousing applause brought roses to Salvicy's sunken cheeks. As the dancers gathered for another set, a swarthy, brown-haired man joined Elijah.

"Lige, ain't you going to give these pretty gals a whirl?"

Elijah noticed his uncle's mahogany-brown eyes looked just like Pa's. "Reckon not, Uncle Jim. "I'd just step on their toes."

Jim smiled but suddenly the brown eyes metamorphosed cold and mean. The music abruptly halted and all heads faced the door. In the sudden eerie silence, Jim's muttered curse seemed loud.

Elijah sucked in his breath. In the doorway stood soldiers dressed in Confederate gray. They held rifles leveled at the crowd. And an officer held a large pistol.

"Hands up!" he barked. "High, where I can see them!" His eyes raked the crowd. When they found Jim Loring, they stopped. A nasty smile overspread his face. He pointed the pistol at Jim's chest. "Well, Loring, we had a little trouble trailing you after you left the Nation, but I told the Captain, you'd turn up back here sooner or later."

Elijah recognized the young officer. He was the surly fellow named Bo who had been bested by Allen at the militia horserace. Now Bo wore a finely tailored uniform, a short double-breasted coat with a double row of gold buttons, a single bar of gold braid on the sleeve, and two gold bars on the stand-up collar. *A lieutenant*, thought Elijah. He also recognized one of the soldiers. It was George Garrison, the boy from Minnow Creek who had moved to town last winter and swept up at Uncle Phillip's office. He looked shamefaced when Elijah stared.

The lieutenant went on, "The governor isn't taking it kindly that you and Fred Reynolds have been trying to convince the Cherokees and the Chickasaws to join the wrong army. And since you both seem to like traveling so much, he's planned a trip to Little Rock for you. When we find out who else is in cahoots with you, we'll hang the lot of you."

Jim stayed rooted. But his granite eyes darted everywhere. Elijah's stomach knotted and his mouth went ash dry.

The lieutenant jerked his head toward the door. "Come on, Jim. Your friend is outside," he goaded. "Let's not keep him waiting."

Suddenly a lantern crashed to the floor, spewing coal oil as it shattered. Fire leapt across the floor. A woman screamed. In the turmoil, a baby cried. Shots rang out from behind the cabin and men shouted. The back door stood open. Jim Loring was gone.

The floor shook with the tramp of soldiers pursuing. Simon grabbed a braided rug and rushed forward to beat back the blaze.

"Stay put!" the lieutenant ordered. Using the pistol, he waved back the men who had started forward to help, Elijah among them.

"You can't jist let my house burn," wailed Polly.

The lieutenant turned the pistol on Allen. "Damn you, Matthers!" he spat out. From the murderous look on his face, Elijah thought he would shoot.

Allen still held the fiddle while he stamped at flames near his feet. He shrugged. "Sorry, Bo. I was shakin' so hard, my bow slipped and knocked that lantern right down."

The flames threw Allen's shadow, huge and grotesque, dancing on the wall. He stopped for a moment to smirk at Bo. It was a taunting look.

Elijah held his breath. Bo's eyes wavered. Then he took a step back. Elijah was amazed. Even without a gun, Allen had the lieutenant buffaloed! Allen Matthers certainly had a way about him.

"Bo,"—Allen nodded to the door—"you'd best get these folks out of here. This coal oil ain't stomping out so good."

Elijah's eyes smarted from the roiling smoke, and like everyone else, he began to cough.

At the back door, a young private stuck his head inside. "Lieutenant, he got away," he said, and then hurriedly added, "but we winged him. There's blood out here."

Opal groaned and Ruby began to sob. Elijah took hold of Opal's arm.

"Take some of these lanterns," Bo snapped, "and comb the woods. Watch out. Loring's keen as a wolf." Glowering, he nodded at the two solders remaining inside. "Get these people outside but keep a sharp eye on them."

At gunpoint the men and women were herded outside and off the porch. The children huddled like scared chickens near the frightened women. The silent, angry-eyed men were ordered to stop. The women were ordered farther away. Polly wrung her hands and stayed as near the flickering chaos as the soldiers would allow.

"Hit's gonna burn plumb down, right to the ground," she sobbed.

"Allen and Simon is still a fightin' it." Granny's sympathetic whisper failed to comfort.

"Ohhhh!" Polly covered her mouth and moaned. "My new stove'll be ruined."

It took several seconds for Elijah's eyes to adjust to the darkness. Some light flared from the burning house, lighting the yard near Belle. She stood stiff-legged franticly barking. In the glow Elijah saw saddled horses bunched together. Three held mounted men. One was the fellow who had passed out pamphlets the day of the mustering parade. His arms were pulled back and tied. His face was a bloody pulp.

Down by the creek, shouts split the night. "There he goes! Across the creek!"

Shots rang out. Then all was quiet. The minutes dragged. Finally the soldiers returned and stood in a group talking low.

Elijah took a tentative step away from the men. When the soldiers paid him no mind, he slipped over to join Opal.

"You all right?" he asked.

She groaned. He patted her arm. "Aunt Opal, don't you worry," he whispered. "I heard one of the soldiers say there wasn't much blood. They barely nicked him. They'll not catch Uncle Jim. I allow he's already slipped down the creek and hidden in some cave."

She reached a trembling hand and gripped his arm. He talked to her a bit and then passed on and patted Ruby on the shoulder before making his way to Polly. He hunkered near where Cindy sat alongside her ashen-faced mother.

"Looks as if Allen and Simon about have the fire put out. One end will most likely need rebuilding but the rest looks fine."

Polly nodded. She bit a trembling lip.

In the moonlight Cindy's face was pearly white and her brown eyes tear-filled and glistening. "I...I hope your uncle is all right."

"I figure he is. Uncle Jim is as tough as whet-leather."

"What's it all about? Why are they after him?"

Elijah shrugged. "Aunt Opal says they think he's in some secret group—like some kind of spy or something. I figure because James is fighting Union it makes them suspicious of Uncle Jim."

The lieutenant strode out of the darkness toward the sullen men still bunched near the porch. He frowned and slapped his leg with a pair of gauntlets. "If you men are smart," he said, "you'll report Loring. Sooner or later we'll get him—along with all of that damned so-called Peace Society. There'll be plenty of hangings before this thing is done—including anyone who aids them." Bo ran scathing eyes over the hard-jawed men. "If you do as you ought and join the State Militia before you're conscripted, it'll go easier on you. The governor doesn't like cowards any more than he likes Yankees."

A tall, thin man spoke out, "Some of us done fit fer him at Oak Hill." He eyed the charred cabin before glaring back at Bo. "Fer all the good it done us."

The lieutenant ignored the remark. "Allen, I see you still aren't in uniform," he said with contempt.

"Now, Bo, you know my folks don't hold with fightin'—us being Quakers and all." Guffaws swept the men. Although Allen sounded jovial, his eyes were as hard as steel. "But I do fancy yore uniform. I just might join...if my pa can rake up enough to buy me some fancy gold stripes fer the collar."

Elijah perceived an insult. Bo's pa must have bought his rank. Uncle Caleb had said it was being done. As the chuckle spread even to Bo's men, an angry flush overspread his face. His jaw tightened and he wheeled. "Mount up," he spit out.

Elijah felt sorry for the man they led away, still tied and bloody.

As the lieutenant rode past, he glared at Belle. "Damn barking dog!" He drew the pistol and fired.

Elijah stood rooted. Belle dropped without a whimper. The lieutenant had put a bullet right through her skull.

That damned Bo had shot Belle! Elijah lunged. He grabbed for George's gun. George's horse sidestepped just as Caleb caught Elijah's shoulder.

"No, boy!"

Caleb spun him around. "Don't be a fool! That feller would bust yer head like a ripe melon! He's just itching to shoot someone." Caleb gave him a shake. "Now you cool off. You hear me?"

Of course Caleb was right. Bo would not bat an eye over killing him. Elijah's hot eyes followed the lieutenant's straight back as he disappeared around the bend.

George looked down. "I'm sorry about your dog." He kicked his horse in the side and rode after Bo.

Chapter 8

There was a gathering to rebuild Simon's cabin. Elijah took no pleasure in it. He was heartsick over Belle, and besides that, Dillon had stayed too close to Cindy. Elijah thought she had looked wistfully at him a few times. That might have been wishful thinking. After the cabin was completed no one ventured far from home. Political opinion became a silently guarded thing.

As days passed Elijah grew used to no joyful yips when he opened the door. He even stopped expecting a wet tongue on his face when he bent to wash at the creek. Time did not lessen the resentment he felt for Lieutenant Bo Morrison.

Now, in the dark, cold loft, Elijah turned back the covers and peeled off his outer shirt. Tonight the woolen long-johns and the heavy quilt would feel good. In the darkness, he breathed in the loft's spicy odors. Bunches of dried herbs and braided strings of dried onions, garlic, and peppers hung from the rafters alongside long threads of leather britches—green beans strung raw and hung to dry.

Before climbing into bed, something caught his eyes. He walked closer to the small window and stared a long while into the night. Suddenly he jerked on pants and boots, ran across the floor, and bounded down the ladder. He missed the last rung and fell. The thud echoed loud in the silence.

"Ma!" he hissed. "Hand me the gun, quick! There's someone messing around the smokehouse."

Becky sat straight up in bed. "Elijah! Don't go out there." In spite of her protest, she reached for the shotgun kept by her bed at night and handed it to him.

"I can't let them steal our meat."

Becky whispered to his departing back. "Meat is not worth getting killed for—or for killing someone either."

He paused. "Food's what keeps us alive, Ma."

Becky acquiesced silently. She stayed out of sight near the window, tensely waiting while he slipped through the darkness, and with iron willpower, she resisted pulling back the curtain for a better view.

Although they had not yet butchered, there was a ham and two smoked shoulders left hanging from the year before. Elijah was determined to keep them.

A shoat grunted, moving about in the pen. Something had disturbed it. Over ground crisp with frost, Elijah crept closer. He could see nothing. His mouth was dry. He could hear nothing except his heart pounding in his ears. There was no moon—probably the reason the thief had chosen this night.

Elijah was thankful to know his way in the dark. With silent tread, he stepped around the big iron hog-scalding pot. Just then someone stumbled. Elijah froze. The culprit was close. The muttered oath had come from just beyond the rain barrel.

Elijah squatted behind the barrel and waited. The dark blotch grew closer. Now he could make out the shape of a man. The fellow was tall and bulky. The foul smell of stale sweat preceded him. When the thief was almost even with the barrel, Elijah stood. He held the shotgun cocked and ready.

"Drop it."

The man froze. A knife clattered to the ground.

"Doc, you weren't aiming to cut down our hams with that knife were you?" asked Elijah. He did not lower the shotgun. Anger swept him. The old thief! He ought to blow Doc's legs off! He and Pa and Ma had worked their fingers to the bone, and Doc intended to stroll in and take it all without sacrificing even a drop of sweat.

Doc turned slowly. He gave a nervous laugh. "Now Lige," he wheedled, "when a man's young'uns is hungry, he gets desperate."

Elijah snorted. "How come you don't raise your own hogs? And how come you don't grow a garden on that place of yours? Guess it's just easier to steal, huh?"

Doc talked fast. "If you let me go, I won't never bother ya again. I promise!" Then he pleaded, "Please, Lige! Things has been bad lately. Ever' living thing I turn my hand to goes wrong."

Elijah's jaw hardened but Doc rushed on, "But I promise I'll get me some hogs and grow some feed corn. And next year, I'll grow me a big garden and then things will be better for us."

Elijah caressed the shotgun hammer with his thumb. What would Pa do in a case like this? He was not sure. "If you ever set foot on this place again, I'll shoot without even giving you a by-your-leave."

"That's fine, Lige," Doc said, almost dancing with relief, "that's fine." He started off at a trot, his fat belly bouncing, but suddenly he stopped and called back in a loud whisper, "Please don't name this to no one...Salvicy and the young'uns would be so shamed."

His boots quickly pounded away in the darkness. Elijah sank down, his back against the rain barrel. With his boot he pushed at the long knife lying on the ground. Had he done the right thing, letting Doc go? Doubt grew. He stood and looked after Doc. It was too late now. He stealthily made his way back to the cabin, going a different route than he had come. Pa had taught him it never hurt to be extra cautious.

"Elijah! Thank God you're safe! What happened?"

"I scared off whoever it was." It was not loyalty to Doc that kept him mum. It was the doubt that he had done the right thing by just letting him go. Better to just let it drop, he decided, than to try to explain his decision to Ma. Besides, he wasn't quite sure himself why he had done it. As lazy as Doc was, it was no surprise to catch him stealing to feed that passel of young'uns. Elijah hated to think of Ruby getting involved with that sorry clan.

"You're sure it was a person and not just some prowling animal?" Becky questioned hopefully.

"No, Ma, It was a two-legged polecat."

With a catch in her breath, she asked, "Do you think it was Lew...?"

"No way," he emphatically denied. "Lew is no common hog thief. Besides, if it had been Lew, I'd not have heard him."

"Whoever it was isn't likely to come back tonight," said Becky, looking past him out the dark window. "Why don't you go to bed, son, and try to get some sleep."

———❧———

The next morning Elijah was surprised when Ma let him sleep late. Usually, she called him at the crack of dawn to start the chores. He stretched and yawned and enjoyed a few more lazy minutes before throwing back the covers to feel the rough, cold boards on his bare feet. It was getting downright chilly. Soon they would need to start keeping fire.

He threw up his head and cocked his ear toward the ladder. He must still be dreaming. That sounded like Pa! With a single bound he crossed the floor and looked down from the loft. He was amazed to see Ned, now sporting a full brown beard, walking through the back door. In spite of toting a full pail of milk, he stopped to give Becky a playful swat on the behind as she stood stirring steaming fried potatoes and turning strips of sizzling bacon in a black iron skillet.

"Stop that!" She laughed, and fairly glowing, raised her cheek for a kiss.

"Pa!" Elijah scampered down the ladder and hammered Ned's back and then grabbed him for a mutual bear hug. "When did you get home?"

"Middle of the night."

Elijah wheeled accusingly to Becky. "Ma! Why didn't you wake me?"

Becky looked flustered and her cheeks grew rosy while Ned grinned ear to ear. Elijah's own face flamed. Of course they had wanted to be alone. Pa must think him greener than a gourd!

Deborah poked her tousled head through the loft opening. "You look like a baby squirrel peeking from the nest," teased Ned.

"Come on down here and let me see if you've growed a foot like your brother."

She quickly descended the ladder and flew to him and threw her arms around his neck, but abruptly she drew back. "I don't like whiskers, Pa. They tickle."

He laughed. "Then I reckon I'll have to shave them off." He tweaked her nose. "Yep, you've growed a foot!"

Then before Elijah could speak, Deborah blurted out the question that was on the tip of his tongue. "Pa, you don't have to go away again, do you?" she asked.

Ned sat down and gathered her onto his lap. Over the top of her head, as his eyes met Becky's, the sunny flush drained from her face.

"Nubbin, I wish I could say never again, but there's a job that still needs doin' and your pa has to help finish it."

Deborah hung her head. "You can stay for all day, can't you?" she whispered.

"Yep. I can stay for all day. And more besides. My company is wintering at Clarksville, so I'll be home for a good bit." He stroked her hair. "I think the captain will be glad for those of us who have homes close by to be off the army feedbag for a while. As long as I show up for drills, I don't think there'll be any problem with me being home for most of the winter."

Becky squared her shoulders and gave a brave smile. "Then I declare this a holiday. We won't do a thing but sit around and visit!"

"Now, Beck," Ned shook his head, "You know I can't enjoy a day of sittin' around with winter coming—the butchering not done and corn still in the field needin' gathering."

"Oh, all right," she relented, "but as soon as that's done, you need to get some rest and let me fill you up with some good food. You look tired and thin.

"I do feel honed down to the bone," he admitted. "Ain't nothing good about army life that I can see."

Elijah knew Ma was right. Pa needed rest. But there was so much that needed doing before the real cold set in. After breakfast, he pulled on a jacket and followed Ned outside. It was cloudy and windy. It would have felt good to sit by the stove today. But if the rain held off, they could finish gathering the corn in a couple of days.

———————⌇∽⌇———————

"Pa, what's it like—the war?" Elijah helped Ned buckle the hames on the mule's harness. Jinks stamped and blew, his breath a white cloud. A crow cawed from the cornfield, and a leaf skittered in a sudden gust of wind.

Ned gazed at the gray horizon before looking across the animal's back into Elijah's eyes. "It's a terrible thing. Don't ever let anyone tell you different." He paused. "You hear tell about glory and honor and such. And there's a bit of that when you march out of your own town—flags flyin', women cryin', men cheering ya on. It brings a warm feeling, for a fact."

"But,"—his eyes clouded— "the truth of war is blood and misery and folks' lives all shot to hell."

Elijah was surprised. Pa never spoke with profanity.

"I've seen boys not much older than you," Ned went on, "who'll never marry and raise a family as the good Lord intended—or ever even see the sunrise again—because their guts is splattered all over Missouri. And it could be, they're the lucky ones. Others will always have twisted, crippled bodies."

Elijah contemplated Ned's words before finally asking, "Pa, do you wish you hadn't gone?"

"Truth to tell, I ain't rightly sure. If the Yankees can be kept out of these mountains, I'm glad I went. But they've got a powerful lot of men and cannons. It's my opinion we was lucky at Wilson's Creek." He shook his head sadly. "Our own generals are feuding. Price and McCulloch are at each other's throats all the time. House divided against itself can't stand."

Pa was different. Before he had seemed so certain that the Yankees could be whipped.

"There's one thing I am shore of," said Ned, "I'll be forever grateful when this war is over. I pray to God you don't have to go."

Elijah silently agreed. He hoped the war would end soon and everyone could get back to the business of living and marrying girls like Cindy and raising a family like the good Lord intended.

"Get up, Jinks." Ned guided the mule and wagon toward the field of tall, brown stalks. Eyes on the ground, Elijah followed.

Ned called back cheerfully, "You done a good job, son. Most of it's already gathered. Looks as if them clouds is liftin' a bit. Maybe it won't rain after all."

At noon there was a special meal waiting. Elijah knew Ma had made all of Pa's favorites: crisp fried chicken, golden biscuits, thick cream gravy, and buttered hominy. With anticipation he eyed the apple pie cooling in the center of the table.

Around the table the mood was happy, lighthearted, almost the holiday Becky had suggested. Elijah wolfed his food like the hungry young animal that Pa accused him of being. But Ned's eyes shone with pride as he took in the broad shoulders and fine look of this almost grown son.

"Let me at that pie 'fore I'm too full to enjoy it," said Ned. After savoring a bite, he breathed a deep, contented sigh. "Becky, if McCulloch had you for a cook, every Yankee in Missouri would surrender fer a chance at the eats."

"Pshaw," she quipped, but her eyes warmed with pleasure. "It's a blessing to have some brown sugar left. It makes an apple pie taste so much better than one sweetened with molasses, or even honey for that matter."

Then she returned to a former subject. "I hope you're right, Ned," she said.

"About what?"

"About Tap. I hope he's still with General McCulloch. If that rumor you heard is true and the general winters in Van Buren County, Tap won't be far away."

Elijah's eyes twinkled. "I reckon Jenny would like that."

When Becky frowned, Ned stopped chewing and looked from face to face. "Becky, you playing cupid?"

She quickly rose to get the coffee pot. Ned's stare held steady. "Could be," she finally admitted with a guilty smile. "You wouldn't object to your cousin also being a sister-in-law, would you?"

"Course not. But I ain't sure Tap is the marrying kind. He's always been a tumbleweed." As Becky refilled the large mug, Ned blew on his coffee and took a sip, his mind abruptly going to other matters. "Soon as the crop is in, I'm going to town. Is Allen still around," he abruptly asked, "or did he join up?"

"Still around last week," said Elijah. "I saw him at the mill when Ma sent me to get some meal ground."

"Reckon I'll drop by and say howdy and thank him for helping Jim get away. And as soon as we butcher them hogs, I'll go check on Opal. And I reckon I'll stop in and see Phillip and Louise. Be time for the November muster by then anyway."

"Thank you, Ned." Becky dropped her eyes. "I would appreciate that very much."

Elijah saw Opal peeking from the window like a scared mouse from its hole. When she saw Ned on the porch, she gave a glad cry and threw open the door. She gave him a fierce hug. "Law Ned! Hit's so good to see you! I thought you was off in that heathen army." Her face reddened. "I mean..." she stammered.

Ned laughed. "I know what you meant, Opal. You thought I was off in that heathen army."

She covered her mouth as she grinned. Elijah joined in the laughter. And as they went inside, he smiled at his cousins.

Uncle Jim's cabin was poor, just a few sticks of crude homemade furniture. And Aunt Opal made no pretense to soften the poverty, no curtains, no rugs, no pretty cushions on the chairs, no colorful quilts on the beds—two of which half-filled the front room. But the room was scrubbed clean without a speck of dust anywhere.

"Take a cheer and sit down," she offered.

Ned sat, but he got right to the point. "Have you heard from Jim?"

Opal looked around at the towheads playing near the hearth. "Children, get on outside and play."

"Hit's too cold, Ma!" the youngest girl protested.

Opal was gentle but firm. "You'll not freeze fer a minute 'er two. Now get. Joe and Tommy, you boys go on with yer sisters."

The boys grumbled but began donning wraps. Elijah hated to see the thin jackets and Joe's bare feet.

Ruby and Pearl remained inside, going on with the dishwashing, but Elijah could see they were hanging on every word. Although the children had gone and the door was tightly shut, Opal lowered her voice and looked around as if a spy were lurking in the corner.

"He's over in the Nation, hid out with some Injuns."

"He healed up from the gunshot?"

"Yes, thank the good Lord. His arm is stiff but he kin still use it."

"If he's over the wound, Jim will make out fine." Ned looked relieved. "Now how about you and the children? You got plenty of food, winter wood?"

"We're fine. Our garden was good," she said.

"How about meat?"

Her face flushed. "We got plenty," she lied.

"Well, I just butchered, so I brought some pork along. If you don't need it now it'll keep."

"That will he'p," she acknowledged. "Our fatten hogs got stole."

"That's too bad. Becky said thieving is getting to be quite a problem around here." Ned shook his head. "Maybe now that there's some menfolk around again, it'll stop." He stood. "Well, I'll bring more meat next time I come. We got more than enough to do us. By the way, Becky sent a couple of pies and some cookies for the young'uns."

"Tell her, thank ya." When Ned stood to leave, she stood also.

Ned headed for the door. "Lige and I'll split you some wood. Your pile looks a little slim."

"Thank ya, Ned," her voice was soft. "Yo're a good man."

"For a Rebel," he joshed her.

"Fer anyone," she said. Just before she covered her mouth, a smile softened her face. In spite of the missing teeth, for a moment there was a trace of former beauty. Shocked, Elijah realized she looked a lot like Ruby. She must have been pretty before the years and the hard work had worn her down.

Before they left, Ruby managed to get him alone long enough to ask about Harley. He bit his tongue to keep from telling her that Harley's Pa was a hog thief. If Ruby married Harley, in a few years she would look worse than her ma. Granny claimed Doc was to blame for Salvicy's numerous bruises. Uncle Jim might be a hard man, but as far as Elijah knew, he never beat Opal.

Elijah had hesitated telling Pa about the hog-stealing incident. He feared his poor judgment in handling Doc would disappoint Pa—that Pa would no longer trust him. If opportunity ever arose, he intended finding out how Pa would have handled it.

———◦———

Near Spadra Crossing Elijah sat in the wagon waiting for Ned. But it was too cold to sit still for long, so he climbed down and stamped his feet and blew on his hands. He wondered how long it took a body to muster. The wind whipping up from the river was icy. He saw men drilling in the distance. They were a puny lot, ragged and unkempt, and some were even limping. When Ned finally returned, his face was downcast.

He climbed up, took the lines, and slapped the mules on the rump. "Sorry state of affairs," he said. "Men dying like flies here, dysentery and pneumonia. Buried so many already, they done named a whole blamed section at the cemetery Confederate Square!"

He turned the mules onto the road. A horse-drawn dray stacked with boxes and barrels passed by, heading for the camp.

"Before picking up supplies in town, we'll go check on your ma's kin. A fellow just told me Phillip is in Little Rock."

Elijah doubted Aunt Louise would take a visit kindly. He dreaded the ordeal but kept trepidation to himself. He always felt out of place in the fancy home with carpets on the floors and big mirrors and candelabras sitting on fine, polished furniture.

When they arrived, however, his mouth fell open. He stared in disbelief. The last time Elijah had visited this had been a fine house, one of the nicest in town. Now the front door was a makeshift affair of rough boards. The window glass was broken and the windows were boarded over like blind, patched eyes. The grounds were neglected. Long grass, dead and yellow, matted the yard, obviously untrimmed last fall. Except for a small thread of wood smoke rising from the chimney, the two-story white house looked deserted.

"My word!" exclaimed Ned. "What in the world has happened!" Soon after he knocked, Nelda opened the battered door.

"Oh! Uncle Ned!" she cried and quickly hugged him. It's so good to see you." She turned to Elijah with a smile.

Elijah hugged her. Nelda had never been curvy, but now she was cornstalk thin, her face all eyes, and her cheekbones even sharper angles than before. She looked tired and worn. Down the hallway stood Aunt Louise. She looked even worse. She was also thin and had large puffy bags under her eyes. Although her blonde hair was neat, her dress was limp and minus the usual wide hoops. He had never seen her in a work apron before.

Her greeting was cool, but this time she did not cut them with angry eyes. She ushered them down the long hall, past portraits of stuffy looking ancestors in wide gowns, tight britches, and high collars. She led on past the closed parlor door and into the dim, chill library where, in spite of the frigid air, only a gnat smoke fire burned. The room smelled of old books and musty leather, and the lingering odor of pipe tobacco held fast in long brocade drapes. She pointed Ned to Phillip's chair. Elijah hunkered on the hearth, leaving the other chairs for her and Nelda.

She began to apologize, "We no longer use the parlor...."

When her voice trailed away, Elijah supposed it had suddenly dawned that they were not parlor folk anyway. But Aunt Louise still sat as stiff and formal as if she were on the satin-covered chairs.

"I suppose you heard that Phillip has been jailed?" she asked.

"What!" Ned was astonished. "Whatever for?"

"Spying."

Elijah's head jerked. Both Uncle Jim and Uncle Phillip accused of spying! How odd.

"Of course it's ridiculous," said Louise. "Phillip went to Little Rock to do a favor for an old comrade from the Mexican War—Mr. C.C. Danley, the editor of the *Gazette*. He was recently appointed to the new military board and had to go to Richmond on business for the Confederacy. He asked Phillip to fill in for him at the paper."

Elijah found it odd that Uncle Phillip would help the Confederate cause. With him being so hard against secession, Elijah figured he stood strong Union. Of course, working at the paper was not necessarily helping the cause, he supposed.

Louise continued, "But Phillip had barely arrived when he was accused of being part of an underground group trying to sabotage the new government. Governor Rector ordered arrests made all over the state." As Louise explained, she drew forth Phillip's latest letter from her apron pocket. "No one who spoke out against secession is safe. Some of our *neighbors*," her voice grew snide, "even tried to burn us out. We're afraid to even answer the door these days."

"So that's what happened," said Ned. "Where's the home guard? They're supposed to keep it safe around here." His mouth had grown hard, and as his eyes thinned, Elijah saw an unusual resemblance to Uncle Jim.

"I have no idea," said Louise. "They certainly weren't in evidence the night we were vandalized."

Ned scanned the letter and then passed it to Elijah. He quickly read while the others talked.

Dear Family, I am well and in reasonably good spirits, although disappointed to have no news of my release. Don't be discouraged, for although the wheels of justice are turning slowly, at least they are turning. Since C.C. returned from Richmond he is twisting arms and using all his influence to aid me. Unfortunately there is a new chapter in the feud between him and the governor. Rector's henchman, General Burgevin, was so enraged over some of the recent comments in the Gazette; he actually challenged C.C. to a duel with the governor acting as second.

Nelda, I think you will get a chuckle from C.C.'s assessment of the situation. "It has seldom, if ever," he said, "been the lot of an editor to receive a challenge from as low a vagabond, or to have it borne by as high a public official."

Elijah grinned. Pa did not much care for Governor Rector and his bunch either.

The letter went on,

Louise, you will be reassured to know C.C. is not going to be goaded into such a senseless act. Since Burgevin aired his grievance by resorting to newsprint, C.C. was honorably relieved by the code duello. I fear, however, that the disagreement has delayed my release. The governor had promised C.C. that he would personally investigate my case, but since the latest dispute nothing more has been done. I have enclosed a clipping of Rector's latest speech. I call it his declaration of war on the Gazette.

Try to keep faith and stay cheerful. Pray for me as I pray for you. The Lord will hear our petitions. All my love, Phillip.

Elijah unfolded the clipping and began to read.

More treason lurks in Arkansas, under the garb of patriotism, than most men conceive of. Libelous 'traduction' of its authorities, gloatingly sought for, and swallowed by snarling cormorants of newspaper filth, well attest this fact. The press—the freedom of the press—once the symbol of liberty,—now the covert and insidious vehicle for undeveloped treason—the hypocritical defender of public justice—its calling, lowered to the dignity of mercenary avarice—a blessing to the people when guided by enlightened patriotism—a dire curse, when marked by malice and ignorance.

Elijah was uncertain of all the words. But it was clear that Uncle Phillip could stop counting on any help from the governor.

Ned struck a balled fist into his palm. "Jailing a good man like Phillip. The governor must be crazy."

"Pa says he is power crazy," agreed Nelda, "but he's the one in the governor's chair and Pa's the one in jail. Uncle Ned, do you have any idea how we could get him out?"

Ned drew a deep breath. "Can't say as I do. I don't know about such things." He looked glumly into the fire. "And I don't know anyone who does." His eyes sought Louise. "But I might be of some help around here. What needs doing?"

Louise sat even straighter. "We're managing very well, thank you."

"Oh, Ma!" Nelda cried. "You know we *very well are not!*" She turned to Ned. "Our girl, Della, ran off. And the army killed the only friend we had left in town. Shot him down right at the courthouse." For a moment she put a hand over her trembling mouth and batted back tears before going on. "And our man Tom is too old to do anything except feed the chickens and milk the cow. A few nights ago some men came and rode off with my mare, Lily." She bit her lip.

Elijah knew she had the same affection for Lily that he had felt for Belle. He touched her arm and she gave him a wan smile.

"They took the cow and everything else in the barn that wasn't nailed down. Tom didn't stop them even though I had given him Pa's shotgun. They took that too." Nelda sniffed and wiped her eyes with her fingers. "Thank God they didn't get the hogs. We hid them down in the woods by the river."

"I reckon them hogs is big enough to butcher?" questioned Ned.

"Yes," said Nelda, "and we do need help with that. We haven't had meat for ages."

"No time like the present." He stood. "I reckon it's cold enough to do it right now. Louise, is that all right by you?"

She gave a stiff, curt nod.

"You know how to handle pork," he asked, "make sausage, lard, and such?"

Her eyes flashed. "In spite of what you think of me, Ned Loring, I do know how to work," she spat out. "I can do all of those things."

Ned took a step back. "No offence intended, Louise. I just knowed you was used to slaves and such...."

She rose and came forward. Elijah's eyes widened when she took Ned's hand.

"Forgive me. I had no right to snap. It is very kind of you to offer help. We do need it." With an unsteady hand she rubbed her head. "Confession is good for the soul, Ned." She glanced at Nelda. "I fear my pride is being laid in the dust. And I richly deserve it."

Wind moaned around the house. Elijah glanced at the glass where a tree limb swayed, tapping the window like nervous fingers. After the butchering was done, he would trim the limb.

Louise pursed her lips. She breathed deeply before adding, "When Phillip met me, I was visiting Ma's wealthy kin in Fort Worth." She looked at Ned. "But when we married, Phillip took me away from a one-room soddy on the banks of the Red River. Pa was a drunk. He never owned a pot to piss in or a window to throw it out."

Elijah's mouth dropped open. Nelda sat transfixed.

"Ma died a year later when Becky was born. Tap had run off from home when he was fourteen. He only came home occasionally. There was no one to care for the baby. I took her...heaven knows Pa didn't care. And Phillip loved Becky like our own." With face paled, she went on, "Phillip came from a wealthy family." She faced Nelda. "The portraits in the hall are your pa's family—not mine like I always claimed." She looked down and her eyes filled. "I'm sorry, Nelda."

Louise swallowed and lifted a dainty handkerchief with trembling hands. She dabbed her eyes and then looked at Ned. "They disapproved of our marriage—but I've been far more unkind to you than they ever were to me. Will you forgive me?"

Ned nodded. He worried the hat in his hands. "We've all got our faults, Louise. I don't reckon yours is any worse than mine."

Looking relieved, she said, "Becky has no idea. I created a make-believe past for her. When Phillip got the opportunity to move here, I was overjoyed. Publishing a newspaper had always been his dream. And I wanted a new start far away from anyone who knew my past." She closed her eyes. "Sweet Phillip...he sympathized and let me go on in my folly."

She gave a dry laugh. "Pride goeth before a fall. And God is certainly punishing me now." She shivered and rubbed her arms. "Yes, Ned, it is a good day for butchering."

Ned cleared his throat. Then he nodded. "We'll get the hams and such salted down today. I'll come back in a few days to help Tom start the smoking. By then the meat will have took on enough salt and be ready to hang." He smiled at Nelda. "Get the knives ready. Won't be long before we'll have sausage to chop."

When they stepped outside, Ned put on his hat. "I'm right glad we came. They do need help," he said. "And your ma loves her sister a powerful lot."

"You aiming to tell Ma?" asked Elijah.

"I'll tell her we helped Louise and Nelda butcher. And I'll say Louise was downright sociable."

Elijah raised a brow. That meant no.

Although he felt some sympathy for his aunt, he did not look forward to spending the day here. He wished she had not raised Ma to be so different from ordinary folks. Ma would be happier. And so would he.

Chapter 9

November gave way to a snowy December. On Christmas morning a bitter wind howled at the cabin eaves and ice clung, thick and white, to the windows. Elijah knew he would always remember it as a cold, bleak day. It had started out well enough. He awoke with pleasure, enjoying the aroma of Ma's baking. The rich smells of pumpkin pie, spice cake, and yeast bread drifted to the loft. And Pa being home made it extra special.

Breakfast was festive. There was a present beside each plate, a new rag doll for Deborah, a keen-edged pocketknife for him, a pink flowered china teapot for Ma, and a new shirt for Pa. They were laughing and enjoying the fried ham, dark thick gravy, and flaky biscuits, when without warning the door flew open. Michael stood there, desolate and gray-faced.

"Ma's dead."

Ned stood, going for his coat. "You sure?"

He nodded. "She was done cold when I woke up."

"Where are the children?" asked Becky, hurrying into her wraps.

"I took 'em to Aunt Polly. Uncle Simon was gone. She said when he gets back—he's sittin' up with some sick feller on the other side of the ridge—she'll send him on over." Michael wiped a sleeve across his face.

"Here, son," urged Ned, "step over to the stove and warm yerself. You look froze to the bone."

Elijah knew he must be. The coat was little more than a rag. His left boot was out at the toe and a bare foot peeked through.

Ned pulled on gloves. "I'll go fetch Granny and Caleb. Why don't you wait here, Michael? Get warmed up."

He barely nodded. Elijah figured he was in no hurry to leave—to go home to an empty house and a dead ma. While Michael hugged the stove, his hollow eyes took in the table. Elijah felt miserable, guilty at the evidence of their celebration. He did not know what to say. Finally, he offered, "Want some breakfast?"

Michael shook his head and turned away. Elijah felt tears roll down his own cheeks. It did not seem right. First Johnny and now Maggie. Why? He wondered what Granny would say. Was this judgment or mercy?

After the dismal funeral, Michael refused the kind offer of a home with Polly and Simon. The younger children, however, did go with them. Elijah thought Cindy was worse than a mother hen, hovering and protecting them. She had barely noticed him when he rode over with Deborah's outgrown clothes that Ma had sent for Mattie. He supposed the young'uns needed some special attention. More than likely this was the first time their little bellies had ever stayed full. He reckoned it was like Granny always said, there was a silver lining to every cloud. But he worried about Michael. What would he eat? There was no game to speak of in the woods this time of year. Deer and squirrels were scarce lately, and bears had gone to den. Michael was too proud to take a handout.

A few weeks later, Elijah had cause to share his concern with Ned. "Pa, on my way to Granny's this morning I saw Michael toting that old blunderbuss of his. And you know there's no game in February. His face was all blue and pinched and he was so skinny his clothes looked about to fall off."

Ned grimaced. "Poor young'un. I been thinking what to do for him. We'll have to tread careful. He's poor proud like his ma was. I wouldn't want to add to his hurt." Ned sighed and slowly shook his head. "Old Johnny left behind a heap of misery."

It was Caleb who finally came up with a solution. He was clearing a new patch of land with both Ned and Elijah helping. Michael agreed to work for vittles.

Elijah knew Michael would earn every bite, for there was nothing much harder than grubbing stumps out of frozen ground. But Uncle Caleb wanted a larger corn patch. The Confederate government was pleading with farmers to grow more food. The Southern army needed to eat.

After a week of working, Michael began to lose the square-jawed defensive look. He even laughed and joked a bit. Everything was going well until the morning Joel Johnston galloped up on a lathered mare.

"What's up, Joel?" called Ned.

"We've been ordered to muster. Rumor is we're heading north again."

"In February!" Ned was incredulous.

"Our scouts reported some unusual activity up in Missouri."

"No one in their right mind would move a army in this lousy weather," said Ned.

Joel galloped away, calling back over his shoulder, "I don't recall the Yankees being accused of having good sense."

Michael put down the mattock. "I'm going with you."

"What?"

Michael rushed on, his words tripping over each other, "I'm a smidgen young, I know. But I can shoot as good as 'ery man. And when the time comes—I figure I can fight as good as the next 'un too. This here job's most over. There ain't no other work around here." He hung his head and spoke low. "I'm sick an' tired of being hungry."

Ned took off his hat and wiped his forehead and the inside brim with a handkerchief. He looked toward the northern horizon. Finally he spoke, "Army don't always eat, son. And there's times you march till yo're so tired you drop in yer tracks and then have to lay down on the bare ground and sleep in the pourin' rain."

"There's nothing for me here," insisted Michael.

Ned drew a deep breath and let it out slowly. "All right. Get your stuff and meet me at my place. We'll leave in about an hour."

Elijah felt sick. Pa was leaving to go off and maybe get killed. And now so was Michael. Up until now the Lane luck hadn't been so good. Would it change for Michael, or would he be one of those Pa had talked about whose guts got splattered over Missouri? Elijah sank down on a stump, feeling as bleak as the bare, cold fields around him.

With both Pa and Michael gone, Elijah was forlorn. He was glad to be working at Uncle Caleb's. It helped take his mind off the loneliness. He had worked all day chopping and limbing trees near the edge of the new corn patch. The thud of the ax splintering the brittle wood echoed like a shot, but the sound was soon muted by low clouds wrapping the mountain with a blanket of fog. Although the day was chill, the exercise kept him warm. He had enjoyed spending the day joshing with Granny. She had worked alongside him keeping the brush pile burning by dragging the smaller limbs onto the fire. For the most part, Viola had stayed inside and that suited Elijah fine.

By day's end, they had made a good showing and Elijah thought Uncle Caleb would be pleased when he got back from town. "Reckon I'll head on to the house, Granny," he said wiping sweat from his brow with the back of his hand and smearing soot on his face.

"Stay to supper," she urged. "You shore worked hard enough today to earn it."

"No thanks. Ma will have mine waiting, and I need to get on and get the cow milked before dark."

"Well, 'til yo're better paid, thanks fer all yer help, son." She threw another limb onto the fire and then used a long stick to stoke it. Smoke blew into her face and she backed away. "Way that smoke is hanging low to the ground, I figure we're gonna get sleet or rain."

"Hope I make it home first," he said. "You ought to get in out of this damp, Granny. You've worked enough for one day." He got Jinks from the nearby thicket and climbed up. After waving goodbye to Granny, he kicked the mule's flanks and started for home at a trot.

Before he had gone far, Granny's prediction came true. The rain began as a slow, cold drizzle which soon wet his hat and jacket. Elijah hunched his shoulders and urged Jinks to go faster. The mule broke into a jogging trot. But as they rounded the bend, Elijah abruptly pulled to a halt. Startled, he sat up straight.

He had ridden straight into a small troop of Confederate soldiers. His eyes widened and then narrowed with hate. Lieutenant Bo Morrison held a pistol pointed squarely at his chest.

"But Bo, he's sort of young...." It was George Garrison from Minnow Creek.

"Do as you're told," the lieutenant spat out. He gave George a withering look. And, Private, don't ever argue with me again."

George rode near Elijah's mule and pulled out a rope. "What's this all about?" Elijah's eyes flashed. "I haven't done anything wrong."

"No, you ain't," George muttered. He dismounted and ordered Elijah to climb down and then tied his hands behind his back. He boosted Elijah back onto the mule but kept hold of the reins himself. The seriousness of what was happening was momentarily lost on Elijah. He was too full of vengeful thoughts.

Bo looked back and motioned some men forward who had waited in the trees.

"Seems we just joined the army, Lige." Dillon Matthers was hogtied and riding double behind a short, skinny soldier. There was a large, bluish lump on his forehead and one eye was swollen almost shut.

Dazed, Elijah echoed, "Joined the army?"

"The dog-killing lieutenant there has him a quota to fill," spit out Dillon. "Since volunteers is few and far between, we got took. Conscription, he calls it."

Elijah slowly took it in. His mind whirled. He needed to get home. Ma would fret herself to death wondering what had happened to him if he did not show up before dark, and daylight was fading fast. He stared at the ropes. This conscription made no sense. How could they expect a fellow to fight for them if he was dragged off against his will? Wouldn't a man run off the first chance he got? Elijah intended to. His eyes darted about. He scooted to get a more comfortable seat on the mule.

"Sit tight. Don't even think about running off," advised George in an undertone. "Bo would drop you in your tracks. He's the best shot I've ever seen—and I've seen some prime shooting."

"Yeah, he shot off Vernon's ear when he tried running off," said Dillon.

Elijah looked all around. "Where is Vernon?" he asked with a sick feeling in his stomach. He had no liking for Vernon, but he hated to think of him lying with a bullet in his head like Belle.

"Oh, he bawled so loud they let him go. Even the lieutenant is more picky than that. He could tell Vernon ain't bright."

"Oh, yeah?" said Elijah. "Well, he's home and we're here. Maybe he's not so dumb after all!" Elijah's insides twisted. To be taken by Bo Morrison!

The lieutenant raised his hand and waved the troop forward. They had not gone far, however, when rounding a bend, Bo suddenly halted.

Elijah's eyes popped. It was Cousin Billy wearing a homespun butternut uniform and sitting on a buckskin mare. Billy eased the horse forward from under the giant cedar that had shielded him. "What's going on here?" he drawled.

Elijah had not seen Billy since he joined up. He had not wintered here like Pa. He was serving with General Hardee, and they had left the state in the fall.

"None of your business, soldier," the lieutenant shot out. "Ride on."

Deliberately slow, Billy used his left hand to pull a twist of tobacco from his pocket. He offered it to George. "Chaw?" George nervously shook his head. Billy bit off a sliver before putting the twist away. He chewed a bit and then spit.

The spittle landed on Bo's trousers. At the same instant Billy drew a pistol.

"I'm making it my business. Don't you bat a eye, Lieutenant." He gestured with the pistol. "Boys, put all them guns on the ground." When the men complied he ordered, "Now untie these boys." He kept his pistol leveled on Bo.

Elijah rubbed his wrists. The tight rope had already chaffed them. He figured Billy would be in a heap of trouble over this.

Bo was livid. "What do you mean, drawing a gun on an officer!" he snarled. Then his eyes narrowed. "I'll bet you're a deserter. You'll hang for this!" he ground out, smearing at his trousers with a gauntlet.

Billy grinned. "Well, since I'm the one holding the gun, you'll more than likely have time to get yore pants pressed before the hang—"

Elijah jumped when the shot rang out. It knocked Billy from the saddle. The soldier returning from a scout rode into sight with his pistol still pointed. Elijah tried to slide from the mule.

"Get back there!" hissed George.

Elijah was relieved to see Billy sit up and groan. Except for a red welt across his temple, he appeared fine.

"He ain't hurt," said George, "just stunned."

"Then he'll be in good shape for his hanging," Bo snarled. "Tie him up. And tight!"

Elijah winced as the rope was lashed onto Billy's wrists. He looked miserable with cold rain plastering his hair. His hat had been lost in the scuffle.

"It's getting dark, sir. Perhaps there's a cabin nearby where we can spend the night in the dry," suggested the skinny soldier in front of Dillon.

While the lieutenant and his men discussed their next move, Elijah took the opportunity to get Dillon's attention. "Psst!" Dillon looked around. "Reckon Allen will trail us up?"

"Shore he would if he wasn't up in Newton County," Dillon whispered. "Jess Holder and his gang of bushwhackers came back and found where Allen had hid their horses. They took 'em back. Took a potshot at Allen, too. He was madder 'an a wet hen when he took off after 'em. Ain't no telling when he'll get back." For the first time Dillon looked a bit shaken as he whispered, "Hope it's before that lieutenant drags us off this mountain."

With water trailing from the brim of his gray hat, Bo peered into the dripping woods. "No, we'll press on. Too many Yankeelovers up here. I don't trust these mountain swine. They're not as smart as their razorbacks but they're just as vicious. Given half a chance, they'll shoot us in the back." He turned in his saddle. "Keep your voices down and gag those men."

George stuffed a handkerchief into Elijah's mouth and then remounted. After Billy was gagged and dragged onto his horse, they set off at a trot through the gray wetness. Elijah began to pray. He knew he was not good at it like Ma or Granny or Brother Simon, but he recollected the preacher saying once that the Lord kept his ears open for a desperate cry. He was certainly desperate.

Bo angled off the trail, cutting through the woods. With renewed hope, Elijah realized they would go right past Uncle Caleb's cabin.

"Cabin ahead, sir." The scout pointed toward the clearing. "We could circle around, but it seems a likely place to spend the night. Doesn't appear to be anyone at home except a couple of old women."

The cold drizzle had already seeped through Elijah's jacket, and even though the lieutenant and his men wore slickers, the wet clay trails would be no fun, especially at night.

"It won't hurt to take a look, I suppose." Bo turned in the saddle and pointed to Elijah. "Take his gag out," he ordered George. Then he asked, "Who lives here?"

Elijah shrugged. He did not try to keep the hate from his voice. "I got no idea."

Bo sneered. "Sure you don't!"

As they drew near, smoke rose lazily from the burning brush pile, and Granny, dressed in Uncle Caleb's old black coat and slouch hat, still dragged limbs onto the fire. Wrapped in a shawl, Viola stood nearby squinting at them through the smoke. Granny's eyes measured the distance to an old musket propped on a stump. Before she could act, the scout rode up, bent from the saddle, and retrieved it.

"Keep shut!" Granny hissed at a quaking Viola. "Not a word, mind you!"

Elijah knew Viola had just espied Billy trussed up like a roast pig with a gag in his mouth for the apple. She looked about to bust or faint or something, but Granny was as calm as a spring day.

Disgusted, she snorted. "I'm gettin' old and careless," she quarreled at the scout, "er you'd not got the drop on me."

Bo rode near. "You're that old fiddle player's mother, aren't you? What's his name—Tanner?"

"Yep. I'm Miz Tanner." She scrutinized his uniform and then she eyed the whole group. "Yo're wearin' gray so we're on the same side. Put them guns away and come on inside." She began hobbling toward the cabin. "And while you dry out," she called back over her shoulder, "I'll fix you a bait of food."

Visibly relaxing, the soldiers expressed relief over finding shelter. They exchanged a few chuckles about the salty old woman who offered it. Elijah was optimistic. Surely Uncle Caleb would rescue them. Granny was salty all right, but it was expecting a bit much to think even she could outdo seven armed men.

Before going inside, two soldiers removed the gags but left tight the ropes on the prisoners. The cabin was dim but warm and dry. The tall spinning wheel and loom filled one end of the small front room. The soldiers crowded around the table and benches and hunkered near the fireplace. Mud now spattered Granny's clean floor.

Granny pulled a Dutch oven from the coals in the fireplace, brushed off the ashes, opened it, and fork tested a venison roast for tenderness. The aroma of roasting meat made Elijah's stomach growl. He thought no one could beat Granny at cooking wild game, especially venison, for she used lots of yarbs and onions.

"Them fellers rob a bank?" she asked, nodding their direction.

"Nope. The two young ones are joining the army."

Granny reached into a pocket, pulled out a tin of snuff, and took a dip. "Jining?" she asked with raised eyebrows.

"Governor's orders. Conscription since the county didn't fill its quota."

Granny squinted at Billy. "What about that 'un? Appears like he done jined."

"Deserter headed for his hanging."

Viola gasped. Granny shot her a threatening look and spoke quickly, "Won't take but a jiffy to bake a batch of biscuits. You fellers make yer'selves to home."

Dillon hunkered against the wall. Elijah and Billy sat on the floor near the fireplace. A blue-eyed sergeant named Prine kept a close eye on them. As of yet, the lieutenant had no idea Granny was their kin, but Elijah feared one close look at Viola would change that. While terror-filled eyes devoured Billy, her mouth worked in silent anguish.

The enticing aroma of hot bread soon began tickling nostrils. Granny pressed her advantage. "Why don't you untie them young'uns so they kin eat? They ain't going nowhere with the lot of you guarding 'em."

"They can eat like that," declared Bo.

His stance softened when Granny gave him a golden-brown biscuit filled with a thick slice of succulent roast. And she fussed over him a good bit, making sure his coffee mug was full and another biscuit was forthcoming before the first one was half devoured.

Then clicking her tongue, she tutted. "Why, look thar—that poor boy's hands is turning blue." She pointed to Elijah. "You ought to back them ropes off just a mite. Hit'll ruin his hands. He won't be no good to the army then."

"George, take the ropes off for now," Bo relented, "but back they go after supper."

Elijah was thankful for the hot food and even more thankful for relief from the ropes. As they ate, Granny managed to convey some news to Billy. "My son, Caleb, has gone to town," she said. "Feller rode through here t'other day and said salt had jumped to twenty dollars a sack at Dover. Caleb hoped to buy us up a good supply 'fore the price goes up at Clarksville. He ought to be back tomorrow night. You might pass him on the trail."

When George put the ropes back, he tied Elijah's hands in front. They were still tight, but at least they did not bite into his flesh enough to stop the blood. He would sleep in more comfort.

Soon after dark the rain stopped drumming on the shake roof, but the temperature plunged. Since the cabin had no stove, the men hunkered near the fireplace, quietly talking and smoking. Rather than banking the fire for the night, they brought in extra wood to keep a roaring blaze. As they began bedding down on bedrolls on the floor, Elijah managed a few whispered words with Billy.

"Billy, you've got to get away. The lieutenant is rotten mean. He'll see you hang or he'll shoot you himself."

"I'll be all right," assured Billy. "Fancy pants ain't getting me hung. I ain't deserting. I'm a courier carrying messages for General Hardee," he said.

"Show him the messages and maybe he'll let you go."

"Can't." Billy tapped his head. "They're up here. But I figure to get away before he kin shoot me."

He hoped Billy was right. Bo was vicious. And his eyes had a crazy look—almost as mean as Lew Willis.

In spite of the fire, Elijah shivered. Cold air stole through the chinking and crept under the door where he lay on the puncheons with no covering except the clothes on his back. Before Granny had gone to bed in the next room she had offered quilts for the prisoners, but the lieutenant refused, saying they needed hardening up for army life. Bo, however, had taken Granny's room and her feather bed, forcing her to sleep with Viola. Although Elijah coveted a quilt, he was certainly glad for the shelter. At least he was not traveling through the frigid night.

Late in the night, when Granny entered the front room, the soldiers were wearily sprawled on bedrolls, the lone exception the smooth-faced private guarding the door. Keeping a grip on his rifle, he rose from the cane-bottomed chair placed beside the front door. He kept his voice low.

"I can't let you go outside, ma'am."

Trying to poke him aside with her walking stick, she ordered, "Look a'here, young feller, I et somethin' that gripped me. I'd advise you to stay out of the way betwixt me and the woods!"

Elijah stirred. What was Granny up to? She had a cast-iron stomach. He'd never known her to have even a touch of the trots. And why was she still wearing a dress—and now with hoops under the skirt? Viola sometimes wore them, but never Granny.

The scout sleepily rose on an elbow. "Oh, Yates, let her pass." With a grunt he rolled over and began breathing deeply again.

Elijah, however, came fully awake. Granny was scheming. He just knew it. With the toe of his boot, he pushed Billy, prodding him awake. Billy roused in time to see her leave.

"What?" he mouthed.

In the dim light of the fireplace, Elijah mouthed back. "Wait."

It was not long before Granny returned, letting in a sharp blast of cold air before quickly shutting the door. She walked slowly past while looking to make sure they were awake. Elijah gave her a wink. With a grin, she winked back.

Before half an hour had passed, the door creaked again. Granny slowly left the room. Sometimes thirty minutes lapsed between trips. Sometimes Granny waited a scant fifteen before disturbing the private's light doze.

A triumphant gleam filled her eye when, after the ninth time, he did not even rouse as she hobbled past. On the next trip, she passed near Billy and prodded him with her toe to make certain he was awake. At a quick move from him, she shook her head and mouthed the words, "Next time."

The old woman's mouth was dry as she rose stiffly from the rocker. That lieutenant was a bad one. He would shoot Billy in a heartbeat and enjoy doing it. There was no fear for herself, but Billy was her grandchild and the apple of Caleb's eye. Her prayers had risen constantly from a trembling heart from the moment she had spied him bound and gagged.

On limbs feeling unusually shaky, she inched to the bedroom door and paused, leaning her head against it. She prayed again and then squared her shoulders.

Amidst the heavy breathing and snores, the door creaked. Elijah peered hard. In the shadow-filled room the only light came from the fireplace. Granny paused, adjusting eyes to the dimness. Then she shuffled toward the door. But this time she stopped near Billy to replenish a dip of snuff. The sleepy private barely moved his outstretched feet to let her by. With a shuffling gait she went around him.

When she returned Elijah risked a whisper. "Give him a chance to get clean away. I can run off later." At her nod, he waited until the bedroom door closed to let out his breath. With a silent laugh, he scooted nearer the fire, taking Billy's place. Then he turned on his side, curled into a tight ball against the chill, and slept.

When Elijah awoke, Granny, minus the hoops, was seated at the kitchen table. Early dawn showed gray through the tiny window. Yates still slumped in his chair, his rifle between his legs. When Elijah slipped over to the table, no one stirred.

White and drawn, Granny gazed at him, her rummy eyes worried. "I wish to goodness you'd got away too."

"Don't fret, Granny," he kept his voice low. "Me and Dillon will get our chance."

Viola came through the bedroom door and crept around the sleeping soldiers to join them. "Thank God Billy got away. Elijah, you all right?" she whispered. At his nod she turned to Granny. "Yer plumb wore out." She worried the shawl around Granny's shoulders and then sat on the bench beside her. "There. Now, tell me quick, however did you do it?"

"I dropped my skirt down over him and snuck him out under them blasted hoops."

Viola's face paled. "The soldiers never seed you?"

"Hit was God's grace shore," vowed Granny, reverently.

Viola agreed. "Hit's a wonder they never noticed the hoops."

Granny snorted. "Men is blind as bats when the skirt covers a old woman, 'stead of a young one."

Bo came through the bedroom door, hair awry and suspenders still hanging. He reached for the coffeepot. "Roll out, men," he ordered. Then he froze. "Where's that soldier!" he spit out. With accusing eyes, he whirled to face Granny.

A glow of triumph on her face, she gloated. "By now I'd say he's a fur piece from here."

His eyes filled with hate. "I knew better than to trust any of you!" He banged the pot down onto the hearth. "Curry, get on his trail," he ordered the scout. "When you catch him, bring him to Clarksville. I want to watch him hang!" He kicked at Sergeant Prine who sat up, still groggy. "Grab what foodstuff is handy and let's ride," he barked. "Get those supplies loaded."

Elijah had little fear that Curry would catch Billy. Billy was canny, especially in the woods.

Stoic, Granny and Viola watched the men stuff leftover bread and meat into pockets and knapsacks. Elijah thought Jess's bushwhackers could take lessons from Bo's men. There was not a crumb left in the cabin.

The horses were saddled and waiting when George prodded him outside. Dillon, still half-asleep, stumbled out just ahead of him. "Blast these damn ropes," he complained. "Ain't got any feeling left in my hands."

Although Elijah had worked his wrists until the ropes were looser, they were nonetheless a nuisance. He wondered how long the lieutenant intended keeping them hogtied.

The day was bitter. The horse's breath clouded with cold. Near the open smokehouse door stood Jinks, now loaded with plunder. The packs across his back bulged with whole smoked shoulders and hams. Elijah could just picture Uncle Caleb's fury when he found the empty smokehouse.

Restive, George's mount pranced while George reached down and hefted Elijah onto the back of his saddle. Elijah looked all around. The bare cornfields stretched bleak and frozen. The holes left by the grubbed-out stumps were frozen puddles. Gray ash was all that remained of the brush piles. He heard the flapping of wings in the barn as chickens flew down from the roost. In the barnyard a cow mooed, placidly waiting to be milked. With turmoil in his breast, Elijah thought it strange that everything looked peaceful and natural.

Rays of pale sun etched the weary, sagging lines of Granny's face as she stood leaning on the twisted cane in the cabin doorway. Elijah wondered when he would see her again. He turned in the saddle and watched until he was out of sight. She raised a shaky hand to wave.

"She's quite a old fox," muttered George. "Glad she ain't a Yankee." He chuckled. "She'd make a bad enemy."

At first the lieutenant set a fast pace but soon was forced to slow on the rain-slicked frozen trail. Elijah bobbed along behind George, rejecting first one and then another plan of escape. He finally decided to wait and see what opportunity arose. He intended to be ready when it did.

As they snaked down the mountainside, leaden clouds settled, looking heavy with snow. Elijah shivered inside his jacket. He wished he had worn long-johns as Ma had suggested, but he had thought them too warm for the hard work of clearing land.

When the lieutenant signaled to leave the trail and head into the woods, Elijah assumed he was afraid of meeting travelers returning from town. They had gone about three miles through the woods when Curry appeared. He was on his sorrel horse, his long coat unbuttoned and his pistol butt handy. After a low conversation with the lieutenant, he fell into line as they rode on. Elijah knew he had given up on catching Billy.

While keeping an uncomfortable perch, Elijah pondered. If he and Dillon did not escape, it appeared they would be packed off to join the men headed for the Missouri border. What about Ma? How would she manage? The miles slipped by with his thoughts in a whirl. He was no closer to any solutions when, just down the hill, Clarksville came into sight. They had made rapid time. The sun had just passed its zenith when they cantered toward the bridge.

A young woman wrapped in a blue hooded cloak suddenly stood in the road waving franticly. She was the pretty girl from mustering day. Then Elijah remembered she was Bo's sister.

"Bo," she cried. "Thank God! I thought you'd never get here. Your captain said you were heading this way, but it seems I've been waiting for hours!"

When the lieutenant stopped, the young woman's eyes swept the group and her brow immediately furrowed. "Why do you have Allen's brother tied up? What's he done?"

"Allen's broth—" Bo whirled to stare at Dillon. He turned back. "Are you sure?"

"Yes, Allen introduced us once in town."

"The little whelp wouldn't tell me his name." Bo's face grew hard as he bit out, "Mary Beth, what are you doing hanging by the road like a common trollop?"

She blanched. "It's Pa, Bo." Her lip trembled. "He's had a bad spell. I think it's his heart. He's all gray and he can hardly breathe." Tears welled in her green eyes and she drew a ragged breath. "Ma's in such a panic, she's no help at all—and there are no doctors left in town." She caught her lip in her teeth. "Bo, I think he's dying."

"Then good riddance." Bo kicked his horse in the flanks.

Elijah turned back to stare at the stricken young woman. It was hard to imagine that pretty girl was Bo's sister. For a moment she looked after them, and then with lagging steps, she turned and slowly started up the long, curving avenue toward a tall brick mansion.

Clarksville was not the prosperous, busy place it had been the last time Elijah was in town. Now it was a ghost town. The only activity was near the courthouse where a handful of soldiers were coming and going and a few graybeards loitered on benches in the cold noon. Store windows were virtually bare. Uncle Caleb had complained of hoarding. He said if the war lasted it was no telling how scarce things would become.

Elijah wondered if there was any way to get word to Nelda. He doubted she could gain his release, but if Uncle Phillip had returned, he might be able to help.

Chapter 10

Bound and gagged, with knees drawn under his chin, Elijah sat cramped on the rough floorboards of a crowded freight wagon. Ropes held him fast to one metal hoop supporting the canvas. After another futile tug, he gave up. His wrists were already raw meat. The lump throbbed on his forehead where Bo Morrison had just whacked him. His mouth, stuffed full of the old handkerchief, was as dry as a dusty field.

In a small patch of gray sky showing through a hole in the ragged cover, he saw the cupola on the courthouse. He had overheard Bo saying they would not be in Clarksville long. If only he could get word to Nelda! But Bo had made sure there was slim chance of that when a short while ago he had pulled him from the horse and hogtied him inside the wagon. With a sigh, he scooted, trying to ease the pinch in his lower back. In the dim light filtering through the tightly drawn canvas, he read the printing on a stack of wooden boxes: 1000 .69 buck and ball cartridges. He shivered and drew deeper inside the jacket. Before nightfall he hoped someone would bring a blanket. Ma would be frantic by now. He wished there was some way to get word—

He threw up his head. Voices were drawing near. If he stamped his boots, maybe someone would come and offer him a drink. Then he froze. He could hardly believe it! It was Nelda! She must be gathering news for Uncle Phillip's newspaper. If she learned about the illegal conscriptions, Bo would be in big trouble. And he would go free!

"Mr. Curry, do you know how strong the invading force is?"

"You'll have to ask Lieutenant Morrison any more questions, ma'am. I'm just a scout. I might get in Dutch if you print something I say. "

Elijah's heart raced. He stomped with all his might.

"What was that?"

"Aw, just the muleskinner rearranging the load."

With fettered feet, Elijah kicked the pile of wooden boxes. The top one crashed to the floor.

"Old Zearl must have dropped something." Curry quickly led her away. The voices grew faint.

Elijah gave a frustrated kick at a fallen ammunition box. A paper cartridge ripped, pouring black powder onto his boots. His shoulders sagged. He was headed for war—a war that still made no sense. Tighter than ropes, an ache of homesickness gripped him. Would he ever again see Ma and Deborah? Or Cindy? Would he ever see home again? Would he ever again watch the mists rise on Little Piney?

He had never felt so alone in his life. He had not sobbed since he was ten years old and the panther had cornered him. Pa had rescued him then. Pa had buried an ax in the big cat's skull, but now Elijah was on his own. He batted his eyes to stop the watering. One thought brought comfort. He was certain Granny and Ma were praying. He had done a good bit of praying himself. Nevertheless, prickles of fear ran his spine when he thought of what was ahead.

There was no chance to escape. In no time at all he and Dillon were in separate covered wagons heading for the front. There were about a dozen more prisoners, town men the lieutenant had conscripted. Elijah gave up hope of rescue. He did overhear one sergeant complain that the lieutenant had overstepped his bounds. The governor had threatened conscription, but had not yet ordered it. Although there were disgruntled mutterings from the volunteers who traveled with them, no one dared interfere. They knew the lieutenant's reputation—Elijah could see it in their eyes.

No matter which way he lay, the wagon bed was still hard. As soon as he grew still, cold began to seep through the thin blanket George had given him. Propped against a sack of flour, he endured the bouncing and jolting for hours, and finally exhausted he slept—unaware that due north through blinding snow, foot soldiers in two armies, with muskets on shoulders, tramped over frozen ruts, some falling fast asleep to stumble, wake, and march again. In Missouri the blue-coated army marched toward battle. The army in gray fled. General Sterling Price, outnumbered, retreated toward Arkansas.

When the wagon finally halted Elijah jerked awake. He tried to move but, stiff and sore, groaned with the effort. "I'm as stove-up as Granny. And I feel a heap older," he muttered, peering out the back of the wagon.

It had begun to snow, but not a gentle, pretty snow. Mixed with wind-driven sleet, the snow pelted the uniformed men hustling to make camp near an ice-crusted stream. The hilly land was covered with frozen timber and plenty of deadfalls. Soon fires dotted the twilight, and the smell of food cooking made Elijah's stomach gnaw. Although the muleskinner had given him a drink of water before they left town, he had had nothing to eat all day. If someone did not come soon to let him out, he would wet his pants.

"Hey, are you in there?" George's voice interrupted a light doze.

Elijah shivered as he poked his head out the back of the canvas tarp stretched over the supply wagon. "Ain't likely I'd be anywhere else."

George chuckled and then untied him and allowed him to climb out to eat and stretch. "Here's some chicken and a pone of bread."

"Chicken! Where'd you get chicken?" Elijah's mouth watered even before he smelled the tantalizing aroma of roasted meat. He quickly stuffed a bite into his mouth.

George grinned. "We went on a little huntin' expedition and ran slap dab into a henhouse."

Elijah's pleasure dimmed and the succulence seemed to leave the golden meat.

George noticed the look. "What's the matter?"

"Aw. I was just thinking how hard Ma and I tried to keep our stuff from being stolen. If the army steals, ain't you just as bad as the bushwhackers?"

Sheepishly, George looked down, his pale face turning red. "If you put it like that, I suppose so. Never thought of it before. Slippin' into a henhouse or drivin' off a hog or a beef just seemed like a lark." He squared his jaw and looked up, defiant. "But, we're fighting fer the farmers and we gotta eat! We'd starve on the salt horse and hardtack the army rations—if they ration us a'tall. I look at it this a'way: If we don't eat, we can't fight. We don't fight, the blue bellies will take it all anyway!"

Elijah supposed he had a point. Maybe it was up to civilians to help feed their own army. Somehow he felt no better, and the meat seemed to lodge in his throat.

"George, I don't see your lieutenant. Where is he?"

"Back in Clarksville, I reckon. Said he'd catch up later. Said he had business." George changed the subject. "Things are poppin'. We've got orders to travel hard and fast."

Elijah felt a chill. "Must be heading for a battle."

"You bet we are!"

Elijah slowly took another bite but found his appetite gone. Not Dillon. He had just been released from a nearby wagon, and Elijah saw him squatting near a flickering campfire to balance a plate on one knee and tear into his food like a starving wolf.

Freedom passed too quickly. George soon retied and thrust him back into the wagon for the night. He lay shivering in the dark, worrying.

After two more days of hard travel they caught up with a sizable army. Elijah was surprised to find the army spread out in a ragged line. He had always assumed an army marched in procession, their feet beating time with a kettledrum. Far from it, these men came and went at will, camping in separate spots to find food and water for themselves and their horses.

"Naw," explained George, "except in hurry-up cases, all that matters is showing up for roll call and even that ain't enforced. Sometimes a feller is left behind for a day or two—hard liquor sometimes keeps a feller from waking up in time." George tied Elijah's hands. Then he cocked his head toward a wagon. "I'll leave yer legs untied, but don't you go trying to run off. The lieutenant rode in last night, meaner than a rattlesnake. I figure from the looks of him, he's bad hung over and just now he's sleeping it off. He'd for sure shoot you for deserting and enjoy doing it."

Elijah didn't consider it deserting if a body was conscripted. But the warning gave him pause. He had no desire to be always looking over his shoulder expecting to see the lieutenant.

That night Dillon awakened him. "Psst!" He was crouched at the back of the wagon where Elijah slept.

Out of light sleep Elijah came awake and crawled to the opening. "What is it?"

"Come on, Lige. I finally got these ropes worked loose. Let's skedaddle!"

"They'll shoot us if we get caught."

"Yeah, and if we stay the Yankees will."

Elijah chewed his jaw. Dillon had a point.

"I'm out of here as fast as I kin run." Dillon grinned, his white teeth gleaming in the night. "But if you stay, I'll kiss Cindy for ya."

Elijah turned and let Dillon untie his hands. With mouth gone powder dry, he slipped from the wagon, expecting any second to hear the bugler sound alarm. Blood pounded in his ears. He followed Dillon's broad back as they crept past flickering campfires and edged on toward the woods. In the darkness behind a tree, they briefly halted.

"Reckon we should steal a couple of horses?" asked Dillon.

"No," whispered Elijah. "There's two men standing guard over there."

"I wish we could at least get us a gun."

"Yeah, me too. But I figure we best get while the gettin's good."

Dillon nodded and then began weaving his way through the trees at a long loping trot. Elijah looked back once. He wondered if Bo himself would come after them.

Frozen briars caught at Elijah's feet and grabbed his clothing. He seemed to be running in molasses, every step too slow. Any noise in the brush made his blood run cold. They kept to the lowest ground, studying the rugged terrain by starlight and always skirting the hills. Twice they splashed through creeks and then waded for a ways to confuse any tracker. Elijah figured Bo would likely send Curry after them. Curry would not be fooled by the trick, but it might slow him some. Then Elijah stopped dead in his tracks.

"Dillon!"

Dillon turned.

Elijah bent with hands on knees to suck in deep draughts of air. "I just thought of something—they know where we're going. They know we'll head right back for Little Piney. Maybe we ought to head east for a ways and then circle back."

Dillon's breath came in ragged gasps. In spite of the cold night his brow glistened with sweat.

"Naw, we got a good head start and I reckon they're in too big of a hurry to waste much time on us. Besides, there's a cave near home. If I make it that far they won't never find me."

Dillon was wrong. Elijah's gut urged that they should head a different direction. Pa always said to err on the side of caution. Elijah looked at the sky. Morning was not far off. The black horizon was already fading gray. They had been running for at least two hours. His chest hurt from running and sucking in the cold night air.

Dillon started forward. Just ahead was a wide gap between two tall hills.

"Dillon, wait up," said Elijah. Then he fell into step with Dillon's long stride. "I still think we should head—" The words died in his throat.

Curry prodded his horse through the brush. His gun was leveled at them.

"Howdy, boys. I've been waiting on you." His grin showed in the fresh dawn. "This gap is the best way through these hills, and I figured two smart country boys like you would find it. Now let's get on back to the army on the double-quick."

Elijah sank down onto a rock. If Curry expected him to run all the way back, he had another think coming! The worst Curry could do was shoot him, and wasn't that what Bo would do anyway?

"No. I ain't going."

Curry's eyes narrowed. "We'll see about that." He kept the pistol aimed as he climbed down and took a rope from his saddle. "You're not as smart as I thought, boy. Getting dragged is no fun a'tall."

Dillon raised his hands. "Hey, I'll go peaceful."

Curry nodded. He motioned Dillon forward. "You tie his hands together real good and tight. I don't want to lose him, yanking through all this brush."

Dillon pulled the rope tight. Curry waved him back and checked the knot. He grunted, and then holding the rope and gun, he climbed into the saddle.

Like a lightning bolt, Dillon leaped and struck Curry's side, knocking him from the saddle. Curry came up shooting. But Dillon had already sprung into the saddle. Elijah did not think Dillon was hit but he could not be certain.

Dillon hunkered low on the far side of the horse like an Indian and raced from sight. Curry lowered the gun and let out a string of profanity. He blew out a deep breath.

"Damn kid can ride—I'll say that for him."

Elijah thought about running, but trussed up like a Thanksgiving turkey, he knew there was no chance. Curry would shoot him before he got ten feet.

Curry reloaded while facing Elijah. "It appears we'll both be walking. But not with you behind me." He took a knife from his belt and cut the rope in two near Elijah's hands, still leaving them tied. He threw the long piece down. "Just try running off. I'm sure in the mood to shoot someone."

Curry's dark eyes glittered. Elijah knew he meant just what he said. But somehow he must find a way to escape before they reached camp!

All along the way, Elijah watched. There was, however, no chance to escape. Curry, as cross as a bear robbed of her cubs, prodded Elijah along. He walked just behind and with the pistol always ready. It was midmorning by the time they neared camp. Elijah was exhausted, but the trembling in his limbs had nothing to do with that. He wondered how it felt to die.

"Damn!" Curry looked ahead. "They've already pulled out. I told Bo to give me a couple of hours. Of course, I never counted on getting my horse stolen." He frowned. "Sit down a minute while I get this rock out of my boot." He shook the boot and a small gravel rolled out. Just as he was stamping the boot back on, a sergeant and four privates rode up.

"Howdy, Curry." The brown-bearded sergeant leaned on the saddle horn and looked all around. "I reckon it was a fine morning for a walk."

Curry shot him a surly look. "Who's going to ride double?"

"Can't do it. We've been out foraging and we're heavy loaded. Besides, the lieutenant will worry about us if we don't hurry on along."

Curry's eyes burned. "Prine, if you ride off, I'll shoot you in the back. I swear I will."

Sergeant Prine laughed and his blue eyes danced. "Keep your shirt on, Curry. I was only fooling." He turned in the saddle. "Uriah and Peters—transfer your loads to those other horses."

Elijah's hopes died as he climbed up and headed for his execution. He wondered how far Dillon had gotten by now.

The train had stopped for the noon meal. Campfire smoke curled into the clear sky, and Elijah smelled coffee. He was surprised to feel hungry when he was about to die. He wondered if Bo would shoot him now or wait until evening. And he wondered if there would be a firing squad or if Bo wanted the fun all to himself.

The train was larger than before. Somewhere along the trail more men and wagons had joined them. Elijah's stomach knotted. As they rode near, Bo rose from sitting on a wooden crate and stared at him with all the venom of an angry rattler. A tall major with long, blond hair pulled back into a queue stood at Bo's side.

"What's this?"

"A man about to be shot for deserting."

The major's brows raised. "More a boy, I'd say. When did he join?"

Bo wet his lips. "He didn't exactly join."

"Conscripted," guessed the major.

Bo gave a curt nod. "Even so, we can't have him running off. It might give the others ideas—especially when Yankee lead starts flying."

The major frowned. "Very well, make an example of him. But I don't want him shot. Tie him spread-eagle to that big caisson wheel and have him flogged. Thirty lashes and have all the men watch."

Bo smiled at Elijah.

For a moment rage eclipsed fear in Elijah's breast. Spawn of the devil! That's what Bo was!

Elijah was pulled from the horse and his shirt and jacket jerked off. While a bugle played assembly, two men tied him fast to the wide wheel. A third returned with the whip. From peripheral vision, Elijah saw a huge arm muscled like a blacksmith with the multi-corded whip dangling from a big hand. He braced his legs wide apart and gritted his teeth. Tensed, he waited while the charges were stated and the sentence announced in a clear, ringing voice.

"Desertion! Thirty lashes!"

He closed his eyes and silently prayed. Don't let me scream. Dear God—don't let me scream!

And he did not, even when the lash landed, ripping open his flesh. His knees buckled. He quivered from red-hot pain. Each time the whip flayed, searing pain racked his back. He had never imagined anything could hurt so much. Tears ran from his squinted eyes. But he did not scream. The ends of the lashes wrapped around and cut the meat of his sides.

He lost count. Again and again the lash fell. He did not know how dying felt. But now he surely knew about hell. As if from a far distance, he heard men begin to grumble.

"He ain't nothing but a boy. This will kill him."

Darkness swam before his eyes. He slumped forward. When the whip landed again, Elijah's body flinched. But he did not feel it.

———⌒~———

"Here, drink this." Someone pushed a canteen to Elijah's swollen, cracked lips.

He turned his head and groaned. "No," he moaned. "Leave me alone." He did not want to wake. He did not want to come alive to the raw, pulsing agony.

"Elijah, you got to drink and you got to eat something." Elijah slowly raised his lids enough to see George bending over him. He blinked. He must be in a wagon. He could see the billowed canvas top and he could feel the movement. Every turn of the wheels brought fresh torture to his aching body.

George forced the canteen to his lips again and he swallowed. Water ran down his chin and splashed onto his chest as he gulped the wetness.

"There. That will make you feel better." George put the canteen aside. "Now I'm gonna put this salve on your back. It's real good stuff. We use it on the horses when they get cut and it heals them right up." George eyed his back with pity. "I'll be easy as I can. But we can't let this fester."

Elijah started to nod, but the movement made him wince. He held himself rigid while George tried to ease on the yellow salve. Elijah could not stop the moan.

George talked as he worked. "Yore Uncle was always good to me. Let me sleep in a back room at the office, and Miss Nelda sometimes brought me meals." His voice grew hard. "I left home 'cause my pa was so cussed mean and ornery." Then he sounded cheerful again, "Yep, when the war is over I just might hit Mr. Phillip up for another job...."

"Just about through," said George. "I almost got it all covered. Then I'll put this nice, soft bandage on you."

By the time George finished, Elijah was wet with sweat and shaking like he had the ague.

"There. See if you can sleep. I'll be back later with some supper."

Elijah wanted to thank him. He was too weak to speak. His eyelids fell shut, but pain kept sleep at bay.

George returned with a plate of food but Elijah could not eat. George sat the plate aside.

"Major Endicott asked about you."

Elijah gave a wry laugh. "Tell him his thirty lashes worked just fine."

"I've seed men get a hundred," George said sharply. "Endicott ain't a bad sort. You can bet yer last dollar if he hadn't been here Bo would have shot you."

Although the next week was a nightmare, Elijah was young and strong and—with George's careful tending—he mended. Finally he left the wagon to walk around. He did not see Bo but he spent hours imagining revenge.

———⌒〜———

Elijah's back was still as tender as Granny's fresh mutton, but he was glad to be out of the jolting wagon and out in the brisk air.

"That there is Fayetteville." George nodded toward the hills just ahead where chimney smoke mingled with gray sky.

Elijah's heart quickened. He might soon see Pa! "Is the 16th Arkansas here?"

George grinned and cocked his cap back exposing shaggy, dark-blond hair. "Every Reb soldier in the whole damned state is here—or headed this way—state guard, militia, Confederate regulars." George offered him a chew. Elijah shook his head, and George cut off a sliver and put it into his mouth. "You stay in this man's army long enough, and you'll get the habit too...helps a feller forget his empty belly."

"We've been eating pretty good so far."

"Shore have," agreed George. Then using two fingers to spit between, he spit a brown arch before adding, "But don't get used to it. Before I got assigned to Bo's recruiting detail, I was hungry more than I was full. At least we eat pretty regular now, but this here army is long on promise and short on pay."

"Yeah, my pa's not drawn a penny yet."

George looked surprised. "Your pa is in the army?"

"Yep. Sixteenth Infantry. He fought at Wilson's Creek. Pa's friend, John Hill, is colonel of the 16th now." Elijah turned. "By the way, who are you with?"

"Fourth Arkansas. But lately I been with Bo on special detail because I knowed the country around Clarksville."

Elijah put in, "I have an uncle serving with McCulloch. He and the general are good friends—served together in the Texas Rangers."

George gave a dry laugh. "Well, wha'da ya know..." His smile widened. "Maybe old Bo will get his yet."

"Get his?"

"For kidnappin' and then beatin' the tar out of you."

Elijah's jaw hardened. "I'd rather tend to him myself."

In the early dusk, freezing rain glazed every bush and tree and hundreds of tents in the crowded camp north of Fayetteville. The encampment at Cross Hollows was bristling with excitement. The Yankees had invaded Arkansas. Rumor said, in spite of sleet, snow, and bitter weather, they were coming fast. Sterling Price's southern troops had fled Missouri only one jump ahead. Sometimes not even that. Some said blood had already darkened the soil of Dunagin's farm only a few miles away.

Soon the Missouri troops, fleeing the Yankees, did spill into Cross Hollows. Elijah had never seen a more weary and disheveled group of men.

He weaved through the chaos, searching for Ned. The 16th Regiment was nowhere to be seen. Disappointed, he headed back to his own camp and arrived just as cheers split the freezing air. Benjamin McCulloch had just returned from Richmond.

The general was a small, bearded man wearing dark trousers, a buff colored coat, and a pair of shiny boots, which Elijah figured had probably cost more cash money than he had ever seen. The men cheered louder and threw hats into the air. Cold rain wet uncovered heads. The general, with a huge smile, rode back and forth on a lathered horse.

"Men, I am glad to see you!" he cried and waved his hat in the air.

The cheers roared louder. Elijah stood near George. He was surprised to see tears shining in McCulloch's bright eyes when the general rode near.

"He doesn't look much like I thought he would," observed Elijah.

"He ought to be taller and wearing a uniform?" guessed George.

"Yeah," said Elijah, "that's pretty much what I was thinking." The pale blue pants and the fancy cut of the gray jacket did not look at all military.

"He dresses like a dude, but I've heared he kin fight like a Comanche," said George.

———⌇———

After supper, in the pouring rain, Elijah tried again. He tramped from camp to camp. "Know the whereabouts of the 16th Arkansas Infantry?" He grew used to the negative replies.

A ragged looking man squinted at him through campfire smoke. "No, I can't say that I do. Troops are strung out up and down the whole valley. We're pulling out at first light, so we should all join up before long."

"Pulling out?"

He nodded. "This position is untenable."

Elijah was surprised by the man's grammar.

"General McCulloch has decided the best thing to do is to drop back into the mountains and regroup." He was glum. "I have the inglorious job of burning a lot of good, much-needed supplies so they won't fall into enemy hands."

Elijah figured the fellow must be an officer, but it was hard to tell. Many men of rank wore no uniform. He wondered how a body knew when to salute. He would have to ask George.

The man stirred a pot of simmering beans. "Can I offer you some supper? You don't look so good, young fellow. Are you sick?"

Elijah shook his head. "No, thanks anyway. I already ate."

Later he lay on his stomach on a cot in George's tent. He doubted he could ever lie on his back again without pain. What kept him awake, however, was wondering where Pa was and what tomorrow would bring.

In the frigid, gray dawn men scurried to dismantle tents and throw open warehouses. With haste they loaded a hodge-podge of vehicles—ox-carts and buckboards and schooners. Elijah even saw a brightly painted stagecoach filled with supplies. The entire exodus was a crazy jumble.

A soldier was throwing dozens of cages filled with terrified bantams onto an overloaded wagon. Terrible squawks arose from the pens.

"Captain says we can't take the roosters!" yelled a sergeant.

"What! These here is the best fighting cocks in all Louisiana. I don't aim to see 'em roasted like no barnyard chickens and et by Yankees!" cried the soldier.

"Leave them! And fall in! Orders are orders!"

The distraught soldier obeyed, but he marched away looking back with distressed eyes. Elijah figured Lot's wife had looked much the same upon leaving Sodom.

The frozen road was soon clogged with thousands of troops in gray and butternut, all hurrying down the icy Telegraph Road toward Fayetteville. Elijah stopped alongside George and watched in amazement as torches were hurled into dozens of log buildings. Soon fire ate the sturdy barracks, huts, mills, and storehouses.

Above the roaring blaze, he said, "It sure seems a terrible waste."

"Yep." George's worried face looked even paler in the morning light and his freckles stood out starkly. "It is a terrible waste."

Cross Hollows was a smoke-filled, smoldering ruin. Elijah looked back in dismay at the havoc the army left behind. Then he sadly shook his head and also retreated over the icy road to

Fayetteville. Along with George, Elijah trudged on, following a lantern-jawed sergeant named Callahan. There was a captain nearby named Culp. Major Endicott rode by on a sorrel. Elijah had not seen Bo Morrison since the beating.

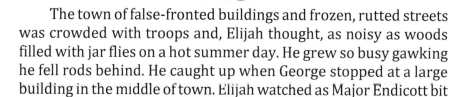

The town of false-fronted buildings and frozen, rutted streets was crowded with troops and, Elijah thought, as noisy as woods filled with jar flies on a hot summer day. He grew so busy gawking he fell rods behind. He caught up when George stopped at a large building in the middle of town. Elijah watched as Major Endicott bit out orders.

"Open the warehouses. Let the troops take what they want. We're burning the rest."

The doors were thrown open. The soldiers began to whoop. Elijah jumped back to keep from being crushed in the stampede. Men ran from everywhere into the building, clutching and grabbing and then stumbling out, arms laden with sacks of flour and meal and sides of bacon. One man rolled out a barrel and split it open with a hatchet drawn from his belt. Apparently salt-pork was not to his liking. He deserted the barrel and headed back inside.

At the next warehouse it was the same. All day the marching armies, Missouri and Arkansas, helped themselves from the opened storehouses as they trailed south, heading deeper into the Boston Mountains. That night Elijah stayed with George in a camp just outside of town, but they were up early and headed back to town.

"I don't relish this detail," said George.

"What detail?"

"Torching the warehouses. These women and children could sure use the food." He let out a deep breath. "But I suppose General McCulloch is right. Curtis would end up with it, anyway. More than likely, the Yankees will have all the food that's left in town before they're through."

The detail of a dozen soldiers allowed a few minutes before ordering everyone out of the first building. Then a major took a torch from the wall and lit it and threw it inside. "Corporal, finish the job."

As the corporal rounded up more torches and more men to light them, George watched the smoke. "It's a crying shame," he said, "to see all that bacon go up in smoke. I keep thinking how hungry our troops got in the mountains last winter—and how it's bound to happen again."

He walked on. Elijah followed, looking back, still incredulous at the waste. He knew General McCulloch was doing what he thought was right. Nonetheless, it seemed a sin to burn food. And there was more to come. At four more warehouses, they stopped and repeated the process.

"Major, sir!" At the far edge of town, a sergeant came galloping to overtake them. "The men have gone wild. They're looting and burning the whole town. They busted into saloons and took the liquor. Women and children running and screaming—it's a terrible mess. No one's listening to orders. Matter of fact, I didn't hear anyone giving any!"

The major spurred his horse, heading back to town with the command ordered to follow on the double-quick. The soldier's report was accurate. Elijah knew Fayetteville would not suffer worse from the invading Federals. Windows lay in slivers on the wooden sidewalks. Flames leaped from stores, even while drunken soldiers still reeled around inside looting goods from the shelves. They tucked what they wanted into bulging shirts and threw the rest onto the floor, then pulled the shelves crashing to the ground.

He saw men carting off scores of smoked hams and shoulders and even sides of bacon stuck on bayonets. He had never seen so much meat. In disgust he saw a soldier throw a whole side of bacon onto a fire just to warm by.

A woman rushed past, a child perched on one hip and two more hanging onto her skirt. She gazed in horror at a house just down the street. Men bolted from the front door, their arms loaded with plunder. Smoke roiled from a broken window where curtains blazed.

Her scream was frantic. "They're burning my house!"

The major was too far ahead to hear. He had kicked the sorrel in the side and hurried forward, shouting orders, rounding up officers, and trying to restore order. Elijah ran toward the house. He rushed through the front door. Smoke filled the room. He jerked down the flaming curtains and stomped at the flames. The blaze ran like quicksilver, eating the cloth. He saw a large china pitcher on a stand nearby. It was full of water. He splashed it onto the drape and then with more stomping managed to put out the blaze.

Pale and panting, the woman arrived. In a daze, she took in the smoke-filled house, every room ransacked, every piece of furniture toppled to the floor. With a groan, she tore off her bonnet and sank slowly down, her hooped skirt a heap in the middle of a sea of broken glass. Elijah noticed her hair was the same color as Ma's. Just then the oldest child began to sob, but the woman stared straight ahead.

"Ma'am," Elijah said softly. "I can't get back what they stole, but I don't think the fire did much damage. I sure am sorry about this."

She merely stared, eyes glazed and suffering like the gut-shot doe Elijah had once killed. He walked toward the door, hesitating in the doorway.

She looked up and, through white lips, spoke. "Our own army.... Why?"

Elijah felt helpless. His thoughts echoed the anguished question. Why?

Outside he started down the street, staring in shock at the wreckage. Smoke! Fire! Terror! He suddenly recalled Preacher Simon's hair-raising portrayal of hell. He passed another frantic woman pulling goods from a blazing house and he stopped to help. This time he was not able to quench the blaze. It was all he could do to hold the woman back from entering the inferno.

Once he saw the major riding up the street shouting orders. Elijah did not think the men were listening. Finally, however, the Rebel troops were rounded up and marched from town. Elijah walked past the silent, white-faced women of Fayetteville who stood gazing with disbelief at the smoldering ruins of their town.

Their angry, betrayed eyes cut him to the heart. What kind of an army did this to its own people? He felt shame to be part of such a group.

―――――∽―――――

Deep in the Boston Mountains in a small valley far from Fayetteville, thousands of McCulloch's soldiers camped near a small creek extravagantly named the Illinois River. Elijah had shivered from fever on the long march from Fayetteville. The sergeant had ordered him to bed.

He threw up his head as the ground beneath him shook. *"What was that!"* he asked George.

"Cannons."

Elijah was wide-eyed. He had had no idea of the tremendous power of cannon shots. "Is Price's camp being invaded?"

The blasts had come from the direction of Cove Creek where Price's men were bivouacked a short distance away. Unconcerned, George looked up.

"Nope. A salute for the new major general. It seems President Davis decided that McCulloch and Price both need a boss to settle the feud betwixt 'em.

"Here,"―George stuck out a steaming bowl―"I brought you some soup."

Elijah gave a weak smile as he took the bowl.

"Thanks, George. Did you find Pa?" He eyed the bowl with skepticism. The odor was none too pleasant. Only a small amount of something that resembled stringy beef floated in thin broth.

"Naw. This army is scattered all over. Everyone's scrambling for forage."

"Well, thanks for looking." Elijah ducked his head to hide disappointment and took a slurp of the soup. It tasted no better than it smelled.

"I know it ain't good," George apologized, "but it's the best we got. And likely we'll wish we had some more of it one of these days."

―――――∽―――――

Two days later Elijah joined the ranks. At dusk he crouched near a small blaze to warm his hands at the open fire. He looked up when George arrived.

"You making out all right?"

Elijah pulled a face. "I've been better."

George gave a knowing grin. Then he sobered. "I located the 16th way ahead."

"Did you see Pa?"

George squinted against the heat rising from the campfire. He lifted a soot-blackened coffeepot, filled a cup, and took a sip. Just beyond the tent a muleskinner swore at an errant mule.

"No. But I talked to Colonel Hill. Your pa is fine." He looked at the ice-rimmed creek and then fixed serious eyes on Elijah. He lowered his voice. "If you think you can make it, home ain't too far over them mountains yonder. Now would be the best time to go."

Elijah looked at the tall hills. He flexed his shoulders. The nerves still tingled. "No. I guess I'll stay put."

———⟨∿⟩———

In the gray dawn Elijah stood at attention alongside George with hundreds more shivering soldiers, as General Van Dorn faced his newly acquired command. The general was a short man. Elijah doubted he was over five feet tall. A shaggy, dark mustache overpowered his thin face. Pale and drawn, he was bundled against the frigid air. It was rumored he had taken a dunking in the river when his boat overturned on the way to Van Buren.

Elijah stamped his feet to keep warm while Major General Van Dorn assumed command with a vengeance. In clipped tones the general announced they would strike the Yankee army. Each man would carry only a weapon, forty rounds of ammunition, a blanket, and three days' rations.

With the distinct drawl of a Mississippian, he addressed the troops. "Soldiers," he boasted, "behold your leader! He comes to show you the way to glory and immortal renown...Awake, young men of Arkansas, and arm! Beautiful maidens of Louisiana smile not on the craven youth who may linger by your hearth when the rude blast of war is sounding in your ears! Texas chivalry, to arms!"

Elijah agreed when George sneered and leaned to whisper, "He sounds like a blamed actor instead of a soldier!"

At Van Dorn's brag to drive the cowardly despots back where they had come from, some soldiers cheered, but not the man on Elijah's left. He had no uniform, just a gray armband. His long, gray-streaked hair was pulled back and tied with a leather thong, and his wrinkled face was covered with a long, grizzled beard. As soon as the pompous speech had ended, he spoke aloud what many were thinking.

"I've fit' Injuns and Mex and Yankees. Them boys in blue at Wilson's Crick didn't appear so cowardly to me. I got a saber cut in my gizzard to prove hit!" While others greeted the order to move out with shouts of jubilation, the old man shook his head sadly. He frowned and muttered, "Don't know what Jeff Davis is thinkin'—lettin' that there fancy-pants outrank McCulloch. West Point graduate...blah! Give me old Ben any day. He's the best Injun fighter and scout ever lived."

He, nonetheless, gathered his gear and fell into the ragged line marching north. And Elijah followed.

For the last few hours, Elijah had given a great deal of thought to returning home. But Bo and Curry had disappeared. Elijah had no desire to run into them again if they were recruiting in the mountains. He was still concerned about Ma and Deborah. Pa had left him with the responsibility, and he did not want to let Pa down. But he felt certain Uncle Caleb was looking out for the family. And as odd as it seemed, Elijah had begun to feel a kinship with these men, a real part of the army. If he left now, right before a battle, everyone would think him a coward. If he stayed, he could go home with his head held high—and he would have done something Dillon Matthers had never done. Cindy was certain to be impressed.

The sky stayed dark, leaden with thick clouds obscuring the hills and far off valleys. An icy drizzle began to wet the road. Wind probed frigid fingers through Elijah's jacket. In spite of feeling weak, he decided marching on such a day was better than riding. At least marching warmed the blood. The weather worsened. By mid-afternoon the drizzle turned into a full-fledged winter storm. On and on they marched over the ice-coated trails. As the miles wore on, Elijah put one weary foot in front of the other. His right heel was beginning to blister.

George, cradling his rifle, marched alongside. Over the winding mountain road, treacherous with ice, men and horses struggled northward. Even though Van Dorn had been struck with a bout of fever and chills, he was merciless in his prodding. He was risking much on the element of surprise, but Elijah wondered how many would survive the march. All along the road, weary, footsore men were falling behind. Elijah marveled that the old Indian-fighter kept pace with him.

When the general's horse-drawn ambulance rolled past, the old man muttered, "Van Dorn has forgot the men's a'marchin while he's a'ridin'!"

Elijah hoped Pa was faring all right wherever he was in the group of weary men. Just then a saddle horse slipped to its knees, halting the progress of the wagons a few yards ahead. Elijah shuddered at its humanlike scream as a leg bone snapped and protruded through the skin. The loud crack of a rifle was followed by silence.

He wondered if men injured in battle screamed like that. In spite of the cold, beads of sweat dotted his forehead. He tried pushing that morbid thought aside by imagining what Ma and Deborah were doing at just that minute. And Cindy.

He thought a lot about Cindy lately, about how it would feel to hold her in his arms, to kiss her soft lips and stroke her long, silky hair. And he imagined even more. His ears reddened. Idle soldier talk had affected him, and he feared not for the good.

He suddenly turned to George. "You were at Wilson's Creek, weren't you?"

"Yep."

"Since so many fellows don't have uniforms, how can you tell who's who?"

"At times it's real hard. Some of them Missouri Yankees has uniforms and them that don't have blue bands. That helps." George gave a wry grin. "Not much chance a' taking you for a blue belly. Only takes one peek to see you been raised on cornpone and fatback."

George turned up his collar and ducked lower into his gray jacket. "I hope them fellers who took my horse falls off a cliff," he muttered. Officers had confiscated a dozen mounts, George's among them.

"I can do fine without a horse but I sure could use a gun. You fellows going to give me one before the shooting starts, or am I just gonna have to throw rocks?" asked Elijah.

George grinned and spit tobacco juice on an ice-covered branch hanging over the trail. "You might need one of these more." He reached into his pocket and pulled out a mahogany-brown buckeye. The normally shiny hull had dulled with age. "A buckeye brings good luck. The longer ya carry it, the better the luck. I been carrying this one since I was twelve years old." He tucked the nut back into his gray pocket. "But I figure to scrape you up a rifle. Rocks won't be much good against twelve thousand blue bellies with fifty big cannons."

"Reckon how many of us there are?" asked Elijah, frowning.

George's pale eyes clouded. "Hey Sarge, how many of us fine, upstanding Rebels are there?"

The lantern-jawed sergeant, tramping a ways ahead, turned. He had thick, black hair and heavy sideburns. "Cap'n Culp claims there's more of us than there are of the Yankees. He says we have more cannons, too."

When the sergeant turned away, George dropped his voice. "I ain't so sure. I doubt we got twelve thousand." Seeing Elijah's worried look George hastened to add, "Aw, you know rumors. There probably ain't half that many Yankees. They probably ain't got that many cannons, neither."

Elijah looked him squarely in the eye. His voice was flat. "I wouldn't bet on it."

By mid-afternoon, Elijah began to drop behind. His feet and hands were numb and there was no feeling in his face. When a halt was finally called near Fayetteville, he collapsed onto the trail.

"Hey, Elijah,"——George shook his shoulder—"wake up. I built a campfire. Come over and get warm before you get sick again. Major General Van Dorn left for town and a hot meal and a warm bed. But us gents in the *Confederate Army of the West*," his words dripped sarcasm, "is bedding down right here on this-here frozen ground without tents—and with only one blanket for each miserable man-jack of us."

Chapter 11

"Roll out!"

Elijah sat up with a jerk and gazed around with bleary eyes, wondering where he was and what had wakened him. George once again nudged him in the side. Stiff from cold and every muscle sore, he groaned and sat up. So began another nightmarish day of placing one weary foot in front of another, struggling through icy sleet, howling wind, and snow. On toward Bentonville. On toward...Elijah wondered exactly what did lie ahead.

After only twelve agonizing, crawling miles, the army again halted for a bitter night of cold and blizzard. Elijah and George, following the old Indian fighter's lead, sought a warmer place to sleep. They pulled aside burning logs to sleep on a spot warmed by the fire. Elijah fell asleep almost before his head touched the lumpy knapsack. At daybreak, however, there were holes in his blanket and clothes where embers had scorched. With clumsy haste, he gathered the damp blanket and rolled it tight.

He smelled coffee. Since he had never really cared for it before, it was amazing how much he wanted a cup. Now wet and frozen, he was surprised to have slept at all. While quickly eating the last cracker from his small stash, he crouched in the frigid dawn and listened to water lapping the nearby creek bank.

After taking a gulp of water, he returned the canteen to George. "I feel hungrier than I did before," he complained.

George capped the canteen. "I figure we'll be hungrier yet before we eat again."

They both fell into step with the straggling line of limping men. Fatigued beyond hurry, they halted at creeks, chopping logs, and crossing single file, going ever slower until the cruel day finally ended.

That evening, Elijah hunkered near a campfire.

"How you doing?" asked Sergeant Callahan. "You look as tired as I feel."

Elijah rubbed his hands above the blaze and hunkered deeper into his jacket. He took a deep breath and let it out slowly. "We're in for a bad fight, aren't we?"

Callahan frowned. Then he slowly nodded.

"What's going to happen, Sergeant? Are we going to get the tar whipped out of us? George says the Yankees have a lot of cannons."

"Well,"—Callahan rose—"we have more cannons than Curtis does. And more men."

Elijah's eyes narrowed. "Really?"

"Yes. We do. Still, there's no way of knowing the outcome of a battle before it's fought. According to our scouts, Curtis is already entrenched on that high ground"—he nodded north—"with his batteries pointed right at us. Van Dorn is scared he'll try to hightail it back to Missouri. He's ordered us to leave these fires burning and a few men to feed them while we sneak around and head him off."

"What!" Elijah was incredulous. "Why! We've marched fifty miles in the last three days! We're too worn out to march another foot! And we haven't had a thing to eat all day. We'll drop in our tracks!"

Callahan replaced the canteen on the saddle horn. "When McCulloch told Van Dorn that very thing, that glory-hungry bastard said we could crawl."

And before the night was over, Elijah felt he would have to crawl. He forgot the Yankees. He forgot the battle. He forgot home and Ma and Cindy. All he thought of was his cold, empty belly and his desperate need for sleep. His insides gnawed as he faltered through the darkness, often treading the heels of the man ahead. He nodded off and then stumbled awake to march some more. He was Caleb's mule turning the mill, round and round, step after step, no destination—no end in sight, just plodding in an endless circle. When the long, dark column finally halted, they stood like icy-backed cattle with backs to the wind, stiff from cold.

George stamped his feet and blew on his hands. "I think my hands is frostbit. I couldn't cap my musket if my life depended on it."

Elijah was almost grateful when Sergeant Callahan whispered orders to move forward. The long halts were more miserable than the marching. When they halted again, he dropped onto the cold ground to sit with his back against a tree. The Indian-fighter lay on the ground nearby.

"Youngster," he said, "lay down ever' chance you get. Hit makes a heap of difference on a long march. Listen to us old heads—like me and Sergeant Callahan. We know a few such tricks that'll stand you in good stead."

Elijah lay down. But all too soon George nudged him to join the line of fatigued men moving on through the winter darkness.

Finally the sky began to lighten. The day dawned clear and cold. Winding out of sight, the narrow, snowy dirt road was filled with exhausted, benumbed men. Suddenly every drooping head jerked and turned toward distant gunfire.

The pop and crackle ahead reminded Elijah of Granny's burning brush pile. He was unsure if it was cold or nerves making him shiver. And his head was swimmy from lack of food.

George came running up carrying an extra musket and a cartridge box. "Here, I got these for you."

"Where did you—"

"Don't ask." George's eyes had a wicked gleam.

Elijah figured somewhere in camp a sleeping soldier would be furious when he awoke.

Just then curses and moans came from up ahead. George swore and kicked at a rock in the trail. When the order finally reached Elijah, he felt like swearing. He shook his head in disbelief.

"About face!"

They were ordered to countermarch back down the road they had come! To backtrack over ground gained with so much suffering!

The army was ordered to split. Price's men were going around the north side of a mountain to come up on Curtis's right flank. McCulloch's men were going south of the ridge to strike Curtis's left.

At midmorning Elijah once again trudged past the Twelve Corner Church. The column turned onto another road and shuffled south. As the unending morning dragged on and on, his stomach gnawed and ached more and more. Just before noon they rounded the mountain, and as they headed east, a tall ridge with rugged outcroppings of sandstone and scrubby timber towered alongside. Here the road traversed a grassy level, but in the distance, Elijah noticed an odd, round-topped hill.

George sat down, took off a boot, shook it, and stamped it back on. "Hey, Cap'n Culp," he called.

The small man stopped and hunkered down. He changed hands with the rifle to take the chew George offered.

"Much obliged." He bit off a generous portion.

"What's going on?" asked George. "I thought we'd be dodging cannonballs by now."

"We will be soon enough," acknowledged the captain. "Hear that firing? Price is just a few miles that way at the tavern."

Elijah tensed. Eyes wide open, he sent up a quick prayer for Pa and Uncle Tap and Michael.

"Cap'n, I can't hear a thing." George grinned. "But with them ears, I bet you can hear shootin' five mile off."

For such a small man, the captain did have huge ears. Elijah thought they stuck out like the handles on Ma's china sugar bowl.

The captain chuckled. "Big ears do occasionally come in handy." He stood. "You boys keep your heads down and listen good to Sergeant Callahan."

Captain Culp stepped aside to let a cavalry brigade ride past. The horsemen were in formation, five columns of fours. The captain said they were McIntosh's men. Elijah shook his head. The gaunt horses looked as famished as the men.

Now he could hear gunfire. From the commotion he figured Price was letting Curtis have it at the tavern—or vice-versa.

Suddenly a thunderous roar filled the air. Elijah had heard Pappy Campbell's tale of the great quake in northeast Arkansas that made the Mississippi flow backwards. Pappy had been an eyewitness fifty years ago. This was no earthquake, but the cannonade made Elijah understand Pappy's wide-eyed awe when he spoke of it. The trees, the air, the ground trembled.

Suddenly a ball exploded nearby. Mangled men and shards of metal hurled through the air. Horses screamed and fell. Dirt and debris obscured the light. As blood and gore splattered on Elijah's arms and face, he recoiled in horror. He hunkered and covered his head, expecting to perish any second. He could not breathe. The air was choking with dust.

Bewildered, he blinked watery eyes and stared at the carnage and then quickly looked away as hot bile rose in his throat. He rubbed dust from burning, watering eyes. Through a blur, he saw smoke rise over the trees. He shrunk back down. Another shell screamed and burst, sending men scurrying away from the blinding hell.

A Confederate battery quickly left the road. With horses shying and snorting, it rolled toward the enemy fire. McIntosh's cavalry returned. Just ahead they lined up, and propelled by the strident notes of a bugle, they charged. The running horses were soon out of sight. How could anyone, Elijah marveled, rush toward that exploding death?

Major Endicott stopped for a hurried conference with the captain. Captain Culp nodded. Then he bawled, "On your feet, men!"

Elijah's ears rang. He barely heard the order. But he followed the men heading pell-mell away from the bursting shells. He was thankful. But in a daze he wondered why they were marching away from the fight. Although the din behind dimmed, the captain hurried them toward a saddleback that separated the tall, rocky ridge from the odd, round hill. Then Elijah presumed they were headed to join Price's men fighting at the tavern.

They hurried along at a fast pace. Soon, however, they halted where tangled woods breasted the road. In spite of a bright sun, snow still carpeted the ground where the long line of anxious men stood waiting while officers held a confab.

What Elijah overhead made him suck in his breath. General McCulloch was back there in the cannonade. McCulloch was leading the 16th and 17th Arkansas. Pa was in all that hell! And more than likely Uncle Tap was with McCulloch, too.

A colonel addressed Major Endicott, "Both we and Louisiana troops will march south through this woodland and push back any Yankee advance trying to flank McCulloch. You will be the right flank, then the 3rd Louisiana and the 14th Arkansas. The 15th will be the far left."

"Be sure to check your load," whispered George. I ain't sure if yore musket is loaded."

Elijah swallowed. With clammy hands, he checked the gun. It was loaded. Every nerve tensed. He forgot weariness.

Naked trees stood ahead like sentinels. He could feel a bullet waiting behind every one. He wanted to run. Why had he come! Why had he not listened to George and gone home! His breath came in shallow pants. Now there was nothing to do but go forward. Sweat popped out on his forehead and trickled down his armpits.

Forward went Elijah into the dark tangle of trees. Foot by foot, the long snake of men wound between trees and bushes with grim determination and rifles ready. They had been ordered to keep the line straight. It was impossible. Fallen logs and tangled briars blocked the way. While scrambling over the obstacles, they pushed deeper into the woods, growing more spread out.

Elijah pushed through brush and briars, peering cautiously ahead. How often had he done the same thing, fearing the sight of Lew. His nostrils flared—if only Lew were all he faced now!

A shallow ravine lay ahead.

Abruptly, Elijah heard pattering all around, like sleet pinging on frozen ground. He glanced up. The sky was clear today. In an instant he knew—it was musket balls! He gripped the gun with trembling hands.

"On the double-quick," yelled Sergeant Callahan.

"Stick close to me," called George.

Elijah swallowed and nodded. As they edged through thick growth and across the ravine, he did indeed stick close to George. As they neared the brow of the rise, the sergeant motioned them to go low.

Once over the rim, Elijah turned to stone. Straight ahead guns stuck from the trees. In sudden flashes of fire, the woods exploded. In the puffs of smoke, men ducked back to reload and fire again.

Elijah dropped to his belly. A shot had dented his cartridge box. He looked down expecting to see blood. By some miracle he was unhurt. He lay in the leaf mold and quaked, wondering how long before a shot would find him.

Then a deafening roar overshadowed the clatter of musket, rifle, and pistol. A tree on Elijah's right shattered into a million splinters. He cast a terrified look. With relief he saw George was still alive.

Shots flew thick and fast, snapping twigs and devastating limbs. Howitzer shells whined and crashed and trees exploded all around. Elijah's mouth was dry as dust.

An answering volley came from the Rebel line. A blue-clad soldier across the ravine grabbed his stomach and fell, rolling and groaning as blood gushed through his fingers. As more Confederates boiled forward, scores of shots, like angry hornets, stung the Yankees. The Union troops gave ground. Men fell back through the trees. The Yankees fired, fell back, reloaded, and fired again.

"Hey, you just gonna watch?" It was George at his elbow. "I figured you wanted that gun fer fightin'."

Elijah nodded and in a daze rose on shaking legs. In the haze, it was hard to see. He aimed where a flash had just been. He fired. In the smoke he was unsure if the bullet found a target. George was moving forward. Elijah made a hunkering run and stopped behind a post oak. Sweat kept coursing down his sides.

"Elijah! Reload!" George yelled above the din.

Elijah's brows shot up. How could he forget! He took the paper cartridge from the box at his belt and, mimicking George, tore it open with his teeth. His hands trembled as he stuffed the contents into the muzzle, pouring in the powder, ramming in ball, shot, and paper, and tamping it down.

Close by the old warrior reloaded, using the ramrod. As a new volley rang out, Elijah saw more Federals fall.

George spoke near his ear, "Keep yore eyes open for a knapsack on a dead one. Could be they had some food."

Then a bugle blew and the sergeant shouted to the men all down the line, "Forward!"

As Elijah moved cautiously forward through the smoke, he came upon a soldier sprawled face down with a knapsack still strapped to his back. George dropped to one knee and, while keeping a sharp eye all around, quickly pawed through the contents. He stood and began moving. He reached a hand to Elijah. "Hardtack," he said and then ravenously gnawed into a piece himself.

Elijah shrugged off revulsion. The dead soldier did not need the food and they did. They were starving, or very near it. His legs were almost too weak to go on. He saw others scavenging for food and ammunition. And from the dead, some pulled boots only slightly less ragged than their own. The sergeant waved them on through the snowy woods.

"Let's go," said George.

At first they edged from tree to tree, stopping when the sergeant slowed. Elijah's ragged breath whistled in his ears. Guns roared. He was reminded of a tornado dipping down into the Piney bottoms. The air was thick with acrid smoke, blinding him to all but George. But the ragged Confederate line was out there. He could hear the shots. Then straight ahead, near a fallen log, he saw a flash.

"Let's go, men!" Sergeant Callahan rushed ahead.

George suddenly let loose with the high-pitched, bloodcurdling Rebel yell. Men along the ragged line took it up. The cry moved Elijah as nothing ever had. It was wild and savage and terrifying, and as he cried it, he became invincible. Suddenly fearless, he plunged toward the scorching shot and smoke. Tangled underbrush grabbed his feet and caught his clothes. His shirtsleeve tore. He jerked it free and dashed on through the trees.

When a sudden volley leveled men all along the butternut line, the heady rush vanished. Elijah's throat constricted. He turned with heart pounding when the sergeant waved them back. They quickly retreated and hunkered behind fallen logs and trees. Fierce booms shook the ground like pudding. Elijah knew it was only a matter of time before another order to advance came. Now his weak knees trembled. He doubted he could do it...not again. Any second he expected to feel the hot burn of lead. His breath sucked in and out, scouring his lungs with smoke.

George fired again. Elijah fired at a blue sleeve sticking past a tree. The arm jerked and he saw it no more. While reloading, he licked caked grime from his dry lips and stared ahead.

A man stumbled past, squint-eyed, running through the smoke—running away. Elijah longed to do the same. Through the smoke, he dimly saw blue-coated infantry with bayonets, long and deadly, like tines on a pitchfork pointed forward. He gripped his rifle. It flashed through his mind that he had never seen a man killed before today. Now he was watching them fall like raindrops, and he had to kill or be killed.

"Fix bayonets!" the sergeant shouted.

Just then the Yankees charged. Elijah fired but missed. He saw the shiny buttons on the blue blouse. He saw the yellow fuzzy stubble on the squared jaw. He saw the clenched teeth and the determined eyes. He saw death coming, but he could not move. Only his eyes widened as the gleaming blade thrust forward.

George lunged to thrust a bayonet deep into the man's midsection. The soldier slumped forward with his fingers grasping the blade. He looked no older than Elijah, and fear was strong on his face.

Elijah began to shake. George quickly withdrew the blade and then removed it to reload. "Reload, Elijah!" he barked.

Elijah shuddered and wiped his mouth. Quickly he bit the end off a paper cartridge. With unsteady hands, he poured powder into the muzzle. Although some spilled, he tamped the charge and bullet down the barrel, pulled back the hammer, and stuck a percussion cap on the nipple. He tried to avoid looking at the leafy ground strewn with body parts and the bloody stumps of what was left of men. He had never imagined the carnage created by men stabbing with bayonets and blazing away at each other from point-blank range. He shook his head to clear the ringing.

For a few seconds everything ahead was still. Then as Elijah crouched behind a scrubby oak, he shook his head again. The strains of *Dixie* came floating on the acrid air. It was a brass band like the one on mustering day...but the Rebel Army had brought no band! He must be hallucinating.

Elijah licked parched, blistered lips. "George, do you hear music?"

George cocked a grime-covered face from behind a tree. "Them damn Yankees! Makin' sport of us." He glowered. "Well, we made sport of few blue-bellies ourselves today."

The day seemed to go on forever—fight, fall back, fight again—a nightmare of smoke, dirt, blood, and sweat. Confusion reigned. Elijah did not think he had killed anyone, but he had almost shot a Louisiana man when the 3rd Louisiana got mixed up with the 4th Arkansas. He wondered how many Confederates were killed by their own army in the mix-up.

Just before nightfall they advanced out of the woods onto a road. The black outline of a Yankee battery of three cannons was prominent in the field straight ahead. The sergeant ordered them onward.

"Out of the frying pan into the fire," George muttered.

As Rebel troops poured over the rail fence into the pasture, Elijah and George followed, running straight for the guns. Through the smoky twilight Elijah saw Yankee cannoneers in a hurried attempt to reload. He followed George's example and, dropping to a knee took aim. When smoke puffed from his barrel, a blue cap and jacket jerked backwards.

Elijah had killed squirrels, plenty of them, and deer and even a bear. Now he had killed a man. He felt no remorse. It seemed unreal. Perhaps it really was just a nightmare.

The cannons fell silent, but a storm of rifle fire spit through the air. A shot riddled the tail of Elijah's jacket. Oddly, he felt no fear. He was numb. Following the running sergeant, he crossed the field. Then the battle stilled. The Yankees had retreated.

Mangled horses and mules brayed and screamed in agony. Wounded men clutched at their pant-legs, crying out, begging for water. Powder smoke, rank with sulphur, hung heavy in the air like a black shroud over men in torment—men with blood-soaked clothes, men with missing limbs, and men with headless bodies. The scene fit Brother Simon's most fearful description of a fire-and-brimstone hell.

The old Indian fighter unslung a canteen from his shoulder and began passing out drinks. The sergeant, George, and Elijah did the same until their water was gone. These were McCulloch's men. Elijah went on, eyes probing the field for Pa or Tap or Michael. He hoped they were not here.

Suddenly the air exploded with screeching shot. Men on each side of him went down. George slumped and fell near his feet. Dropping the musket, Elijah grabbed for him.

"George, are you hit bad?" He already knew the answer. George's left side was covered in blood and his leg lay at a crazy angle.

At first George's tone was bantering. "Reckon the buckeye let me down." Then eyeing his shattered body, his blue eyes went wide and desperate. He gasped. "I don't wanna die!" He clutched his side, groaning.

Trying to staunch the blood spilling onto the ground, Elijah stuffed George's handkerchief into the open wound. "You'll be all right, George." He knew it was not so. "I'll get help." He started to rise but George clutched him.

"Don't leave me," he gasped.

Elijah knelt and watched the handkerchief redden and begin to drip. He had never felt so helpless in his life.

"Ain't there something yo're supposed to pray before you die?" George panted.

What was it Brother Simon had said at Maggie's funeral? Elijah's mind went blank. When he was nine years old, Elijah had been washed in the blood of the Lamb. At a camp meeting, Simon had baptized him in Little Piney Creek, but now he could not recall a word of the sermon. Granny claimed a body was responsible for leading the lost to Jesus; otherwise, on Judgment Day their blood would be on your hands. He did not want George's blood on his hands.

"Elijah—" George's voice was weak.

Elijah lifted his head. "I'm right here, George." He squeezed the limp hand reaching for him. Elijah choked back a sob.

George's eyes were cloudy. Without a doubt he was dying. Elijah had no idea how to give comfort. Head bowed, he sensed rather than saw someone bending down. A long squirrel rifle in one hand, it was the old veteran.

He hunkered down. "Yo're bad hit, youngster."

George left off gripping Elijah's hand for a moment to pluck at the man's arm. "I'm dying, ain't I?"

"Yep," said the old man, "you air'."

George gasped and coughed. Bloody spittle wet his mouth. "I done a heap of wrong in my life. Wish I hadn't! I don't wanna go to hell!"

The old man cleared his throat. When he spoke his words were gentle. "Well, boy, doing wrong ain't what keeps a body out of heaven. If t'was, wouldn't no human ever go there. Forgivin' is what the Lord does best."

George's eyes flickered. "Pray for me!"

While Elijah took George's hand and tried to will life into him, the old man nodded. He swept off a slouched, round-topped hat. "Lord, forgive this here youngster...."

The old man had hardly begun when the calloused hand in Elijah's grasp went limp, but not before a smile touched the hard, tobacco-stained mouth, leaving it as soft as a girl's.

Elijah gripped George's limp hand. In a daze, he watched blood drip from the ragged handkerchief in George's side, the same handkerchief George had once stuffed into his mouth. Somewhere along the way George had stopped being the enemy.

So this was war as Pa had seen it. With shot peppering all around, Elijah sat and stared.

"Come on, boy!" The old man prodded Elijah with his foot. "We're movin' forward, and you can't do yore friend no good now. He's dead."

Woodenly, Elijah stared. There was blood on his hands. He wiped it onto a clump of dead grass and then he stood and gazed back down. "Who'll bury him?" he asked.

"There'll be a burying detail along when the battle's over." The old man cut a chew from a plug and offered Elijah a sliver.

Elijah recalled how many times George had done the same thing. Fighting tears, he shook his head and swiped his nose on a shirtsleeve.

"We'll need these." The soldier unbuckled George's cartridge box, and after handing Elijah George's canteen, he shouldered his musket. "Come along, youngster. Stick close. I ain't no good-luck charm, but I've lived through many a battle—Injun, Mex, and Yankee."

Rifle fire still came from the far end of the field. The old man reached out for George's gray uniform cap and handed it to Elijah. He took it. George would want him to have it. Cradling the musket, he trailed behind the old soldier. Before climbing the fence, he glanced back at George lying crumpled on the frozen ground.

George was dead! It could not be true! And yet it was.

"Get a move on," urged the old soldier, quickening the pace.

Elijah passed near a grove of trees. In his peripheral vision movement flickered. He turned. A Yankee aimed his rife and pulled the trigger.

Elijah froze, expecting any second to fall. Nothing happened. He went limp. The shot had missed!

Relief was short-lived. He was staring into pale eyes that were stark with fear. The soldier was about Pa's age. Although grim just now, he had a broad, pleasant face and the furrowed, brown skin of a farmer. His wide hands shook while trying to attach a bayonet.

This was different than shooting at a blurred, blue-coated figure in the distance. Elijah hesitated, but only for a heartbeat. He raised the rifle and fired.

The man jerked backwards. The hole in his throat squirted blood. He could not speak but the guttural sounds were gruesome.

Elijah dropped to his knees alongside him. "I'm sorry, mister."

The old Indian fighter pulled him up. "He'd a done the same to you. Still would if he could." He pointed to Elijah's rifle. "Reload. And if you intend stayin' alive, don't wait fer me to tell you."

Elijah's insides twisted. He knew the old man was right. But it did not make killing any easier. When he fumbled and dropped the shot pouch, the old man took it and reloaded for him.

He handed Elijah the gun. "I don't see no officers nowhere. Let's go find out who's in charge."

Elijah took two steps and then looked back. He would never forget the man's anguished look.

Soon after they arrived at the crossroads, the old man sat down with a tired sigh. "There ain't no one here who knows what's going on. McCulloch is dead and so is McIntosh. And hit looks as if Hubert got hisself captured. Everyone is just waitin' fer someone to tell 'em what to do."

Elijah froze. McCulloch was dead! *What about Pa?* Captain Culp had said McCulloch was leading the 16th. Despair choked Elijah.

"Where did they take the dead?" he quickly asked.

"Plenty of 'em still laying out there on the ground. The dead don't care—one way or t'other. Poor pilgrims I feel sorry fer is the wounded. But I reckon there's a hospital set up somewheres." He looked at the lowering sun and then faced east where terrible and constant gunfire boomed. "Ain't no supply train here. Still lots of fightin' over yonder—train must be there. I'm most out of ammunition. I aim to mosey over that way. You want to come?"

Elijah nodded. He wanted to find the field hospital and search for Pa, Tap, and Michael. Elijah, except for the scratches on his arms and face, had escaped injury today. He wondered how it was possible.

With slow, dogged pace they started down the road. A large moon had risen, lighting the way as they skirted the mountain. Elijah decided the old fellow tramping alongside must be as tough as nails for it had been thirty hours since the army slept and, for the most part, longer since they had eaten. Although men had dropped like ripe plums all afternoon, the old warrior stayed abreast, his long strides almost pulling ahead on the downhill pulls.

The moon climbed higher, reflecting eerie light off the white sandstone cliffs. Elijah determined not to think about George and his blank, staring eyes. Nonetheless that picture danced in his brain. Other gristly images came to him like daguerreotypes from the darkness—the men he had seen die, the men he had killed.

After nightfall the gunfire stopped. Instead of silence, Elijah heard a constant ringing in his ears. He and the old man often slipped into the bushes to let some unknown rider pass. They trudged on through the darkness until, finally, up ahead campfires dotted the night. Without mishap they had reached Elkhorn Tavern.

In the moonlight the homey, two-story inn appeared a haven. As they cautiously crept near, Elijah saw the large elk horns on the roof that had given the inn its name. With relief he saw the troops in the yard were Confederate.

The veteran stood and strode forward and Elijah followed. While passing a group of men gathered near a huge barn, he overheard angry voices.

"With McCulloch and McIntosh dead, half the army didn't fight today. Van Dorn's leadership is an outrage!"

"For a fact!" agreed another, and then added, "And so is Pike's! Scalping soldiers! I don't care if they were blue-bellies. It's not decent. Pike should have kept his Indians under control!"

Elijah shied away from the group, but the grizzled old fighter turned back and stopped. "Don't know why you Rackansackers would expect otherwise. Hit's the Injun way. And Pike ain't fixin' to change Injuns just by puttin' little gray coats on 'em."

Elijah walked on. But as he drew near the inn, he stopped.

It was no haven. It was a house of death!

The porch was stacked with dead men. And outside the back door, lying in moonlight, were piles of severed limbs—arms, legs—some still wearing blood-soaked sleeves and tattered boots. He had found the hospital! With gritted teeth he braced himself. He went inside just as a surgeon in blood-soaked apron drew a knife across a man's shattered leg. The man screamed. It sounded worse than the injured horse back on the icy road. Elijah covered his mouth. He quickly searched all the grimy faces. Without success, he hurried outside. He leaned on the rail and breathed deep. Then he gagged when a putrid odor filled his nostrils.

If Pa were dead, he wanted to know. He squared his shoulders, and in lantern light spilling from the window, he painstakingly viewed every dead face—old and young, red and white. There was no one he knew. He leaned over the rail and wiped cold sweat.

The old fighter joined him on the porch. "Find yore Pa?"

Elijah shook his head and wiped his mouth on a ragged sleeve.

The old man hunkered alongside a body. He drew forth a knife from a dead Indian's leggings. He handed Elijah the knife.

"Here's something the human buzzards missed. Put it in yore belt. Many a time I been spared by having a extree weapon handy." He pointed to a knife handle sticking from his own leggings.

Elijah shoved the knife into his belt and then staggered away, trying to escape the cries of suffering. But he could not. The screams of the man getting a leg amputated followed him.

He stopped to warm by a campfire, watching it flicker on tree limbs as white as skeletons. Others squatting near the fire rehashed the day—how Curtis had been driven from the high ground. They were in disagreement regarding why the last desperate Rebel charge across the cornfield had failed. Elijah gleaned that Price's men had bravely charged across the open fields and been slaughtered like sheep.

He stepped away. He wanted to hear no more of war. He wanted to be alone. The road was bright in the moonlight. He started walking.

Then he saw them, hundreds of them, men still lying on the cornfield as lifeless as the brown, riddled stalks that stood like lifeless sentries.

He had a bizarre thought—"Why had the farmer not gathered last year's fodder?"

Drawn by some morose impulse, he stepped over the rail fence. In the frosty moonshine the upturned faces and uniforms were ghostly white. Men lay every which way with gaping jaws and glassy stares. This reality was worse than any nightmare. Elijah sat on the cold ground and wept.

When the old man touched his shoulder, he jerked.

"You've see'd too much today, youngster. Let's go warm by the fire. I found us a bite to eat."

Elijah followed. But he was no youngster. Not anymore. Not ever again.

———~———

The next morning there was no food. There was no ammunition. The supply wagons had not come forward. Men rose from the hard ground with even harder feelings for Van Dorn. What kind of idiot did not resupply the troops? How did he expect them to fight without ammunition, without food?

Elijah thought of all the ruined food in the scorched warehouses just a few miles south. He wondered if God was taking revenge on them for what they had done to Fayetteville. It seemed right that the army should go hungry along with the women and children they had left to suffer. But he wished the good Lord had been more selective in the punishment. Not all of them had looted—but they were all starving.

Soon after daylight, in a hazy sun, the shelling began again. For two unbearable hours the sky rained cannon balls that shook the ground. Bursts of flame and smoke and thunderous noise—Elijah recalled Granny's dire warning of the soon-coming end of the world. He wondered if it had come.

He fought alongside the old Indian fighter, running and then hunkering to fire a volley, sometimes advancing, sometimes falling back. It seemed senseless—such loss of life to capture a cornfield. Elijah knew if he lived to be a hundred it would still make no sense.

"Let's sashay over yonder to that creek," the old man pointed, "and fill our canteens. I'm dry as powder."

At a running crouch, Elijah arrived first and, flopping onto his belly, took a long draught of the icy water. It hit his empty stomach like a rock. He stood and groaned.

"You check that there water for blood?" asked the old man, out of breath, dropping alongside him.

Elijah retched. Then he dropped to the ground and retched again as less than three feet away a man and horse were blown apart. Although bloody debris spattered his face, Elijah was still unharmed. He figured it must be Ma's and Granny's prayers. He hoped prayer had worked as well for Pa, Uncle Tap, and Michael.

"Fall back! Fall back!" Men rushed past, splashing through the creek.

The old Indian fighter pushed up from the bank and shouldered his rifle. "Reckon that means we're licked," he said and shook his head. "Ain't no wonder. In all my born days I never seed anything like the bloody hell they just give us. Must of fired a million cannonballs at us today."

Elijah left the creek bed at a trot with the old man at his heels. It crossed his mind to wonder what the fellow's name was. If they both lived long enough he would ask.

It had all been a total waste! George and hundreds like him had died for nothing. Van Dorn had ordered them into the gates of hell, and they had gone. Now, he ordered what was left of them to retreat, running away like scared rabbits. Curtis's army had held firm. The hills still vibrated with the boom of lobbed cannon shells.

Elijah wondered how many of the Clarksville men were left. Most of all, he wondered about Pa, Tap, and Michael. Tiredly, he joined a ragged line of men converging on the Huntsville road. Not marching, the men shuffled with a dragging tread. Humiliation lay heavy on them, mixed with anger. They had come to fight but not to charge blindly across open country under a leader whose strategy was totally void of common sense. It stung that hundreds had been left wounded on the field at the mercy of the Yankee army.

Elijah's head shot up. There was Uncle Tap! He was dismounted and walking alongside a wagon. Elijah ran forward. When he drew near, Tap looked up.

"Elijah! What in the world—"

"I got conscripted." Elijah managed a wobbly grin. "Uncle Tap, I'm sure glad you made it through that battle. Have you heard from Pa?" he asked quickly.

Tap was too sober. Elijah's heart skipped a beat.

Tap nodded toward the wagon that was now passing from sight, up the next slope. Elijah tried to run but was too weak. He managed a slow trot and soon caught up with the wagonload of wounded men. Ned lay near the rear, white and unconscious. His shirt was off, and there was a large bandage across his shoulder and chest. There was a small vacant spot on the wagon bed alongside him, and Elijah climbed up and sat down, dangling his feet off the back of the open tailgate. He put a hand on Ned's shoulder. Tap rode ahead and spoke to the muleskinner and then waited while the wagon drew abreast.

"They're taking the wounded to Little Rock. I talked to the muleskinner. You can ride along and help care for your pa."

"Will I get into trouble for deserting?"

Tap gave a wry smile. "No. Tell anyone it was Colonel Brook's orders."

Tap gave Elijah a grim look. "But if Ned dies, promise me you'll head straight home."

Elijah swallowed. "I promise," he said and meant it.

"Was everyone at home all right when you left? Your ma and those neighbors—Mr. Campbell and Miss Jenny?"

"They were fine."

"Good," said Tap.

"Uncle Tap, do you think Pa is going to die?"

"He might."

Elijah swallowed.

"I have to get back to my command. I'll try to get in touch with you later. Take care of yourself, Elijah."

Elijah nodded. As Tap rode away he called after him. "Uncle Tap, I think Jenny would like to see you again."

Tap looked around and his begrimed face broke into a grin. "I'd enjoy that myself."

As Tap waved, Elijah looked back down the trail and saw the old Indian fighter climbing the last hill. He had forgotten to ask his name.

Chapter 12

Little Rock turned out to welcome the cavalcade of wagons loaded with hundreds of wounded. There had been no doctors or medicine on the trip. Many had died and many more hovered near, their anguish hard to behold. Droves of women volunteered to nurse the grimy, blood-caked men. Elijah knew it took courage. Some of the mutilated flesh had already begun to putrefy, and the stench was awful. Although Ned had regained consciousness, he was extremely weak.

Elijah, still seated by Ned's side, gaped at the numerous store buildings. Little Rock was the largest town he had ever seen. The wide streets were lined with gaslights. He had never dreamed of such marvels.

Stores, churches, warehouses, and private homes opened their doors. Elijah was disappointed when place after place was too full. Ned's wagon was turned away. Finally they stopped at a neat stone house near the edge of town. The owner, short, plump Miss Lucy, made them welcome. Both Ned and another wounded soldier were placed in a canopy-covered bed in a room with rose-colored drapes and ruffled white counterpane. Elijah suspected it belonged to one of Miss Lucy's pretty daughters.

Elijah thanked the girl who brought a bowl of hot water and some clean bandages. She was fine-boned and fair-skinned, but her hair was as black as a crow's wing and just as shiny. She gave him a timid smile.

"Here are some bandages and salve for your pa's wounds. If you need anything else, just call." She looked shyly down, shielding blue eyes behind dark, curly lashes. "My name is Sarah."

"Thank you, kindly." He took the rag from the water and squeezed it. With dread he soaked loose the old, caked bandage. He gave a relieved sigh. There was still no sign of infection. But Elijah wished for Granny with her know-how and herbs. On the second night, the man who lay alongside Ned died. Elijah was glad the man's suffering was finally over. He began to feel more hopeful when, with each passing day, Ned began to improve.

For the first week Elijah stayed right by his side, feeding him, dressing the wound, and bathing him. He also cared for three more men crowded into the small bedroom, lying on pallets. All three were in less serious condition than the other six men crowded into the small rock house. Miss Lucy, her servants, and her two daughters cared for them night and day. The anguished moans and cries were terrible. Sometimes Elijah put his fingers into his ears to mute the suffering. He wished Van Dorn had to nurse every one of them. Before the week was out, two more died.

At night drums beat in Elijah's brain and he saw men lying—butchered like beef, oozing and raw—wallowing in their own blood. Night after night he jerked awake and sat up shivering. He began to comprehend that all wounds were not visible.

Slowly, the other patients grew stronger. Soon Ned was walking about and spending more time sitting up than lying down. He even helped roll bandages.

When Miss Lucy declared war on lice, Elijah cropped the men's hair close and even shaved the ones too weak to shave themselves. He began doing other chores, hauling countless buckets of water from the well, chopping wood, firing the stove, and dumping chamber pots. There was always a pile of dirty bandages and linens to scrub. Sarah, whom Elijah guessed was about age sixteen, was in charge of laundry. He was glad to offer help. Her eyes were as blue as a mountain sky.

"Thank you, Elijah." her voice was soft and cultured.

He held the empty bucket, unaware that he stared until she looked up from bending over the washtub and smiled. Heat flushed his neck. He had been staring at the neck of her dress where the flesh pushed up rounded and firm. He felt guilty, as if he had been unfaithful to Cindy. He wondered if Dillon had made it home—and if he had kissed Cindy.

Sarah's older sister, Dolly, stood nearby stirring a simmering pot of soup. She was short and round and resembled hefty Miss Lucy. However, Sergeant Daniel Upton did not seem to mind. He stood nearby peeling potatoes, but his eyes were not on the task.

Elijah took the afternoon off. He wanted to mail a letter to Ma. And he wanted to find Uncle Phillip.

Although April had arrived, the day was raw. Elijah turned up a collar against the cold wind whipping through litter-filled streets. His nose wrinkled at the horrible odor caused by rotting flesh and poor sanitation. He thought how different the city was now from the pleasant place Uncle Phillip had described before the war. The stores, almost empty of merchandise, were stuffed with wounded men. Passersby were without exception a tired, worried lot. The sight of too much horror and suffering had marred the haggard faces of women who dragged home from nursing the sick and dying. The convalescing sat in sunny spots sheltered from the wind, their eyes vacant or hard—Men who, as Pa had said, would never be the same again. Elijah knew he would not.

He searched every face, hoping to find Michael. Ned had last seen him the day of the battle, and although Elijah had asked and asked, no one knew his whereabouts or if he had survived.

Elijah mailed the letter. He hoped it would not be long before Uncle Caleb went to town or someone else took the letter to Ma. Finally, he located the *Gazette* office and went inside. Since Uncle Phillip had worked for the editor, Elijah figured Mr. Danley would know where to find him.

A stooped, skinny man in an ink-covered apron was busy working at a tall-legged table. His fingers were blotched with ink.

"Excuse me, mister; I'm looking for Mr. Danley."

Without looking up the little man pointed across the room to a hefty man seated behind a cluttered desk.

"I'm Danley. What can I do for you?" the big man asked around a long cigar.

Elijah, gray cap in hand, stepped over and nodded. "I'm looking for Phillip Horton. He's my Uncle. I reckon he works for you...or at least he did."

Danley stood. "So you're Phillip's nephew," he said extending a hand.

Elijah shook it. "Could you tell me where he is?"

Danley said, "Better yet, I'll take you to him."

"I don't want to bother you, sir, just point the way."

Danley flicked ashes from the cigar, and after taking up a walking cane, he grabbed a hat from the rack near his desk. "I go see him every day about this time." He stopped for a moment to speak to the stooped man. "Edward, don't set that last page yet. I want to do a bit more fact checking," he said. "There's already enough misinformation in print about this plagued war."

Elijah followed him outside. He slowed his steps to accommodate Danley's limp.

"Compliments of a dark-skinned soldier," drolly said Danley.

"Mexican war?" guessed Elijah.

Danley nodded. "Buena Vista." He cut his eyes sideways. "Were you at Pea Ridge?"

"Yes, sir, me and my pa."

"Crying shame how that attack was mismanaged. Seems to be a Confederate habit lately. Your Van Dorn...." he began but Elijah cut him off.

"There's nothing about Van Dorn I claim."

Danley chuckled. "You're a shrewd young man." He went on, "Van Dorn has single-handedly managed to ruin us. He lost over two thousand men in that battle, and no telling how many more starved in the retreat through those barren mountains. Then with Curtis perched on our gable ready to swoop down like a hawk, Van Dorn has left us as unprotected as fledgling chicks. He took the army—plus all the weapons, equipment, stores and animals. We'll have to start from scratch."

"Where did he go?" Elijah quickly asked. "My Uncle Tap is with him."

Danley stopped to let a wagon pass. "He headed to Tennessee, intending to join Beauregard and Johnston in a big push at Pittsburgh Landing—Union Newspapers call it the Battle of Shiloh—but by the time Van Dorn arrived it was all over." He drew deeply on the cigar and then withdrew it from his lips to study the red tip as it paled. "Grant," he muttered. Then he cut his eyes sideways again. "Ever hear of U.S. Grant?"

"No, sir, can't say as I have."

"Well, I'm afraid you'll be hearing plenty about him." He frowned. "Unconditional Surrender Grant. Got the nickname when he captured our forts on the Tennessee. When he took Forts Henry and Donaldson, he refused terms. 'No terms but surrender,' said Grant." Danley quirked an eyebrow. "They say he's a drunk, but from all I can tell, he's a fighting son-of-a-gun. And this last battle proved it." With an ominous shake of the head, Danley went on, "Johnston and Beauregard were no match for him." He slowed and leaned heavily on the cane. "Twenty-three thousand men dead or wounded."

"Twenty-three thousand," echoed Elijah in disbelief. He could not comprehend a slaughter worse than the one he had seen at Pea Ridge.

"Yes, more than all the other battles in this war put together. And not one thing gained. Johnston is dead and Beauregard is pushed back to Corinth." Danley bitterly added, "This will end all bragging of a quick and bloodless victory."

He scowled and stopped in front of a squat brick building with small windows. "Here is where my good friend the governor is holding your dangerous uncle." Sarcasm dripped from his voice. "We'll get searched. Do you have a weapon?" he asked.

Elijah drew the knife from his belt.

"Give it to him." Danley nodded toward a man with wide shoulders sitting near the door with a hat pulled over his face. "If the guard isn't in a foul mood, we should be allowed to see Phillip."

———⌒———

The room was small. It held a desk, bed, and chair. There were no bars, merely windows too small for escape. Phillip sprang from the chair, his eyes lit with joy. The gray at his temples had spread to his hair. It hurt Elijah to see how thin he was. When Phillip gave him a bear hug, Elijah felt his bony ribs.

"Aren't they feeding you, Uncle Phillip?" he asked. "You look like you've been marching with Van Dorn."

Danley gave a hearty laugh and even Phillip chuckled. "They feed me...it just seems I have no appetite."

"Worry does that to a fellow," put in Danley as he pointed his cigar at Phillip's head, "and it causes gray hair too. I keep telling him I'll get him out of here but he doesn't believe me."

"C. C., I'd have been hanged long ago if it weren't for you...but you can only do so much."

"I'm not through trying though—not by a long shot." Danley stuck the cigar into his mouth and spoke around it. "But since Rector's in such a tear about Van Dorn deserting the state and Curtis advancing, I don't think now is the time to press your case. I figure we're better off biding our time a while longer. Guess you read his proclamation?"

Phillip nodded. "But after all that's happened, with no pay, no food, and no success, I doubt men will be flocking to the state army even with the promise of not being turned over to the Confederacy."

"You're right. And Rector has certainly stirred up a hornet's nest by threatening state secession." Danley grinned. "Sounds like treason to me. Talk about the pot calling the kettle black...." He chuckled. "Dick Johnson is blasting him hard in print. For a change, the governor is furious at someone in the press besides me." He put on his hat. "Well, I'll get out of here and let you two visit." He took a step and as an afterthought stopped to ask, "Phillip, you need anything? Paper, tobacco, anything?"

"Thank you, no. You brought the best gift possible,"—he slapped Elijah's shoulder—"my kin."

When Danley had gone Elijah sat on the bed while Phillip pulled the chair near. "What are you doing so far from home?"

"I got conscripted." Elijah paused. "Just in time for Pea Ridge. I reckon you heard about that?"

Phillip nodded.

"Pa got wounded." Upon seeing Phillip's concern, he quickly added, "Oh, he's all right. It's just taking him a while to get his strength back, but he's gonna be fine. He's one of the lucky ones." Elijah looked at the cap resting on his knee. "George Garrison got killed. He was standing right beside me."

"Poor George. That's a shame. He was a fine young man." Phillip was quiet for a moment, and then he said, "I'm sorry you had to experience that. It's a hard thing. But men face hard things and go on."

Elijah nodded. "Uncle Phillip, any idea how I can get word to Ma that we're all right? I know she's worried sick. I mailed a letter, but the fellow at the post office told me it might not get there."

"I'll have C. C. send a telegram to Clarksville. But it may be a while before anyone takes it to her."

"Uncle Caleb goes in to get the news pretty regular. He'll get it."

"I don't suppose you've seen your aunt or Nelda recently?"

"Pa and I helped them with the butchering but that's been a while back. They were fine," he said. "Then the day I got conscripted I overheard Nelda interviewing a soldier outside the wagon. But I was tied and gagged. She never saw me." He hesitated. Honesty made him add, "The last time I saw Aunt Louise, she had one of those bad headaches."

Phillip's shoulders slumped. "Poor Louise. I wish there were some remedy." Then he said, "I certainly appreciate your help with the butchering. They couldn't have managed alone."

Then Phillip changed the subject. "Before you left home was there any news of your uncle Jim?"

Elijah's brows shot up. How had Phillip heard about Uncle Jim? And why was he asking? They barely knew each other. Or so he thought...

"Last we knew he was fine." Elijah looked closely. Phillip's expression gave nothing away.

―――――⌒〜〜――――

Each day Elijah drilled with the troops. Soon Ned, albeit on shaky legs, was able to join him. Curtis advanced within fifty miles of the capitol, and the pale, worried faces of Little Rock turned northward, listening, waiting, watching, dreading. The stench of putrefying flesh poisoning the air slowly began to abate, replaced by the fragrance of lilacs and honeysuckle.

A letter finally arrived from Becky. They were all fine and rejoicing to hear from Elijah and to learn that Ned was alive and getting stronger. With Caleb's help, she and Deborah had a fine garden started and a small field of corn already planted. Granny, Caleb, Jenny, and Pappy all sent their love. In spite of the good news, both Elijah and Ned had long faces. The letter made them homesick. Elijah was especially disappointed that Ma had made no mention of Cindy.

One balmy afternoon in May, while Elijah and Ned were visiting Phillip, Mr. Danley arrived.

"Listen to this," he said, putting on glasses and withdrawing the paper tucked under his arm. "Not the *Gazette*," he said, nodding at the paper. "This is Johnson's editorial last week." He began to read, "We would be glad if some patriotic gentleman would relieve the anxiety of the public by informing it of the locality of the state government. The last that was heard of it here, it was aboard the steamer *Little Rock*, steaming up the current of the Arkansas River."

He removed the glasses and put them into a crumpled, white shirt pocket. "Sad state of affairs. Rector has moved the government papers down river and then overland to Hot Springs. But it might be good news for you, Phillip. With the government on the run, Rector might consent to your release." He smirked. "Even I might get a rest," he said. "He's so livid over Johnson's editorial, he challenged him to a duel." He went on with a wry grin, "And, Phillip, you'll never guess who will be his second."

"The honorable General Burgevin?"

Danley joined in with Phillip's laughter. Then he explained to Ned and Elijah, "A few months ago Burgevin challenged me to a duel with the governor acting as second."

Danley put on his hat. "I figure this duel will fizzle out as fast as that one did. I dare say, both of them are better at rhetoric than pistols." He headed for the door. "I'd better get back to the office."

Phillip halted him with a question. "What's your opinion of our new general?"

Danley stopped. He contemplated for a moment. "Hindman may be a runt," he said, "but he knows how to get things done. It takes know-how and guts to impress a million dollars from Memphis banks—even in war time—and get away with it." Danley grinned. "And Hindman did just that. He's already managed to put together another army and set up factories to make the things we're desperately short of." Danley went on, "Of course, Rector is steaming mad that he took over the state army. Rector wanted control of it. And considering how Van Dorn raped the state, I can't say as I blame the governor. But there's no arguing with success."

"But Hindman is riding roughshod over everyone," said Ned, "taking everything that ain't nailed down. I especially don't like having to answer to no provost marshal and needin' a pass to travel right here in my own state."

Danley flipped an ash from his cigar. "Yes, personal liberty has certainly suffered," he acknowledged with a frown.

Ned added, "And all that cotton! Even to keep it out of Curtis' hands, it seems a shame to burn it."

Phillip nodded. "I agree."

"Well, boys," said Danley, "at best war isn't pretty, but if we're going to win this one, we need a man like Hindman who will stop at nothing. He dug up those cannon fence posts and put them back into service. He even raided the library to use the books for cartridge making."

"Oh, no! Those books are irreplaceable!" Phillip groaned. "Is there going to be anything left to fight for?"

"I don't like it either," agreed Danley, "but I can't help but admire his resourcefulness." He left the cigar dangling as he spoke. Elijah noticed the manicured hands propped on the cane were as smooth as a woman's.

Elijah looked up. "He may be a different breed of polecat than Van Dorn, but I'm not looking forward to serving under him any better," he said with a woebegone shake of the head.

"Since you were conscripted, why don't you just leave?" Danley asked.

"I'd just be hiding and looking over my shoulder all the time." Elijah did not mention the flogging. Although there was no shame in it, he felt shamed.

Danley let out a deep breath. "I suppose you're right. Everyone old enough to hold a gun is being conscripted now. And I hear deserters are being killed like flies."

Elijah nodded, "Yeah, and if I left, I figure the general would for sure consider me a deserter."

Chapter 13

Elijah received orders to report for duty. Confederate scouts reported the Yankee army was cutting a swath of destruction down the east bank of the White River unequal to any yet seen—stealing all the food, burning fields, houses, barns, cotton gins, and fences. Curtis was emancipating all the slaves as he went, giving them bogus freedom papers. Now hundreds of freed blacks were trailing in his wake.

Ned was still unfit for a long march. This time he watched with sorrowful eyes as Elijah went away.

Sarah waited until he was outside and then hurried before he had shut the front gate. "Elijah, wait."

Surprised, he turned. He had already told her goodbye along with Dolly and Miss Lucy, and thanked them for their kindness.

Sarah carried an armful of clothes. "I...I picked these out for you. I think they're your size." Her cheeks glowed as pink as the sunrise.

"Why, thank you." It was a much-needed gift. His pack held only one change of underwear. His laundered pants and shirt had to dry while he slept. "That was mighty nice of you." From the size of them, he figured the clothes had belonged to Tommy Sloan. He had died from a head wound his third day here.

As Elijah reached for the bundle, their hands touched. He was amazed that tears suddenly rimmed her eyes. She looked down and smoothed her apron.

"I think you're the nicest, most handsome soldier in the entire Confederate Army." She looked up. Her face had paled. "Oh, Elijah!

I'll never see you again. I wish I'd spoken out sooner, but Ma says a lady doesn't...."

Elijah blinked. Sarah had been nice and sweet, but he had no idea. He was speechless.

She laid a hand on his arm. Then she bit her lip. "I suppose you'll think me the worst kind of woman"—her head tilted defiantly—"but I'm going to kiss you. At least I'll have that to remember."

Her mouth was warm and firm. Elijah stood in shock while she kissed him.

She drew in a breath. Her eyes shone. "I'll be praying for you, Elijah Loring." She turned and fled into the house. He took a few stunned steps and then looked back. She stood at the window holding back the lace curtain. Tears ran down her white cheeks. He felt as though a cannonball had struck him dead center. He had never intended to give Sarah any such notions.

After a long march, Elijah and dozens more ragged soldiers reported to a command in northeastern Arkansas. It was a motley group of men standing at attention, some in uniform, some in butternut, and some in finely tailored but worn jackets more befitting a parlor than a battlefield.

They had not waited long before a colonel strode onto the field. Tall and slender, he walked with the brisk military stride that Elijah had begun to associate with trained officers.

"I am Colonel Stedman, but to you men—I am God Almighty." Moments passed before he spoke again. Elijah supposed Stedman wanted his threat to sink in. For a threat it was, plain to see in the stern face and unrelenting mouth and jaw.

"A foreign invader has plundered our land. General Curtis has destroyed everything in his path. He has cut a swath of destruction unequalled in the South—burning our homes, burning our crops, and leaving our women and children to starve. He must be stopped!

"I will tolerate no seditious mutterings, no shirking, and no insubordination. You will do as ordered immediately and without question. Punishment for infractions will be severe. Without exception deserters will be shot." He turned on his heel and left.

An Irishman with sandy-colored hair, a wide chest, and short legs, took over. "Save yourselves some trouble, gents, and do as he says. By the way, the name is Potts." His merry blue eyes and jovial manner were a relief. "No doubt, we've a nasty job of work to do, but, all in all, driving out the varmints will be grand."

As time passed Elijah grew to like Sergeant Potts and his new captain named Goodman. But the job of driving out the varmints was not grand! He learned the ugly meaning of guerrilla warfare. They struck at Curtis's front, rear, and middle with quick onslaughts like pestering horseflies intended to keep him off balance but never with enough force to halt the advance.

Elijah never bragged and joked about the men he shot as some soldiers did. He was, however, able to level the rifle without wavering now, and without suffering nauseating remorse, see a man fall.

Potts ordered the line of men to straighten up. Colonel Stedman curtly addressed them. "Because of low water on the White River, the Union flotilla has been unable to reach Curtis with supplies. His army is still living off our land, taking food from our people! General Hindman has ordered everything in Curtis' path destroyed. We leave him not a pound of meat or flour, not a grain of corn, not a stack of fodder, oats, or wheat. We will block roads, destroy bridges, and contaminate every well. What we do may seem harsh, even barbaric to some. If so, keep your opinions to yourself."

When Stedman spun on his heel and walked away, Potts pulled at his mustache and fixed tired eyes on the men. "Gents, when we're done, there won't be chitlins left for Curtis' army. 'Tis a nasty job, but orders is orders. So let's get to it!"

The day was fine. Elijah breathed deeply of the cool spring air. The road following the White River was dust free, hard packed, and shaded by big oaks full of songbirds. He saw polk stalks growing beside the road. At home Granny was probably cooking a mess of the greens seasoned with bacon fat and served alongside a hot slab of buttered cornbread. His mouth watered. Home seemed a lifetime away. He rounded a bend and saw a picturesque farm with tall barns, a stately white house, and rolling fields green with new cotton. In the spring sunshine, the wide pastures full of fat, slick cattle made him homesick.

"Cattle first," yelled Potts. "Dress out what we can eat before it rots. Then burn the barns and the stored cotton."

A group of slaves gathered at the far edge of the field to watch but came no closer. After the first volley of shots, Elijah stared in revulsion as, one by one, cows, calves, yearlings, steers and bulls fell dead. His rifle had not fired, but he joined in to help butcher what the army could eat. The rest would be left to greenflies and buzzards. He squatted and split the steer down the middle while thinking how the gutting would be easier if the animal were hung. He worked mechanically. He had helped butcher all his life. The killing of beeves did not bother him. It was the wanton destruction, the bold thieving, the waste. Only the choicest meat was cut and wrapped into bloody skins and thrown onto the wagons along with hams and shoulders from the smokehouse and goods from the cellar.

The slaves suddenly raised a fuss, their voices high and scared. He looked up. A lighted torch arched high to land atop a hay-filled loft. Black smoke roiled from both barns. A woman stood on the porch of the big white house.

Elijah washed his hands and knife in a horse trough and joined the ranks approaching the house. The old woman still stood on the porch, glaring. Although her dress was fine, she reminded him of Granny. She tore down a Confederate flag hanging by the door. Then she threw it down and spit on it.

Potts stopped near the gate. "Check the pantry. Remember, gents, what you leave will wind up in Yankee bellies. Curtis will take what we don't."

The woman stepped back into the doorway and grabbed a double-barreled shotgun. Elijah sucked in his breath. She had Granny's determined eyes. He knew death was only a hairsbreadth away. He figured they deserved it. They might as well be raiding with Jess and his fat-bellied friend.

"Not one step closer, you bandits!" Her fierce eyes swept them all. "My two grandsons died at Pea Ridge and this is the thanks they get. No! You'll not take one more thing from me!"

Elijah was relieved when Sergeant Potts wisely ordered them to let the old woman be. He looked back as they left the yard. She still stood, a shrunken figure on the big white porch, holding the pointed gun. He was heartsick and worried. With two armies and all the bushwhackers ripping the state apart, no one was safe. He hoped Ma and Granny were keeping weapons handy.

At the next farm, it appeared no one was home, although the doors and shutters of the large, white house stood open. "Careful," whispered Potts. "The hair on the back of my neck is standing at attention like it does just before bullets start to fly."

Elijah nodded and tightened the grip on his rifle.

"Search the barns and outbuildings. Load any meat from the smokehouse into the wagons." Potts looked at Elijah and a wiry, half-Cherokee scout named Hawk. "Find the cellar and clean it out." Then he waved other men forward through the open front door.

The cellar was behind the barn, built into a tall bank facing east. Hawk tried the door but it would not budge. He gave a mighty kick and it burst open, revealing a large, dark hole. Elijah held the gun cocked and ready.

"I'll find us a torch," Hawk said and turned away.

Elijah hunkered a ways from the entrance to wait. There was a small scurrying inside—a rat or a mouse, he supposed. The sun was warm on his back. After enduring the cruel cold of last winter, he enjoyed soaking it up like a lizard, but he did not mean to doze.

He sensed a bulk above him. Hawk must be back with the torch. His eyelids fluttered. With a grunt he lunged just as a long knife bore down into his left shoulder. He twisted away as the attacker jerked out the knife and raised it again. The rifle lay where it had fallen, just out of reach. Swift as a cat, the big man grabbed Elijah's hair and raised the knife again.

Almost without thought, Elijah grasped the knife in his belt. He brought it up with all the force in him, with all the power driven by fear and the desire to live. He drove the blade deep into the man's belly and thrust upward—just as the old Indian fighter had told him would quickly kill a man. At the same time he twisted away from the onslaught of the man's blade.

The gray eyes above him widened and then grew dazed and glassy. With a groan, the man fell forward and hit the ground hard with a thud, like a sack full of grain.

"You bastard!" muttered Elijah, gripping his shoulder.

"Bushwhackers have been here," called Hawk as he rounded the barn. "They killed…" He saw the dead man and stopped cold. "I see you already found one," he said. He came forward and with one foot rolled the man over. "Deserter, I reckon. Or else a bushwhacker that stole a Reb uniform." He pulled out the bloody knife. "That's as good a job gutting as I ever saw."

Elijah stood. Weak-kneed, he quickly sank back down. His shoulder throbbed. But he was glad to be alive!

Hawk eyed the bloody shoulder and then ripped away the mangled fabric. "Good clean wound. Don't reckon it will even slow you down much. You got off lucky. The two old folks in the house are dead. He stabbed them and then cut 'em up some for good measure."

Elijah shuddered. He was sick of the horror, sick of the killing, sick of the war. And he understood the Yankee's loathing for Hindman. His famous Order Number 17 had sanctioned the formation of independent companies of irregulars. These men, known as Partisan Rangers, had tortured, murdered, and even mutilated captured Federals. All across the state, atrocities were happening daily. As hatred grew, Elijah feared the regular army was also growing too vicious. It was rumored General Curtis had finally ordered his own men to take no more prisoners.

Although Elijah would not speak it aloud, he sympathized with all the Rebel soldiers who had deserted in droves, some even going to join Curtis's Army. Of course, Hindman had put a stop to that. Mr. Danley was right, Hindman was a man of action—but to Elijah's way of thinking, much of it was wrong. The last men apprehended were given no trial, just an execution for six of them. Elijah had seen them shot. Since then, to his knowledge, no other Rebel had tried to join Curtis.

To Elijah the worst thing of all was living off the land, taking food and fodder from their own people. He found that intolerable. In his tent at night he relived each torturous day—the teary-eyed women standing at smokehouse and cellar doors, begging them to leave food for their children. He writhed in shame. Could any cause be worth this!

Elijah awoke the next morning in a cold sweat. The nightmare was horrible. Raiders had hit his home. It was hard to shake off the vision of Ma and Deborah at the mercy of bushwhackers. He hoped it was not prophetic.

Everyone was solicitous of him and his wounded shoulder. He was embarrassed by the attention, especially by Sergeant Potts's loud and overstated narration of his valor. To hear Potts tell it, he could walk on water. Elijah knew better. He had been stupid for falling asleep and was merely lucky to be alive.

The sergeant convinced the colonel they should camp near the river and take a day or two off to wash clothes and rest up. It was a pretty place with water running over a bluff into twin falls. Elijah knew the delay was an excuse for him to regain his strength. Sergeant Potts was a good friend.

———~———

One morning Potts rousted them from their tents and stood them into line. Elijah rubbed sleep from his eyes and watched the gray dawn grow pink on the horizon.

Potts's brow was furrowed. "Colonel Stedman needs a firing squad. Now straighten up that line before he gets here."

Elijah hardly knew the shivering man who stood nearby. He was a lanky man named Gorman, a quiet fellow. The night before Gorman had been captured less than an hour after slipping away from camp. Now he would have little time to make peace with his maker, for the army must hurry ahead.

The colonel came from his tent and went swiftly down the straight line of men, pointing. He pointed at Elijah. Elijah's stomach tensed. This was not the first execution he had witnessed, but it would be his first duty on the firing squad. The other times he had squeezed shut his eyes. This time they would have to remain wide open. He squared his shoulders and drew a deep, ragged breath. How many more horrible things would this army require!

Along with eleven others, he handed over his musket to be loaded. Six guns would be given heavy charges of shot and powder. Six would be loaded with blank cartridges. With a bleak face, he shouldered the loaded rifle and marched in formation a short distance from camp. In the clear morning air, the adjutant read the proceedings of the court martial. The charges: desertion. The sentence: to be shot to death by musketry.

Just then from a nearby tree floated the golden notes of a wren's happy call. Gorman looked toward the sound. For a moment he hung his head, and then unflinching, with head high, he marched forward alongside his guards. He was ordered to stand with his back to a small blackjack tree. Hands at sides, he was lashed with ropes to the oak. Without a murmur he obeyed.

Colonel Stedman sat a horse. "Private Gorman, do you have any last words?"

Gorman stared at him. "We're not soldiers. We're bandits, stealing from our own people."

Captain Goodman nodded to Potts, who tied a handkerchief over Gorman's eyes and marked off ten paces. As Elijah fell into line, sweat poured down his armpits. The soldier alongside him cursed under his breath. "Damn fine man about to die."

At the order, Elijah raised the rifle. He was a good shot. He could bark a squirrel from the tallest tree along Piney. The sights were on the left pocket of Gorman's butternut shirt. He was tempted to pull left. Then he realized, no matter what, Gorman was going to die. It may as well be quick. He held steady.

"Fire!"

Shots exploded. Gorman slumped.

Elijah lowered his rife.

The soldier beside him spoke. "He died game."

"Yeah," Elijah said bitterly, "for all the good that did him."

—⁓—

A week later Elijah sat on the bank of the sparkling White River, drinking a cup of brown water, a foul-tasting concoction made from parched corn served by the camp cook as a substitute for coffee. The loud twitter of birds rose above the lap of the clear water, and in the distance through the mists came the croak of a lone bullfrog. It was a peaceful morning, the rosy sunrise shining through lacy clouds. He wished for a cane pole and the time to use it. With a sigh he wondered about everyone at home. He had written several letters to Ma. Although disappointed, he was not surprised to receive no reply. His company was constantly on the move. He often thought of Sarah, but the face he saw in the flickering campfire was always Cindy's.

He scratched at an itchy tick bite. Ticks and chiggers had never bothered him before. Granny's sulphur must have worked. This was the first year he had not been forced to swallow the bitter stuff, and now he was tormented by the pests. He eyed a dozen red bumps and scowled. He would never argue about taking sulphur again.

"Howdy, youngster."

He glanced up. It was the old Indian fighter from Pea Ridge days!

The old man squatted beside him. "Course you don't look so young now with them whiskers. And you've growed a heap since Pea Ridge. Glad to see yo're still in one piece."

Elijah's eyes lighted. "Good to see you too! When did you get here?"

He paused to yawn. "Bunch of us rode in late last night. Reckon you and me is in the same outfit now."

"Good! I wondered what happened to you. Glad you're in our outfit."

"That there colonel is sort of puffed up with hisself, ain't he? He's got enough chicken guts on his sleeve to be a general."

"Yeah, he is right fond of gold braid." Elijah looked off across the creek. "And shooting deserters."

"I take it you ain't fond of Stedman?"

Elijah snorted. "I like Captain Goodman and Sergeant Potts, though."

"Yep. Potts is a good sort. I've knowed him fer years."

"Hey, before I forget again, what's your name?"

"Cowen—Levi Cowen. And yor'en?"

Elijah stuck out his hand. "Elijah Loring, but I answer to Lige for short."

Levi transferred the steaming cup to his left hand and shook hands. Now he blew on his drink. "This war can't be over quick enough to suit me. I'm almighty glad we're headed to the fort this morning and not out yonder"—he waved his cup toward the countryside—"burning cotton and taking food." He wagged his head. "Baah! That sticks in my craw."

Elijah nodded. "Mine too. I hate taking stuff from our own folks."

Levi went on, "I reckon Hindman has turned more good Rebels into Yankees than Curtis or Lincoln ever will."

Elijah nodded agreement and then lowered his voice. There were men scattered up and down the river, lolling at numerous campfires. "I ain't too high on this war myself," he said bitterly.

Levi fiddled with the handle of his tin cup. "Me neither." He swatted a mosquito and looked up, his black eyes tired above the straight beard. "Blood and lice and stink and flies...I'm sick to death of hit all. But I swore on for the fight, so reckon I'll stick—win, lose, or draw." As an order to break camp rang out, he slopped the rest of the drink onto the ground, rose stiffly, and shouldered his rifle.

Elijah stood and shouldered his own rifle. "I reckon I'll stick too. I've seen what happens to deserters."

The fall of Memphis earlier that month had cleared the way for Federal gunboats to move up the river to resupply General Curtis. It was hoped the Confederate fort at St. Charles would stop that resupply. Elijah was relieved his company was assigned to the fort. He was sick of scavenging and brush fighting.

After a few hours of marching, he was grateful when Sergeant Potts called a halt. He and Levi gulped water from canteens and rested a bit before shouldering their packs again. They had taken only a few steps when a blast shook the earth, trembling the ground under them.

"What the!" Levi swore and, in a flash, dove for cover, immediately raising his rifle.

Elijah was right behind. All down the line men swore and stared in big-eyed wonder. Elijah had endured one of the worst cannonades in history at Pea Ridge, but this explosion had sounded and felt like all those shots rolled into one. No cannon had made that noise! But what had?

Now an eerie silence reigned.

Hunkering down, Potts made his way over. "That was one helluva blast. Hawk, you and Cowen go forward and see what it was. Yankees may have blown the fort to smithereens."

Elijah crawled closer. "Can I go too?"

The sergeant chewed at an unkempt black mustache. "I suppose so, but don't get your fool head blown off."

Levi, Elijah, and the scout, Hawk, cautiously edged forward, rifles ready, crouching, running, crouching again, peering carefully through the brush and trees. Up ahead the noise of battle reverberated along the river. But this was normal rifle and cannon fire, nothing like the earlier blast. At the next ridge, Hawk motioned them to wait while he went first. He halted at the brow of a hill and studied the land ahead. Then he quickly scooted back down for a whispered confab with Levi.

"Best I can tell, shelling is coming from gunboats on the river and return fire from the fort." His breath came in quick pants. "Woods ahead are crawling with men."

"Gray or blue?" asked Levi.

"Can't tell yet, just heard rifles barkin'."

"Well, let's go and find out," said Levi, inching forward with Elijah right on his heels.

They skirted the next rise and hugged the riverbank, shielded in thick brush as they drew near the fight. When they disturbed a pool of stagnant water, mosquitoes rose like mists. As Elijah inched forward, he swatted them from his neck.

Rounding the next bend, they halted, mouths agape. Black smoke hovered the bloody river. The water was strewn with mangled, dead bodies which floated amid burning debris. Some of the blue-coated wounded lay just a few yards ahead, moaning on the muddy bank, slick with blood. Elijah fought hot bile rising. He thought he was becoming hardened to carnage. He did not want to vomit and shame himself. But a quick glance showed a grim Levi. Even stoic Hawk looked stunned.

Elijah wanted to put his fingers in his ears to drown the cries and curses of the suffering. Instead, on his stomach behind a moss-covered log, he held his rifle ready. A frightened buck bolted past, its white tail tucked low as it ran, going less than a foot from the log, but Elijah knew the deer had not even seen him.

Hawk signaled them to wait as he crawled ahead. Downriver a half-dozen gunboats continued lobbing shells toward the bluff. It seemed forever before, wet with sweat and panting, he returned, craw-fishing backwards, keeping his rifle trained ahead.

"Yankees swarming everywhere," he whispered. "Seems one of our shells exploded the boiler on that Yankee gunboat yonder. It's blown to smithereens. Men from the other boats"—he nodded toward the river— "are trying to take the fort."

Levi half-stood. "We best go tell Potts and the Cap'n."

Elijah warily inched backwards and then crawled along behind. When they had traveled beyond the river's bend, they rose and ran, staying low and watchful.

After hearing the news, Potts chewed his mustache. "Gents, let's go tell the captain we want to kill some Yankees," he said.

Soon they slipped through the woods. On top of a rise, they hunkered and held, waiting for the colonel's signal. In the trees below were blue-coated figures carrying rifles. Mouth dry and heart pounding, Elijah waited behind a thick tree. Also shielded by a tree, Colonel Stedman dropped to his knee and aimed, but he held his fire. Elijah risked a peek. The wave of blue coming through the woods had them greatly outnumbered. Emblazoned on their flag was the word Indiana.

Elijah went cold. *Indiana!* Grandpa Loring, Uncle Jim, James—the names churned through his mind like a paddlewheel on the river.

With a cautious, upraised hand, Stedman urged restraint. No one fired. Hawk soon slinked up, returning from reconnoiter.

"They took the fort."

Stedman nodded. "There's nothing we can do. We're too outnumbered."

Potts sidled over. Elijah and Levi wasted no time in following as he signaled retreat. Slowly, the wary group headed back the direction they had come.

It was days before they learned what had actually happened along the banks of the White River. A cannonball had exploded the boiler on the *Mound City,* scalding to death one hundred fifty men and maiming and wounding more. No one in the regiment had ever heard of a single shot killing so many. Yet it was no Confederate victory. Now both the fort and the river were in Union hands.

Elijah had heard a rumor that his own regiment would soon return to Little Rock. Unpaid, ill clad, and many unarmed, the Confederate Army was, Elijah thought, a pitiful mess. He was unsure about the Confederacy back east, but he wondered how long the war could go on this side of the Mississippi.

Chapter 14

Elijah rose on one elbow. Something had disturbed his light doze. He did not sleep deeply these days, so he was alert to any noise. Nothing unusual stirred. There was just the sound of a slumbering army camp and the night sounds of summer—crickets and night peepers and an occasional scurrying in the brush. The army had been without the luxury of tents for ages. Stars twinkled overhead, bright dots in the vast darkness. He wondered how far away heaven was. He wondered what God thought when he looked down and saw the mess things were in. If he were God he would put a stop to it. No, on second thought, if he were God he would be doing exactly what God was doing for then he would be God....

Elijah did not understand the suffering. But Preacher Simon said man was as bent on evil as the sparks fly upward. Perhaps they were all getting what they deserved. Himself included. He had flown into a rage the day before and almost beaten Newt Fetters to a pulp just for stealing his blanket. Newt had been drinking. Elijah should not have hit him so hard. And yet one thin blanket was all he had to sleep on. Newt should not have stolen it. Elijah hated a thief. With that thought—and the hope he had not blasphemed—he closed his eyes. He rolled onto his side and tried returning to sleep. With a sigh he gave up and rolled to his back, realizing that it no longer hurt. But he knew the welted scars would never go away.

When the detachment was ordered back to Little Rock, Elijah's heart quickened. It would be good to see Pa. And it would be good to sleep in a bed for a change. He occasionally whistled as he walked. Then it began to rain, a slow, steady downpour. In no time he was wet to the skin. His whistling ceased.

After days of slogging through mud, they arrived footsore and hungry. There were no cheering throngs to greet them, just weary, dispirited people. The wounded still filled the city, where disease had taken as great a toll as saber, gun, and cannon. These hollow-cheeked, sallow-faced men watched from doorways as the army passed. A few called greetings, but most watched pokerfaced with disinterested eyes. Every woman Elijah passed looked old.

General Curtis had come within forty miles of the town. The Rebel Army kept him at bay but did not drive him back. Finally, too far from his supply base, he had withdrawn and turned east. Now his troops were entrenched at Helena, where they had thrown up earthworks around the small but strategically important Mississippi River town. Curtis had proven his ability as a general. His men had marched over 700 miles deep into enemy territory and managed to live off the land. He had achieved all of his objectives—except the capture of Little Rock.

The town was still on tenterhooks. It was only a matter of time, people thought, before there would be an assault on their city. For an entirely different reason Elijah was anxious. He wanted to see Pa again, but he felt as nervous as a treed coon. On the march he had wondered again and again what to say to Sarah. Now he took a bath and scrubbed his worn clothes. He smoothed the thick, ragged beard and studied his face in a chipped mirror. The beard made him look older. He decided to keep it, but he would trim it nice and even.

As he crossed the shady street and went up Miss Lucy's rock walk, he still had no idea what to say to Sarah. No denying Sarah was pretty and sweet—but he had Cindy waiting at home. At least he hoped he did!

Sarah was gone.

A neighbor said that during the Federal advance the family had migrated to Texas. Elijah was both relieved and disappointed.

He supposed Sarah was right. More than likely, she would never see him again.

Ned was also gone. The neighbor knew no details, just that Ned had been ordered elsewhere. Elijah was at least comforted to know Pa was able to march. He headed back to town and went in search of Phillip.

"I suppose I should be grateful," said Phillip, with a wry grin after hugging Elijah and slapping his back, "that the governor has forgotten me. Jail beats hanging." Then he looked Elijah up and down. "Your mother won't know you. You're taller than your pa. You get that height from your ma's side. Her pa was a tall, wiry man like you. But at that, you don't look as beanpole thin as most of Hindman's men I see out yon window." He nodded toward the dab of glass that substituted for a window.

Elijah glanced down. He was lean from the constant marching. However, his arms were sinewy, and his shoulders strained at the shirt Sarah had given him.

"Part of the time we did eat good on this round." His face sobered. "But where we've been, they won't be eating too good."

"I take it things are pretty bad along the White River?"

Elijah nodded.

"What got hold of you?" Phillip asked, taking Elijah's chin in his hand to study the large, red welts on his forehead.

"Skeeters. And don't look too close or you might see something crawling, too. This army is low on men and ammunition but we've got plenty of gray-backs and ticks and chiggers to go around."

Phillip laughed. His own white shirt was no longer starched and ironed with the empty sleeve neatly penned at the shoulder. He was thinner than ever and his gray eyes were tired. There was no recent news from home. The telegraph lines were down and the mail uncertain.

He listened intently to Elijah's news. Upon hearing of Hindman's latest tactics, his eyes narrowed. "I'll swear, Pike is right!" he bit out.

Elijah's ears perked up. "Pike—the fellow commanding the Indians at Pea Ridge?"

Phillip nodded. "Albert has his faults, but that scalping incident was not to his liking. I've known him for years. He was a good lawyer before the war. But now he's under arrest too."

"Because of the scalping?" guessed Elijah.

"No. His crime was with a pen, not a knife." At Elijah's perplexed look, he added, "Albert detests Hindman's policies, especially the provost marshal system. He attacked Hindman in print with a vengeance. And Hindman is no man to anger."

"Don't I know it!" Elijah thought of all the men he had seen shot for deserting.

Phillip went on, "His provost marshals act like God, telling people if they can come or go and dolling out passes...or not, as the mood suits them. Speaking of coming and going, do you know where they'll send you next?"

Elijah shook his head. "No idea. I don't even know where they sent Pa."

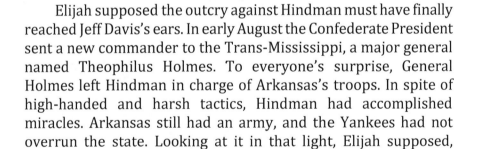

Elijah supposed the outcry against Hindman must have finally reached Jeff Davis's ears. In early August the Confederate President sent a new commander to the Trans-Mississippi, a major general named Theophilus Holmes. To everyone's surprise, General Holmes left Hindman in charge of Arkansas's troops. In spite of high-handed and harsh tactics, Hindman had accomplished miracles. Arkansas still had an army, and the Yankees had not overrun the state. Looking at it in that light, Elijah supposed, Hindman was a good general.

Two months later Elijah and Levi, along with much of the First Corps of the Army of the Trans-Mississippi, boarded steamboats headed for Fort Smith. It was good to at least be headed in the direction of home. As the boats steamed along the calm waters of the Arkansas River, Elijah watched as bored soldiers played cards on deck. He had never played the game and knew better than to attempt it, especially when he saw both coins and tobacco quickly pile up in front of Sergeant Potts. Elijah did, however, join in the entertainment when a boxing match began. He watched spellbound as a wiry, bandy-legged sergeant, not more than five feet tall, bested men who were much larger and younger. Colonel Stedman stood on deck wearing a sour look, but he did not interfere with the sport.

"Hit's the feet," Levi pointed out. "See how he dances around? He moves in and out like a weavin' shuttle while that big feller just wades right in and goes to slugging. Dixon there wears 'em out by dancing and ducking, and the other feller don't never lay a fist on him." With an elbow, Levi nudged Elijah. "Give him a go. I seen you whip Fetters. Yo're quick as a cat."

Elijah frowned. Newt was drunk, so it had not been a fair match. Still and all, Elijah was intrigued. No one else was imitating Dixon's style. Elijah had watched closely. He thought he could do it. He flexed his shoulder. It was not even sore anymore.

Impulsively, he stepped forward. "I think I'll give it a try," he said. When Dixon danced up, Elijah began to bob and weave.

Dixon wiped sweat from his forehead, "I see you're playing me own game." It was minutes before his fist finally connected. Good naturedly, Dixon grinned as he landed a blow to Elijah's chin, snapping his head back.

Elijah managed to land a few quick but ineffective blows. Before long, the older man had him reeling. The match ended with Dixon's friendly arm around his shoulder.

"You have good reflexes. I think in a few lessons I could make a fighter out of you."

Elijah grinned through a split lip. "If I lived through 'em," he said.

"If you want, I'll teach you what I know."

So began Elijah's lessons. As promised, Dixon spent hours showing him how to use feet and fists to better advantage. When Dixon's company disembarked at the Post of Dardanelle, Elijah hated to see him go.

"With a few more lessons, I'd whip you," jested Elijah, while shaking the small but powerful hand.

"Why do you think I'm getting off the boat?" Dixon laughed and stepped down the gangplank.

"Thanks for the lessons," Elijah called. "If this war ever gets over, come see me. I live northwest of here over in Johnson County on Little Piney Creek."

Dixon looked back over his shoulder. "I'll do it." With a wave and a smile he called, "Keep that left up."

In the mild October sun, Elijah stood on deck and watched the swift waters of the Arkansas roiling past. A rare thing in Arkansas, the sky was bright blue and completely cloudless. He imagined it was like the Texas skies that Uncle Phillip missed. On just such a day he had once taken Belle and gone hunting.

Along the banks goldenrod grew, the tall, straight spikes heavy with bright blossom. Sumacs blazed with upright candles of crimsoned seedpods and leaves of ruby red. Tall oaks were russet brown and hickories were dazzling gold. A buckeye bush loaded with fruit grew near the water, each nut still inside the belly of a tear-shaped pod. Elijah thought of George and his lucky buckeye.

He gazed north. From here he could see neither the mountains nor a hint of Little Piney, but they were there, just a short ways off. He figured it was a good thing the boat passed Spadra without docking. He would have been more than tempted to desert—firing squad or no.

———⌁———

Fort Smith was a buzzing beehive. Hindman had combed the state to amass a sizable army—over 20,000 by some reports—of conscripted men along with regulars and volunteers. Most of that army was now at the fort. It was a poorly equipped group. Supplies were low and morale even lower. Elijah was astonished at the emaciated state of the livestock. Horses and mules had bones that stuck out like the ribs on Ma's washboard, and many of the men looked just as honed. It was obvious they had not been pillaging in prosperous territory. The camp was rife with rumors of soon being sent to aid the colossal struggle at Vicksburg. Elijah did not think these rickety wagons could make it over a mountain, much less across a state.

He searched for Ned. Uneasiness grew in him. There was no sign of Pa and no one even remembered him.

On Saturday Elijah visited the town. After a short walk down the main street, he almost expected fire and brimstone to rain down. It fit Granny's description of Sodom and Gomorra, a place filled with sin and vice—grog shops, gambling dens, and trollops, women so brazen he had to pull away when they grabbed his arm. One was a hard-eyed blonde, a woman young in years but haggard of face. He had just disentangled his arm from her grip when someone yelled his name.

"Lige! Hey! Elijah Loring!"

He looked across the busy, dusty street to see Michael Lane striding toward him, a heavier, older version but Michael, nonetheless. Elijah rushed forward to pound his back and then grab him in a bear hug.

"I hardly knowed you!" said Michael, wearing a huge grin. "You're a tall, skinny drink of water now, ain't ya?"

"Well, look at you—big as a Texas mule. I'd say you've put on about thirty pounds." They clasped hands and then hugged. "Pa and I feared you got killed at Pea Ridge. I looked for you everywhere."

"Come through without a scratch," Michael said. "Then yer pa—he's all right?" he asked quickly, his eyes joyful.

"He was wounded at Pea Ridge and pretty bad off for a while. He spent weeks at Little Rock getting over it. I stayed with him until I got new orders to head for the White River."

"Fighting Curtis," guessed Michael.

Elijah nodded. "The last I heard Pa was fine. They sent him somewhere else while I was away. I've looked all over for him here, but no one knows him."

"When did you end up in the army?" Michael asked.

Elijah chuckled. "We have a lot to catch up on!"

Michael beamed. "I'm glad I spotted you. We just rode in from Ozark. Let's go to that cafe and get a bite to eat." As they walked, Michael related how since Pea Ridge he had been serving in Marmaduke's cavalry. "I like riding a heap better than marching," he said with a grin. "Reckon that's why I ain't skin and bones no more."

"I know what you mean," Elijah agreed. "I must have tramped a thousand miles the last few months."

The fare was disappointing, undercooked beans still hard in the center and stringy fried meat. Elijah suspected either horse or mule.

They did, however, enjoy their visit. After going back to camp, they talked late into the night. When Elijah finally went to bed, he stared at the tent roof. He felt more homesick than he had in months. He supposed that accounted for why he thought he saw Uncle Jim today. While leaving the cafe he had gotten just a glimpse of the fellow, but he had sat a horse just like Jim. Elijah rolled over and pulled up the blanket. The nights were growing cold. He hoped there would soon be a letter from Ma. He had written soon after arriving in Fort Smith, but he had not heard from her in months.

Early in November Hindman learned of an advancing Federal division led by General James Blunt. Blunt was leading his men south down the Military Road, the border between Arkansas and the Indian Territory. Now, only miles away, Hindman saw them as a plum ripe for picking.

His strategy required splitting his own troops. Marmaduke's cavalry of two thousand would be a frontal diversion to screen Hindman's own advance with the main force. The unsuspecting Federals would be overwhelmed, and the door to retake Missouri—Hindman's personal passion—would be open once again.

Before Michael mounted the bony, black mare, Elijah gripped his shoulder. "You take care," he said. "I'll see you in a few days."

Michael nodded. He swung up and kicked the mare's flanks and looked back to wave, his cap pulled down over his dark hair and the canteen bouncing on his saddle.

Elijah had a sinking feeling.

Days later, on a loaded ferry, Elijah stood alongside Levi and stared at the swirling waters of the Arkansas. He was worried. Reports from the front were disheartening. Hawk had returned from the Boston Mountains to report Marmaduke's men were greatly outnumbered. Blunt had stormed forward with five thousand men and thirty cannons. The unequal forces had collided at Cane Hill and a nine-hour running fight had ensued. But Hindman, or so Hawk said, was delighted. Blunt was only thirty miles away, almost a hundred miles from possible aid from Springfield, and therefore more vulnerable than ever. And Marmaduke had lost few men. His cavalry now waited at Dripping Springs, ready to join again in the fight when Hindman arrived with the army.

On the cold, clear December morning, Elijah and Levi stepped from the ferry at Van Buren to join eleven thousand men and twenty-two cannons of the First Corps of the Army of the Trans-Mississippi in a long, ragged wave heading north. Elijah did not especially fear the coming battle, but it was a poor plan. Each man had only enough ammunition for a single day of fighting. When he eyed the skinny draft animals and the rickety wagons in a train loaded with only a few days' rations, he shook his head. It seemed foolhardy...

And it was, for General Blunt, alerted by his spies, had already rushed a telegraph to Springfield. In hours an entire force was hastening from Missouri to Blunt's relief.

Elijah cocked his head. Yes, that was artillery he heard. "Marmaduke must still be keeping Blunt busy at Cane Hill," he said.

"Yep. I reckon we're gonna slip around and flank him," said Levi.

Elijah was worried. On the march many of the men had dropped out from sickness and fatigue. He hoped there was enough left to whip Blunt.

Hawk arrived and dismounted. He dropped onto the ground to rest. "We fixing to advance?" asked Levi.

"Could be, but not exactly like the general planned." Hawk groaned and leaned back to rest against a tree. "Two more Federal divisions just arrived at Fayetteville. They're a worn out bunch, but I reckon they still have some fight left in them—even though they did march more than a hundred miles in three days."

"Why, that ain't possible!" avowed Levi.

Hawk replied, "Well, they did. I saw them before I hightailed it back here to tell the general. They're heading this way right now. At least the one's that can still march are. They're so tired; they're dropping like ripe fruit." He cast a worried look toward the firing at Cane Hill.

"If Hindman plans to fight 'em all, I'm afeard his eyes is bigger than his stomach," grumbled Levi. "We ain't got enough ammunition to fight one army, let alone two. He ain't kerful, hit'll be us gets whipped."

Elijah's eyes shadowed. It was true. They might soon be going at Goliath with nothing but slingshots and stones. He hoped God owed Hindman a favor.

Hawk was grim. "One thing sure, we can't risk an attack on Blunt now. It would expose our back to Herron—he's the Yankee officer heading this way."

"Hindman has bit off more than we kin all chew," growled Levi.

Elijah shook his head in disbelief. Levi was right. This time Hindman had surely bitten off too much! When the order came to move out, Levi rose with a groan and Elijah stood wearily to his feet. He ducked his neck deeper inside his jacket, thankful the December weather, although chilly, was mild today. He recalled the march last winter to Pea Ridge and shivered.

On the double-quick they hurried to join Marmaduke's main body. They would advance on Herron while a smaller force of men would, hopefully, keep Blunt's division occupied at Cane Hill.

Midmorning they arrived where Marmaduke's main force waited. His cavalry had skirmished with the vanguard of Herron's men ten miles west of Fayetteville and fallen back to a hill where a small church stood. Elijah squinted to read the name, *Prairie Grove*

Presbyterian Church. He hoped it was a good omen. He reckoned Presbyterians were all right, but Granny was a Baptist. He would feel better if it were a Baptist Church.

He hoped they would rest a bit before going on. He was dog-tired and hungry. He gratefully took the small piece of dried jerky Levi offered. Tearing off a bite, he caught a glimpse of General Hindman drooping in his saddle.

"Doggone," said Levi, "if the general don't look about as used up as I am."

Just then a scout rode up, saluted, and gave a report. Hindman threw up his head and looked west. Then his shoulders drooped even more. Elijah had a sinking feeling it was more bad news!

———∽———

Herron ordered his twenty-four rifled cannons and his thirty-five hundred men to commence firing on the hill where Elijah and the First Corp of the Trans-Mississippi waited. They were engulfed in shot and smoke and the roar of battle. Elijah crouched near Levi. He fired. A blue-coated man pitched backwards. Elijah used his teeth to rip open the paper cartridge. He poured and then rammed in the load and fired again. Shot spatted all around. The blue sky seemed to rain cannon balls. In the continual booming, time and again, they were driven back.

He hunkered low and ran behind Levi through shots falling like rain. It was Elijah's habit not to look at the bodies and pieces of bodies strewn on the ground—although if a man called for help, he always tried to stop. Levi had stopped just ahead to lift a wounded man to his feet. Several men had fallen here, ripped apart by cannon fire. Elijah glanced down at a mangled body. It was Dixon sprawled on his back with a grotesque twist to his face. The bottom half of his body had been blown away.

Elijah reached and shut the wide open eyes. He wished there was time to stop and bury the little boxer, but Levi had already moved ahead supporting the wounded man. Elijah ran to catch up.

———∽———

Eventually the Confederate cannons fell silent and the superior firepower of the Federal guns held sway. Elijah hunkered on the cold ground in a little draw at the edge of an orchard. He could imagine it in springtime covered with blossoms. The limbs were naked now and the trees too small to shield from the grapeshot peppering all around. He jerked as a shot thudded the dirt nearby.

"Levi, reckon we should fall back again?"

Before Levi could answer a line of blue coats appeared on the ridge above. Colonel Stedman, waving a braid-covered arm, gave the loud order to charge. They hefted from the ground and rushed forward. On they went, shooting and yelling and pushing back the wave of shocked Federals who had not expected the counterattack. Only a few Yankees were left to run away. The majority had been mown down like ripe hay. Exultant, the Rebels tasted victory. Elijah saw few casualties in their immediate ranks. However, Colonel Stedman took a ball in the leg. He was carried from the field. Elijah noticed his fancy uniform was now a bloody mess.

When Blunt's division arrived to challenge their left, the tide of battle turned. The First Corp was again driven back. Elijah stayed near Sergeant Potts and Levi at the front. They had to keep falling back. Men fell all around. The fight lasted late into the afternoon. Near nightfall Confederate hopes faded.

In the dusk Hawk joined them. "We're licked." With a grimy face, between panting breaths, he told Potts the latest bad news. "Blunt ordered up three thousand fresh troops, his reserves from over at Rhea's Mill."

Potts swore. Elijah knew they had no reserves. There was nothing to do but flee. He hurried along behind Hawk, Potts, and Levi.

More by feel than sight, Elijah helped wrap caisson wheels so they could slip away like thieves in the darkness. He had the distinct feeling he had lived this moment before. It was Pea Ridge all over again—leaving behind hundreds of dead and wounded. How had he managed to live though another long day filled with death and defeat? Remembering Dixon, he goose-fleshed and hoped Michael was all right. Thank God, he and Levi were still whole as they stumbled along through the cold, dark night. But hunger was a gnawing pain in his belly. Except for the small bit of jerky, Elijah had not tasted food in two days.

They traveled through the night. When the Yankee army was far enough behind, the beaten army dropped down to doze a bit and then rose to push on. There was no way of knowing if Blunt would follow.

Elijah grew faint from hunger. By mid-afternoon of the next day, he voiced no opposition when Levi leveled his rifle at a hog. It no doubt belonged to the farmer in the cabin they had just passed, but if they did not eat soon they would drop. The razorback fell where he stood.

"I'll skin and gut him. You get a fire goin' over there." Levi pointed to the scraggly timber near the edge of the field.

Elijah piled dead sticks together and then put flint to powder. The spark caught and a tiny curl of smoke rose. The sticks began to burn. He was on his knees blowing the tiny blaze to life when a group of horsemen rode up.

He jumped to his feet and saluted. Levi stood from kneeling beside the dead hog, and moving the bloody knife to his left hand, gave a cursory salute. It was Hindman, himself. And his staff. Before leaving Van Buren, the general had ordered no depredations. Elijah figured he and Levi were in big trouble. He eyed the naked, skinny hog and wished they had at least eaten before getting caught.

Hindman looked at the hog. Then he looked at them.

"Boys, is it fat?"

Levi squinted up at the general. "Fat enough."

Hindman grinned and rode away.

Elijah—along with about ten more men—watched with hungry eyes as the meat dripped into the fire. He licked parched lips. The fat sizzled. Had anything ever smelled so good? As more men approached, Levi sent them on their way.

"This hog's spoke fer. There's more in them woods yonder. Go help yerselves."

The roasted pork was devoured before it had barely cooked. Even without salt, they wolfed it down. Soon nothing remained but the bones. Elijah was still hungry, but it had stopped the gnawing in his gut.

Chapter 15 ⎯⎯⎯∽⎯⎯

Elijah heard the rumor: seven hundred fifty killed and wounded, nine pieces of artillery and over three hundred prisoners lost to the enemy. But Michael Lane was fine. Elijah had spoken with him when Marmaduke's cavalry galloped past.

The weary, hard-faced men finally arrived at Van Buren. On the barge, while crossing the river, Elijah and Levi were ordered to stand guard over some of the Federal prisoners.

"What do you think will happen to us?" asked a nervous, young private with a squeaky voice. He had pale, pockmarked skin and hardly any chin.

"I reckon they'll treat you all right." Elijah did not relate the prisoner mistreatment he had seen. Besides, it was not always the case. It depended on who was in charge.

Levi snorted. "Iffen they treat you as good as they treat us, you'll soon be skin and bones." Everyone in earshot laughed.

It is true, thought Elijah. They were a sorry looking lot. He had lost weight until his pants barely stayed on his slender hips.

⎯⎯⎯∽⎯⎯

Sergeant Potts lined them up straight in the chill morning sun. "Look lively, men. We've orders to get gussied up for a full dress review. General Holmes is coming from Little Rock."

"Dress review!" snorted Levi. "Granny Holmes will get his eyes full, all right," he muttered. "But hit won't be no pretty sight. These rags is our best."

Elijah looked down at his ragged clothes and agreed. How could they have a dress review in these tatters?

In spite of the lack of uniforms—with glittering bayonets, regimental flags, and hundreds marching on Massard Prairie in perfect time to fife and drum—the drill was impressive. Elijah stood at attention on the field as General Holmes galloped a fine horse through the ranks. The general might be nicknamed Granny, but Elijah thought he sat a horse every bit as good as Allen Matthers.

As Marmaduke's Cavalry passed in review, Elijah understood Michael's pride of General Marmaduke. He was handsome and young—less than thirty years old, Elijah guessed. With the general's long, thick hair blowing in the breeze, Elijah doubted King David's son, the thick-haired warrior Absalom, had looked much better.

Just then he spied Michael on a glossy bay. It was a fine looking horse compared to the bony mare he had ridden before. The flags, the fife and drum, the drill, and the galloping horses—Elijah was reminded of muster day in Clarksville. It seemed years ago. How the victory bragged of that day had vanished!

An army camp was the last place Elijah wanted to spend Christmas. It was his first away from home. All day he fought melancholy. The bran-filled cornbread and tasteless, stringy beef (if it was beef) was a far cry from Ma's Christmas dinner. What he wouldn't give for a slice of dried apple pie! He was worried. There had been no letters from Ma. He had written again after the battle to let her know he was fine. Of course, Uncle Caleb rarely went to town in the winter. That was more than likely why Ma had not written, he told himself, and yet worry still niggled.

Midmorning he hunted up Michael. Since it was the first anniversary of Maggie's death, Michael was morose. They visited a while but Michael seemed drawn inside himself. Elijah gave up and returned to his tent and took a nap. He dreamed of fried ham and hot buttered biscuits soaked with dark sweet molasses and tall glasses of cold, creamy milk.

The next week a train of wagons brought supplies. It was hailed with delight; however, spirits fell when the load proved to be only corn for the livestock.

"Don't reckon they think we need any better eats than moldy beef and half-bran cornmeal," Elijah grumbled as he helped unload the shelled corn. Lately he could barely choke down the poor fare.

Levi leaned on his shovel. "If these animals die, we'll be in a pickle."

"I reckon so, but it looks like they could have sent a few wagons of food. When I get home, I'm gonna eat a whole apple pie all by my—" He stopped short as a group of men with hammers and nails went to work nearby. "What are they up to?"

Levi glanced over. "Building a gallows. Hawk caught a spy giving information to Curtis."

Elijah remembered his part in the execution of Gorman, the deserter. "I wonder which is worse...getting hung or getting shot. My Uncle Caleb saw a man hung. He said it was the worst sight he ever saw."

Levi grew still. "He's right."

Elijah chewed his lip. Whom had Levi seen hung? Or had he hung someone himself?

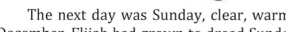

The next day was Sunday, clear, warm, and bright for late December. Elijah had grown to dread Sundays. Unless there was necessary work to be done, they lolled about camp, resting. It made the day drag. This Sunday was no exception. While Levi napped in the tent, Elijah played cards with Michael and then, restless, he walked near the river under bare trees through silvery-gray grass that hung dead and limp over the steep banks. Everything was quiet. Even the river made little noise. The water was low. In places a horse would have no trouble crossing. He could see docked steamboats in the distance. They would be going nowhere until it rained. He realized with disappointment, neither would supply boats be heading this way.

Finally he returned to camp. He strolled among the tents and occasionally stopped to hear singing or banjo or French harp music. He hurried past a fiddler. Fiddle music made him woebegone. What wouldn't he give for the sight of Uncle Caleb's bald head tucked over his old brown fiddle!

At the far edge of camp, near Hindman's headquarters, the regimental band was practicing. Elijah ambled that way. He passed the new gallows and felt a shiver trace his spine. It would be an awful thing to be in the guardhouse knowing that a noose waited. At least today the poor fellow was hearing music rather than ominous hammers pounding out his fate.

Elijah drew near the band to listen. It was a fast-paced catchy tune. As his foot tapped, his own spirits lifted. Wouldn't it be grand to whirl Cindy to such a tune! He could picture her now in the pretty white dress with her long hair flying as she sashayed and whirled at the party. In his mind's eye it was his hand rather than Dillon's that circled her tiny waist.

He looked toward the road. Someone was riding fast. It was Hawk. He raced past.

"Hey, Hawk," Elijah called. But Hawk did not slow until he pulled the lathered horse to a stop at Hindman's headquarters. Then he jumped down and rushed inside. It was only seconds before officers scurried from the building. The music abruptly ceased. Men began to run.

Federal cavalry was on the way to Van Buren!

Abruptly the word spread—Hindman was ordering retreat. Elijah headed for camp, but when he saw Levi and Sergeant Potts, he hurried to join them. They stood near the gallows alongside a tall, chisel-faced colonel whom Elijah did not know. A new yellow rope now dangled from the gallows. Elijah supposed the Union advance would not help the spy. He would hang before they arrived.

Elijah wormed his way through the frenzied crowd.

Levi looked up. "Why don't you go on and break camp, Elijah. I'll be there directly."

Before he had finished speaking, two guards led a prisoner forward. Elijah froze. His mouth fell open. The lean man mounting the steps with legs shackled and hands tied behind was Uncle Jim!

Elijah ran forward. "Wait!" he cried.

Jim turned. Then he grimaced and his jaw worked.

Elijah ignored the quick shake of Jim's head. He did not intend standing silent while his own uncle was hung.

"Colonel," he burst out, "you're making a big mistake. He's no spy!"

The colonel turned. "You know this man?"

"Yes, sir. He's my uncle."

"I'm very sorry to hear that. But there's no mistake. One of our informants in the Federal camp overheard him passing information to General Blunt."

Elijah's heart dropped.

"Go on, Lige." Jim shook his head again. "There's nothing you can do for me."

"Yes, there is." Elijah stood firm. "I can be here. You won't die alone—without family."

In appreciation Jim tipped his head. Then, in spite of the noose dangling near, he jested, "Lige, hit appears you've been eating plenty of bear meat."

Unconsciously, Elijah touched his short, thick beard. He recalled the incident as if it were yesterday. He was seven. Uncle Jim had just shot a big bear tearing into Granny's bee gum. Jim, with eyes twinkling, told Elijah he would grow whiskers if he ate enough bear meat.

The colonel nodded and Potts slipped the noose over Jim's head. There was no blindfold, no last words, no mercy. As the trap door dropped, Levi gripped Elijah's shoulder. Elijah's own breath cut off when Jim fell with a thud. Jim's face purpled. His neck had not snapped. It would be a long, agonizing choking.

Elijah clenched his fists. There was nothing he could do. The kicking, the choking, the jerking! He stood stoic and watched it happen. Images flashed: Uncle Jim giving him piggyback rides, Uncle Jim foot racing with Pa, Uncle Jim dropping the bear with one shot and then skinning it while it dangled from the hickory in Granny's back yard. But the bear had hung limp and still, not doing a Saint Vitus dance like Jim with his tongue lolled out and slobber dripping from his chin. *If only the gagging and jerking would stop!*

Elijah thought he had seen enough death, enough suffering, to never again be affected with this hot, sweating nausea. It was as if the rope kept choking his own neck—cutting off his own gasping breaths. He closed his eyes.

Finally it was over. Jim dangled limp and still.

Sympathetic, the colonel looked at Elijah. "Soldier, we'll bury him before we go."

Elijah nodded and turned away. He thought of Aunt Opal and Ruby and all the cousins. He glanced across the river. Was James with these Federal troops? Was that why Uncle Jim had spied? Or had he been spying all along as Bo Morrison had accused? Elijah's brows shot up. He groaned. Was Uncle Phillip also a spy? Would they hang him too?

Levi's voice was husky, "We best get our gear loaded."

Elijah followed him toward the tent. He longed to be alone. But there was no solitude. Panicky men milled like frightened sheep, their anxious eyes darting toward Van Buren. Elijah stopped to watch a plume of black smoke rise over the trees along the river where the steamers *Eva* and *Arkansas* were docked above Van Buren.

"Yankees are burning our boats," he muttered.

"Naw," said Levi as he tossed a tent pole into the wagon. "Burning 'em ourselves—to keep the Yankees from getting 'em. And we got orders to burn all that feed corn, all three hundred bushels of it. No time to haul it." He sadly shook his head. "Damn shame, too, with us needing it so bad." He looked toward the town. "And I reckon those poor pilgrims will be hungry soon."

Elijah weaved through the melee. Frenzied men tossed tents, blankets, pots, and pans topsy-turvy into wagons. Weak mules hitched to wobbly wagons jumbled high with supplies could not run even though teamsters poured on whips. Instead, they jerked along at a ragged trot.

With anxious looks over shoulders, the infantry fled down the river. Elijah and Levi shouldered muskets and joined them just as cannons began to boom near the river. Smoke rose over the trees and drifted on the wind as Confederate guns rained defiant shells on Van Buren. Soon a thunder of shots answered. The enemy was returning fire.

Sooner or later Elijah halfway expected to perish in this awful war. Just now he felt numb to fear. He hurried only because Levi urged him on. Granny said there was no suffering in heaven—no hunger, no thirst, no death, and no tears. Perhaps Uncle Jim was lucky....

The hurried march downriver was nothing new. It seemed to Elijah as if the Rebel Army, at least in Arkansas, had mastered the art of fleeing. First at Fayetteville, then Pea Ridge and Prairie Grove, and now Fort Smith. They were always just one jump ahead of the Yankees. But he knew—as worn and tattered as they were—someday soon one jump would not be enough.

All afternoon they cast worried looks back, expecting any second to be overtaken. Eventually, however, even the sound of cannons died. Daylight faded with no sign of the enemy. Cold crept in as the moon rose, a luminous full orb in the cloudless sky. Elijah could plainly see feathery pines and leafless hardwoods and far-off shadowy hills and the river threading like a silver ribbon alongside the road. He plodded around deserted, broken-down wagons and around tired men, who with the anxiety of capture passed had dropped exhausted.

Officers allowed fires built and soon the cooks weaved through the men, passing out food. Elijah started to gulp his down. The stringy, sticky meat was so awful that he gagged. Even his ravenous belly would not tolerate such rotten fare. He did, however, wolf down the sorry mess of half-baked dough—cornmeal and water without salt. It barely stopped the gnawing in his middle. He felt as hungry as ever. He lay down and rolled into a knot and closed his eyes. But dread for poor Opal and Ruby and all the children robbed him of his rest. He sat up and stared at the fire. Hours later he still sat with his back to a tree when Levi nudged him.

"Get up! Enemy cavalry comin' fast!"

Elijah stumbled forward, brushing sleep from his eyes. Men formed a line and stared into the night. In bright moonlight the regimental flag fluttered alongside the Stars and Bars. For hours Hindman's army waited on tenterhooks. But no Yankee cavalry galloped into camp. It was a false alarm. Vigilance relaxed and with the sunrise came a general dispelling of gloom. Even Elijah felt less despondent as they set out again along the south edge of the river. If the army survived and moved on toward Little Rock, they would be in Clarksville in a day or two.

Potts drew abreast. He cut a look sideways at Levi and Elijah. "I thought you fellows would appreciate knowing that this army isn't running away." He rubbed the end of his nose with the back of a finger. "I just got it straight from our new colonel—Hindman had already been ordered to Little Rock. The Federals just hurried the move along a bit." Potts chuckled as Levi snorted.

"Yeah, well, I heared we're heading for Vicksburg, and Hawk says Arkansas Post. I ain't sure Hindman knows hisself!"

It was immaterial to Elijah. He had made up his mind, and with the decision came a great sense of relief.

Hours later he stood in the pouring rain along with thousands of wet, miserable men. He chewed on hard, dry kernels of parched corn while looking across the churning Arkansas at the Spadra bluffs. While ferries and steamboats carted load after load of troops across the rising water, he hunkered in the downpour and waited impatiently. He was almost home on this first day of 1863. A shiver of excitement traced his spine. It seemed ages since the day he had ridden from Granny's yard. What would he find now? What had happened at home? If Pa were alive, Ma surely would have gotten a letter by now.

Finally Elijah and Levi were ferried across the river and began setting up camp at Spadra. When the tent was up, Elijah sat on his knapsack near the campfire.

"Levi, my home is right over yonder, across the mountains."

Levi looked up expectantly.

"And I'm heading there just as soon as we march through town."

"Right smart decision, I'd say," said Levi.

On impulse Elijah said, "Come with me. You've fought enough for this army. You know it doesn't have a chance. The Yankees have already won."

Levi looked into the fire. "You might be right, but we ain't licked yet. And I got nothing better to do." He looked up and raised a droll eyebrow. "I ain't no farmer...but I thank you fer the invite."

Elijah had not really expected him to come. But he would miss Levi. And Levi and Uncle Caleb would have gotten along famously.

Elijah hunted up Michael and made the same suggestion. "Go home with me, Michael. The war is as good as lost."

Michael looked into the campfire. His eyes were dark in the shadows, but Elijah could read pain in his voice. "I don't reckon I'll go back...at least not just yet." He raised his bowed head. "Too many bad memories. But I would appreciate it if you'd look in on the young'uns—see how they're faring at Simon's and tell them I said howdy."

Elijah stood. "I'll do it. Take care of yourself, Michael."

As Michael stood, they shook hands. He was slow to release Elijah's hand. "Go careful, Lige. Hindman still shoots deserters."

Elijah nodded. He walked toward Potts's tent. The sergeant sat before his tent drinking a cup of corn bran coffee. "Sarge," he said, hunkering down. He stretched his hands toward the blaze. After looking around, he dropped his voice. "I'm heading home tomorrow. I don't figure it's deserting. I never signed up. I got conscripted."

Potts' face was unreadable.

Elijah grew defensive. "I fought all the way from Pea Ridge to the White River to Prairie Grove and back. I figure I've done my share. You can send someone to arrest me but I'm going home." He stood.

"Not as if you'd be the first," said Potts. "I figure we've lost a few hundred since we left Fort Smith." Then Potts chuckled. "Besides, I doubt I could find a willing soul to go after you—everyone's seen how you handle a knife." He stood and shook Elijah's hand. "Let's say you're just going on a bit of a leave. I'll be looking the other way tomorrow. Take care of yourself."

"You too, sir." Elijah turned to go and then looked back. "You're a good sergeant."

Potts smiled. "And you're a good soldier—a mighty good soldier. I hope you'll come back soon."

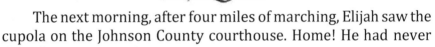

The next morning, after four miles of marching, Elijah saw the cupola on the Johnson County courthouse. Home! He had never thought to see it again.

The troops formed in regular order for a march through town. It seemed General Hindman intended an impressive show. Fifes and drums began the rollicking new tune *The Homespun Dress.* Elijah envisioned Cindy in her homespun dress. He gave a silent but hearty amen to the words "three cheers for the homespun dress that Southern ladies wear."

Old men, women, and children lined Main Street. Elijah's eyes swept the crowd. There were scores of tearful ladies waving white handkerchiefs, but no Nelda. Of course, considering her Union sentiments, he was not surprised. But he had hoped to see her sunny face. He wondered if Uncle Phillip was still in jail.

A soldier was tacking a notice on the front of Phillip's office where the broken windows had been boarded up. Elijah had heard in camp that Hindman was issuing written orders for the citizens of Clarksville to act as pickets. Perhaps the general still feared an enemy advance.

Just then, all up and down the line, the troops began the hair-raising Rebel yell. With a dart of sadness, Elijah thought of George; no one could do it like him.

As they smartly marched down Main, the covered bridge loomed ahead. Sergeant Potts whistled. "Would you look at that bridge! Must be a hundred fifty feet long!"

Levi looked ahead with a grin. "Yep, we've done come to the end of the Confederacy—yonder is the spout."

Elijah was not smiling. His mind was set, but as the time drew near, he felt regret. He would not miss the moldy cornmeal or the musty beef or the bitter cold without proper shelter, but he had enjoyed the camaraderie. Most of all he would miss Levi.

He marched across the bridge, his worn boots along with hundreds of others making a hollow, thumping sound. On top of East Hill, he glanced toward the tall, red brick mansion. It seemed a lifetime ago he had seen Bo Morrison's pretty sister standing in the road. He wondered if their pa had died. Elijah's mouth grew hard as he wondered what had happened to Lieutenant Morrison. He must still be off conscripting; at least Elijah had not seen him again.

Now he looked ahead at the long line of ragged men tramping down the muddy road heading toward Little Rock. How many of them would live to go home? When he saw the cut-off leading toward the mountains, he prodded Levi in the back and motioned toward the side of the road. They stepped aside unnoticed into the brush.

"Levi," Elijah said, "You've been like a father to me. I wish you'd come with me. We've got a pretty place on Little Piney—the fishing is mighty good."

"When the war's over I just might drop in and say howdy." Levi's voice was husky.

Elijah looked down at his dusty boots. "I reckon I'll keep this rifle."

"You've earned it."

Elijah gripped Levi's calloused hand. "Levi..."

"Get along with you." The old man cleared his throat and swallowed. As Elijah slipped away, Levi called softly, "Keep that-there knife handy."

Elijah looked back and raised a hand. Yes, he would miss Levi.

He looked north toward the mountains and his heart quickened. He headed through the woods at a slow trot. But before going home, a sad chore awaited.

Opal answered his first rap. He suspected she had been peeking through the curtains. Her face was haggard and suspicious as she stared from the doorway.

"Aunt Opal, don't you know me?"

Her hand flew to her mouth. "Laws a'mercy! Elijah, that ain't you! Why, yo're tall as a tree—and just look at all them brown whiskers."

The remark made him cringe. It brought back the horror of Jim's hanging. "I have something to tell you, Aunt Opal." Like taking a dose of Granny's bitter tonic, he wanted to get this over with quickly.

She grew apprehensive. "Come on inside. From the look of ya, I don't reckon hit's good news."

He followed her inside and nodded to the cousins who were as still and big-eyed as owls. They had all grown considerably, he noticed. Ruby was nowhere in sight.

Opal sat down and drew a deep breath. "Let's have hit."

Elijah fumbled with his pack and looked out the window. How did you tell a woman that her man was dead? How did you tell young'uns they would never see their pa again? His gut twisted and this time not from hunger.

"Hit's Jim, ain't it? I knowed something was wrong. A few nights ago his dog commenced howling and wouldn't quit." Her face contorted into a wrinkled mess. "He's dead, ain't he?"

Elijah dropped his head. "He got hung for spying—but I was with him, Aunt Opal." He looked up. "He didn't die alone."

She nodded. Tears dripped onto the hand over her mouth. When she gave a ragged sob, Pearl rushed over.

"Oh, Ma." She bent and took Opal into her arms.

Elijah stood, heading for the door. Garnet followed.

"Elijah, would you go tell Ruby—and tell her to come on home. Ma needs her."

"Where is she? Living at Doc's?" he guessed.

"Yes, her and the baby."

Elijah had a sour taste in his mouth.

"Tell Harley to bring her right on home. Ma is partial to Ruby, and having the baby around will help." She began to cry.

"I'll tell her," he said, patting Garnet's skinny arm. "And I'll come back in a few days to see if you need anything."

Chapter 16

It was after nightfall when Elijah finally reached the trail fronting the creek. Still a long way from home and dog tired, he rolled into his blanket and slept on the ground without even building a fire. Before sunup he awakened shivering, stiff, and cold. While rolling up the blanket, he bent double from a stomach cramp. Hunger was, he thought, might nigh as bad as Yankee bullets. But he was almost home, almost tasting Ma's hot buttered yeast bread and fried meat and thick pan gravy. His mouth watered and he groaned. As the sun rose behind leaden clouds, he traveled as fast as weak legs would go. Cold penetrated through his thin clothes. The miles seemed to creep. Finally he passed the Matthers place. Everything looked the same. It was the same cluttered mess with the same leaning barn and the same dilapidated cabin with the same sagging porch. Strangely, it almost looked good to him. My! He was glad to be back!

He passed Doc's lane without turning. Ruby's bad news could wait. He would come back after he had seen Ma and Deborah.

He tramped wearily on. His steps quickened when he saw a faint curl of chimney smoke. *Home!* Finally there stood the cabin as solid and welcoming as ever. Until that moment he had not realized how he feared to find it burned. Lately he had seen too many blackened chimneys. He fairly flew across the creek and, without knocking, threw open the door.

"Where is every—" The happy words died in his throat. Becky sat hunched over the table, her thin face a ghost of former beauty. Her dress was unkempt. Although her hair was in the customary knot, strings dangled as though it had been days since the last combing.

She jerked a hand toward a butcher knife lying on the table. Then she froze, her green eyes wide with surprise.

"Elijah," she whispered. "Oh! Elijah, is that really you?" She stood and fell into his arms. "Oh, dear God! It is...it is you!" She embraced him with frantic arms. She pulled back, and then grabbed him again. "I didn't think I would ever see you again!"

"Where's Deborah?" he asked as his eyes swept the bare room.

"Out in the barn milking."

"Pa? Have you heard from Pa?"

Her joy dimmed as her shoulders drooped. "He got captured. Later there was a prisoner exchange but Ned was not with the rest." She dropped sorrowful eyes. "He must be dead. I faced the fact months ago."

Elijah felt numb. *Pa dead?* No. Not Pa. Ma was wrong. Many men were taken prisoner and not released. Pa would come back to them. Elijah was not willing to face any other reality—not yet anyway.

Becky looked up. "But I thought you were dead, too," she cried, "and here you are!" She touched his face and her own face glowed with some of the old radiance.

"Ma." He eased her into a chair. "What's happened? What's going on here?" She was too thin. And as his eyes again traveled the room, he saw empty shelves, bare cupboards, and missing furniture. Gone were the pretty quilts and the pictures, and even the padded rocking chair no longer sat near the fireplace.

"Bushwhackers," she said, "a big band. They struck months ago."

He was dazed. "*They even took the rocking chair?*"

"Loaded it right onto their wagons along with all the blankets and quilts and our clothes—except what was on our backs. They took the mule and the wagon. They took all the meat from the smokehouse and all the food in the house. Deborah and I stayed in the cellar with the door barricaded. I had the shotgun to hold them off, so we managed to keep the food in the cellar."

"Ma," he quickly asked, "what about Brother Simon and his family?"

"They were robbed too, but Cindy is fine." Becky gave a tiny, knowing smile. "They're living hand to mouth just like the rest of us."

"Johnny and Mattie?"

"Growing up and doing well. Cindy has them both reading and writing."

Elijah wanted to rush right over and see Cindy. But first things first. His mind reeled with the new reality and what to do about it.

Becky went on in a tired voice, "Even after the bushwhacker raid we managed. Granny had extra quilts stored in her attic. Even though the bushwhackers struck there too, for some reason they never climbed into her attic." She drew a deep breath and went on, "And when the weather turned cold enough, Jenny helped me butcher."

He shot her a quick look. "You and Jenny butchered!" He was incredulous. "Where in the world is Uncle Caleb?"

"They got word that Billy was wounded at a battle in Mississippi. Caleb and Viola went to get him. We haven't heard a word since they left." Her voice grew choked as she went on, "We were doing fine until a few weeks ago. Deborah took a high fever. I needed herbs, so I left her here asleep and went to your Granny's. When I got home the cellar door was wide open and the smoke house—everything was gone. Deborah didn't hear a thing. Since then we've barely managed. We've had no meat except what game Lew brings occasionally."

Elijah's head jerked up. "Lew?"

She nodded. "Yes, Lew. And thank God for him. He drops off a squirrel ever so often."

"Ma, how much food is left?"

"Nothing much except the corn in the crib. Most of the hogs are still in the woods. The bushwhackers only drove off the cattle that were grazing close by—all but one milk cow. She was in the little field behind the cellar and they missed her. I imagine we have more cattle up and down the creek, but I don't know for certain.

Most of the corn is still in the crib, and a sack that was already shelled is in the barn. Caleb and I raised a big crop last year—everyone did. I suppose corn is too plentiful for bushwhackers to bother stealing...or else their horses and mules were already too loaded. Whatever the reason, I'm thankful they left it. Deborah and I have been grinding it in the coffee mill. I make a bit of bread every day."

As she went on, her voice grew flat and defeated. "Worst of all we're almost out of salt. Even if I had butchered again, there was no way to keep the meat from spoiling. The last thieves even took the salt barrel from the barn."

"Why didn't you just borrow some from the neighbors?"

"It's a different world now, Elijah. Folks have gotten tight fisted, and who can blame them? No one knows how long this war will last. Besides, I've discovered that many of our neighbors are loyal Union. There is an independent Union Company here now. Even Simon is part of it."

Elijah groaned and dropped his face into his hands. His bright dreams of plenty vanished in one agonizing heartbeat. And Cindy's pa was a Yankee! He looked up.

Deborah came through the back door holding a milk bucket. "Less than a quart, Ma." Suddenly her mouth flew open. "Elijah!" she shouted.

How, Elijah wondered, *could a body feel overjoyed, sorrowful, and angry all at the same time?* He gave Deborah a big hug. As he felt the bony thinness of her young body, anger grew paramount.

"Did Allen go after the bushwhackers?"

Becky shook her head. "Before Caleb left he heard that Allen was seen riding with a group of Red Legs up in Missouri...but I don't know if that's true."

Elijah slowly digested that. Allen might be pro-union. He had not cheered and thrown his hat into the air on muster day.

As Becky looked out the window, her face was gray in the thin morning light. "Since the Rebel conscription officers come through often, men have gone into hiding—some living in caves like bears.

A conscription agent shot and killed Red when he wouldn't tell where his boys were."

The news made Elijah mad. He realized with a twinge that he had not disliked big Red Matthers so much after all.

"Poor Kate," Becky went on, "is barely scrimping by."

"Who all got robbed?" he asked.

"Several right around here. Jenny and Simon and Granny and Kate—that's all I know of for certain. Oh, yes, the Millsaps too. It was not long after poor Vernon died."

"Vernon died?"

"The same ones who conscripted you shot his ear off. It got infected."

Elijah muttered, "Another kill for the lieutenant."

"Oh, dear!" Becky jumped up. "Here I am serving you up troubles when what you need is something to eat! Here, have some cornbread. You can crumble it in the fresh milk."

Elijah eyed the small wedge of golden cornbread lying on a plate on the table. It would hardly make two good bites. He swallowed against the gnawing in his middle. Memory flitted of Michael on molasses making day, stuffing food into his pockets for his family.

"No, Ma. I'm fine. I'll drink a little milk. You and Deborah eat the cornbread. I have to go see Ruby, and I want to get it over with."

"Ruby?"

Elijah took a deep breath and retold the story of Jim's hanging. As with Aunt Opal's version, he left out the grisly details.

Becky was silent. Then she spoke. "I don't care who wins. I just want this awful war to end."

——————⌁——————

The weak sun peering through thickening clouds did little to warm the biting air. It felt like snow. Elijah turned a ragged collar up and strode along briskly in hopes of warming his blood. But his energy waned too quickly. He was forced to slow. He felt like Pappy Campbell, an old man with no strength. With every step he worried. What would he do? How could he feed his family in the dead of winter—and hungry neighbors too? There would be three or four months of bad weather yet and even longer before crops would grow. Of course they would not starve. There should be plenty of meat. Pa had more than a hundred head of hogs. And a big herd of cattle. Elijah had no idea how many the thieves had made away with. But surely there were some left. Although Pa's herd had free range, they seldom strayed far, preferring the good grass in the pastures near the house. But it would not be an easy job to round them up.

He frowned. A body got tired of just fresh meat. There was an old fish trap in the barn. He would drag that out when he got home and sink it into a deep hole in the creek. Even after harvest, there were a few potatoes left in the ground. He would carefully spade each hill. And Granny knew different edible roots. As soon as he gave Ruby the sad news, he would go see Granny. My, how he had missed her!

The Lucas hovel looked worse than he remembered. Dead grass stood high in the yard, and the porch had fallen in on one corner. Dirty rags stopped up holes in the skins stretched across the window, a substitute for window glass. He had to step across a hole to get to the front door.

No one heard his knock. Somewhere in the cabin, a baby cried loudly. He pushed open the door a bit, intending to call out. Then he froze. There in the corner was Pa's salt barrel! It was the one Ma said was stolen from the barn. Elijah knew it by the odd markings on the keg. He pushed the door wide. Rage swept him—worse rage than he had ever known. On the dirty table were remains of a bountiful breakfast, crumbles of biscuit, rinds of golden fat that had bordered fried ham, and on the plates were dark, sticky traces of molasses. In the center of the table sat a molasses jug. The golden syrup had dripped down the side and made a small puddle on the table.

Elijah heard a noise and turned. It was a small Lucas boy, black-haired, blue-eyed, ragged, and dirty.

"Where is your pa?"

The child cowered at the harshness in Elijah's voice. He raised a shaking finger and pointed toward the barn. Elijah left the room and crossed the yard in a few long, angry strides. The barn door was closed. He was furious, shaking with rage, but army life had taught him to be cautious. Doc might have a gun. Elijah quickly edged around the barn and peeked between the logs.

Doc was pouring corn into a trough for the mule. There was a shotgun propped nearby. Elijah stepped through the door. Doc grabbed the gun.

In a heartbeat Elijah pounced. The gun blast splattered rotten logs, sending splinters and dust flying. He knocked Doc to the ground, wrestling away the gun. Twice he brought it down on Doc's head like a club. Doc yelped and rolled away. Elijah went after him. With a boot to the back, he kicked him again and again, unrelenting at Doc's tormented cries. Then Elijah saw a rope hanging on a stanchion.

When the kicks ceased, the fat, whimpering man rolled over. Doc's eyes grew wide with terror when he saw Elijah knotting the rope.

"Ever see a man hung, Doc?" Elijah threw the loop over the rafter. He drew the knife from his belt to cut off a piece of rope. "Well, I have. And of all the terrible things I've seen, nothing was worse than a hanging when the neck didn't break." He gave a brittle laugh. "And I aim to make sure yours doesn't!"

When Doc tried to run, Elijah caught him by the scruff of the neck and shook him like Old Scrapper shook a coon. He tied Doc's hands and then dragged him by the collar. Under the noose he hauled the struggling man upright.

"No, Lige!" Doc's pale brow was a sheen of sweat. He began to cry. "I promise ya..."

"Seems to me"—he dropped the noose over Doc's head—"I've heard that before." He yanked it tight. He pulled the rope slowly, leaving the balls of Doc's feet on the hard-packed ground. When the rope rose more, Doc's eyes bugged. His toes barely touched the dirt.

Then Elijah pulled again. Doc's feet cleared the ground. He began to choke. Face blood red, he twisted, thrashing and struggling. Saliva dripped from his distended tongue.

"Elijah! Don't!" Ruby rushed toward him. She grabbed his arm. "Let him down!"

He shrugged off her imploring hands.

"Please! Lige! Don't kill him. My baby—all the young'uns—we'll all starve."

He turned. "You mean like Ma and Deborah are starving right now?" Stone-faced he turned back to stare at the flaying feet.

Ruby burst into tears.

A shadow fell in the doorway.

"Elijah!"

He barely heard the trembling, whispered word. He turned. *Cindy! What was she doing here?*

White-faced-she stood in the open doorway, her brown eyes large and scared. Now she stepped forward.

"Please don't. Hit's wicked—'Thou shalt not murder.'"

His memory had not done her justice. In the gray light slanting through the barn door, she stood tall and straight, wrapped with a shawl. She was more beautiful than ever.

He blew out a deep breath. He supposed she was right. This was murder. It was not as if he had shot Doc in the act of stealing. Elijah felt no compunction at killing. But murder was different. He had little fear of man now. But he did fear God. Then his mouth hardened. For a few more seconds he let Doc dangle.

Doc hit the floor with a thud. With hands still tied, he coughed and gagged and sucked in air.

Elijah stood over him. He touched the edge of the knife blade with his thumb. "If I see you even close to our place again, I'll kill you."

He picked up the shotgun and reached for the mule's bridle. "I'll bring back the mule and wagon when I'm done," he told Ruby. "You'll need them. Your pa is dead. Your ma wants you to come home."

She gasped and covered her mouth. Elijah felt no pity as tears streamed down her sallow face. This slovenly girl with stringy, dirty hair and mussed dress was not the Ruby he knew and loved.

He hitched Doc's mule and drove the wagon to the cellar, resentful at how fat the mule was. It had been ages since he had seen a fat mule, but this one had been eating fine on the corn Ma had planted and hoed and harvested.

Just as he had supposed, the cellar was full. He took most of the food. Some he left, enough—if Doc did not hog it himself—for the family to scrimp by on until spring. Ruby and the children would not starve. He loaded most of the meat from the smoke house. Last of all, he went to the house. Salvicy stood in the kitchen wringing her hands.

"Lige, don't take hit all. Ya don't want Ruby's babe to starve," she wheedled.

He shot her a disgusted look. When the salt keg was loaded, he drove away.

———————

Cindy walked down the trail. She quickly drew aside as he came near. She no longer wore a childish braid. Her hair was drawn back into a thick knot at the nape of her neck. Even in the thin sun, the crown of her head glowed. The threadbare brown dress and the worn shawl only emphasized the full-breasted, perfect figure. *Nothing,* thought Elijah, *could hide her beauty.*

"Cindy."

She drew a good way back when he stopped the mule.

It was a far cry from the glorious reunion he had planned. "Would you like to ride?" he asked.

"No," she said.

He winced. It should come as no surprise, he supposed, that she was reluctant to accept a ride. He was wooly and ragged and probably smelled like a polecat. With a sinking sensation, he knew that was not the reason. He recalled her horrified look in the barn. And now there was no mistaking the wide eyes and the shrinking back.

"I'm heading for Granny's. I'll be going right by your cutoff—besides, I'd like to give your ma a side of bacon and—"

She drew up stiffly. "We don't want your stolen food!"

Then his brown eyes widened. "*You think I've turned bushwhacker?*" He was incredulous. Him a thief! How could she think that! And worse yet he could tell she was repulsed. She thought him a vicious animal!

"I'm not sure what to think." She hesitated. "Pa says war changes men—makes some of 'em hard and mean." She bit her lip.

He gave a wry laugh. "Hard and mean." His mouth grew grim. He let out a deep breath. Well, in some ways he was vicious. The war had changed him until he hardly knew himself. "Well, that may be so," he said, "but this is our food. Doc's the one who stole it—right out of our smokehouse and cellar." He gripped the reins with white hands. "Besides, I left enough for the Lucases to make out. I meant no offense by offering the bacon. I told Michael I'd look in on Johnny and Mattie."

She stepped closer. Her voice was anxious. "Is he all right?" She laid a hand on the wagon. "When did you last see him?"

"Yesterday." Elijah added, "He's fine—at least as fine as anyone else in the army. No one is having a good time of it these days."

"I reckon I'll ride a ways with you."

He nodded and put out a hand. She hesitated before taking it. Suddenly he felt unfit to touch the shapely, strong brown hand. He guided the mule and sat in miserable silence.

It was minutes before she spoke. She looked at a cloth sack in her hands. "I forgot to leave it," she whispered to herself. Then she explained in a stiff voice, "Granny asked me to take some willer bark to Ruby. Her baby's teething." She kept her eyes straight ahead.

Elijah was emboldened enough to slide his eyes sideways. Head high, back stiff, and finely molded jaw tensed, she was, nonetheless, a lovely woman—certainly prettier than any girl he had seen in Little Rock.

Elijah suddenly said, "I haven't seen Dillon since we both got conscripted. How is he?" His stomach knotted when she grew rosy to the roots of her hair.

"I have no idea," she said.

Because of the blush, he figured she did know. She twisted a ring on her finger. He had never known her to wear one before and his heart skipped a beat. She saw him glare at the ring.

"For your information," her voice was haughty, "this little ruby belonged to my grandma. Ma gave it to me on my sixteenth birthday last spring."

He swallowed and rode the rest of the way in cold, pained silence. At the crossroads she climbed down unassisted. They each said a stiff goodbye. Elijah felt sick. He drove to Granny's with an active imagination—vivid scenes of Cindy meeting Dillon in some remote cave. With difficulty he wiped the scowl from his face as he climbed down and went to Granny's door.

Chapter 17

Elijah stepped through the door without knocking. Granny looked up from stoking a fire that was burning brightly in the fireplace. She gave a glad cry, propped the poker on the hearth, and hobbled toward him with outstretched arms.

With a hearty laugh, he enveloped her in a huge hug. "Ma hardly knew me, but I reckon you knew me right off." He pushed her away to study her beaming face. He grinned. "Unless you've took to hugging wooly strangers."

She smoothed his beard with a trembling hand. "I'd a'knowed you on the darkest night that ever was." She hugged him again. Tears flowed down the wrinkled cheeks. "My boy's come home," she whispered. "Thank the Lord. Praise the good Lord." Her eyes devoured him with a starved look. "I had just about give up hope—I should'a knowed better," she scolded herself. "Ain't I prayed fer this night and day."

"I reckon that's all that saved me," he said ruefully.

Her eyes sharpened. "I don't reckon the war is over?"

"No. I took what you might call a recess."

"Deserted, did ya?" She chuckled.

"I don't figure it was deserting since they took me without my say so."

"Me neither. But you'll have to look sharp," she cautioned. "Conscripting is worse than ever. That there lieutenant come again. Or I allow it was him shot Red—"

"Ma told me Red got shot. So you think Morrison did it?"

"The way Kate described, hit sounded jest like him."

"I hope he does come after me," said Elijah. His jaw hardened.

She studied his face. "Don't you go letting hate take root. Hate poisons a body worse than larkspur poisons a critter."

He changed the subject. "Granny, I found out who robbed Ma—at least the last time. It was Doc."

Her nose flared. "I ain't surprised! That old reprobate!" She snorted. "He always was too lazy to hit a lick at a snake. I reckon there ain't much work in stealing." She shook her head and closed her eyes. "Pretty little Ruby a'marrying into all that scum...hit makes me sick!"

With a deep frown, Elijah heartily agreed. He pointed outside. "I got our stuff back. It's outside in Doc's wagon. Ma said bushwhackers hit you, too. I'll bring in some stuff to tide you over, and then I best get home. Ma will be worrying." He asked, "Do you have any salt?"

"I got just a mite. Hit's as scarce as hen's teeth."

"Now we've got plenty. Give me a bowl. I'll fill it up."

He carried in the bowl of salt, along with a smoked ham and a shoulder, a sack of potatoes and another sack of turnips, and some dried beans. Last of all he hauled inside a huge orange pumpkin. "This be enough for supper?" he teased.

Her eyes were bright. "Thank you, son," she breathed. "Victuals was getting scarce. This very morning I was a'feared of mighty hard times if Caleb didn't make it back—but now just look! All this bounty! Elijah, the Lord must be plum ashamed of me. Like the good book says— even in seven."

Elijah's brow knit until she loosely quoted, "He'll deliver ya in six troubles. Yea, even in seven, no evil will touch ya. In famine he'll redeem ya from death, and in war from the power of the sword." She smiled and quietly added, "Book of Job, chapter five." She touched his face again. "And ain't he done just that—delivered from the power of the sword and brung ya back." She sniffed and wiped her face on her apron. "There now. Get along with ya."

Elijah could hardly enjoy Becky's and Deborah's delight as he unloaded the wagon. All he could think of was the horror on

Cindy's face and how she had shrunken away from him. He would have to forget the rosy dreams conjured on the long marches and dreary nights by a campfire. There would be no courting at the Mason cabin, at least not by him. And as he recalled Cindy's blush, he set the salt keg down with a bang.

When Becky jumped, he was chagrined. "We'll keep it here in the kitchen," he said. "I'll not risk someone stealing it from the barn again."

She frowned. "Do you think Doc would dare come back?"

"No. He won't be stealing anything else from us."

She put a hand to her throat and fixed him with troubled eyes. "You didn't...?"

He blew out a deep breath. "No, I didn't kill him, Ma. But I let him know I would."

She searched his face. "I hate to imagine what all you've seen—"

"And done," he finished for her. "Don't worry, Ma, I reckon I'm still more human than not." Silently he asked, "Am I so tainted even Ma is shocked?"

"Son, I've been thinking; there shouldn't be much conscripting in this bad weather," she said, "but in the spring, it will begin again."

He figured Ma was right about the conscriptions. If he knew General Hindman—and he did—the general would be trying to scrape together all the men who had drifted away. Even if his army were on its last leg, the general would go down kicking. Elijah, however, intended staying out of the fray.

Becky added, "And there's Simon's company..."

Elijah was quiet for a long while. Finally he spoke, "Well, if they leave me alone, I'll leave them alone. I've had all the fighting I want. This spring I won't be marching. I'll be plowing. And I won't be getting conscripted again." His mouth was a hard line.

The next weeks Elijah drove himself. Like a maniac, he chopped wood—even when the pile was stacked to the eaves of the cabin—and hunted the barren woods as if the smokehouse and cellar were not, once again, fairly well stocked. Only when ice and snow forced him inside did he sit by the fire and brood, knowing soon spring would bring the hard work he craved—anything to take his mind off Cindy.

The temperature dropped below zero. Becky complained the cabin was always cold no matter how hot the fire. But Elijah recalled a thin blanket on frozen ground. The cabin seemed snug to him. In spite of his gloomy mood, he had to admit it was good having a warm place to sleep and a full belly.

Before the bitter weather had arrived, he had taken more food to Granny and to Jenny and Pappy Campbell and to Kate Matthers. Kate had thanked him over and over again, saying things like, "Oh, Holy Mother of God!" and "Saints be praised!" But she had stayed mum on the whereabouts of her boys, and Elijah had not pried.

He often wondered how things fared with the Masons. Since Simon was still at home, Elijah figured, they were managing. He longed for the sight of Cindy but dreaded facing her scorn. The hurt was too raw.

Fat Tom Sorrels brought the latest news from Clarksville. He stopped by Granny's on his way up the mountain and gladly accepted the offer of a chair near the fire and a bowl of hot stew.

"Things in town is a sorry mess. No flour left a'tall. Some folks is downright hungry, I reckon."

Elijah also took a steaming bowl and thanked Granny. Tom slurped the soup while still managing to talk.

As Tom prattled on with war news, Elijah shook his head in disbelief. *Hindman was on the offensive!* It seemed impossible. Only days after Elijah left the army, General Marmaduke had left Lewisburg with over two thousand horsemen to make a successful raid on Springfield. Tom bragged the general had captured hundreds of Federals and then paroled them. Marmaduke had returned with wagonloads of much-needed supplies, guns, and ammunition.

"Jack Wallace says the Yankees has tucked tail and skedaddled out of Fayetteville back into Missouri again," said Tom while accepting a second bowl of soup. "Shore is tasty, Miz Tanner." He belched and then said, "Laveney is frettin' herself to death. Todd is with Marmaduke. But I reckon he's fine or she would a' heared by now."

Michael must have also gone on the raid. Elijah hoped he was still in one piece.

Tom gave a deep laugh, which shook his bulging middle. "Yes siree—Marmaduke stirred up a hornet's nest in Missouri. He swore in new Rebels right and left fer Anderson and Quantrill. All a feller had to say was 'yes' when he got asked if he would kill anyone who served the Union."

Elijah had heard of both Anderson and Quantrill. According to Levi they were bloody guerillas, worse even than bushwhackers. Southern Missouri was in for a bloody time.

With a sly look, Tom added, "Reckon we need Marmaduke to thin out the nest of vipers we got crawling around here, too. Yankee Company—hump!" he scoffed.

Elijah gave an inward groan. He fervently hoped there would never be a battle here. The old windbag had no idea how awful war was.

"The news from Fort Hindman ain't so good," Tom went on. "Some Yankee general name of Sherman might-nigh throwed the whole Yankee Army at the fort. Holmes had ordered General Churchill to hold on 'er die trying, but Churchill didn't have a snowball's chance in hell against forty thousand —and him with less than three. Hit would have been mere foolishment to try."

Elijah had met Churchill when his troops were camped at Clarksville and Pa had gone to muster. He had been a colonel then. Elijah hated to think of the fine man being a Union prisoner.

Tom shook his head. "Nope, I don't know iffen he got paroled 'er not." After another slurp of soup, Tom added, "At least things is looking good back east. Lee whipped 'em good at Fredericksburg—Yankees lost more than twelve thousand men."

"*Twelve thousand men!*"

"Yep, so Jack says." Tom passed his bowl for more, and Granny dipped it from the big kettle keeping warm on the hearth. "I reckon things will start looking up around here too," he said, "now that Kirby Smith has took over and Hindman has resigned."

Elijah was more shocked than ever. He leaned forward.

"*Hindman resigned?* Are you sure?"

Tom looked offended. "I'm telling it gospel—just like Jack told me."

"Did he say why Hindman resigned?"

Tom shrugged. "Don't reckon he liked being passed over again for command of the whole shebang."

Elijah doubted anyone could outdo Hindman at managing the army. Although he did not approve of all the man's tactics, Hindman was an amazing organizer. But Elijah did not waste his breath arguing with Tom. Tom was hardheaded and not overly smart, anyway. Elijah ate the stew and mulled over all the news.

It was a blustery day in March when Elijah learned Michael was alive and well. He rode up unannounced just as Elijah was leaving the barn with a fresh pail of milk. He rode a fine mount and had a shiny new rifle.

"Hey!" Elijah called, jovial. "Good to see you all in one piece. Where did you get that good-looking rifle?"

"Borrowed it and the horse off a Missouri Yankee—hit's a Whitney and the best gun I ever shot."

Michael appeared hale and hearty but unkempt. His long, dark hair hung past the flat cadet cap and partially hid the ragged collar. The threadbare gray coat strained tightly across his broad shoulders.

"Good to see you, Lige." Michael dismounted and glanced all around. His eyes were troubled.

"What's the matter?" asked Elijah as he dumped the milk into the hog trough.

"Have you seen Mattie and Johnny lately?"

"No. But I know they're fine. Cindy visits with Granny, and Granny gives me the news."

Michael leaned over the pen to watch as a dozen fat little pigs ran to stick pink snouts into the warm foam. "Our pigs never done good like yers. O'course, we never had no milk to feed." He glanced at Elijah. "Things must be right prosperous if you got milk to waste on pigs."

Elijah propped a foot on the rail. "Cow just freshened. The calf doesn't take much and it's too soon yet for us to drink it." He cast a sideways look at Michael's downcast face. "Did you know your uncle Simon is part of an independent Union company up here?"

"Yeah, I heard. I'd like to see the young'uns, but don't reckon I will. No use looking for trouble. And I shore don't want to cause Uncle Simon no harm." Michael chewed his jaw and looked over his shoulder. "And bad feelings are running real high in town just now. There's a big stir about McConnell getting killed."

"McConnell?" Elijah asked.

Michael looked at the trail again. Elijah wondered why he seemed nervous.

"Major McConnell—old Doc's son. He left town with a scout of about two hundred. They skirmished with some Yankees up near the headwaters of the White, and the major got shot off his horse. He hit the ground dead." Michael pushed back from the fence and looked toward the creek again. "I never knowed him, but they say he was a fine fellow."

"Pa spoke well of him. I saw him once on muster day before the war." Elijah faced Michael. "Now, are you ready to tell me what's wrong?" he asked. "You're as jumpy as a bull frog."

As Michael stared at the ground, Elijah heard horses coming. Michael looked up. "I tried to lead 'em shy of here but the captain insisted on coming this way. We're foraging, Elijah."

Elijah set grim jaws and his stomach knotted. Foraging! He knew what that meant. Hadn't he done it himself often enough? Hadn't he helped Hindman leave families with barely a mouthful? If only he had more warning! He could have hidden the food! Why hadn't he thought to do it sooner? He had counted too much on being able to drive bushwhackers away with a gun. But the army was a different matter. He could not drive them away. Now visions of hunger—of Ma and Deborah with gaunt faces— whirled in his brain.

"I'm mighty sorry, Lige. I told the captain that you're my best friend and to go easy—not take no more than he has to."

Elijah looked up. "It's not your fault, Michael. Don't blame yourself."

Michael let out a deep breath.

Elijah eyed the mounted men splashing across the creek.

"I'm sorry." Michael's apology faded into silence. As the patrol of hard-bitten soldiers approached, he quickly said, "I'll do all I kin to see they don't take too much. But it might not do no good," he finished lamely. He looked sheepish. "The captain did bypass Uncle Simon's. I told him there might be dozens of Union men there. We're keeping our eyes peeled real sharp."

As the captain rode up, Elijah's jaws set tight.

"Good day." The captain was a middle-aged man with wary eyes. He looked ready to meet trouble. "We need corn for the stock and meat and potatoes. I'll have the men load the corn—but you can bring out the other provisions so we won't disturb your family."

Elijah clenched his fist. *Not disturb my family! Take our meat, our corn, our potatoes—oh, no, it won't disturb my family!* He wanted to shout. If only he could shoot the captain! But that would do no good. There were at least fifteen soldiers.

He silently groaned when one of them left the barnyard leading the cow with the calf trotting at her heels. He knew they would eventually butcher the cow, but the calf would be their supper. It was too young to travel.

Still carrying the empty milk bucket, Elijah wheeled and strode around the house heading for the smokehouse and the cellar. Becky peeked from the curtains. As he rounded the house, she opened the back door and called, "What is it, Elijah? What do they want?"

"Army forage party."

She sucked in a sharp breath.

With gritted teeth, Elijah cut down a ham and two shoulders and two sides of bacon. That left only one more ham for them and some bacon. He threw the meat onto the wagon that a soldier had drawn near the door. Then he opened the cellar door and sacked up two bushels of potatoes from the bin. A scant two bushels remained. He had been sharing with Jenny, Kate, and Granny, counting on a new crop before these ran out. Now it would be doubtful if he had enough left to eat and have seed, but he feared if he were not open handed with the army the captain would help himself.

His ears grew hot as he watched the gray-clad men shovel corn from the crib into sacks and pile them onto a wagon. He remembered the work, the sweat, the effort to grow a crop—now with what ease they took it! He had done the same to others, but it was no easier to endure.

Michael led his horse over and stopped. He held the reins loosely while the animal cropped the short grass just beginning to grow beside the cellar.

"I shore am sorry, Lige."

"Why are we keeping on?" Elijah asked. "I thought we'd have give up by now."

"Oh, we ain't whipped—not by a long shot. Kirby Smith is running things now. He made a feller named Cabell a brigadier general. And Cabell and Marmaduke are planning a fresh push soon. We're downright bold again. That last Missouri sashay put fresh blood in us—ammunition, supplies, mules, horses. I know things still look bad yet, but the tables is turning. Not just here, but for the whole army. Guess you heared how Lee won big at Fredericksburg. 'Course we lost Arkansas Post—Fort Hindman—but look how Grant has been stumped at Vicksburg. He's tried to take it forever and can't."

Michael broke off a twig of sassafras growing near the fence and began to chew. "If I was you I'd hide some food. This won't likely be the last forage party through here. And there's been thieving and murder and houses burned to the ground all over the county." He rolled the twig around in his mouth. "Granny Holmes sent special orders to get rid of the bushwhackers around here first. That's why Cabell and Marmaduke has both been in Clarksville lately. With two generals around, the bushwhacking has slacked up a bit. But we'll pull out soon. Hill's company is staying behind to patrol things. I doubt they can catch many bushwhackers, though. That kind hits fast and rides hard."

"Yeah, they do." Elijah recalled Jess's raid. As soldiers kept loading sack after sack of corn, distracted, he said, "Bushwhackers hit here once already."

"Well, they'll be back. Keep yer eyes peeled. Now that the weather is warmin', they'll come out of hibernation like the skunks they ere." Michael added, "I heared folks in Fort Smith almost starved after we left. Just lately—since Brook's men started patrolling the river—a couple of boatloads of corn finally made it up there."

Elijah wondered how long a body could live on just corn. He might soon find out.

When the corn was loaded, the men remounted. Michael spit out the twig. "I hope you all get along all right. It'll be a while before I get back. Marmaduke is planning another sashay into Missouri to settle a grudge against some Yankee general. Seems this McNeil feller put ten Reb prisoners in front of a firing squad. Marmaduke wants to teach him a lesson." Michael kicked a dirt clod with his boot. "But I don't know—I feel sorta funny this time."

"Don't reckon I could talk you out of going?" asked Elijah. When Michael grinned and shook his head, Elijah griped his hand. "Then take care."

"You, too." As Michael rode away, he turned to wave.

Elijah lifted a hand. His mind was already churning. It was still months until harvest. And he would need much of the corn and potatoes that were left for seed.

He chewed his jaw. Michael was right. It was foolish to leave the corn and all the food where any passerby could take it. Where would be a likely hiding place? He started toward the house. It must be a dry place, a place no one was likely to stumble across.

Suddenly he knew. He would borrow Jenny's horse. Then he would try to salvage the old broken down wagon sitting in the weeds behind Uncle Caleb's barn. He set off in long strides. He would not rest until the job was done.

Elijah circled through the woods, guiding the horse and wagon through bushes and around trees. It was a roundabout route to get past the Matthers' cabin without Kate seeing. Under normal circumstances he would trust Kate. But bushwhackers had begun torturing to get hidden valuables. Tom Sorrels had said they were burning folks' feet. Just now this corn was more valuable than gold. Kate not knowing would keep it safer.

The schoolhouse door stood half open on sagging hinges. Last year's grass stood tall and yellow around the rickety porch. Elijah stopped the wagon a short distance away. He would not risk making wheel tracks in the yard. He crossed the ground gingerly himself. Once inside he took moments to adjust his eyes to the dimness. Near the back of the dusty room something scurried away. Spider webs and mouse droppings covered the room. Elijah hoped the rats and mice would not steal too much corn. He had put the flour, meal, and potatoes into barrels. The cured meat would hang with twine on the rafters.

He toted in sacks of shuck-covered corn. And after climbing the wobbly ladder into the loft, he placed the sacks in a spot where the roof had not leaked. He returned to the wagon to get the other sacks.

He worked quickly. It was going to storm. Rising wind rattled the oaks in the schoolyard and moaned through the pines along the creek. Thunder rumbled in the distance. The sky had grown almost black. Suddenly, the towering bluff on the far side of the creek stood out bold against a backdrop of lightning, its sandstone ledges showing white and jagged. Elijah hurried faster.

When the last sack was in place and the meat hung, he descended the ladder. His eyes fell on the log seats—his desk and the one behind that had been Dillon's. Then they lingered on Cindy's. *What a lifetime ago! What bright childish hopes and dreams he'd had!*

His shoulders drooped. He went outside and pulled shut the door and latched it. After a searching look to make sure he had left no trace, he trudged to the wagon just as the first splashes of rain fell.

Chapter 18

Each long day Elijah was in the fields from sunup to sundown. Straight furrows opened under his plow and pushed into ridges, dark and crumbling, along both sides. At first the earth had been too wet, clinging in wet clumps to the plow. He had to give up for a few days and wait for drier weather. Now, plodding behind Jenny's horse, Elijah thought it was a godsend that Jenny had been visiting Ma the day the bushwhackers had raided. She was on the way home and had hidden as they rode past. Elijah had no idea how he would have managed without the horse. In return for the loan of the mare, he had promised to raise enough corn for Jenny and Pappy. And he would need to grow enough for Granny.

He wished Uncle Caleb would come home. Granny never named it, but he knew she was worried sick. He had assured her they were waiting for Billy to get strong enough to travel. It would not be easy to send word. Mississippi was a boiling pot. The river was crawling with Federal troops and gunboats.

Midafternoon, when Deborah arrived with a bucket of water, he whoaed the horse, pushed his hat to the back of his head, and drank deeply. The cool water slid deliciously down his dry throat. It was hot for April. He looked at the dirt and frowned. It did not matter if the rain held off until he got the corn in the ground, but what if the dry spell held and the corn seeds remained shriveled and lifeless? He pulled his worried thoughts back from that path. As Granny always said—no need to borrow trouble when ya own enough already.

He thanked Deborah for the water and watched as she walked away. She was still thin. She did not skip and run about as she used to. But both she and Ma had lost the gaunt, hollow-eyed, scared look from when he first returned. Fervently he hoped it was gone forever. He must try to be less harsh with her. Pa was not around now telling him to watch his temper, and he had been so cross lately that both she and Ma walked on eggshells.

With a deep breath, he put calloused hands on the smooth plow handles and slapped the lines against Brownie's neck. At the end of the row he would head for the creek and let the horse rest and bring it a bucket of water. He would enjoy a break himself. It was always cool and damp near the creek.

After the mare drank, Elijah knelt and dunked his head into the cool water and let it run deliciously down his hot face and neck. He took the handkerchief from his pocket. Then he threw up his head and faced down the creek. Gunshots! They were faint. At first he heard only two, and then dozens erupted close together. Army? Bushwhackers? Whoever—it was a sizable battle. If it was bushwhackers they might be here soon. He led the mare deeper into the woods and tied her. Then on a run he headed for the house.

The firing ended, but through the long afternoon he stood vigilant watch. Becky and Deborah were safely barricaded in the cellar and the horse hidden in the woods. Finally, before dark, he ventured forth to scout around. He had gone less than a mile down the creek when he heard hoof beats. After a quick look around he dove into the brush and hid behind a tree. Soon Simon's voice drifted.

"Naw, Ben, after that dusting we give 'em, I misdoubt them soldier boys will be back anytime soon. I know we kilt at least a couple and maybe more."

"Yo're too cheerful, Simon. They was over a hundred men in that patrol. I knowed that major leading 'em. Believe me, getting three soldiers killed ain't likely to stop Adams. He won't rest until they've wiped out our company."

Simon's voice grew fainter. "I figure yer right, but fer now they've scurried off to town. They'll be a while lickin' their wounds."

Elijah stepped back into the trail. Pa had died to stop it, but the fighting had come here anyway. Like Simon, Elijah doubted this was the end of it. With a deep breath, he started home. At least this time it had not been thieving, murdering bushwhackers.

Elijah stayed vigilant. He kept the rifle nearby. But the plowing must go on. Each night, almost too tired to remove pants and shirt, he dropped into bed in the slant-roofed loft. Sleep came quickly, but it was restless. The plow still tugged at his shoulders.

When the nights warmed he traded the loft bed for a pallet on the porch. In the army he had grown accustomed to sleeping outside and actually preferred it in good weather. He enjoyed the singing of katydids and crickets and night peepers. When he was not too fatigued, he found pleasure watching stars twinkle over the hollow where he knew, later in the season, there would be countless fireflies winking back at the stars.

One day at noon the ground was finally all plowed and the cornfield awaiting the golden seeds. Although the sky was blue, the rain crows were cawing for rain. He needed to hurry.

Elijah stuck his head into the cabin. "Ma, I'm going to get the seed corn. I'll be a while. I have a bit more left to shell."

"All right," she called. "Be careful. Now that it's spring, that conscription man might come back."

"I'll keep a sharp eye out," he assured her and then went swinging down the road in easy, loose-limbed strides.

The day was mild. Birds twittered in the newly leafed trees and violets carpeted the shady places alongside the dim deer trail. While coming and going to the schoolhouse, he never used the main road. After cutting through the woods, he stopped before entering the clearing and took a good look around. The door was shut. Everything looked undisturbed.

He went inside. It was stuffy in the airless loft. He decided to toss the last few sacks down and husk and shell the corn in the classroom. With a firm grip on two sacks he started for the loft opening. Upon hearing hoof beats, he stopped. Taut as a fiddle string, he crouched near the hole. The hoof beats stopped. Soon boots climbed the steps. The door creaked on the hinges. Elijah could not see the intruder, but from the thudding of boots, he was a big man.

Elijah dared not move. The cracks between the boards would sift down dust like rain. He wondered how long he would be treed in the loft like a scared coon. Restless, the man paced back and forth. Then he stopped and Elijah heard a match strike. Soon tobacco smoke wafted upward. The pacing began again. This was no bushwhacker on a raid. But who was he? What was he doing at the tumbledown schoolhouse?

Elijah held the rifle ready. Someone else was coming. He heard a tread on the steps and then lighter, swift steps entered the room.

"Dillon, what's wrong?" Cindy was breathless from running.

A deep laugh rang out. "Not a thing now that yo're here."

Elijah's ears went hot and his heart raced as if he too had been running. He must have the worst luck in the world! He wondered with a silent groan how much he would have to endure.

She sounded puzzled. "But Pete said he saw you on the trail and you said I should come quick. "

The boots thudded and then Cindy spoke, "Stop it, Dillon."

"Aw, come on, Cindy. Yo're my girl ain't ya?"

"I never said I was." She stepped away. "No! I mean it, Dillon. You smell like whiskey."

"Shore I've had a nip. In that old cave, ain't nothing to do but drink and play cards with Shawn. I'm sick of hit. O'course of a night I dream of you." His voice grew husky, "Cindy, yo're the prettiest woman I ever seen. I'm gonna kiss—"

"Dillon Matthers!" she cried, insulted. "You're drunk! I've never even let you hold my hand—and I sure ain't going to now!"

"Aw, you're just a playin' bashful, Cindy."

Then she cried out. "Let go! You're hurtin' me!"

Elijah heard her shove Dillon. Her footsteps beat quickly on the board floor.

Elijah, holding the rifle, leaped through the opening. Cindy had gone.

Dillon spun around. "What the—"

Elijah smashed him in the face with the gun. Then he hit him hard in the stomach, and as Dillon clutched his middle, he smashed him with the rifle on the chin. Dillon shook his head and blinked. Jealousy drove Elijah. He pounded Dillon's face. Each time the rifle slammed into flesh he felt a surge of joy.

Dillon's nose spouted blood and one eye was swelling. His nostrils flared and his lip rolled out in an ugly snarl. His fists dropped to his belt. He jerked a knife. Dillon still had one good eye wide opened. When he lunged, Elijah dodged. Crouching and brandishing the knife, Dillon circled. He swiped sweat from running into his eyes and then shook his head to clear it. If he had been drunk, he seemed sober now.

Elijah watched like a hawk. When Dillon lunged, off balance, Elijah kicked the arm that held the knife and it went flying. As Dillon dove for the knife, Elijah kicked him in the back. Dillon fell hard. As he struggled up, Elijah jerked his own knife and grabbed Dillon's hair. Jerking his head back, he put the knife to his throat.

"I ought to slit your throat." His words came through clenched teeth. He wanted to. He wanted to feel Dillon's blood run through his hands. But something stopped him. He seemed to hear Pa's warning in his head. He drew a shaky breath.

"If you ever so much as touch Cindy again, I'll gut you like a hog. You understand?"

"That's plain enough."

Elijah put his arms down and backed off.

Dillon stood. He picked up his hat and dusted it off. "I was out of line. But I never meant to harm her. I was a little drunk, but drunk or sober I'd not force a woman—not like that."

Elijah, reading honesty in his eyes, nodded.

"Kin I get my knife?"

Elijah nodded again. Dillon got the knife and limped from the room.

Elijah righted the overturned bench and sat down at his old desk. He put his head in his hands and groaned. Perhaps this was what Pa had always feared—that he would fly into a rage and do murder. He could not help that the war had hardened him. That was to be expected. But Pa was right. He could help losing control of himself.

In May the word came. Vicksburg was under siege. If it fell, along with it went the last hopes of keeping the Yankees at bay in the Trans-Mississippi. Even though growing fainter, the hope for months had been: fight on! Look to Vicksburg! Grant and his thousands can't take Vicksburg! Now, so it was said, not a mouse could come or go without Grant stopping it.

Elijah was not surprised. For months he had felt sure the Confederacy was doomed. Although he had not been an avid secessionist; nonetheless, it made him sad. He had witnessed the valiant struggle and sacrifice—right or wrong—made by the South. He pitied the soldiers still fighting and dying for a lost cause. Michael might argue and the Rebels in Arkansas might fight on, but Elijah knew it was only a matter of time. The North had the men, the money, and the machines, while the South was daily growing more destitute.

Concerns of another sort kept Elijah frowning and studying the sky with a grim countenance. The corn had sprouted and pushed through the hard, dry clods. Now the shoots stood stunted and yellowed. Brown edged the curled leaves. The vegetables in Ma's garden looked no better. When June brought no rain, he began carrying water from the creek. Watering the cornfield would be impossible. With drooped shoulders, he gave it up as lost. But he fought to save the garden. Tom Sorrels had said flour was selling for two hundred dollars a barrel at Little Rock and there was none to be had in Clarksville, not at any price. Granny said she had no taste for milk and gave them her cow. Elijah knew she did it for Deborah, who was still pitifully thin.

Impotent to change things, Elijah felt helpless. Clothes and shoes were wearing thin. Coal oil for the lamps had long since been depleted. They horded the candles and rarely kept a light. Until he butchered there would be no more tallow. But most oppressive of all was the constant dread of hunger! He had to watch Ma closely or she took small portions to make certain he and Deborah had more. In nightmares he relived the torture of days and nights without a bite to eat. He shuddered at the likelihood of enduring that again, of the vision of Ma and Deborah with sunken eyes and bony bodies.

So Elijah drove them all. When Deborah accused him of being cruel, he set his jaws. It would take hardness to survive. Each morning he, Becky, and Deborah made trip after trip to the creek with buckets of water for the meager crop. When that job was done, he went to the meadow with the scythe and cut hay. It was slow, backbreaking work. The grass was short and sparse. Hours of scything netted hardly enough to make a load, and it was of such poor quality when dried, he doubted it was worth the trouble. But Granny's cow and calf and Jenny's horse would need something in their belly for the winter.

Perhaps Granny was right, perhaps the ground was cursed because of the shedding of innocent blood. Innocent blood had certainly been shed. Hardly a week passed without horrific news of some outrage. Just across the ridge, Ben Pelts' boy was killed, and Elijah had seen the rope burns on James Cheek's neck. Some conscription officer had hanged him while trying to get information where local men were hiding. The description fit Bo Morrison. When James vowed he knew nothing, the officer let him down. James had been lucky. Plenty of men were not. Back in March two brothers who lived down the creek had been dragged from their beds and shot. Just a few miles away, Limestone Valley was plundered and every house robbed. Seventeen men had disappeared. Elijah figured they were murdered and thrown into a well or a cave. He figured it was the same band of bushwhackers who struck on Big Piney killing Batson Cox and Thomas Fiddler. Pa had known and liked both men. The country was just too big for Hill's men to patrol. They had chased the culprits, but it was no surprise the weary soldiers returned empty-handed. There were too many hiding places in the rough mountains.

Elijah worked with the shotgun ready and his eyes vigilant. Each night before going to bed he walked to Granny's to check on her. One evening, near twilight, he rounded a curve and came face to face with Cindy.

"Howdy. How are you?" he asked.

She drew up tall and cut him with cold eyes. "I know what you did to Dillon"—her face blazed—"and I don't appreciate you spying on us!"

"I wasn't spying," he denied. "But I won't stand by and watch anyone hurt you."

"Dillon is not the one who needs watching. He's not the one who goes around hanging folks and beating them to a pulp!"

Without thinking he reached out.

She shrunk back. "Don't touch me."

He watched her leave. He was desolate. What was that old saying of Granny's...a body could win the battle but lose the war.

Chapter 19

Elijah was hard at work in the field when Deborah came running. She could hardly speak for panting. "Conscript man's coming! Little Johnny just ran over to warn us. Ma says hurry! She's hiding the horse!"

Elijah dropped the scythe and grabbed the rifle. He loped across the field, heading for the creek. He angled toward a spot on the bank shielded by underbrush. It was steep and rough. Almost sitting down, he slid on haunches to the bottom and then splashed across the shallow water toward the bluffs on the far side. The hiding place was not a deep cave, just a depression masked by brush and trees. For just this contingency he had stashed a blanket and a cache of food. He would stay here until Deborah came for him. It made no difference that he had already served in the Confederate Army. It seemed every man able to walk was being called in. He had imagined meeting the lieutenant and taking revenge, but too much depended on him just now to give into foolishness.

Elijah checked closely for snakes and then hunkered and went in. The sun inched overhead. Hours passed. He wondered why Deborah was so long in coming. The only sound was the rustle of leaves in the breeze. Even the creek was silent. In the drought it had stopped running. In many stretches the rocky bed was laid bare to the sun. He grew drowsy. Hunkered with his back to the cool rock, he slept.

He was awakened by a squirrel squacking in a tree across the creek. With caution he stepped from the bluff. The sun was past one o'clock. Something was wrong. Deborah should have come by now. Possibilities churned in his brain. Perhaps the conscription man waited at the house. The plowed fields were a dead giveaway there was a man on the farm. Whatever the trouble, he could not sit here wondering. He would go careful and circle far around.

While staying on the far side of the creek, Elijah climbed the bank and looked at the house. All was quiet there. If the conscription man was there, he had hidden his horse. At the trail Elijah bent to study the ground. There were no fresh horse tracks. That puzzled him. A horse would certainly leave tracks in the powdery dust. There were fresh prints made by Ma's small boots heading down the road but none returning. With a premonition of doom, he set off at a trot, following the footprints. Soon they disappeared. The hair on his neck rose—just as Potts had said his did before lead flew.

Near Granny's he left the trail and with long steps slipped through the trees. He would not approach the cabin head on. Nothing stirred. The woods were still and drowsy in the warm afternoon sun. He had not gone far when he saw, straight ahead, a horse browsing on brush. The reins dangled and the saddle was empty.

Elijah froze. The laugh was no ordinary laugh. It was a diabolical cackle that made his hair stand on end. He crept forward. Then he stopped cold. Near the old hickory where Belle had treed her first squirrel lay a mutilated body, sprawled on the ground face up. Blood had soaked the blond hair and the gray coat and britches. Lew Willis stood over the man, hacking the buttons from the uniform jacket with a long bloody knife.

It was Bo Morrison. Elijah did not feel cheated. The contorted face said death had not come quickly.

Elijah had lived this moment before. He held his breath. The knife, the bloodstained leggings, Lew's evil face as he spun around—but this time Lew neither grinned nor dropped the knife. He darted a glance toward a rifle propped close by, and then his eyes quickly swept the woods to see if Elijah was alone.

"This here idiot thought he could conscript me. Them other soldier boys run off when the lead started flying."

Elijah stepped closer with his gun on Lew. "You ought not to have butchered him like a hog, Lew. The law hangs a man for such—like they hung Dub. You're the one murdered Bessie, aren't you?"

Lew's white-hot eyes narrowed. "Nobody's gonna hang me."

Elijah leveled his rifle. "Drop the knife, Lew."

"You ain't gonna shoot me, boy. I know you better than that."

Lew's knife cut the air. It sliced Elijah's arm just as he fired. Now he had difficulty holding the rifle, but he barely felt the pain. Lew grabbed his own gun. Elijah dodged behind a tree and drew his knife. His breath came fast. He crouched and waited for Lew's attack. When Lew did not immediately attack, Elijah, still keeping the knife ready, hurried to reload the rifle. Now his arm burned and in his haste, his movements were clumsy. He cocked his head. There was a rustling on the bench below and then he heard hoof beats. When he ran forward, he caught a glimpse of Lew clinging to Bo's saddle. The horse ran toward the creek. Lew swayed. He had been hit. Elijah threw the rifle to his shoulder. But it was not a clear shot. There were too many trees in the way.

He looked back at the blood covering the ground near Bo's body. There was no way of knowing how much might be Lew's. Elijah trailed him a short ways, relieved to find a considerable amount of blood splattered on the leaves. The wound would hinder Lew even if it did not kill him.

Elijah chewed his jaw. He must go after Lew. But he needed ammunition and he needed a shotgun. A rifle was too apt to miss. Uncle Caleb had taken his pistol but had left his good double barrel with Granny. Elijah glanced at Bo's body and then headed for Granny's cabin at a run, looking back often to check the woods.

Even before climbing the porch, he heard moans. He crept near the window and looked inside. Dread washed over him. Then he quickly burst through the door. Granny lay on the floor, writhing in pain. As he sucked in a shocked breath, the sickening odor of burned flesh filled his nostrils. One look told the story. A fire, blazing in the fireplace, filled the room with oppressive heat. Granny's feet were crispy-black and oozing. She had been tortured.

"Granny, can you hear me?"

She groaned. "I never told...I never told."

Suddenly he knew! Bo had tortured Granny to find him! Rage welled. Blood pounded in Elijah's ears as he clenched and unclenched his fists. It gave no comfort to know Bo was probably roasting in hell. Elijah craved to cut Bo's heart out—to watch him twist and scream as Granny must have done.

"Granny, are you home?" Cindy pushed open the door. "What on earth?" She quickly covered her mouth and nose against the stench. Horrified, she knelt alongside the writhing woman. "Oh, the poor thang!" She whispered, "Who would do such a thang!" She retched and turned away. White and shaken, she looked up. "Water. Elijah, get some water! There's some burn salve on that shelf yonder. It's in a blue jar."

Elijah snatched the ointment and then he grabbed the water bucket. It was only half full. He dumped the contents into a bowl and handed it to Cindy.

"Petee, fetch some clean rags," ordered Cindy.

Pete stood near the door in a stream of sunshine where dust motes glittered, his eyes large and scared. Elijah pushed past him and hurried to the creek and dipped the bucket. His mind reeled. He must get after Lew before Lew could hole up somewhere! But he must go careful.

Poor Granny! How she must be suffering! He rushed back to the house with the dripping bucket. Cindy spoke when he came into the room.

"She was teaching me all about yarbs and such, but we never talked much yet about burns...just this ointment. She doesn't hold with using butter or lard like most folks do." Cindy pushed wavy hair back from her forehead where beads of sweat had gathered. "She needs a doctor."

Elijah met her scared eyes. "There isn't one."

"James Cheeks knows doctoring," she said quickly. Then her voice fell, "But no one knows where he's hid out since they tried to hang him." Cindy bit a trembling lip. "I sent Pete for your ma." She eyed the mangled feet. "Reckon I'll do the best I can. I wish Ma was home."

When Cindy had finished bandaging the charred flesh with strips of clean rags, Elijah lifted Granny onto her bed. Cindy eyed the red drops staining the white coverlet.

"Why, Elijah, you're bleedin'!"

"It's just a scratch," he said.

She shook her head. "A scratch doesn't bleed so. Put some of that salve on it and bind it. There's some more bandage over there." With tears misting her eyes, she looked at Granny. "I don't know what else to do for her." She looked at Elijah. "Go tend that wound. I'll stay with her."

Elijah was glad to leave the bedroom, glad to be away from the pitiful sight of Granny tossing and moaning on the bed. Granny might die. The thought pounded in his brain. Yes, she was tough...but she was old. And such a hurt was likely to kill even a tough man.

He looked at his wounded arm. He chaffed to be after Lew. But it might take a long while to find him. It would be foolish to let the arm get infected. After rolling up the sleeve, he washed the blood from his arm. The wound was long but not deep. He dabbed the cut clean and then applied the yellow ointment.

He lifted the shotgun from over the door and took down the ammunition pouch. He was loading the gun when Cindy came to get a rag and a bowl of water.

"I'll sponge off her face. It's hot in that room." she slowly lifted the dipper from the bucket. She stared at the water for a long moment. Then she looked at the gun and raised her eyes to his tight face. "Vengeance is mine, sayeth the Lord," she quoted. "Elijah, if you still care for me, don't go," she implored. "All the time you were gone to war, I prayed for you night and day and I ached for you to come home. But I won't have a bloodthirsty man. I won't live under such a curse."

He picked up the shot pouch and walked out.

On Jenny's horse, Elijah crossed and crisscrossed the woods and trails. Daylight was fading when he finally found where Lew had left the creek and headed north toward rugged Newton County. Elijah wanted to follow. He had no desire, however, to come upon Lew in the dark. Lew would be as dangerous as a wounded cougar. He halfway suspected Lew could see in the dark.

With reluctance, Elijah turned the horse and headed homeward. He did not rush. He feared to find Granny dead. He stopped along the trail near Bo's body.

Wild hogs had found it. They ran when Elijah's horse approached. He dismounted and stood over the remains and realized that he had felt more pity for a dead deer. Bo deserved no burial. But his mother and pretty sister might someday want to visit his grave. Bo's boots were fine. Elijah bent and pulled them off. He hefted the body onto the sidestepping horse and led it to the barn to get a shovel.

He opened the barn door but kept tight hold of the mare. She was skittish of the load on her back. He led her inside and reached for a long-handled shovel propped against the log wall.

He whirled. One hand covered Cindy's mouth. She had a bucket in the other. Her horrified eyes studied the mutilated body. Then she stared at Elijah. She sank slowly to sit on the floor. Hands covering her face, she leaned forward. Her hair, held back with a wide ribbon, fell in silken waves over her shoulders.

Elijah had seen many such things. But he would have spared her the gruesome sight—the awful memory etched on her brain. "What are you doing here?" He had not meant to sound gruff.

She uncovered her face. Eyes dilated, she hitched herself up with hands behind holding onto the logs. She shrank as he stepped near.

"I didn't do it," he said. This time his voice was gentle. "Get on home. Ma and I will tend to Granny."

She wrapped a thin shawl tighter about her body. Then she went out the door. He watched her leave. She looked back once and then fled from the barnyard.

Although Elijah had spent a week searching for Lew, there was no trace. Finally he had given up and come home. He was bone tired from the search but mostly from the tension. When would Lew put a bullet or a knife in his back? He had lost sleep wondering.

Granny was still alive. But listening to her moans, Elijah wondered if that were a good thing. He could barely stand to stay by her bedside and watch the unimaginable torment as her head rolled from side to side and her feeble hands plucked at the coverlet. Becky, Cindy, Polly, Simon, and Jenny took turns nursing her. Through the long, grueling days and nights, they bathed the burns in vinegar water—Cindy recalled Granny said that was good—and they applied the ointment from the blue jar. Slowly, ever so slowly, the fever ceased and she began to heal.

Now as Elijah sat nearby, she awoke and looked all around.

"Well, I had a right good visit with yer Grandpa Tanner—but I reckon hit ain't my time ta go," she said in a cracked whisper.

"With Grandpa?" Elijah's hackles rose.

"Yep, and with sweet Reeda May."

"What did they say?"

A flicker of smile crossed her face. She tiredly closed her eyes without answering. He wondered if she had merely dreamed or if she had actually parted the eternal veil.

That night at home he fell asleep with his head on the table. Becky pushed back his hair and kissed his forehead. He stirred and roused.

"Get to bed, son. You fell asleep over your food."

He stretched and yawned and watched as she scalded the milk crocks in readiness for the morning's milk. She looked exhausted. She was not sleeping well. He knew. Far into the night, when she thought them all asleep, he had heard her crying. How she must miss Pa!

Elijah had never shared the days and years and nights that made two flesh one. He had not joined bone with Cindy's bone, nor flesh with her flesh to form a new life to love and mourn and bury as Pa and Ma had done. Yet he understood Ma's loss.

She turned and saw his scrutiny. "Something is troubling you, son." She waved aside his hoot of derision. "I don't mean Granny, the war, the crops, the bushwhackers...it's something else."

She sat down. The candlelight played on lines in her face—lines he had never noticed before. Ma was getting old. The realization made him sad.

"If you want to talk, I'm a good listener."

It might feel good to talk to someone, to pour out his frustrations, his self-doubt and his guilt over the uncontrollable rages. But Ma had enough troubles of her own.

"I'm just tired, Ma."

"Well, go on to bed and try to get some sleep."

He could tell by her worried scrutiny, she knew he was keeping something from her.

Chapter 20

In the warm afternoon sun coming through Granny's window, Elijah dozed. He jerked awake when she stirred.

"You ain't resting good of a night, are ya?" she guessed.

"Not very," he admitted. "Too many ghosts I reckon."

She surprised him with her insight. "I don't reckon ghosts is the only problem. I see how you look at Cindy. What's the trouble between you two?"

He swallowed hard. Then it all poured out, the hurt, the frustration, the bitter dregs of—if not lost love—at least lost respect. "She despises me, Granny. And worse yet, she fears me. I see it in her eyes. And who can blame her! When I get mad and fly into a rage, I can do most anything."

Granny studied his face. Elijah was quick to fly off the handle. But after what he had been through who could blame him? How could anyone fail to see the goodness—the generousness of heart? Aloud she said, "Sooner er later, truth always comes out." She put a hand on his arm. "Don't despair. If Cindy is worthy of ya, someday she'll see you for what you ere." She closed her eyes again.

When she slept, he pushed the chair back from the bed. Arms on knees, he bent forward and studied his clasped hands. *But what was he?*

He jumped. Without opening her eyes, Granny spoke.

"When yer pa was young, he had a terrible temper."

"Pa?"

"Hit cost him a sweetheart. Rachel wouldn't stand fer his tantrums." Granny opened her eyes. "She was a pretty little thing. I always liked that girl."

Elijah stared. Poor Granny's mind was wandering. She had Pa confused with someone else. Why, Pa had been the most even-tempered man on earth! And surely he had never loved anyone but Ma.

Elijah sat up straight. Johnny Lane had a sister who ran off years ago with a cowboy. If he remembered correctly, her name was Rachel.

Just then Deborah came into the room, carrying food for Granny. The door squeaked. Elijah jumped up, pulling at the knife. Deborah dropped the plate. Her eyes were big and scared and she drew back.

"Oh! Lige, I'm sorry." Her voice shook.

He slipped the knife back. With a weak smile, he said, "I reckon I'm pretty jumpy these days."

Her frightened eyes hurt him as she stared at the spilled plate. "Oh, I ruined all that good food—after all the times you've told me to be careful and not to waste! I'm so sorry!"

The poor child was shaking. Did she think he would punish her for an accident? Had he been that harsh? He put an arm around her shoulder and kissed the top of her head. "It's all right, honey. No harm done. I'll go home and get some more food while you sit with Granny."

Deborah took a step toward the door. "Not by myself—please, Elijah, I'd rather go get the food."

He looked up, surprised to see Cindy in the doorway. She was watching intently.

"I called but no one answered," she said quickly. "The door was open so I came in."

She wore a blue dress. Her hair, pulled back in a ribbon, was hanging down. He loved it loose like that—a golden brown river running down her back. He swallowed.

"I'll stay too," she said.

After giving Deborah a reassuring squeeze, Elijah dropped his arm. "Then I'll be back soon."

"Deborah and I will manage fine," she said and gave Deborah a smile.

Elijah left the cabin and looked back.

Although Elijah often saw Cindy, they rarely spoke. But always he felt her stare. She quickly averted eyes if he looked her way. One hot afternoon he arrived early. Cindy did not hear the door open. He took the opportunity to study her. Her back was turned and she stood at the bedside sponging Granny's face with a wet rag.

Granny took a deep breath. "I knowed you had the gift. You got the gentle touch of a ministerin' angel. I reckon I kin sleep a bit now. You set yoreself down and get some rest, too."

"I just might do that," she said and plumped the pillow under Granny's head. She rinsed the rag, dumped the bowl into a slop jar, and poured fresh water into the bowl. She unbuttoned the top of her dress and began sponging her own throat. She turned and gasped. Her face flamed. Water droplets glistened on her creamy skin. Elijah dragged his eyes away from her beauty but not before his insides twisted with longing.

On Sunday Caleb came home. He was alone. Viola had stayed with Billy. After Billy's wounds had healed, he developed a lung problem and hovered near death for weeks.

"He's still weak yet but he could a traveled," said Caleb sitting at Granny's bedside where she lay with bandaged feet uncovered. He and Granny took the glasses of tepid water Becky served.

"I'm sorry it's so warm," she apologized. "The spring went dry and your well's so low the water is almost hot."

"Hit's wet. That's good enough fer a parched traveler," said Caleb.

"Ain't no hotter than my feet," teased Granny with a crooked smile. "Thank ye kindly, Becky."

Caleb grinned. "Ma, if you ain't tougher than whang leather." Then he went on, "Like I was sayin', Billy could a come but there's a sight of murder being done by the Yankees. Not a day went by but some poor traveler got shot or hung fer spying. Viola said they'd kill Billy sure. And I figured she was right. So we went real kerful about thirty mile to her brother's place. Billy is hid out there on Bill's farm."

He took a sip of water. "I had many a close shave myself getting here. Even had to steal my own mule back onc't. And another time, I thought I was a goner! But I convinced 'em I was a fiddle player goin' to a hoedown. Glad I had my fiddle along."

Granny kept looking at his face with hungry eyes. Elijah knew she had despaired of ever seeing him alive.

"Reckon you all knowed Vicksburg surrendered."

"No, but I'm not surprised," said Elijah. "Grant had them bottled up for weeks."

"Yep, they finally starved out. And things ain't going so good fer yer old army neither," Caleb added. "Price and Marmaduke tried to take Helena back and got whipped real good."

"I reckon if Michael is still alive he was in on it. He's a scout for Marmaduke."

"I hope he's all right," said Caleb. "I allus did like that boy." Then he asked, "Had you heared about that big battle in Pennsylvanny a couple weeks ago?"

Elijah shook his head.

"Place called Gettysburg. A real humdinger—lasted three days. Old long-face Abe changed generals again—some feller named Meade this time. I'll sware, Abe changes generals more regular than most men changes socks. Seems this 'un done him a good job, though. Lee got his tail feathers singed. More than fifty thousand dead. And more than half of them was Lee's! Appears to me, iffen this war ain't over soon, there won't be a man left standing!"

Elijah nodded. The terrible count did not impress as it once had. He supposed the awful truth was a body finally grew numb to hearing such numbers. The withered bodies at far off Gettysburg were of less consequence just now than the withered corn in the fields. At least it was comforting to have Caleb home. Now Elijah would have someone to help share the load.

But having Caleb home did not improve the weather. The harvest was the worst Elijah had ever seen. While Caleb guided the middle buster behind his mule, Elijah lifted a plant and shook it. He swallowed disappointment with a taste as bitter as alum. The small potatoes clinging to the vine were hardly worth digging. Caleb stopped the mule and looked back.

"Ain't much of a crop," he said.

"We won't be filling up on Irish potatoes, that's for sure." Elijah lifted worried eyes. "Hope we can raise some fall stuff."

"Me too," Caleb agreed. "If not—by the looks of our empty cellars—I'd say we best tighten our belts."

———〜———

Lew Willis had vanished. Elijah wondered if he had crawled into a cave and died. But Caleb figured that, like many other outlaws, he was hiding out in the Indian Territory. Elijah never relaxed his vigilance. He would not feel safe until he knew Lew was dead.

Finally the withering summer drew to an end. For months Union troops, pestered by Rebels like Cabell and Shelby, had jumped like checkers on a board in and out of northwestern Arkansas. Now came word of a Union advance deep into the state. On the first day of September, Union General Blunt along with Colonel Cloud and his Kansas troops took Fort Smith, sending Cabell's Brigade fleeing toward a ridge known as Devil's Backbone. There was a hard-fought battle ending in defeat for the Rebels.

When Caleb returned from Clarksville, he found Elijah gathering skimpy ears of dried corn. The sky was bright and cloudless. A screeching hawk sailed far overhead.

Caleb pushed his hat back and looked up. "If we had any chickens left, I'd shoot him, but don't reckon there's any need." He hunkered and rolled a dried clod in his fingers. "I got no word of Becky's kin. No one even knowed where they was."

"Ma will be disappointed."

Caleb nodded. Then he related news of the recent battle. "Cabell give 'em a good taste of artillery, but he still had to light a shuck to keep from being captured. He headed fer Waldron at a fast clip. But Clarksville was in a dither. Everyone was pasty-faced—scurrying around like mice before a cold snap because the Yankees was coming. I was in front of the courthouse when they marched through heading fer Dardanelle. They was stepping out right proud like. Never paid no mind to no one—'cept some of 'em hollered at a pretty gal when she stuck her head out the winder." Caleb drew a deep breath and shook his head. "Never thought to see Yankees marching down Main Street."

"Where are Hill's men?" Elijah asked.

"Don't rightly know. I heared they fought at the Backbone. They're saying a hundred men deserted Cabell and joined up with that-there Yankee Colonel Cloud. I ain't certain of the number, but I seen men with Confederate belt plates marching right alongside them blue-backs just as bold as brass. And I recognized some of 'em as John Hill's bunch. I reckon he's fit to be tied."

Elijah wiped sweat from his brow and watched the hawk circle. So, the Yankees had reached the county. They would take the post at Dardanelle with ease. Then he figured they would march on down the river and take Little Rock. General Price had held the city far longer than Elijah thought he could, but with both Fort Smith and Arkansas Post falling as ripe plums into Union mouths, it was just a matter of time before they swallowed Little Rock as well.

He hardly cared who was in control—just so the war ended. The dire threat now was not the Yankees. It was hunger. The fall garden had only produced a few peanuts and beans and peas and a small crop of sweet potatoes.

They could get by if, as Uncle Caleb said, they tightened their ragged belts—and if no bushwhackers or forage parties made off with the meager stores hidden in the schoolhouse. His eyes roved the wilted fields. It was no longer the land of plenty. The cattle were gone. The mules were gone. There were no slick, fat hogs in sight. The chickens had long ago disappeared into some bushwhacker's belly. Both cellar and smokehouse were almost empty.

He looked down and his shoulders sagged. His clothes were rags and his boot soles flopped unless he tied them. He was saving Bo's boots for winter. Then his lips curved into a slight smile. There was no great loss, he supposed, without some small gain. Ma spent a lot of time with Granny. She was learning to spin and weave. And she loved it. Even more surprising was the pleasure Granny took in the teaching. From her chair drawn near the loom, she supervised like a top-notch sergeant. It warmed his heart to see them together. He wished Pa had lived to see the pleasant sight.

Elijah's ax fell. The upended stick of black oak parted like soft butter. He pitched the split sticks aside. Before standing up another chunk, he wiped his face on the shirt hanging on the woodpile. Sweat glistened on his lean torso. He glanced at the sky. The September sun felt like July. He figured when Caleb got back from the mill, he would be pleased to see this stack of wood all split. Swinging an ax hurt Caleb's back. Elijah let out a deep breath. It hurt to see Caleb aging. Lately he had really slowed down, and his face looked drawn and almost as wrinkled as Granny's. Elijah figured the worry was part of it. Caleb fretted a lot about Billy and Granny. Elijah propped the chunk on end and made a high, arched swing. He jerked the ax free.

It seemed the war had blighted every living thing, sucking out the life as mistletoe sucked life from a tree. It had sapped him. He felt dry and callous. Cindy thought him a murderer. And in his heart, maybe he was. He let out a slow breath. When rage swept him, he felt capable of anything. He felt shame that it was so. He had always admired Pa's self-control. Elijah recalled Granny's council from Proverbs about how a body who controlled anger was better than one who conquered a city. Pa had certainly conquered himself—he had been ruled by neither anger nor fear. Elijah drew a deep breath and let it out slowly. He wished he were as good a man as Pa.

"Elijah!"

He whirled to see Cindy stumbling through the woods toward him. She ran but was so out of breath, she almost fell at the edge of the field.

Elijah sprinted toward her. "What's wrong?" he yelled.

"Bushwhackers!"

She was still yards away. "Wait there and catch your breath!" he called as he turned back and grabbed the rifle. Throwing open Granny's cabin door he yelled to Becky.

"Ma! Bushwhackers at Simon's! Take Granny's shotgun. Get everybody into the cellar. Stay there until I get back."

While he spoke he collected Caleb's shotgun and an ammunition pouch. He frowned and then tucked an ancient cap and ball pistol into his waistband. It was not much good but it would still shoot.

He crossed the field at a lope. If only Caleb had not taken both mules! Glancing back he saw Becky and Deborah supporting Granny on the way to the cellar.

Cindy, white and panting, leaned against a tree. "There's five of them. I hid in the woods as they rode past. I know they're bushwhackers headed for the house. And Pa is off cutting wood!" With terrified eyes, she added, "Oh, hurry, Lige! I think I heard a shot while you were in the cabin!"

He began to run. He called back, "Get into the cellar with Ma and Granny."

Simon's cabin was a mile away by the trail, but much less if he cut across. And the woods were open here, browsed close by Granny's sheep and goats. His feet flew over the ground. He had to slow while making his way down a rocky bluff, but after crossing the creek he could run again. He heard shots. When the cabin was just over the next hill, he slowed and approached the rise, staying shielded by trees.

There were five horses and four pack mules in the yard. The mules had large, bulging packs. One horse held a man who stood watch with a rifle. The cabin door was open. Then Elijah froze. Pete's blond head was hanging off the porch where he lay without moving. Elijah's jaws worked.

Jess stepped from the barn leading Simon's best brood mare. At the same time, the fat man came from the cabin pulling up his suspenders.

"That never took you long, Heavy," called the mounted man.

Elijah did not hear Heavy's answer, but the man holding the horses haw-hawed. Elijah gritted his teeth and slipped closer while Heavy picked up a rifle lying near Pete. Pete had always been full of grit. Elijah knew he had tried to fight back before they shot him.

There were two men in the back yard near the smokehouse. Elijah wanted them all. But he especially wanted Jess and Heavy! It took all his will power to wait. When the two disappeared inside the smokehouse, he made a hunkering run down the hill to the back of the barn. He was vulnerable while holding the rifle in one hand and the shotgun in the other, but he needed them both!

Every second he expected to feel hot lead. It seemed a miracle that no one spied him. Gulping deep breaths, he leaned for a minute against the back barn wall.

Then he slipped around the side. The front yard was now out of view. There was a large pecan tree near the rock well house. From there he would have good view, and the range was close enough for the shotgun. Flower bushes grew nearby. They would offer some cover. He drew a deep breath and ran.

While Jess mounted his horse, the other men rounded the cabin carrying two loaded sacks.

One spoke out, disgusted. "Not much here. I guess the old woman was telling the truth. Somebody else beat us to it. Good thing we found that one place way off the trail or we'd have empty sacks this trip."

Elijah reached the well house, his breathing so hard he feared they would hear. He leaned the shotgun against the rock wall and wiped sweaty hands before readying the rifle. He risked a quick look. Heavy had started for the chicken house with his pistol drawn. Elijah ducked back.

"Come on!" ordered Jess. "There aren't any chickens. I already looked."

"I'm looking for that brown-haired gal. I seen her in town once with that old hag in the house. I bet she's hiding someplace."

Elijah clenched his jaws until they ached.

"Come on I said!" Jess was sharp. "Someone likely heard that shot."

Elijah waited until Heavy, grumbling, turned. He took aim at Heavy's back, but Jess was leaving! Elijah swore and turned the rifle on Jess. He fired. Jess jerked and fell and landed near the porch with his skull bleeding. Heavy whirled. He fired and ran. A shell broke rock right above Elijah's head. Heavy ducked behind a plunging horse and dove behind the porch. The mounted man kicked his horse and sped down the trail. Elijah turned the shotgun on the two men near the porch. One yelled and grabbed his side. The horses milled and the string of pack mules bolted.

Elijah ducked behind the building, thankful for the speed he had acquired in reloading. Once he quickly glanced out. The wounded man was grabbing at a sidestepping horse. The other man had grabbed a horse and mounted. Heavy had disappeared on the far side of the house.

Elijah finished loading. He looked out. Two shots shattered the wall, narrowly missing his chest and head. Ducking back, he drew a deep breath, raised the rifle, stepped forward, and fired. The man pitched off the horse and then lay still on the ground. The wounded man struggled with a foot in the stirrup.

Elijah jerked the pistol. It had always pulled left so he aimed to the right when he took a bead on the head. This time the bushwhacker fell and lay still.

Elijah searched for Heavy and then quickly stepped back. He reloaded and then grabbed the shotgun. More than likely Heavy was still on the far side of the house. He was too big to move fast. Elijah was certain he had not caught a horse. They had all bolted except Simon's mare. She stood near the barnyard fence. Heavy would be waiting for him to stick his head out again. He stepped to the opposite end of the rock wall and eased along the far side.

Heavy's belly and legs stuck out past Polly's washtub where it hung on the south wall of the cabin. Pete's feet almost touched it.

Elijah waited. He wanted a head shot. Then his eyes darted. Polly had stumbled out the front door. Her clothes were half torn off and her face was a bloody mess. She screamed. Falling to her knees she grabbed Pete and held him.

Heavy stepped out, grabbed Polly's hair, and pulled her off the porch. He stuck a pistol to her head.

"Step out and throw down yer gun or I'll shoot!"

Elijah had jumped back behind the building. Heavy would not shoot Polly. He needed her for a shield. Elijah was certain Heavy would go for the mare. But he would not ride away. Not after what he had done here! Elijah loaded the pistol.

Heavy's big fist jerked Polly's hair. She screamed for Pete. Heavy shook her like a rag doll and dragged her toward the horse. He kept his eyes on the rock house.

"Throw out yer guns. I'll shoot her!"

Heavy mounted, pulling Polly up alongside him. She hung like a limp rag doll dangling at his side. He kicked the horse's flanks. Elijah waited until Heavy had passed the barnyard and the cellar and the bee gums. Then he leveled the rifle and fired. Heavy's head jerked. Polly dropped, splattered with Heavy's gore as he fell from the mare.

Elijah walked forward. Polly looked up, her eyes horrified.

"It's all right, Polly. It's me, Elijah..."

A blast shattered the calm. Elijah spun around. Cindy stood in the edge of the woods by the barn. Black powder smoke wreathed her. She lowered a shotgun. Elijah's eyes followed her stare.

Jess was on his knees. A pistol dropped from his lifeless hands. Blood spurted from his neck. His eyes were wild as he grabbed at his throat. He weaved for a moment, and then he fell.

Elijah strode forward and checked each outlaw. He was taking no more chances. They were all dead—except the two who got away.

Cindy went to the porch. Clinging to the rail, she went up the steps. She kneeled by Pete's body and moaned. "Oh, Petee, oh, my little Petee."

Polly still sat in the dirt and cried. Elijah went and lifted her like a baby and carried her into the house. He laid her on the bed in the front room and then went back outside.

"Cindy."

She kept stroking Pete's back.

"Come on,"—he gently lifted her by the elbow—"you can't help Pete, but your ma needs you." Then Elijah remembered. "Where are Johnny and Mattie?"

Cindy looked up. Her eyes were dazed. "I don't know."

Elijah ran through the house shouting. No one answered. Dread gripped him like a vise. Then he ran to the outbuildings. He finally found them, big eyed and shaking, huddled together in the loft.

Johnny held a pitchfork. "I ain't gonna let 'em hurt my sister," he said. Tears ran down his pinched face.

"They won't hurt anybody, Johnny—not ever again." Elijah, holding to the loft ladder, dropped his head. He had been too late for Pete. And for Polly.

———∽———

Cindy turned from sponging Polly's battered face. "Thank God they're all right," she said as they all walked through the back door. He had brought the children far around, away from Pete's body.

"Oh, Mama." Cindy's voice broke and she began to cry softly with big tears rolling down her pale cheeks.

Elijah wanted to pull her into his arms and comfort her. But he knew to her that would be no comfort. Instead he told Johnny and Mattie to sit down. He pulled a quilt from another bed and went to get Pete. He had just wrapped the body when Simon came, whipping the mule. He eyed the carnage and jumped down.

"Elijah! Is everyone all ri—" The words died away as he saw the quilt. "Who?" he whispered.

Elijah's insides twisted. "It's Pete."

"Pete!" Simon grabbed the porch post to keep from falling. His mouth worked but no words came.

Elijah led him a ways from the door. "Simon, get hold of yourself. There's more bad news. No. No one else is dead. But Polly is in a bad way. They...they hurt her. She's inside on the bed."

Simon pushed past him and ran into the house, his long legs stumbling. Polly cried out when she saw him, and he rushed to hold her sobbing body. Cindy fled from the room. She stopped on the porch and looked where Pete had lain, and then her eyes traveled to the quilt. Her face crumpled.

Elijah led her to the rocking chair and knelt down. He held her while she covered her face and wept. "Oh Elijah, why? Why?"

It was not the first time a stricken woman had asked him that question. He still had no answer.

Her gaze went to the yard and rested on Jess. "I've done murder."

"No. You just saved my life," he said. He stood. "You all right? Then I'll go dig a hole to throw the scum in." There was no law to notify, no courts to convince of justice. In the warm weather the bodies would need burying soon. He would go through their pockets. Perhaps they had kin who would care to know they were dead. First, he must ask Simon where to bury them. On second thought, Simon might not want them buried here.

Elijah knocked softly. "Simon, could I see you for just a minute?"

Simon stepped through the door and pulled it shut behind him. Tears streamed down his seamed face. "Elijah, I shore want to thank you for what you done. I know you saved the rest of 'em." He looked at the quilt and his lips trembled.

"Well, sir, Cindy saved me."

Simon's brow knit.

Defiant, she looked up. "Pa, I shot one of them. And I'm glad I did—even if I am a murderer."

Simon looked old and stooped. He had aged in the last ten minutes. "Daughter, protecting yore family ain't murder. Never was. That ain't what God intended when he give Moses the command." He squeezed Cindy's arm.

That was how Elijah believed. So had Pa. But he was relieved to hear Simon say so.

"Simon, I was wondering about the bodies...I mean the others. Do you want me to haul them off? I can bury them someplace else."

Simon looked toward the tall, rounded pecan tree growing beyond the rail fence. "I can't see burying them in the plot alongside of little Sally Ann and"—his voice broke—"now Pete. No, bury them out yonder." He pointed to the far side of a field.

"I don't mind taking them somewhere else," Elijah offered.

"No. They're done gone on to judgment and they can't hurt us now. When yo're done, I'll say a few words over 'em."

"Yes, sir. I'll come get you." Elijah started off the porch in search of a shovel and mattock. Simon and Cindy were talking low. He could not hear the words, but they were both crying. Simon had lifted Pete, and Cindy held the door as he carried him inside.

Elijah found a sled and a shovel. He hitched the mule to the sled and rolled the bodies onto it. It took one trip just for Heavy. Then he picked up Granny's shotgun where Cindy had dropped it. He knew Ma and Granny would be frantic, but he would tend to the burial first. Already two of Simon's hogs were roaming near. If it were up to him, he would just as soon let the hogs eat them—especially Heavy. But it would be bad for Cindy and Polly if the hogs and dogs dragged in bones, so he would dig a big hole and put them all in it.

Elijah was digging when Caleb rode up. He had stopped at Simon's cabin and learned the worst, but now he wanted Elijah's version. Caleb offered to dig, and Elijah was glad for the help. But first he asked Caleb to reassure Ma and Granny that he was alive. Caleb hurried off to do so, and he took along Granny's shotgun.

———⁓———

"I don't in no wise feel love for these here, Lord," Simon prayed with his head bared and wearing his black preaching frock coat, "but I choose to forgive 'em. Vengeance is mine sayeth the Lord. You be judge, Lord, and don't forget what they done here. Amen." He put the black slouch hat on and turned to Elijah. "With Polly in the shape she's in, I don't plan on having no service for

Pete. I'll just say a few words myself. But be shore and thank Caleb fer offering to lay out the body. Hit was mighty kind of him. But I've done it many a time." He swallowed and looked toward the cabin. "And I reckon I can do hit fer my own."

The dead men had had little in their pockets, not even enough to identify them. Caleb was spreading the word. He would try to find the owner of the goods in the packs. Simon had offered Elijah his pick of the horses and the mules, but he did not have feed enough for more than one. He decided to take a mule. He still missed Jinks. Elijah figured the rest of the livestock would end up in the Union Army.

Elijah put the shovel in the barn and haltered a big red mule. He would return early tomorrow and dig another small hole for Pete. He turned. Cindy waited in the yard. Elijah led the mule forward and then stopped.

"I just wanted to thank you—for everything. It's a miracle you got so many of them without getting killed yourself."

"I reckon I learned some things in the army that come in handy."

She looked chagrined. He had not meant it as a reprimand, but she had taken it so.

"Caleb told Pa it was Lew who killed the soldier. I've been trying to get up the nerve to come over and apologize. You must despise me…"

The mule pulled away and Elijah drew on the reins.

"Whoa, there!"

When he turned back, she had fled.

Chapter 21

Two weeks later Elijah raised his head from the creek and squeezed water from his dripping hair. His shirt was off and his suspenders hung down. After rinsing the sweaty shirt, he used it to wash dirt from his arms and chest. Although there had been few sweet potatoes, digging them from the granite-hard ground had been hot, dirty work. The September days still baked like an oven. He wondered if fall would ever come. He heard a gasp and whirled. Cindy stood a few paces off. Her eyes were wide from shock and a hand covered her open mouth. He wondered how long she had been standing there—probably since he had dunked his head in the water or he would have heard her.

"Your poor back! Oh, Elijah, who beat you?"

He wrung out the shirt and put it on. Then he stood and pulled up the suspenders.

"When the army says to fight, a man better fight—whether he wants to or not."

"I'm so sorry…"

He picked up his rifle. "How are your folks?" he asked.

She drew a shaky breath. "That's why I came. Oh, Elijah, I'm at my wit's end. Pa won't eat. He hardly sleeps and the work is all just waiting." Her eyes had filled with tears. "If anything, he's in worse shape than Ma. He just sits and stares. And I don't know what to do! Heaven knows I have my own trouble eating and sleeping. Oh, Lige, every time I shut my eyes, I see that man's face and all that blood spurting from his neck. And I feel like I'm the worst person on earth. But then I get to thinking about Petee with his little head hanging off the porch, and I feel glad I shot that fellow. I suppose that is pure wicked. I'm just so mixed up!"

His eyes were compassionate. Cindy was facing the same ghosts he had wrestled. "I know," he said gently.

"Did you ever feel that way?" she whispered.

"Yes, a thousand times. I don't think I had a restful night for a year after Pea Ridge. But Cindy, like your pa said, you did no wrong. If a man lives by the sword, he dies by the sword. If ever a body lived by the sword, it's a bushwhacker." He laid a hand on her arm. "The hurt of all that's happened will pass in time. You look plum worn out. I'll go talk to Simon, if you'd like."

"I'd like that very much."

She began to sob, great wracking sobs that shook her whole body. Elijah took her into his arms. She clung to him. His lips brushed the top of her head. "It's going to be all right," he said. He longed to kiss her, but Cindy had come to him for help and not love making. He stroked her hair and let her cry.

Finally, she raised her head. "Thank you," she whispered. She sniffed and wiped away tears with her fingers. "I better get home. I never told Ma I was leaving."

"I'll be over soon."

She nodded and gave him a trembling smile.

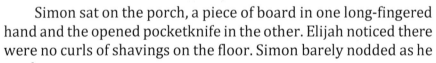

Simon sat on the porch, a piece of board in one long-fingered hand and the opened pocketknife in the other. Elijah noticed there were no curls of shavings on the floor. Simon barely nodded as he sat down.

"How you making out?"

"The trials of Job." Simon's face twisted. He dropped his face. "I used to preach—tell folks how a man's faith will sustain him." Simon's shoulders shook.

Elijah took the board and the knife. "Well, will it?"

Simon looked up, confusion on his face.

"Will it, Simon? I heard you tell Maggie when Johnny died that the Lord would never put more on a body than he could bear."

Elijah looked hard at him. "Has the Lord put more on you than you can bear?"

"Hit feels so." Simon's face crumpled and tears rolled down his furrowed cheeks. "But let God be true and every man a liar," he said.

Elijah nodded. "I've never lost a son or been through what you're facing—but I have had some trials. A man faces what he has to and goes on. I figure that's what the Lord intended. Right now Polly needs someone strong to lean on. And Cindy is just about to drop because you're sitting here feeling sorry for yourself. It is a hard thing that Pete is dead. You can't bring him back. But you have family left that needs you."

Simon stared into space. "Now he is dead," he quoted. "Wherefore should I fast? Can I bring him back again? I shall go to him, but he shall not return to me."

Elijah recognized the words of King David grieving for Bathsheba's dead baby.

Simon drew a deep, shaky breath. "No, I can't bring Pete back—but if I keep faith, I'll go to him. I been forgetting that. Lord forgive me." Simon looked at Elijah. "You got a lot of wisdom for a boy."

Elijah's jaw tightened. "Simon, I been to hell and back—at least a man-made hell—and I'm no boy."

"I never meant no insult." Simon shook his head. "No, yo're right. In some ways, you've done lived more life than I have."

Elijah relaxed. He used a light touch. "Reckon I'm old enough now to drop around here occasionally?"

Simon gave a tiny smile. "I reckon you are at that."

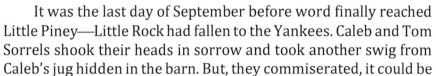

It was the last day of September before word finally reached Little Piney—Little Rock had fallen to the Yankees. Caleb and Tom Sorrels shook their heads in sorrow and took another swig from Caleb's jug hidden in the barn. But, they commiserated, it could be worse. Price had escaped with his army to Arkadelphia. Elijah wondered when folks would realize that Price and his army were whipped. But he stayed quiet. Everyone would know soon enough.

He shook his head at the offer of a swig. "I never developed a taste for whiskey or turpentine either."

"This shore ain't turpentine. Hit's the last jug I got of Red's good liquor," Caleb said with sorrow. "I hope them boys of his recollect the recipe."

Two weeks later Michael returned, not riding a fine horse, but astraddle a broken down army mule. Elijah was cutting sorghum cane when he splashed across the creek.

"Appears I'm just in time to he'p," he called. He laughed, swung down, and took a limping step.

It was then Elijah saw the soiled bandages peeping through holes in the ragged trousers. They shook hands.

"Well, looks like you made it back—but not all in one piece."

Michael grinned, exposing even, white teeth. In spite of the wound, he was much improved from the skinny boy who had once helped make molasses. His shoulders were broad and his arms muscled. He looked all around. "Good to be back," he said. "Never thought I'd say that." His eyes swept the bright, cloudless sky and took in the rugged ridges and the shaded creek bottoms. "I missed this place—especially when I figured I'd never see it again."

"Have you been to Simon's?"

Michael sobered. "Yeah. Awful about Pete." He looked off. "And poor Aunt Polly. I'm mighty grateful you were around. Glad you killed them sons-a-bitches."

Elijah pointed at the knee. "Where'd you get that?"

"Right near Little Rock. I was hid behind a log at Fourche Bayou that would scarce have covered a scared rabbit—helpless with a two-inch piece of metal in my knee, and Yankees a swarmin' around like a bunch of stirred up yellow jackets. Ain't sure yet how I got away."

"We heard they took Little Rock."

Michael nodded, looking glum. "We fought hard but hit was four to one—and them with tons more artillery."

"Seems like Price and Marmaduke ought to be about ready to call it quits," said Elijah.

"Oh, no! You don't know them two birds! They're still ruffled up worse than two jakes with one hen. That Marmaduke would rather fight than eat." Michael grinned. "Why—with Yankee shells flying thicker than skeeters—he took time out to fight him a duel. Killed General Walker."

Elijah's eyebrows rose.

"Walker never covered our left flank at Helena like he was supposed to. Him and Marmaduke had been feuding ever since. Nosiree, the Yankees ain't heard the last of Marmaduke and Price."

Elijah snorted. "Then they've got less brains than a jake turkey—even a jake knows when an old tom has him whipped."

Michael chuckled. "You might be right. But when this knee heals up, I figure to give it another go myself."

"Haven't you had enough of this stupid war?" asked Elijah, incredulous.

"I don't know, Lige, seems like I sorta like it—the excitement at least. I ain't wild about the mud, cold, and heat. But I take to the rest right natural."

For the first time, Elijah noticed how much Michael resembled his pa. He was a fine looking man now. There was a jaunty twinkle in his eyes that had never been there before.

"Not me," said Elijah. "I hope I never see another army camp."

Michael grinned. "You always was way smarter than me. But I can probably still outshoot you," he teased.

"You always were the best shot around. Even Pa said so."

"I sure miss your pa." Michael cleared his throat. "Everyone else all right?" He looked toward the cabin.

"Pretty much now. Granny almost died." Elijah told of the many events since Michael's last visit.

Michael gave a low whistle. "Lew always was a strange one. You best watch yer back."

"Oh, I do," he said. Then he asked, "Why don't you stay here with us?"

"I appreciate it, Lige, but I reckon I'll stay at the house." Michael took a deep breath. "Hit's a cinch I can't stay at Uncle Simon's the way his Union Company drops around. Have they let you alone?"

"Yeah. I see them riding around every now and again. They haven't said a thing to me. I figure that's thanks to Simon." Elijah took a whack at a cane stalk and tossed it onto the old wagon. "Back in the spring they had a big shootout with some Rebs from Clarksville and killed some of them. Since then I reckon they've pretty much been left alone."

"Let me put this here magnificent steed in the shade and I'll give you a hand. I can't walk much yet, but I kin sit and head that grain."

Elijah grinned. "Be like old times."

Michael gave a derisive snort. "Hope it's better than them!"

With raised eyebrows, Elijah looked about. He envisioned the farm as it used to be. Now there was nothing but lack. Then he realized that such scarcity had been normal to the Lanes. It stood to reason that Michael would not chafe at this as he did.

By the last week in October there had been no frost, but rain occasionally wet the parched hills. Most nights Elijah slept on the porch, not pulling up the blanket until near sunrise when the air grew chill.

Although Becky and Deborah had combed the woods for persimmons and nuts, the harvest was disappointing. Trees growing near the creek that usually produced plump, sweet fruit, this year yielded shriveled, meatless persimmons, barely larger than the oblong seeds. The diminutive hickory nuts and black walnuts were hardly worth gathering.

When the meager pea crop and the last of the small pumpkins and fall squash were gathered and the few gallons of molasses divided with Caleb and Cousin Jenny, and the rest stored in the root cellar and some hidden in the schoolhouse, Elijah began cutting wood for the winter. He had refrained from going to the

Mason's cabin. Cindy needed time to mourn. But soon he intended to start calling in earnest.

Today while he worked, he ruminated on Jenny's news. She had arrived just after dinner to visit with Becky. The day before she and Pappy had visited other kin in Newton County. On their way home, a large force of mounted troops—Pappy estimated over two thousand—had passed them on the road near the county line. Pappy had talked with a captain. It was Joe Shelby's command, heading back from another raid into Missouri. They had helped themselves to dozens of hogs and all the corn in nearby cribs. It appeared Michael was right. The Rebel Army was not about to give up. But Elijah was certain—neither would the Union!

Midmorning he stopped for a breather. He leaned on the ax handle and stared across the creek at the far ridge. The foliage was drab, without a hint of color. Drought-curled leaves, brown and dead, turned loose and fell. They sifted down onto the still, murky pools in Little Piney.

Everything was drab and dead. Life was as dreary and bleak as the woods. When winter came Elijah knew things would grow worse. He shook his head. This war should never have been. So far as he could tell, this fight had been for the sole benefit of the slave owners. Rich man's war—poor man's fight. He agreed with that oft-repeated assessment.

Now Pa was dead—and thousands more besides. Granny was a cripple and Ma was little more than a hollow shell. It should never have happened. He wondered what the rabble-rousers thought now—now that the armies had mauled and fought over the country like two dogs with a bone until it was chewed, gulped down, and devoured. Hunger, death, and poverty! So far as he could tell, that was all this fight had gained.

Once again, he lifted the ax but froze in mid-swing. Shots! And they were close by, just down the creek. He buried the ax into the log and grabbed the shotgun. In a long lope, he crossed the creek and headed through the woods. Nearing the top of the far ridge, he slowed and crept to the summit. Down below, beyond a sharp bend in the stream, men were hunkered behind trees, exchanging fire across the creek. The five soldiers directly below were not in uniform, but the dozen or more on horseback on the far side of the creek were dressed in Yankee blue. Elijah could have picked three Yankees off with ease. But this was not his fight. He hunkered and stayed quiet.

The Yankees soon grouped together and charged. Shots rang out and puffs of black powder smoke rose from behind the trees. As the horses splashed into the creek, a lieutenant pitched off a lathered black horse and fell backwards into the water. Elijah saw two more Yankees jerk, hit by thudding lead. The attackers abruptly pulled back and did not give chase—not even when the Rebels broke into a run, grabbed their mounts, and raced south down the trail.

Elijah watched until the patrol retrieved the lieutenant's body and threw it across the back of the black horse. They went back up the trail, heading north. He chewed his jaw while wondering just how many Yankees were nearby. It was a sure bet there were more than a dozen. This had been a small skirmish between Shelby's rear and the Yankee vanguard. More than likely the main force would be along soon. Armies meant foraging. He must check the schoolhouse to make certain he had left no tracks. And he must hide the mule and warn Jenny to hide the horse.

As he turned there was a flicker of movement in the trees. Then it was gone. Elijah tensed. For a long while, he looked. Nothing stirred. He relaxed and drew a relieved breath when he saw a wild sow heading down the hill at a trot. He started for home but kept glancing back over his shoulder.

When he arrived at home, Michael was there. Deborah, eyes shining, sat on the porch step near him. Her face fell when Elijah said, "Deborah, run along and let Michael and me talk." Elijah watched her go. If he didn't know better, he would suspect she was sweet on Michael. She was way too young for such notions. At least he thought she was...

While Becky set dinner on the table, Elijah and Michael stood outside and talked.

"Did you hear that skirmish a while ago just down the creek?" asked Elijah.

Michael's face tensed and he spit out a twig and stared downstream. "No. I just now rode in. Who was it?"

"About a dozen Yankees and I reckon some of Shelby's men. They killed a Yankee lieutenant and stung a couple more before they lit out."

"I knew the Yankees were hereabouts," said Michael. "Little Johnny said Quinton Beasley had stopped by Simon's last evening." Michael frowned. "Beasley and all that bunch are as happy as kids at Christmas. Quinton is even acting as guide for them. Hit's McNeil's command, the Yankee general I told you about."

"The one who shot his prisoners?"

"Yep."

Michael went on, "I'd like to have McNeil in my rifle sights. Maramduke would make me a colonel."

Elijah looked down at a slow-crawling ant trying to scale his worn boot. He raised a brow. "Dead men don't make good colonels, Michael. Don't do anything crazy."

Michael chuckled. "You sound like Cindy."

Elijah threw up his head. "Cindy?"

"She came over to warn me about the Yankees. I told her I'd lay low."

"How is she?"

"Fine."

Elijah's heart quickened. "I've not seen her lately."

Michael cut his eyes at Elijah. "Well, she still lives the same place. Why don't you go see her?"

Elijah raised a brow. "With Simon's company meeting there to muster, I don't figure that would be too wise."

"Yo're probably right"—Michael grinned—"unless you want to be the first fellow on Piney to be conscripted by both armies."

Elijah snorted. "Not hardly!"

"I figure Shelby is heading for Clarksville," said Michael. "With McNeil right on his tail, I figure he'll cross the river and then make a stand. Hope he makes it."

Becky stepped to the door. The aroma of fried pork filled the air. "Dinner's ready. Michael, there's plenty for you too.

"Thanks, but I reckon I best get on. I got work waiting."

"Ma, I'll be back in a bit. I want to go check on something."

As Michael also turned to leave, Elijah once again cautioned, "Keep out of trouble."

Michael chuckled and lifted a hand.

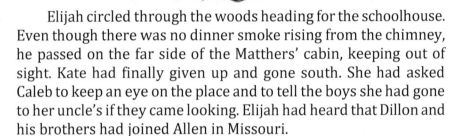

Elijah circled through the woods heading for the schoolhouse. Even though there was no dinner smoke rising from the chimney, he passed on the far side of the Matthers' cabin, keeping out of sight. Kate had finally given up and gone south. She had asked Caleb to keep an eye on the place and to tell the boys she had gone to her uncle's if they came looking. Elijah had heard that Dillon and his brothers had joined Allen in Missouri.

A brisk breeze stirred the dead leaves in the schoolyard and sent them skittering. Since bare feet no longer trod the hard-packed ground, grass and weeds had encroached. Nothing had been disturbed since Elijah's last visit. He studied the ground for tracks and, satisfied there were none, started homeward, once again cutting through the woods. He had not gone far, however, before the sound of riders sent him scurrying behind a boulder high on the hillside. The riders soon passed on the trail below. The troop of Yankees stopped first at Kate's. As Elijah watched, one soldier broke open the cabin door while others rummaged the barn and smokehouse. They returned empty-handed. Apparently Kate had left nothing behind that interested the Union army.

Elijah held his breath as they rode toward the schoolhouse. He sprinted through the trees for a better view. When a tall, black-haired trooper kicked open the door and went inside, the others soon dismounted and followed. Elijah's heart fell. They had found the provender! He lowered his head. His knuckles whitened on the gun. He knew it was useless to fight. There were too many of them, almost twenty in the foraging party, and more bound to come if there were shots. But it galled in the worst way to watch them carry off his livelihood.

The black-haired soldier came outside with a sack of grain slung over his shoulder. Just as he threw it into a wagon, he jerked and then crumpled to the ground. The shot had come from just behind. Elijah whirled but saw no one.

He heard angry shouts. They would be combing the woods soon. He looked down to see them mounting up. He grabbed the gun tight and ran. If he could circle and make it back to the creek, he could hide under the bluff near the schoolhouse. There was a niche there that was impossible to spot unless they rode right into the water. He sped between the trees, dodging the branches and tearing through the brush. Sweat ran into his eyes and his breath came in ragged pants. He ran down a steep incline and swerved to avoid some boulders. The creek was just ahead. He could see the water.

A shot clipped the branch in front of his face. He ran on. Then the world went dark as he fell dazed to the ground. Far off he heard the shout.

"I got him, Cap'in Frasier! Down here by the creek!"

Elijah felt a kick in his ribs. He opened his eyes to see four hostile soldiers.

"Get up. You ain't killed." The sergeant, a fair-skinned man with a long blond mustache, prodded him with a rifle.

Elijah stood on shaky legs and felt his head. A long welt lay on his skull above the temple. He winced and his hand came away bloody. When he stumbled, the sergeant whacked him in the back with the rifle butt. "Rebel scum," he growled, "I just wish you'd try running off—Simmons was a good friend of mine."

Elijah knew military justice occurred quickly in the field. He wondered if it would be a firing squad or a rope. He staggered up the hill. With a bevy of hard-jawed soldiers looking on, Elijah's hands were tied and he was seated on a stump while a man rode off to consult with officers of higher rank. The dead soldier lay nearby in the wagon bed alongside the sacks of corn.

Elijah sat and waited. He worried about Ma and Deborah. His death would go hard on them. He felt panic wondering how they would survive without provisions. He wanted to pray but he could not. Always before he had felt safe from hell. Now he was not so sure. Granny had warned him about bitterness and anger. He wished he had listened. He did not like what he had become. A chill traced his spine. He suddenly felt a great and reverent fear. After all he had done, how could he face God! Elijah recalled George dying on the rocky ground at Pea Ridge. What was it Levi had said? Elijah quickly sent up a fervent prayer asking forgiveness.

A thin-lipped major arrived. He stepped from the saddle and briskly approached the men.

Elijah stood. "Major," he said, "I never shot your man. It was someone else on the hill behind me—I figure it's some of Shelby's men. A rifle killed your man. I was carrying a shotgun. " He was not surprised at the sardonic rise of the major's eyebrow.

"No matter. You were with them." Then the major ignored him. "Captain, we must press on before Shelby crosses the river. The general said to hang this man. There's a rope on my saddle. A firing squad would be a waste of time and ammunition." With that the major stepped back and crossed his arms and waited to witness the proceedings.

The soldiers lost no time in grabbing the rope and picking out a likely-looking strong limb. Thoughts whirled in Elijah's brain, the most poignant, perhaps, how he had often sat under that very oak and watched Cindy cross the schoolyard as graceful as a princess. *Cindy!* He would never see her again!

Elijah pulled back as men laid hold of his arms and began dragging him toward the noose swaying in the stiff breeze. He could not get visions of Uncle Jim from his mind. These men were not expert hangmen and doubtless a dangling torture awaited. Although Elijah had a passionate desire to live, just now he would welcome a quick bullet. He struggled, but in vain. The rope dropped over his head and the noose jerked tight. Then he stood resolute, with jaws tight, as a dozen men vied for a handhold on the far end of the rope. He was going to die.

The major stepped forward. "I hope you have made peace with your maker." He eyed Elijah with contempt. "Although I find it hard to believe, I suppose God might forgive even Rebel scum."

As if fearing the major's wrath, a nearby soldier spoke low, "Not by works of righteousness we've done, but according to His mercy He saved us."

Elijah nodded his thanks to the man. It was a verse Simon was fond of quoting. That remembrance brought Elijah a strange calm.

The major raised his hand.

Just then more shots rang out. Two men holding rifles pitched forward. As the rest dove for cover and more shots whizzed past, the major turned and jerked his pistol.

"Major!" The call rolled down from the rocky bluff across the creek. When the major whirled, Michael shouted, "Drop that pistol. I got this rifle pointed right at the back of yer head. In case you got any doubt, let me tell you that I can bust yore skull with no trouble a'tall. Now, have all them soldier boys raise their hands while you cut my friend loose."

"Do as he says." Dillon Matthers stood nearby in the edge of the trees. "I got your boys in my shotgun sights."

The major tossed the pistol aside. Dillon ordered all the soldiers to stand and walk forward. Dazed, Elijah watched as Dillon eased over, and with shotgun leveled, picked up the pistol. Then he gathered up the stack of rifles and put them into the wagon. "You fellers won't be needing these so I'll just—"

A shrill whistle split the air. Dillon threw up his head as the call rang out, "Riders coming!" Elijah recognized Shane Matthers' voice.

"Cut me loose," hissed Elijah.

Dillon kept his hand on the trigger while he drew a knife and cut the rope binding Elijah's hands. Although he kept the shotgun on the soldiers, one man broke and ran toward the wagon. Dillon fired. The side of the wagon splintered and three men fell in the blast.

Elijah yanked the noose from his neck and bolted. Just as shot pattered around him, he dove over the creek bank.

———————～———————

Elijah stopped. The breath rasped so loudly in his throat, he was unsure if anyone followed. He started on, but this time at a more cautious pace. In a slow trot, he cut through the edge of the woods near the Matthers' cabin and then descended again into the creek bottoms. Sweat poured down his armpits and his insides trembled. He could hardly believe he was alive.

The troops might come to the house, so he headed for the bluff. The autumn breeze cooled his sweat as he slowed and began to calm. A flock of geese flew over honking, and he smelled a faint whiff of muscadines. The world almost felt normal again.

He had just slid down the bank and barely gotten out of sight when a large group of horsemen rode by on the trail above. He drew his knife. The hoof beats faded. He let out a deep breath when they rode on without stopping. His pounding heart slowed and he lowered the knife. The Union Army in hot pursuit of Joe Shelby would not waste much time looking for him.

Chapter 22

The sun was low in the sky when Elijah heard a noise. He tensed. He jerked the knife and cocked his head and strained to listen. It was just a whisper of sound like soft footfalls. It sounded like a woman—Ma or perhaps Deborah. Pebbles rolled and dirt sifted past the opening.

Cindy drew back before Elijah had time to lower the knife. Her breath was fast and ragged. "Michael sent me," she stammered and stuck out a holster and an ammunition pouch. "He said you'd need this. He said to tell you Lew Willis is back. He saw him today."

Elijah snatched the gun. "Thanks. And be sure and thank Michael for me. He and Dillon saved my life today. Do you know if they both got away?"

She nodded. "Yes, they did," she said. "Elijah, please be careful."

As she talked, Elijah checked the load in the pistol and the ammunition in the pouch.

"You ought to let me bandage that head."

"I will later."

She added, "I think the soldiers are all gone now, chasing Colonel Shelby. General McNeil told Pa's company to go to Fort Smith to join up with the Union there. Pa stayed behind but the rest of them went. You should be safe now."

He pulled the holster around his waist.

"Don't go after them, Elijah. Let them go!" She grew frustrated as he pulled the strap tight and buckled it. "Are you always going to fly off the handle? Or do you just enjoy killing? Hasn't there been enough blood spilled already?"

His jaw clenched. "I'm not going after the Yankees. I got no quarrel with them." He stepped around her into the sunlight to check the load in the pistol. "But I intend being safer by nightfall."

"Lew Willis?" she guessed.

He stepped away.

"Elijah! Stop!" She grasped his arm. "I don't want to lose you, too."

He hesitated.

"Elijah!"

He did not turn back. The light would soon fade. He did not intend spending another day looking over his shoulder. This time Elijah felt neither rage nor revenge. Lew was a menace, a danger to everyone. Like a predator, he needed killing. Of course, Lew would only be found if he wanted to be. But Elijah had a suspicion that he did. Lew had long enjoyed this game of cat and mouse. He would welcome Elijah getting a glimpse again.

Elijah, however, was caught off guard at how quickly it happened. He had barely topped the bank when Lew stepped from behind a tree with an aimed rifle. His eyes glowed with a predatory shine and his lips curled back. Spittle gleamed on his sharp, yellowed eyeteeth.

Elijah ground his teeth. How could he have been so careless?

"Elijah, please wait—" Eyes wide, Cindy stopped beside a willow tree and her voice faded. She laid her hand on the trunk.

"Unbuckle that belt and throw hit and the ammunition into the creek." Lew glanced at Cindy. "Ya wouldn't want anything to happen to her, now would you, boy?"

"Lord Jesus," Cindy whispered. "Help us!"

Elijah tossed the holster and bag. They splashed into the water. "Now, let her go, Lew. You got no quarrel with her."

"Oh, you might not be so careful of her if you knowed what I know!" Lew grimaced. Disgust filled his voice. "Oh, I've see'd her—I've see'd her slip away to meet Dillon, the same time as she's making up to you. She ain't no good. Woman like her ain't fit to live."

Elijah went cold to the marrow of his bones. He had a sudden vision of Cindy hacked into pieces. He took a step but Lew pointed the gun at Cindy.

She gasped, covering her mouth with one hand. Lew stared at the ruby on her finger. For a moment he seemed mesmerized.

"That's purty," he muttered.

Elijah dove. Lew whirled and fired. Elijah fell. Pain seared his leg. He groaned and rolled away as Lew clubbed him in the head with the rifle butt. Though he had managed to avoid the full force of the blow, he was stunned. His eyes flickered open. Lew had drawn a knife.

"I like a knife better." Lew propped the rifle nearby.

Elijah struggled up. His leg was bleeding, but he could stand. He wobbled and shook his head to clear it. Lew brandished the knife. Elijah sidestepped, hoping to turn Lew's back to Cindy. Crouching and weaving, Lew inched forward as Elijah hobbled back, clumsy from the wound. Then Lew lunged. Elijah jumped back, barely escaping the slashing blade.

"Run!" Elijah shouted.

Instead, Cindy sprang toward the rifle. Lew, with a wave of the knife, sent her scurrying back. From the leer, Elijah knew that Lew was enjoying this. Like a cat with a mouse, Lew was playing with them. Lew was confident—too confident. Lew's eyes suddenly narrowed. *Dixon had warned to always watch the eyes.* Just as Lew sprang, Elijah grasped the knife in his own boot. Elijah jumped aside and slashed upward. Lew's intestines spilled out. Shock washed his face. His knife fell. His eyebrows knit and he groaned and clutched his belly, staring first at Elijah and then at the bloody knife. *He shuddered*—thought Elijah—*just like the big, black panther when Pa had axed it.* Lew crumpled. He writhed on the ground with blood and gore streaming between his fingers. Elijah gripped the knife and watched.

He glanced at Cindy. She had covered her mouth. Then she retched and vomited.

"Are you all right?"

She nodded, leaning weakly against a tree. "He was going to kill us both," she whispered.

Elijah picked up the rifle. "I suppose I ought to put him out of his misery," he said, staring at Lew thrashing and moaning.

"No! Don't!" she cried.

"Sometimes," he said, "killing is mercy."

He hunkered, searching for an ammunition pouch. He reached for the buckskin bag on Lew's chest and cut the leather thong. He dumped the contents into his hand. No shot rolled out. Instead it was trinkets, sparkling buttons, pieces of shiny glass, and jewelry. There was the button from Deborah's dress.

Cindy gasped. "There's my shoe button. I lost it at Uncle Johnny's funeral."

His gaze froze on a tiny gold watch. It was a broach. He had seen it before. Bessie Hadley had always worn it pinned onto her collar. Elijah slowly shook his head. He laid the stuff on the ground alongside his knife while he searched Lew's belt for a shot pouch. He jumped. Lew's claw-like fingers had grasped for the knife.

Elijah grabbed the rifle and raised the butt. Lew groaned and fell back, his dark eyes staring dull and sightless at the October sky. Elijah stared for a long minute. He felt a great weight lifting. No longer would he have to dread every tree and bush and expect a bullet in the back at every turn. It was over!

He picked up the knife, walked to the creek, and knelt. A red bird flew down and lit on a nearby limb. It warbled a golden call. As the cool water wet his bloody hands, he pulled his mind from the horror of the day. The water was growing cool. Winter would soon be on them. How would they manage? He knew Granny would insist that the good Lord would provide—well, He would have to if they survived.

"Elijah."

He sheathed the knife as Cindy drew near. Then he grew still as her eyes went over his face.

She drew a ragged breath and her lips parted. "I've been wrong about so many things." She glanced away. She shivered and rubbed her arms. "But as Pa says—I am starting to see the light." She looked back and tears had filled her eyes. "You are a good man, Elijah. You've only done what you had to do. I've been so foolish. I wouldn't blame you if you never spoke to me again." Suddenly she stared. "Oh, you're hurt! There's blood seeping through your pants!"

"It's just a scratch."

"Elijah Loring, you'd say that if your leg was blown off!"

The next day Caleb buried Lew alongside Bo. Elijah thought it fitting as those two would likely be spending eternity together. He chafed to be up and around, but Granny and Becky insisted he stay off his leg.

"It's a clean wound, Granny. The shot barely nicked me. With such a little scratch, Sergeant Potts would have me marching on the double-quick."

"Well, around here"— her black eyes snapped— "I outrank him. Now you stay put! Or I'll dose you with black powder and sulphur." She grumbled, "Men ain't got a lick of sense when hit comes to taking care of theirselves." But, hobbling around with rags on her feet, she fluffed up the pillow under his leg and fussed over him as if he were a baby.

Poor Granny, thought Elijah, with tenderness. *She'll never wear shoes again.* He kissed her withered cheek when she left and assured her that he would obey orders. Then he insisted that Becky and Deborah go along to work on the weaving. He would be fine alone at home for an hour or two.

That afternoon he was surprised by a knock on the door. He reached for the pistol. "Come in."

Dillon removed his hat and then his broad shoulders filled the room. He sat down when Elijah invited. He grinned. "Glad to see you still got most of yer hide."

"Thanks to you, Shawn, and Michael."

"Aw, it was a good day for shooting Yankees."

"I thought maybe you boys were on the other side."

"Some of us maybe." Dillon grinned. "Mostly we ain't on any side but our own. We always were an independent bunch."

Elijah grinned. "I really appreciate what you did. Especially considering how we last parted."

Dillon squirmed. He studied the dusty hat in his hands. "That's really what I come about...that last time." He cleared his throat. "I was a real jackass that day, no doubt. But, Lige,"—he paused and looked up—"I got true and honest feelings for Cindy. And I aim to court her, right and proper, if she'll have me."

Elijah stayed as still as stone.

Dillon watched him for a moment and then said, "I figure you still got feelings for her too?"

"I do." Elijah looked out the open door. A sudden breeze sent leaves skittering across the yard. The coolness had a touch of fall. He locked eyes with Dillon. "I intend to court her too. And I'm not about to say may the best man win—because I might lose her."

"Same goes for me." Dillon stood. They shook hands.

———— ∾ ————

Elijah waited a week before putting on a clean but ragged shirt and his best—as sorry as they were—trousers and Bo's shiny boots. He had shaved using Ned's straight razor and now stood looking into the mirror over the basin to comb his wet hair. He frowned. It could use a trim but he didn't want to wait that long. Now that he had made up his mind, he was anxious to go.

"Ma," he called, "I may not be back for supper."

She stuck her head from the pantry. "My, you look nice. Tell the Masons I said hello." Her face grew soft and wistful. "Have a good time, son."

He wondered if he would find Dillon seated on Cindy's porch.

———— ∾ ————

Simon sat on the porch. But this time there were piles of shavings alongside his chair. He stood when Elijah climbed the steps.

"Have a seat," he offered. "Cindy," he called. "You got company." Simon started to leave as Cindy stepped to the doorway.

Elijah halted him with a question. "Simon, I want to ask Cindy to marry me. Do you have any objections?"

Simon rubbed his chin. "Hit'll take some gettin' used to—having a Rebel in the family. Well," he said with a twinkle in his eyes, "the Union don't win 'em all." Then he grew serious, "If she's willing, hit will pleasure me."

Cindy stepped outside. "I'm willing, Pa."

Simon held up a satin-smooth board with delicately carved leaves and flowers along the edge. "Then I reckon hit's a good thing I've almost finished this doodad shelf fer yore hope chest." He smiled and went inside.

Elijah drew her into his arms. She clung to him. He breathed in the fresh scent of her hair. He kissed her. Her lips were soft. He savored their sweetness as he had so often done in dreams. "I love you," he breathed.

But he had to know. "Has Dillon been here?"

"Yes."

"Did he ask you to marry him?"

"Yes."

"You turned him down?"

"Well, you're here and he's not." She took his face in her hands. "I love you, Elijah Loring. I always have."

When she nestled her head against his shoulder, he smiled. "If I have my way, Simon will have to get used to a Rebel son-in-law mighty soon. I don't want to wait. Do you?"

She shook her head.

To seal the bargain Elijah gave her another kiss, this time long and seeking and not so tender. He drew a deep breath. Just as quickly as the preacher would allow, he intended to marry Cindy and raise a family as the good Lord intended.

To learn more about Nancy Dane Books
Nancydane.com

Join Nancy on Facebook
facebook.com/nancydanebooks

Made in the USA
Coppell, TX
08 November 2023

23972092R00182